KAREN HEENAN

Shifting Stages

Shifting Stages

A Philadelphia Theater STory

E-book ISBN: 978-1-957081-31-1

Paperback ISBN: 978-1-957081-32-8

Hardcover ISBN: 978-1-957081-33-5

With every door that closes a new one opens.
— *Alexander Graham Bell*

Also by Karen Heenan

The Tudor Court
Songbird
A Wider World
Lady, in Waiting
The Son in Shadow
The Tudor Court Omnibus (ebook only)
***

Ava & Claire
Coming Apart
Coming Closer
Coming Together
Coming Home (Omnibus books 1-3, ebook only)
Home for Christmas (novella, ebook only)
French Lessons
Shifting Stages

Part One
The Dancer's Dream

1

"Kimber Byrne! Byrne!"

The director's voice vibrates through the airless backstage area. I don't respond until another dancer pokes me between the shoulder blades.

"Byrne!" she whispers. "He wants you."

"Coming!" I spring forward onto the stage, as if I haven't been dancing for hours already. We learned the routine as an ensemble and then danced in small groups while we were picked off, one by one, and sent either backstage or home.

The stage is lit by a single bulb. Three people are already there: the director, the choreographer, and the dancer whose job I would like to have. More men sit out in the shadowy seats, watching.

"Sorry, sir."

While the director's tie is snug at his collar, both men have their sleeves rolled up to show forearms in varying states of hairiness; the dancer wears tights, shorts, and a blouse tied at her midriff. All their faces show the strain of the long day. The air smells of sweat and the vestiges of a half-dozen perfumes.

Stan Arkright shakes his head. The light glints off his glasses so I can't see his eyes. "First day with a new name?" he asks, his voice caustic.

"First week." Kimber is my last name. My parents named me Thelma, which isn't bad as names go—I went to school with a girl named Araminta, for Pete's sake—but it doesn't sound like a professional dancer, and that's my goal. Last week, after losing yet another part to a girl no more talented but with a name snappy enough for a theater marquee, I renamed myself. My father's surname, then my stepfather's: Kimber Byrne.

It sounds enigmatic. Seductive. Successful. All of which I will be or die in the attempt.

His brows lift, his tanned forehead creasing like corduroy. "Well, Miss Byrne, you weren't listening, but I hope you were paying attention. Did you see what Belle did there?"

"Yes, sir." Belle Watson isn't the star of this show, but she's the principal dancer, the highest I can aim right now. I know her steps, her gestures, the way she tilts her head when she takes direction—and how men react when she does it.

I tilt my head at Stan Arkright and look up at him through my lashes. "The whole routine or the solo?"

Something flickers across his face. He's on to me. "Do you know the whole routine?"

"Yes, sir." I edge past Belle, adjusting the sway of my hips to match her subtle rhythm. I've practiced her walk in front of the mirror until I have it down pat. My younger sister also has it down, which incurred a lecture from my mother about teaching Grace to sashay around like a tart.

She wasn't calling *me* a tart. Mama's not like that. She understands I need to be someone other than Thelma Kimber to make my dreams come true; she doesn't want her fifteen-year-old daughter to behave in the same way.

I take center stage, imagining a real spotlight around me—a real audience out in those seats—and wait for the music. When it comes, I hold for the proper count and begin.

It's the end of the day when the director strides back onto the stage. He crackles with energy, though the dancers are as wilted as the men in the seats. Glancing over at us, then down at the list in his hand, he says, "Rayburn and Collins."

A brunette and a redhead step forward, reaching for each other's hands. I ignore the tightness in my chest and hold my head high, as if watching Stan Arkright will bring forth my name from his lips.

"You'll fill the spots in the chorus. Thomas and Miller, chorus and the second act song."

They squeal and join the other girls.

It hurts to breathe. If I don't get this part...

"First dancer in the chorus, and understudy to Miss Watson"—he gazes off into the distance—"Byrne."

Relief floods through me, weakening my knees. I come forward, this time as myself, and take my place in the line of dancers. When he looks at me, I smile my thanks, hoping my tangled emotions don't show on my face.

He turns towards the now-silent group waiting at the side of the stage. "That's all. Thank you for coming in."

There is a muffled sob from the back row. I press my lips together; I would sooner fall through the stage than publicly show my disappointment. After three years of near-constant auditions, I've been turned down in every way imaginable. Mr. Arkright was kind, all things considered.

When they are gone, he turns his attention to us. "Good job, ladies," he says. "Be here tomorrow at nine."

"But the call sheet says eleven," the redhead—Thomas?—says.

His laugh is more of a smoker's cough than a sound of mirth. "That's for dancers who already know the choreography. Get your beauty sleep, Miss Collins, and be here at nine. You have a lot of work to do."

I'll be there by half past eight. And I already know most of the choreography, but I'm not enough of a dumb bunny to say so.

It's a huge stroke of luck—bad for them, good for us—we've been taken on to round out the engagement. The play will only run another five weeks, but that's fine by me. Even if I don't get the opportunity to dance in Belle Watson's place, it'll be the best job I've ever had. Certainly, better than the one I have right now.

I'll be on stage by the weekend, dancing in front of all of Philadelphia.

It's an ensemble cast, which is a fancy way of saying I'm a chorus girl, but I've waited my entire life for an opportunity like this. Maybe I should be terrified, like the other girls, but my body is buzzing with anticipation.

The next morning, all the girls are there before nine. Collins is the second to arrive, right on my heels, nursing a paper cup of coffee in her mittened hands. Her bright hair is covered in a woolly hat which she drags off and tucks into her pocket.

She looks at me curiously. "How did you know Belle's routine so well?"

"I usher here five nights a week." When we've finished rehearsals for the day, I'll have to give notice. If time allows, maybe they'll let me work out the week.

Most ushers are struggling actors or dancers, with the occasional fifty-ish man whose worshipful devotion to theater equals my own. While ushering pays less than waitressing, it's easier on my feet, and I can watch the shows for free. Also, theater patrons rarely pinch my bottom. It evens out.

Calling out sick doesn't happen in this business, so when one of the younger chorus girls failed to appear last Friday, everyone began speculating. Then a stagehand and two more girls fell ill. Chicken pox, we were told. I'd never been so happy *not* to be on stage in my life. As soon as the call went up, I dashed back to put my name on the list.

The choreographer arrives at quarter past nine, walking out from the wings and dropping a caped overcoat over the back of a chair. He is unrecognizable from the rumpled despot of the day before.

"Sherlock Holmes," someone whispers. The coat, at least, fits the description. Oliver Barnet, well-known choreographer and habitue of a certain gentleman's bar frequented by my brother, bears no physical resemblance to the famous detective. He's of middling height but appears shorter, with a fussy manner and an old-fashioned mustache.

He's tougher than he appears, though, putting us through our paces for four solid hours, not letting us stop for breath or questions. Some of the sequences are simple time steps with variations, but others are more complicated. By one, we have the basics of each routine down. I'll be dancing them in my dreams—if I can sleep.

When he calls the break, we all sag with relief. I've managed to maintain the ribbon in my hair, but my shirt is pasted to my back, my shorts are creased, and my ballet tights are damp all the way into my shoes.

Some of the dancers are wearing black tights, and Rayburn is bare-legged. I like the look of black, but because my ballet mistress won't allow it in her classroom, I have three pairs of pink tights; it would be extravagant to buy new ones simply because pink feels like a little-girl color.

Many of the girls throw dresses and heavy coats on over their sweat-stained practice clothes and head off to a luncheonette around the corner from Arch Street, chattering like sparrows. I didn't want to take my nicely warmed muscles out into the cold, and the very last thing I need in the brief time we are given is to be surrounded by people.

My avoidance of other dancers is why I haven't made many friends working in this business. I could try harder, I suppose. I'll lend a lipstick or borrow a tampon, but that's the extent of my efforts; we're all too wrapped up in plans for our futures to expend much energy on the present.

The Durang is an old theater, with fat, graceless cupids holding up the gas lamps at the entrance and a beaded velvet curtain that saw its best days before my birth. Named for an early light in the Philadelphia theater community, it attracts a crowd simply for its low prices and constant array of unchallenging comedies and musicals. It hasn't hosted an out-of-town preview in decades.

To me, the theater—even one as unfashionable as the Durang—feels like home, whether I'm on stage, in the audience, or guiding people to their seats and making sure they have programs. There is something special, however, about the areas never seen by the public: the nooks and crannies where I can hide away and watch others without being noticed; the flies, high above, tightly controlled by the stagehands and not to be accessed by curious girls; the dressing rooms, for those fortunate enough to warrant them, where privacy is absolute. The audience sees the front of the house; knowing the backstage areas gives me a sense of belonging.

The stagehands and dressers know me by sight and merely nod as I pass. I find an out-of-the way trunk, sit down, and pull an apple and a sandwich from my dance bag. The temporary stillness eases my aching head, but there is nothing to be done for my feet, which feel as if I've been dancing on hot coals. It's worth it.

The director yesterday was hard to read; did he appreciate my mimicry of Belle or was it a step too far? He must have seen something in me, if I was chosen.

Although my audition got me the job as Belle Watson's understudy, it's unlikely I'll ever go on in her place, which leaves me in the chorus with fifteen other ambitious girls—nothing more than a pleasant backdrop in the big musical numbers.

Every morning, before I get out of bed, I prop myself up on my pillows and take stock of my career, staring at the array of programs and photos around my mirror and wondering how to make my dreams of becoming a professional dancer come true. I audition constantly, and yet I'm not much better off than when I started.

At my age—almost twenty-three!—I should be farther along in my career. If only I could sing properly! Dancers who can sing are much more likely to climb out of the chorus. I'm not terrible, which would have comedic value, but no matter how many singing lessons I've had, I can't do carry a tune.

If I were in New York, it would be different. There would be more opportunities for a non-singing dancer. There are plenty of theaters in Philadelphia, but many are venues for out-of-town shows working their way toward Broadway. If I moved to New York and got cast, I might be sent back to Philadelphia with the show before it opened.

Moving takes money I don't have. All my wages are spent on dance classes. Although my sister, Pearl, lives in New York, she shares a tiny apartment with her English husband. They don't have room for me, other than as an overnight guest, and they're newlyweds, besides. It feels funny to call a man Julian's age a newlywed; he must be nearly forty.

I've taken the train up several times for auditions, but I've never made the second cut. It was embarrassing to have Mama yell at me for sneaking off when there was nothing to show for it but disappointment and sore feet.

After the break, we are joined by the other dancers. Mr. Barnet files us between them to more easily hide any lapses. Other than one instance when Thomas turned left instead of right and cried when she was shouted at, we are remarkably cohesive after a single day's hard work.

I step back from the others, turning upstage so I can rub my hip while listening to Mr. Barnet. After eight hours, it aches worse than my feet. The director is far out in the middle row of velvet seats, watching us appraisingly.

The theater isn't far from home, but because it's after eleven and absolutely freezing, I splurge on a taxi and ask the driver to let me out at the corner. The downstairs lights are on; Mama rarely goes to bed before I come in. Instead of my mother, I find Pop in his big blue armchair with the newspaper and a glass of beer. I wind my arms around his neck and kiss his cheek, inhaling his comforting scent, a combination of cologne, cigarettes, and—faintly—disinfectant.

"Where's Mama?"

"In bed." He folds his paper away in case I want to talk. "She spent the evening with Claire and came home with a headache."

I know the feeling.

"Is everything all right?" My uncle died not long after the war ended, and although Aunt Claire is nearly as strong as Mama, the loss hit her hard; they'd been married since she was seventeen.

"I think they needed some girl time. Claire gets lonely, rattling around that big old house with only Teddy for company."

"You're not waiting up for me, are you?" I lean on the arm of his chair to remove my shoes. My leg muscles quiver from the strain of standing all day. "I do have a key, you know."

"Not really." He shrugs and it turns into a stretch. "What can I say? Like the rest of you, your mama has me well trained. I'm glad you got this part, but you're putting in awfully long hours, kid. Have you eaten?"

"I had a sandwich."

A tray had been delivered at three and we'd fallen on it like we were starving, then danced for another two hours. When we were released, I changed into my usherette's uniform and went to work. I no longer take pleasure in watching the show. Still, my feet moved to the music—a routine in miniature—as I stood along the back wall.

"I'm wrung out." I love spending time with Pop, but if I don't get away soon, I'm going to embarrass myself. "I need a bath. It's all I've been able to think about for the last two hours."

"Your sister had a tub earlier," he says, squeezing my hand. "I hope she left you some hot water."

"She'd better have." I shut the door and for a moment I stand there, shoes in hand, letting the room's silent comfort wrap around me. It is my nest, my hiding place, its subdued wallpaper almost hidden behind theater programs, movie star photos, and my first pair of pink satin pointe shoes. The lure of the bed is overwhelming, but common sense kicks in. If I don't have a bath, I'll be in pain tomorrow. I drop my clothes on the floor and pull on a silky blue kimono.

As soon as I open the door, Grace's leggy frame, clad in bright red flannel pajamas, pops out of her bedroom. "Hey, Thel. You're late."

"That's not news to me." I lean against the wall. "Did you use all the hot water?"

Her brown eyes widen. "Gee, I hope not. You look like you need it."

"I do." I shut the door in her face and turn the faucet. Hot water gushes, and my tears follow suit. Opening the medicine cabinet, I pour Epsom salts into the tub and shake two aspirin into my palm. I stretch my arms above my head until my back gives several small pops. I try to ignore the worrying tug in my hip. Finally, I take off my robe and sit on the edge of the tub to massage my calves so they don't cramp in the night.

If Mama knew how much it hurt to keep up with the other dancers, she'd tie me to the stair rail to stop me from leaving the house. Pop, on the other hand, would ask what he could do to help. He can't do more than he has: I still do the exercises he taught me when I was little. Sometimes they work, and sometimes I work so hard that they don't.

This is one of those times. I step into the tub and lower myself gently. The scalding water hurts my skin, but soon it will seep into my sore muscles and meet up with the aspirin and then I'll be able to sleep.

2

When I was little, nobody had a name for what was wrong with me. My crooked legs made me slow and often refused to bear my weight, forcing my brothers and sister to push me around in a wheelbarrow. We later learned I'd been born with rickets, which caused a deformity that made walking difficult.

My stepfather—who was then just my uncle's friend—proposed a regimen of exercise and vitamins, plus metal braces for my legs. It might work, he said; it might not. But he thought it was worth trying.

I wanted it to work. When my mother asked if I was willing to try, I couldn't answer fast enough. My trust in the man I called Dr. Max was instant. That my treatment would keep me in the city with the aunt I adored added weight to the argument.

Mama went home to the rest of the family, while I stayed in the city with my aunt, uncle, and baby brother Teddy, who they had recently adopted. Aunt Claire encouraged me to spend time with him because it made the transition easier for both of us. Life in Philadelphia, even with Dr. Max's painful exercises, was far more pleasant than life at home. My aunt's house was clean and bright; food was abundant; and I had my brother and a puppy to play with. I pretended far too often they had adopted both of us.

The treatments did work, slowly. I could walk longer and longer distances with less discomfort, and when my braces were removed at night, my legs might not have looked any different, but they *felt* straighter. It was all the proof I needed: I pushed harder, until I hurt myself and they made me take a break.

Six months after my arrival, we were called home to Scovill Run because there had been a collapse at the mine. Daddy was dead and my oldest brother Dan was gravely injured. Being so small, I didn't know how to explain to the adults in my life why I was inconsolable, that my father had once said aloud he wished he'd been stricken in my place. In my mind, his death was tied to my recovery.

When the funeral was over, we moved to Philadelphia to start a new life. I continued my treatments, and after a year, my braces were removed. After bearing their clanking weight for so long, I felt like a girl reborn. Dr. Max—who had by then fallen in love with my mother, though she wouldn't marry him for years—suggested dance classes to strengthen my legs.

Aunt Claire often took me to the movies as a treat after my doctor's appointments and I was wild for Fred Astaire and Ginger Rogers. I threw myself into the lessons with everything I had. I couldn't bring my father back, but I could do something that would make him proud.

I suppose it happens in all large families, the pairing off. Pearl and Dan, Toby and George, Grace and Teddy. The other half of my pair has always been Aunt Claire. She paid for my dance classes and took me to the theater, showing me a world outside of the closed space the rest of my family happily inhabited.

Dancing has consumed me since my first lesson. I began with tap, so I could pretend I was dancing with Fred Astaire. When I was twelve, I added ballet. The other students had started much younger, so I worked hard to catch up. I'll never be a true ballerina, but I can dance en pointe—briefly—without losing my center.

After years of sitting and watching everyone else living their lives, I couldn't imagine ever sitting still again. Dance was freedom and the sense that I very nearly *could* fly. Ever since Aunt Claire took me to the theater for my seventh birthday, I've wanted to be the one on stage. Dancing alone wasn't enough; I needed to perform, as well.

This singular focus has kept me in a bubble for fifteen years. School was a matter of marking time until I could escape, either to dance class or practice at home. When I got older, there was a steady stream of boys. I needed dates for dances, and I enjoyed the bits Mama warned me to be careful of—the kissing in cars, the furtive hands under my sweaters. Going beyond that with Jerry on the night of our senior play. They were a pleasant distraction, but they were always secondary.

For the most part, my family understands. Mama has cautioned more than once that if I'm not careful, my dreams will cost more than I'm willing to pay.

I don't know what she means. My dreams are worth everything.

Rehearsals run from eight in the morning until the crew appears to set up for the evening's performance. The cast drifts in to watch us work, glad that in two more days there will be a full complement of dancers again.

When they shoo us offstage, we are sent for our fittings. The costume shop is located at the top of the theater, a place I've somehow never visited before. Up two flights of winding stairs, then down a narrow corridor and up a final flight, we find a dusty wonderland rich with the scent of old fabric: velvet and satin and spangles. The space is lit by hanging bulbs and occupied by five women who sigh when we present ourselves.

The women—three white and two colored—appear annoyed but unsurprised as six of us troop across their threshold.

"Why didn't they wait until Friday?" the oldest woman asks. "They think we can perform miracles."

The other dancers are silent. I step forward. "My mother is a seamstress," I say, "so I know you *can* perform miracles, but it would have been helpful if they had sent us sooner. What can we do to make it easier?"

Some of the tension eases and Collins shoots me an appreciative glance.

"We need to measure y'all first," says one of the women, producing several cloth measuring tapes and handing them around. "Get down to your unders, we'll do that and see how much work it's going to take."

With some laughter, we arrange ourselves in the tight space, hanging our practice clothes on the nearest hooks. I end up in a corner surrounded by neatly labeled cartons—plumes, color; plumes, white; gloves, black; gloves, white; gloves, opera.

It makes me think of the treasure trove of Aunt Claire's attic, where I've scavenged some wonderful pieces over the years. Because of her generosity, I have an extensive wardrobe that is twenty years out of date. I've garnered some strange looks and the occasional comment when I wear her beaded 1920s dresses in public, but I don't care. Even her everyday things are nicer than most of what is available in the stores. An added benefit is that many of her garments were sewn by my mother, which means they're as well made as they are beautiful.

One of the women comes over to take my measurements, introducing herself as Mabel. She's no more than twenty, with warm brown skin and tightly waved hair.

"You're lucky you're so slim," she says. "You'll fit into almost anything."

"After this week, I'm lucky I'm not a toothpick," I tell her. "Mr. Barnet is trying to kill us."

"Oh, that man." Mabel runs the tape around my hips and makes a note on a tiny pad. "He likes to come up here and paw through our boxes of bits and pieces."

"For the show?" Collins's figure is fuller than mine in both bust and hips, though her waist is small; they're going to have a difficult time popping her into a costume without alterations.

The room fills with soft laughter. "No, honey, for himself. He likes his finery."

"Remember last week?" The older woman peers through the boxes. "Prancing around with that long white scarf like he was Mae West."

Guilt tightens my throat as we make fun of Mr. Barnet. My brother is like him—while not being like him at all. I can't imagine Dan prancing; he's even more serious than Pearl. Then again, Mr. Barnet has nearly driven us into the ground. I'll allow a few unkind thoughts on that basis alone.

Our first costume is a bit of pink sequined fluff, resembling an abbreviated, shiny tutu. It fits me well enough, but Mabel makes notes on a slip of paper and pins it to the strap when I slip it off.

"I thought it was fine."

She shrugs. "There's fine, and there's better than fine."

"Oh, my mother would like you." Mama might have phrased it differently, but she would have agreed completely with the sentiment.

The sequined costume comes with flesh-colored tights and pink satin shoes. I buckle them on and immediately the toes pinch. "Ow."

"They run small," the woman in charge says, coming over to look at me. "Go up a size."

The larger shoes don't squeeze, but when I stand, there's a faint twinge in my hip again. I'm going to need another hot bath.

Two more costumes, with slightly more coverage, are easily dealt with. One by one, the other dancers disappear, their steps sounding hollowly in the stairwell.

When my fittings are done, I reach for my clothes.

"Not yet," Mabel says. "We need to put you in Miss Watson's costumes, to see how much work they'll need if you have to go on for her."

"We'll have to stuff the bosom," the older woman—who has finally introduced herself as Hettie—cracks. "Belle's got melons, compared to you."

I look down at my bust. "I wouldn't mind a little more, if you could build it into my dresses."

Hettie shakes her head. "The more you have, sweetheart, the more they fall. Someday you'll be grateful for those little plums."

Collins is seated on the bench in the dressing room when I return, wearing a sharp blue dress and matching beret. "I waited for you," she says, shifting over so I can get to my things.

I pull off my practice clothes for the second time in as many hours. "Haven't you had enough of this place?"

"Of course." She stands, catching hold of the door handle and leaning to one side to stretch. "I thought we could get a coffee around the corner."

"Why?"

"You can't be that thick." Collins shakes her head, auburn curls bobbing. "If you want to be standoffish, then fine. I just liked how you calmed those costume ladies and wanted to get to know you better."

I stop in the middle of rolling on a stocking. Whether it's the temporary nature of our work or being in a profession that pits pretty girls against one another, I've never understood the point of female friends.

"I'm sorry. I'm not used to people being friendly."

She sits back down on the bench. "Because you're in your own world all the time, Byrne. Or can I call you Kimber?"

"My name is Thelma." I hold out my hand. "You can call me that if you want."

"Good choice on the stage name." She nods approvingly. "Thelma's never going to knock 'em dead in the aisles, but Kimber might."

"That's what I'm hoping for." I fasten my garters and pull my dress over my head. It's another one of Aunt Claire's cast-offs, a lavender flowered rayon I remember from my childhood. Now skirt lengths are longer, it doesn't even look out of style. "If you're going to call me Thelma, I can't keep calling you Collins."

"I'm Vivian," she says. "Or Viv. I answer to most anything."

"Well, then, Vivian." I check my hair in the mirror and touch up my lipstick. "Let's get that coffee. I'm due back to work by seven."

The next day, after Mr. Barnet pronounces himself satisfied, we don our costumes and the full cast is brought in for a dress rehearsal. Once we find our places in the whole, it is easier to believe the show will go on. If my biggest break thus far is in this cobbled-together rescue of a show which already has a closing date, I'm not going to argue.

It's very different being onstage with a full complement of dancers. The space feels crowded and the sound of our tap shoes makes the floor shake. When the run-through is finished, the director holds up one hand and everyone remains where they are.

"That was... not bad." Raising his voice, he directs his next words to the choreographer. "Oliver, you've pulled off a miracle. They look like they know what they're doing."

"We should," Vivian murmurs behind me. "He's beaten it into us."

It is late enough that I won't have time to go home—again—or even to duck out for a bite to eat. I change into my black and white usherette's uniform and make my way through the theater to the lobby, hoping I can scrounge a snack before the evening performance. Several people linger near the counter, and I duck past them.

"Miss Byrne?" Mr. Arkright's brow creases in confusion. "What are you doing here?"

"Working, sir." I meet the eyes of the counter girl, and she nods, discreetly sliding something under a program.

"You *work* here?"

"Tonight is my last night, obviously." I can't be rude to him—the theater world is far too small—but I'm pretty sure there's a sandwich under that program and I want to eat it while I have time.

When he smiles, his face changes utterly. "That explains a lot."

"Does it?" My stomach growls loud enough for him to hear.

"You've seen Belle Watson perform every night, haven't you?" He grins now, like he's in on a secret. "So you have all her lines, as well?"

"I have everyone's lines," I say, hungry but not at all abashed at having been found out. "But I'm a dancer, not an actress, so that's not helpful."

"What you are, Miss Byrne, is a clever girl." Mr. Arkright tips one finger to his brow in salute. "Have a good evening. And if I don't see you tomorrow, break a leg."

3

Aunt Claire has purchased tickets for Friday evening's performance. She'll be coming with Mama, Pop, Grace, and Teddy. My brothers aren't available; they rarely are, and the thought of them dozing in the audience would have put me off my game, anyway.

"Since Claire beat me to it on the tickets, I'll take us for a treat after the show," Pop says at breakfast. "To celebrate your big night."

"It's not that big." *Trials and Tribulations* is as fluffy and insubstantial as my first act costume; nevertheless, I'm thrilled down to my toes, unable to keep down the excitement surging through me.

He raises his mug. "Don't give me that nonsense. You've been dreaming about this since you took your first dance lesson."

I smile sheepishly. "You're right."

"I'm looking forward to it," Mama says. "I want to see what's been keeping you out until all hours and sending you home so tired."

"I'm not tired." After my final shift, I dragged myself into the house at midnight, but I woke up this morning bright-eyed and full of energy. Tonight, I'll be the one on the stage instead of watching from the back of the house. It was enough to get me out of bed and dressed for my morning dance class.

Since it is a big night, I dress carefully in a black and silver beaded dress I recently liberated from my aunt's attic. I'm looking forward to her reaction when I make my entrance. When I walk into the changing room, fringe swinging from my hips, the other dancers look up.

Vivian whistles. "What a getup."

I give her my best dancer's curtsy, then begin to work my way out of the dress. It weighs a ton, and I have to be careful of the fringe; I don't want to have to ask Mama to repair it, even assuming I could find all the beads. "I'm going out with my family after the show."

"That must have cost a bomb when it was new."

It probably did. Not only did Uncle Harry worship the ground she walked on, but he let her spend lavishly on whatever made her happy. Which often involved things that made *me* happy. If Mama ever realized how many of my afternoons with my aunt were spent shopping or at matinees, she wouldn't have been amused. She's got nothing against the theater, but she wanted all us kids treated equally, and Aunt Claire quietly played favorites.

I place the dress carefully on the shelf and tuck away the rest of my things, then retrieve my sequined costume from the crammed rack in the center of the room. Wriggling into it, I turn so one of the other girls can do up the back, then do the same for her. A dresser will check on us to make sure we're ready to go on, but otherwise we're meant to manage for ourselves.

The dancers who've been here since the beginning help with our makeup, which consists of a thick layer of Pan-Stik until our faces are blank, identical masks, then bright rouge, liquid eyeliner, and false eyelashes. I swear quietly as I stick on the lashes, squeezing my eyes shut until the glue sets; fake lashes always make my eyes thick and clumsy. My brows are unfashionably pale, so they require a going-over with dark pencil, and we have been given lipstick in the same aggressive shade of pink as our costumes. When I have finished, Belle Watson drifts over and looks me up and down.

"Pretty good, kid," she says. "But your eyelashes are crooked."

I peer at my reflection.

"Thanks." I peel off the outer edge and stick it back down in the proper place.

By the time a boy bangs on the door and calls, "Five minutes!" we are warmed up and ready. We make our way to the wings, where we will skim out from both sides of the stage as the lead actress falls into a deep slumber. Belle, as her dreaming self, will rise up from behind the bed while the rest of us flutter around her in a shimmering orbit.

I'm second in line for the entrance. My chest is tight, my breath fast. The butterflies in my stomach are trying to force their way out through my ribs. I stare at the dark head of the girl in front of me and think of my first steps, where my marks will be, where I must look once I'm onstage.

There is no time for more—we're gone, out from the wings, moving in intricate patterns around Belle. When the male dancer springs forth to—wordlessly—declare his love, something the actor won't do until intermission, we fall back, then swirl around them, our arms moving rhythmically, the feathers in our headdresses swaying with each step.

I spin one last time, passing Viv as I do. Our eyes meet and something electric passes between us.

The applause rises as the scenery moves on its tracks, hiding us from view.

"We did it!" Viv throws her arms around me. We laugh with joy as we run back to the dressing room.

"You looked good out there," one of the stagehands says; it's not a pass, but a compliment, as he's in a place to watch this routine every night.

The dressing room sounds like the monkey house at the Philadelphia Zoo: sixteen girls, all talking excitedly, all celebrating that none of the new dancers fell on their faces or embarrassed themselves.

I strip off the sequined outfit—soaked now with sweat—and remove the uncomfortable pink shoes, wrapping myself in a robe until it's time to change into my next costume. My existing makeup will do; other than changing my lipstick color, nothing else is required. I touch up my eyeliner and poke again at the pesky lashes, which appear to have decided to stay in place.

Viv comes over to remove my feathers, then sits down so I can take hers out of her hair. Her dressing gown is woolly as a sheep, and she's pulled on thick socks over her tights.

"Cold?"

"Freezing," she says, with a mock shiver. "First night terrors. I'll be fine."

We've had several conversations by now and I've fallen swiftly for her quick wit and charm. While she's currently dancing in the chorus, her ambition is to be a comic actress. In the meantime, she'll take any job that keeps her in the theater—aside from ushering. She'd rather waitress and dodge handsy men than be tormented by the presence of others in her rightful place.

Our opinions diverge there; to me, there is nothing to be gained by dealing with handsy men in a restaurant. One day I'll give in to the impulse to tip a tray of drinks over one of their heads and that will be the end of my employment.

She respects my goal to be a dancer on Broadway or at Radio City, asking, the first time we went out for coffee, about my favorite dancers.

I almost said Ann Miller but then told the truth. "Vera Ellen."

"But she's so skinny!"

"She's also talented." In the first movie I saw her in, a forgettable film called *Wonder Man*, she displayed a dizzying number of techniques. I determined then and there to become as versatile as she was.

"And who would you most like to dance with?"

"Gene Kelly," I said promptly. During my childhood, I would have answered Fred Astaire, but once I'd grown up and realized what sort of man appealed to me, it would have been dishonest to give any other name. Gene Kelly's grin makes me melt; his footwork makes me swoon. It's an unbeatable combination.

The stage manager comes in and we all fall silent, listening as he tells us what worked—most of it—and what needed correcting—coming too close to Belle at one point, being too far upstage at another. "The audience isn't supposed to focus on you," he says. "You're background. You're scenery. Remember that."

Background or not, my family is in the audience, and they are focused on me. Even though I can't think beyond the next number, part of me is already with them, listening to their praise of my performance, and drinking the champagne Aunt Claire will nag Pop to buy for me.

The second number goes by in a blur and then it is intermission. I linger in the wings and once everyone has gone past, I tip my head to the nearest stagehand. "Can I take a peek?"

"Go ahead." He smiles understandingly. "Don't let them see you."

The heavy curtain keeps me from the sight of the audience. I move to center stage, then delicately part the curtain with a fingertip and place my eye to the opening, gazing out at hundreds of seats, where people are beginning to mill around. Most will go to the lobby for a drink or a bite to eat, but the dedicated theater-goers will remain in their seats throughout, paging through the program or waiting, as we will be, for the show to resume.

I don't know where my family's seats are. Scanning the audience, I look for Aunt Claire's pale hair and finally spot her about halfway back on the right side—not her usual excellent seats, but these were bought at the last minute. Mama is beside her, then Pop, with Grace and Teddy on the other side. Grace has her nose in the program, and Teddy's head is turned attentively toward her. The three adults appear to be talking—hopefully not about how silly the show is. The velvet panels swish together again, and I make my way to the dressing room, brimming with triumph, affection, and more than a touch of anxiety.

Our final number is the most rational of the show—we're actually dancing instead of being part of the main character's dreams of love. As she and the hero come together at last in a soaring duet, we chassé across the stage in groups of two and three, scattering flower petals and joy over their union.

It's absolutely ridiculous and I love every moment of it.

The applause washes over us at the end, and when the curtain closes so the key players go out for their bows, I stay behind again to listen and pretend it's for me. Then a sound cuts through the applause.

A long, shrill whistle, over and over.

Grace.

Mama is undoubtedly embarrassed, but my sister knows I'll recognize that sound anywhere and understand they're applauding me, whether I can see them or not.

It takes time to wipe off all the makeup and put on a real face, get my hair back to normal, and resume the beaded dress, but when I finally make it out to the ornate lobby with two other dancers, they are waiting in an alcove near the doors.

Pop looks proud enough to split a seam, and Mama is beaming in a most unfamiliar way. Aunt Claire is lit up like a candle, but it's Grace who hurls herself at me.

"You were amazing!"

"You really were."

"You were excellent, Thelma."

I bask in their praise. I've worked for years to have something more than a tiny part, and their words fill me with joy. I want to celebrate, but equally I want to be alone in my bed to go over the evening, examining it from all sides like a jewel, and polishing it in my memory.

"Are we ready?" Pop is in one of his less offensive suits, a muted check, with a truly heinous tie. Mama has learned over the years to choose her battles. She's wearing a black velvet cocktail dress she made before she and Pop got married. Despite being able to whip up a dress out of fabric and a daydream, she rarely sews anything new for herself.

Aunt Claire is in dark blue velvet with diamonds at her neck and ears, while Teddy appears older than his age in a dark suit and tie. Grace hangs on his arm, her black hair in coronet braids, wearing a dress Pearl left behind when she went to Paris.

We are a family of scavengers; we even made Mama's wedding outfit from old clothes we found in Aunt Claire's attic.

The nearby restaurant Pop leads us to is packed with a post-theater crowd. Thomas and two other dancers are with a noisy group at the bar. I wish I was the type of girl to fit in effortlessly with them. I asked Viv to meet my family, but she had a date and disappeared before I had even finished smearing cold cream on my face.

A bored waiter leads us to a table far from the dancers and we spread out. I'm between Mama and Grace, facing the door. I keep an eye out for other cast members, curious to observe how they behave outside what I think of as their natural habitat.

"I wish Pearl could have been here," Grace says wistfully as Pop orders champagne. "She's so proud of you."

"She would have come if she'd had more notice. I talked to her before you did." Pearl had called in the late afternoon, when she had the best chance of catching us all at home, chatting away like she wasn't calling long distance in the middle of the day.

"I know. But still."

The waiter returns with the bottle and an ice bucket. He pops the cork with a flourish and pours glasses for everyone, including Grace and Teddy, who take large gulps before anyone can think to stop them.

"She's old enough for one glass," I murmur, as Mama bristles.

"Can I please keep one of my children an actual child?" she asks with a sigh. "Just for a little longer?"

I shake my head. "I don't think so."

Since everyone in my family loves dessert, we order a selection of pastries for the table and eat them with champagne and much merriment. Before we leave, Lena Gilbey, the lead actress, comes in on the arm of her manager. There is scattered applause throughout the restaurant, and she bows her head in acknowledgement before sitting at a small, round table. Immediately, several men pull up chairs, and I think of Scarlett O'Hara and how she wouldn't sit at a long table because she would only have room for two suitors.

I watch her every move, filing them away like the lines to a play. Someday that will be me.

$$4$$

The faint sound of Frank Sinatra's voice, smooth as maple syrup, drifts from the kitchen. I pick up my pace. If Mama's in there doing dishes, I've slept entirely too long. She looks over at my entrance. "Morning, sleepy head."

"Morning. Sorry I missed breakfast."

"You deserved a little extra sleep after last night." She pauses. "Though you were probably too excited to sleep anyway."

"I was," I admit. "But now I'll be late if I don't eat quickly."

"Where are you off to?"

"Ballet." My Saturday morning class is worth getting out of bed for when I'd rather lie in, turning over the events of the night before in my mind.

She turns from the sink, surprised. "But you're dancing every day."

"Not ballet." I pour a cup of coffee and drop two slices of bread into the toaster. "I can't stop taking classes. I'll get rusty."

"You don't give yourself time to rust." She wipes her hands on the dish towel and sits at the table, where a basket of mending waits for her attention. "You worry me sometimes, you know?"

The toast pops. I put the slices on a plate, grab the butter dish from the counter, and carry it all to the table.

"Why? I'm fine." Last night was everything I could have dreamed of, but I woke up this morning with new, bigger dreams.

"I know you are." Mama takes a sip of coffee, plainly trying to marshal her words in a way that will not offend. "But you work so hard—I don't think Dan's job is as hard on him as yours is on you."

My brother is a shipyard welder; I'm sure most of his days would put my aches and pains to shame.

I chew slowly, gathering my thoughts. "This is what I want," I say finally. "It's all I've *ever* wanted. You know that. Why are you trying to take away from what I've accomplished?"

Mama's face falls. "Honey, I'm not trying to do take anything away. I'm sorry if that's how it sounds. I've never been good at careful speaking." She takes my hands. Her skin is rough despite the amount of cream she rubs into it. "I just worry all this is too much on your body. I'm a mother, it's my job to worry."

"Well, you shouldn't." I retrieve one of my hands and continue eating. "I know how much I can handle."

She nods and turns her attention to her cup. She's not finished. I can feel the next question hovering. Most of the time, she's pretty live and let live, but when she gets her teeth into something, she's relentless.

"When was the last time you were out with friends?" It's an innocent enough question, on the surface.

"I see my friends at dance class," I say airily, even though none of those girls are my friends. Viv appears in my mind, a bright spot. But we aren't close, not yet. "We don't have time otherwise."

She takes that in stolidly, then asks, "When was the last time you saw Sofie?"

"She wasn't there last night." Sofie came to live with my aunt and uncle before America entered the war. Our childhood closeness dissolved by the time we entered high school, when Sofie proclaimed my interests to be shallow and American. "I suppose she was busy."

Mama carries her mug to the sink and rinses it. "She's not well again."

"Not well" is a euphemism for the black cloud Sofie carries around with her. It was always there, but since she went to Germany and discovered that her entire family had perished in the war, it visits more often. A pang of guilt makes me wrinkle my nose. It's hard enough to be friends with normal girls; Sofie is far too much work.

"Maybe you could stop and see her later? She's at Claire's through the weekend, but she'll be taking the train back to New York on Sunday night."

"Class isn't over until twelve," I say. "And then I have to come home and get cleaned up. I need to be at the theater by four at the latest. If Sofie wants to see me, she can come over."

"But you have a show tonight."

Which was what all the dancers had said when we were told to come in after last night's performance. "We're too new. We haven't had enough practice."

Her shoulders go square; she's holding something back. Probably disappointment that I turned out ambitious and anti-social instead of the other way around. "I'll be sure to tell Claire you said you're busy."

"Don't." I hate the way she uses her sister as a weapon, knowing I want Aunt Claire's approval. "I might not have time to go over, but I'll call when I get in. Maybe she'll want to come over here. Is that enough?"

Mama turns from the sink. The morning light strikes her face in such a way that it emphasizes the lines at the corners of her eyes and the way her mouth turns down. She looks tired. Staying out late and drinking champagne doesn't agree with her.

"I just want you to be happy, Thel," she says at last. "You think you're an island, but you're not."

Her words remain with me when I get off the streetcar and trot the remaining block to Madame Duchay's ballet academy. It's a place I could find in my sleep, having gone there for ten years. When I burst through the front doors and head straight back to the changing room, it is already filled with a dozen girls and young women, getting into their practice clothes, chatting and laughing. No one looks up.

"Good morning!" I say brightly.

There are a few murmured greetings, but no one slides onto my bench, and no conversation is interrupted for long.

It's silly to let it bother me. The girls here have never been particularly friendly. Like at the theater, we all have our own agendas and ambitions. It takes time to cultivate friendships. Time we don't have.

Except everyone else is talking to someone. They've found time to make what could be casual or genuine friendships; I don't know, because I barely know their names.

A glance at the clock makes me speed up. Madame values discipline above all, and one way discipline is shown is to be punctual. I like to be among the first to arrive in the practice room and be thoroughly warmed up by the time Madame Duchay strolls in, tongue sharpened and pointer in hand.

She's told me for years that I have no future in ballet. "Your turnout is not good. You cannot stay en pointe long enough."

It's true; my legs don't turn from the hip in the same way as girls who've taken lessons since they were five or six. The problem, which I have tried to ignore, is that it hurts. Everyone's hips hurt, Madame said, the same way everyone's feet hurt. My feet can take it, but in the beginning, my hips ached deep inside, and it worried me. I never told Madame, because she might have told my parents. And they—caring as they do—would have stopped me from dancing. And then I would have died, and it wouldn't have mattered if my hips hurt.

I'll never be one of Madame's success stories, leaving school to join a ballet company. I started too late to be truly good at it, but I love ballet for the strength and discipline it demands. It also gives me a grace that doesn't come naturally in more modern forms of dance. When Mr. Barnet told me I had good arms, it warmed me through, and I mentally thanked Madame, though I would never have the nerve to tell her to her face, knowing her feelings about musicals and popular plays. I'll stick with being an enthusiastic student who will never be good enough.

It is a long three hours before Madame releases us, and conscious of my promise to Mama that I would call Sofie, I do not make another attempt at socializing and instead change rapidly and head for the streetcar stop.

There's a stiff wind blowing down Broad Street, and I turn my collar up and stamp my feet as I wait for the trolley. When it grinds to a halt and the door opens, I realize with dismay that either the schedule has changed, or there has been a change in the driver's schedule. The young man who grins at me from beneath his peaked cap has asked me out a half dozen times. To date, I have not even given him my phone number, but it never stops him from trying. If this is his new schedule, I'll have to start taking the subway.

"Pretty lady!" he sings out. "I haven't seen you in forever."

"And here I was hoping you'd forgotten me. No such luck?"

"No such luck." He waves away my fare. "Not for you."

"I'd rather pay." I drop my coins in the box and take a seat several rows back. When I look up, he's watching me in the mirror. It's a midday trolley; it should be packed with people heading downtown to do their shopping, but instead the empty seats in front of me do nothing to block his view.

"Still going to your dancing school?" He raises his voice over the traffic.

Why had I ever told him that I danced? I'd done it back before I knew I'd never be rid of him.

"Still going."

"I'd like to see you dance sometime." He hits the brakes, and we shudder into the next stop. A woman across the aisle glares at me for distracting him and tucks her bag prissily onto her lap.

"I'm in a show right now," I respond, to spite the woman and in the hope of getting rid of him. "At the Durang. You should bring your girlfriend."

He waits until several people pass, then starts the vehicle. "No girlfriend," he shouts. "I'm holding out for you."

"Don't hold your breath," I mutter. "Blue's not your color."

Why can't some men take no for an answer? This one has been trying his best for well over a year. I refuse to believe he's pining for lack of me, and if he is, the more fool him. Grace would tease me and say I'm too much of a snob to date a PTC driver, but that's not it. While I might prefer a man with more money to spend, what I want is to be left alone. No man I've ever met, barring Pop and my uncle, has ever understood that dance is more important than anything.

When we get close to my stop, I make my way to the rear door, but it's no use. The car doesn't move until I reach the corner. Then the door flaps open and he says, "I look forward to our next meeting."

I'm definitely taking the subway from now on.

The house is quiet when I let myself in. Mama's at her shop, Pop is doing something with Toby and George—trying to get them to act like part of the family—and Grace is either out running with her tribe of girlfriends or clinging to Teddy like a growth.

Should I call Sofie? Just because we were close ten years ago doesn't mean we have anything in common these days. I don't want to disappoint Mama, nor do I want her to say anything to Aunt Claire. I drop my bag on the sofa and sit down at the telephone table, running my fingers through my sweaty hair. Finally, I dial the number and listen hopefully as it rings. Maybe they're all out.

"Warriner residence."

"Hi, Cecie. It's Thelma." I shift to the sofa, shoving my bag to one side and stretching the cord. "Is Sofie around?"

"She's up in her room," comes the soft voice of my aunt's maid. "Let me get her for you."

Her footsteps recede and I wait, wondering what I can even say to Sofie.

"Thelma." I hadn't even heard her approach. "I hear you did wonderful things last night."

She's trying. I force a smile into my voice and say, "It was good. I'm sorry you weren't there."

"No, you are not." Silence. "I would have brought nothing to the party."

"You'd have been there." I wince. Now I feel terrible for *not* missing her last night. "We all said you would have rolled your eyes and declared it was terrible, but... I missed you."

I hear a creak, and I picture her sitting in the fragile chair at Aunt Claire's desk.

"I am happy to be missed, but I wasn't in the mood for frivolous things, you know?"

Personally, I'm not sure Sofie has ever been in the mood for frivolous things. Even when she was a little girl, she was thin and dark and watchful. She's the same now, just taller.

"Are you feeling up for some frivol today?" I ask. "I'm fresh from dance class, so I have to take a shower, but I don't need to be at rehearsals for until later."

"I have to study."

"You always have to study." I laugh. "Come on, Sofie. You can study on the train back to Barnard. Meet me at the little restaurant on Pine Street, we'll get coffee and a piece of pie."

Sofie hesitates, then says, "Fine. It will make Claire happy."

We're both trying to make Aunt Claire happy. I notice she doesn't mention if it will make *her* happy.

Once I'm showered and my hair is dry—an easy thing thanks to the hair dryer Pearl gave me for Christmas—I leave a note for Mama and start up Pine Street, shoulders hunched against the cold. I hope to get there before Sofie, but it's not likely. Not only is our meeting place closer to her house than mine, but she's punctual for everything and I'm never on time unless it's for work or dance class.

The plate glass window of the café is fogged, but I can discern her silhouette as I approach the door. She's in a booth, her spine straight, gaze downcast. Just looking at her makes me tired. I swallow my dread and open the door.

Sofie looks up as I slide onto the seat across from her. I'm startled by how different she looks. She's always been thin and naturally pale, but there's something more going on here.

"Good to see you," I say, reaching over to squeeze her hand. "You didn't have to start without me."

"Who knows when you would get here," she responds. "You are always late. You have so many places to be"

"Just the theater." I glance quickly at the menu and when the waitress arrives, order coffee and a slice of lemon meringue pie. "You would have laughed at the show last night. It's so silly."

"The family was there." She shrugs. "I am not your family."

"Yes, you are." Sofie has spent more than half her life in Philadelphia; Aunt Claire thinks of her as a daughter, even when Sofie makes her want to tear her hair out. "But I know how you feel about musicals. You wouldn't have enjoyed it."

She doesn't respond, addressing her attention to the apple pie and ice cream on her plate.

"How is school?" I couldn't wait to graduate, but Sofie always loved it. She convinced Uncle Harry to send her to boarding school, and when she came home from Germany, she went straight to college in New York. She doesn't even make it home for every holiday, which hurts my aunt, though she tries not to show it.

"Very well." She gives a small, satisfied smile. "After I graduate, I will attend law school."

"You can't get enough, can you?" I try to make it sound like a joke, but her gaze doesn't waver.

"You are too unserious. Education is important." She pokes at the ice cream with her spoon. "And the law is important. There need to be responsible people trying to enforce the laws."

"Aren't there?" This conversation is as much my style as musicals are hers.

"Not everywhere. Bad people can manipulate the law to their own ends. Good people must stop them."

I look up gratefully as my coffee and pie arrive. "You make it sound like America is going to turn into Nazi Germany. We're not like that."

I see raw pain in her dark gaze, the kind she never shares. "We weren't like that, either."

Pop is pulling up to the curb as I arrive home. "Where were you?" he asks, hauling his doctor's bag out of the front seat, where it has pride of place when there are no passengers.

"I met Sofie for coffee," I say, trying to mask the exhaustion in my voice. "Now it's time to go to work."

He offers me his bag. "Take that inside and get your things. I'll drop you off. You've worked hard enough for one day, and you haven't even started."

5

My failure to connect with Sofie rattled me so much that as the week went on, I made a concerted effort to be nicer, not only to Viv, but to the other girls at the theater. As I began to listen to the dressing room conversation about auditions and dance classes, interspersed with warnings about lecherous directors and spotlight-hogging actors, I realized my tunnel vision had prevented me from acquiring valuable information.

These girls aren't my competitors. Until we are up for the same role, they are my colleagues, willing to share knowledge I might not have. I need to get off my high horse and start making friends.

Between room and board and the cost of dance classes, my pay from the Durang is gone as quickly as it arrives. Pop would let me slide, but I want to pay my way. My older siblings contributed to the running of the house from the time they were old enough to hold a job. Pop makes decent money now, so the rule changed. We don't contribute until we graduate high school, which was a break for me and my sister. It would cost far more to live on my own—even sharing an apartment with several girls, assuming I could find anyone I wanted to live with—so it's easier to stay home, especially since only Grace is left. Now that she's older, we get along much better.

I look at the few dollars I have left in my wallet and take the plunge. "Who wants to go out for something to eat after Saturday's matinee?"

Heads swivel around the room, surprised by my sudden proposal. In the end, a half dozen girls agree, and we make a plan for an early supper at a diner before returning for the evening show.

"It's not like I can fit in a date between four and six anyway," one girl complains. "Not one where he'd have time to spend any decent money on me."

"You could pay in advance," Thomas suggests snidely. "That way when he takes you out on Monday, you've already paid for your dinner."

The girl says something rude and everyone laughs. I feel strangely more part of the ensemble than I do when we're on stage.

When it comes time to go, we're joined by two of the younger actresses and three actors, who make much of walking out of the building surrounded by eight women.

"We need one more girl," Joe Dexter cracks. "Then it would be three apiece."

He plays the leading man's best friend and has several colorful but tasteless jokes which make the audience roar with laughter. I've had little contact with him thus far; from what I've seen, he's as slick as his slicked-back hair, and his winning attitude fails to win me over.

"I'm an old man." Andrew Bellamy slings an arm around my shoulders. "I'll stick with two. This little doll and that brunette over there."

"I don't think so." I dip from beneath his arm. "You're too old for me."

"Touchy!" He is no more than forty, but if he can make a joke of his age, then I definitely can. "Watch out for this one, boys."

Viv comes up behind me. "Don't undo all your hard work. Playing the ice queen isn't going to earn you any points with this crowd."

"I'm not playing the ice queen," I tell her indignantly. "I just don't like men assuming things."

His heavy arm assumed quite a lot. I don't care what the actors think of me. We hadn't invited them; they piled on because they saw a bunch of pretty girls going out and couldn't leave us in peace.

Somehow our original plan of going to the diner is changed to a nearby hotel bar, where we take over several empty tables. The men immediately begin hailing the waitress, who is hiding behind the bar with a cigarette.

"I don't have the money for this," I say to Viv, as menus are distributed. I could eat a whole meal there; here, I'll be lucky to get a bowl of soup and some crackers. "That's why I suggested the diner."

"Let the men pay," she advises. "You might have to kiss somebody, but fair trade, right?"

I wrinkle my nose. "I don't want to kiss anybody."

"You mean to say"—Rayburn leans in—"you haven't kissed some-body you didn't want to? In this business? How have you managed that?"

"I didn't say I haven't." My face heats, thinking about some of the situations I've been in. "But I'd prefer not to."

Andrew Bellamy reminds me viscerally of a director I met at one of my first auditions. I'd made it through the first round and when I arrived at the callback the next day, I ran into him in a hallway backstage.

"You did good yesterday, kid." He put a hand on my shoulder. "There's no reason why you won't end up in the chorus."

"I'd like that," clueless me had said, as his fingers slid down my arm.

"Good girl." He pushed me behind a tall stack of crates and pressed me up against the wall. "How about a little thank you in advance?"

There was something exciting about being manhandled in an almost public place, but his breath smelled like cigars, and I didn't like the way he was rubbing himself on me.

"How about I do my audition and say thank you afterward?"

He took my hand and placed it over his crotch. His zipper was already down. "Because you're not going to get that audition unless I get a little sweetness first."

That afternoon, I learned a few things: how to give a hand job; to be glad of that semi-public hallway because he couldn't push me to go farther; and to never trust a man who offered me a part in exchange for sex, because after all that, I didn't make the chorus. He winked at me when I left, like we had a secret.

I went home, locked myself in my room, and cried from the unfairness of it all.

There had been another, similar situation, but instead of crying, I used what I'd learned from the first director, convincing myself that it was a transaction, one hand washing the other. Not every job makes such demands, and I've gotten pretty good at sensing which directors will want more than an audition.

Actors, on the other hand... they're constantly creating drama. Even with my limited experience, I've seen more romances begin and implode than I thought possible. Backstage is as fraught as a Saturday afternoon movie, with tears, cursing, and occasional threats of violence.

I would stay well away from all that.

"What kind of soup do you have?" I ask the waitress when she comes back around.

"Chicken noodle or beef barley." She looks exhausted and the evening rush hasn't begun.

"Beef barley and coffee, please." I ignore the jeers of my companions, all of whom have ordered drinks and sandwiches. "I don't like dancing with alcohol in my system."

I'm not much of a drinker, anyway, because I don't eat a lot and it goes to my head too quickly. I can't risk a loss of control.

"You're smarter than most of us," says the third actor, who I think is named Conrad. He looks about my age, with a thick swoop of brown hair falling across his forehead. "More than one drink and I'll forget all my marks."

"It's a good thing you don't have any lines, then," Viv says pertly. "You'd be lost **and** silent."

"Most directors I've worked with would prefer me that way." Rising half out of his seat, he peers around the dim bar. "Speaking of directors, ours isn't here anywhere, is he?"

"Don't worry," Dexter says from the next table. "He doesn't come here."

"Thank God!" The young man falls theatrically back in his seat, then gives me a sideways glance. "I'm young enough to handle three of you girls, but given my choice, I would prefer our dashing director."

"Is he dashing?"

His brows lift. "You've met him. Didn't he make your heart go pitter-pat?"

I think back to the stern man I'd met at auditions and the slightly softer version in the theater lobby. He's attractive enough, I suppose, in a tightly-wound sort of way, but I hadn't considered him in that light until now.

"The only thing that makes my heart go pitter-pat," I tell him truthfully, "is dancing. I'm not going to get drunk and fall off my shoes."

"I've heard that about you."

"Heard what?" The other table is rowdy, and I lean closer.

He smiles conspiratorially. "You're ambitious. Driven. Gunning for Belle Watson's job."

"Who says that?" I'm not sure I like people in the theater talking about me.

"Stan Arkright, for one. And he thinks you're good enough to get it."

My family complains that I'm never home, but with seven shows a week and dance classes every weekday except Wednesday, when there is a matinee, there's nothing to be done about it. I'm doing what I love. Getting paid is a bonus.

It won't last; no show ever does. But I will enjoy every moment of *Trials and Tribulations* until it closes, and then I'll go back to auditioning every chance I get. At least I won't be alone. Viv and some of the other girls have already made plans to audition for the same shows, so we can all work together again.

Viv was the one who told me I could trust Conrad Toll, the young actor who called me ambitious. "He's not like the others," she murmured. "You're safe with him."

I didn't tell her I already knew. Theater people are more accepting of such things, but I couldn't be sure if Andrew and Joe were aware of his inclinations. I can't imagine they are. Or perhaps they like having less competition for the chorus girls.

Connie, as everyone calls him, bumps into me one night as I'm leaving. "Kimber," he calls. "Do you have a moment?"

"Just about." I want to get home; it was a two-show day, and I've been dreaming about a hot bath. My feet hurt and the nagging pain in my hip has cropped up again.

"I won't keep you." He pushes his fingers through his hair. "I was going to get a cab. Can I drop you somewhere?"

"Sure. Camac, between Spruce and Pine." I see the surprise on his face; it confirms what I already know. "You're familiar with the neighborhood?"

"A bit." He wraps a vivid red scarf around his neck and takes my arm. The few people lingering at the stage door look up hopefully, deem us unworthy of attention, and go back to waiting for the show's stars. "Have you lived there long?"

"Over ten years." I duck as he hails a cab. His gesture is large enough to be seen across a packed house, but perhaps somewhat excessive for Arch Street.

We settle into the snug warmth of the back seat, and he gives the driver my address. Although Connie was the one who wanted to talk, he remains silent.

"Did you want to ask me something?" It's comfortable sitting with him, knowing I'm not going to have to fight him off.

"Mmm. Yes." His fingers are in his hair again; if he cut it fashionably short, or wore a hat, he would have nothing to do with his hands. "Would you"—he clears his throat— "would you like to have dinner sometime?"

"Sure, I guess." I hadn't expected him to ask me out. "Why?"

The cab turns onto Twelfth Street and heads south. We'll be there in a few minutes

"My family is coming to town the week after the show closes," Connie said, speaking very fast. "And I've told them—well, I've told them I have a girl."

"Oh." I consider the prospect of an evening pretending to be an attentive girlfriend, and how grateful he will be if we pull it off. "Will it be a nice restaurant?"

A relieved laugh bursts out of him. "The nicest," he says, giving me a smacking kiss on the cheek. "Only the best for my best girl."

6

Trials and Tribulations closes on the second Saturday in February. The show ran for over three months. I performed onstage with the replacement dancers thirty-five times.

"I'm sorry it's over, but I'm beat." Viv pulls down a few photos tucked into the frame of the mirror. "I'm going to take an entire week off before my next audition. What about you, Thelma?"

"I'll sleep in tomorrow." Sunday is church, but Mama will understand my desire to stay in bed. "I have ballet on Monday."

I've missed so many classes lately. Madame Duchay couldn't argue about Wednesdays—I could hardly skip a matinee—but I've missed Saturday mornings, as well, because the thought of two Saturday shows after one of her grueling classes made me not want to get out of bed at all.

"You could give yourself a break." She stuffs her personal items in her bag and looks in the mirror. "Do I look good enough for the cast party?"

"Of course." Viv always looks good, if a little flashy. Tonight, she's wearing a snug red dress that clashes with her hair but highlights all the curves we don't have in common. "Do you have your eye on someone particular?"

She shrugs. "Joe Dexter's been giving *me* the eye lately. Now that I don't have to see him every day, it might be fun."

I doubt that, but I'll leave her to it; I've learned it's better not to tell people when they're making bad decisions, only to comfort them afterward.

"You are going, aren't you?" she asks, gesturing at my dressing gown. "Do you have one of your ridiculous costumes?"

"Yes and yes." I bring out a dark blue velvet dress with a dropped waist and a hem that dips low in the back. "You and Connie wouldn't let me live it down if I didn't."

All I want is to go home and take a handful of aspirin and a hot bath. Over the past week, my hip pain has increased to the point where it's getting hard to conceal it. Obviously, I've managed, because Mama hasn't said anything. Neither has Viv, but she doesn't watch me in the same way.

"You and Connie have really hit it off, haven't you?" She zips my dress while I hold my hair out of the way. "He's a sweet guy, even if he's a little flitty."

"He should be getting better parts." I fish my lipstick out of my bag, then look critically at my face. "Did taking off my lashes mess up my eyeliner too much?"

Viv peers at me. "You're fine. And the bar will be dark, anyway." She spins around impatiently in the tight space, brushing against one of the other girls, who is putting on her stockings. She swears when Viv knocks her off balance.

"Jesus, Collins! Be careful."

"Sorry." She drops a hand on my shoulder. "I'll get out of here. Meet you at the back door?"

I'm fighting to get my sweat-dampened hair to behave. "Give me five minutes."

It is no more than ten minutes later when I arrive, heels clacking on the scarred wood floor, but only Connie remains at the stage door. "They went on ahead," he explains, shivering theatrically as he winds a deep red scarf around his throat. "I waited for you, but I'm freezing."

The cast party is being held in one of the smaller banquet rooms at the Bellevue-Stratford. I've been here before, back when my aunt was involved with a yearly charity event at Christmas. The room is buzzing, women's light voices overlaying the men's deeper tones. The clink of glasses is audible from the door.

We check our coats and venture in, finding a table away from the crush of people. I see Viv almost immediately, a champagne glass in one hand,

Joe Dexter's arm wrapped around her waist. She's laughing, her head thrown back.

"Well, she got what she wanted," I murmur.

"Him?" Connie makes a face. "She can do better."

"That's not for us to say." I lean against him, suddenly exhausted. "My feet hurt. Get me a drink?"

"Your wish is my command." He bows deeply. "Bubbly or something else?"

"Bubbly, please." Champagne doesn't go to my head in the same way as wine or hard liquor. "I deserve it."

There are more people here than I expected, not just the cast, but men in dark suits with expensively dressed women on their arms. The money men, I guess. Producers, investors. Theater management. People I should speak to, if I had the energy. Maybe the champagne will help.

I close my eyes for a moment, opening them when someone drops down in the chair beside me. It's not Connie but Belle Watson, wearing a spectacular sequin dress that covers slightly more than her first act costume.

"Sorry you didn't get to go on." A waft of liquor and perfume drifts off her. "Bad luck."

"Not for you." I can smile at her now, though during the run I'd fantasized about minor things that could keep her from going on—a bus stuck in traffic, a twisted ankle. Nothing dire, because I don't want to risk my bad wishes coming back on me.

"No," she agrees. "Not for me. But you'll get there."

Her praise is gratifying; she certainly doesn't have to be nice at this point. "Thank you."

Connie arrives with my champagne, and Belle removes it from his hand. "How did you know I was parched?" She tosses it back, waves her fingers languidly, and drifts in the direction of a plump older man in a tuxedo.

"I guess that's my cue to get you another one." He goes to move but I put my hand on his arm.

"I'll get it this time," I say. "No one's going to take it out of my hand."

The bar is crowded, and there is a four-man band setting up on a small platform beyond. I didn't realize there would be music. Music means dancing, the last thing I want to do right now. My hip throbs, and I press my hand against it under the shadow of the bar.

"Two glasses of champagne, please," I say to the harried young man with two bottles in his hands already.

"Two? Do you have an invisible friend, or are you thirsty?" It's one of the older men, and he's leaning far too close.

"I'm thirsty," I tell him, accepting my drinks, "and I have a friend waiting for me over there."

"The pretty ones always have friends." He tilts his head, staring at me with narrowed eyes. "You're in the chorus. Kimber, is it?"

"Yes. Kimber Byrne."

"I'm Lou Hartley." He holds out a hand, forcing me to put down one of the glasses. "The manager of the Durang."

During my time at the theater, Mr. Hartley has spoken to the ushers several times, but it never occurred to him that I already worked for him. I certainly look different out of my uniform. I let his sweaty hand encompass mine; it never hurts to be pleasant. "There are so many people here I haven't met."

"Well, we can remedy that." Mr. Hartley keeps hold of me and I catch Connie's eye across the room, telegraphing he'll have to get his own drink. "You're one of our pinch-hitters, aren't you? The girls who came in to rescue us from the damned measles."

I follow him across the floor; he pushes forward like a ship through choppy seas. "I thought it was chicken pox."

"Whatever. Damned inconvenient." He comes to a stop in front of two men in suits. "Bob. Roger. Let me present Bernice Kimber, one of our chorines."

The men don't hear—or don't listen—when I correct him and are already calling me Miss Kimber, which feels wrong in this setting. I want to take my drink and go back to Connie, but Mr. Hartley has me by the arm and is telling them all what a fine job I've done in the chorus, and how he hopes to see me on his stage again sometime soon.

"It would be my pleasure." It would, especially if I didn't have to spend any more time in his company.

"Well, then." He bestows a broad smile on me. "There's an audition next week. We're looking for chorus girls for *Love Letters*. You'd suit for that."

"I'll be there." Unlike Viv, I hadn't planned to take the entire week off, but I also hadn't expected another audition so soon. "Thank you."

Finally, I get away from the men and hunt Connie down. He's standing in the center of a knot of girls, critiquing their dresses and causing them to weep with laughter. I listen, drinking my champagne entirely too fast, and when he pauses for breath, ask, "What about me, then? What's wrong with me?"

He sobers abruptly. "Not a damned thing, darling."

I discover the next morning how much my family has missed me when everyone stays home from church and Mama cooks a big celebratory breakfast. Dan comes, along with Tommy, and even George, one of my other brothers, makes an appearance. He is yawning and smells of smoke, explaining he got off a very late shift at the firehouse.

"I'm glad you're here." It's unusual to be happy to see George; he and Toby tormented me as a child, but the war changed him and now, with a wife and baby, he's almost tolerable.

"Sorry I didn't see the show," he says gruffly, accepting a plate from Mama. "The baby's had colic and Ruthie wanted me home."

"There will be other shows." I think of Mr. Hartley's mention of an audition this week. I'd told Viv before I left and she'd jumped up and down, drunkenly proclaiming we had to do it, so we could work together again. "Hopefully something Ruthie will enjoy. Maybe Alice could stay with her parents."

"Maybe." He hunches over his plate, shoveling in food as if he expects a bell to go off any second.

Grace leans her head on my shoulder. "I've missed you."

"I've missed you, too. I've missed all of you." Most nights, she's been asleep when I've come in and I exchange a few words with my parents before dragging myself upstairs. I know Mama struggles to stay awake until she knows I'm home safe, but some nights I've been so late even she has gone to bed.

"How was your party?" Mama asks, laying a light hand on my shoulder as she refills my coffee. "You got in very late."

"Later than I even wanted." It had been difficult to leave when everyone was having such fun. Connie hauled me out onto the dance floor and made me jitterbug, not an easy feat in tight, twenty-five-year-old dress, and I had three more glasses of champagnes to dull the pain in my head and hip.

Finally, as the music subsided and many of the partiers had paired off, I snuck away, picked up my coat, and walked the few cold blocks home to enjoy the silence. I fully expect Connie to call later to reprimand me for abandoning him.

"Are you taking a break now?" Dan asks. It's the first time he's spoken, which is not unusual.

"Do you take breaks from work?" I bring a piece of bacon to my lips. "I have an audition on Thursday."

We linger at the table until Pop looks up and says, "If we stay here much longer, I'll bring out lunch."

Sunday lunch is his responsibility: he makes enormous, messy sandwiches that require bibs to eat.

"I think you can take today off, along with Thelma," Mama says. "There's another pack of sausages in the kitchen if anyone's still hungry."

Wordlessly, Dan picks up his plate and takes the one George holds out to him. Moments later, the smell of frying sausages reaches us.

George perks up. "Say, Thelma, how does all this dancing girl stuff pay?"

"Not well enough," I tell him. "But I love it. How about running into burning buildings?"

"Not well enough, either." He grins. "But I love it. Ma, how did you manage so many of us? Ruthie and I don't know what to do with the one."

"Momentum," she says. "If you don't stop having babies, you never have enough time to think about how hard it is to have them."

"So by the time I was born, you had time to think." Grace, youngest of all, makes a face. "I'm sorry."

"You weren't a hard baby," Mama says. "A little demanding, maybe—"

"But then I came along," Pop interrupts. "And you just loved me."

She did. And Pop is the only father she's ever known. We'd even agreed, as a family, to let him adopt her so he had one child who bore his name.

Grace gets up and leans over the back of his chair, her arms around his neck. "Still do," she says and kisses him on his bald spot. "Aren't you lucky?"

I've warned the family in advance that Connie is a friend, not a boyfriend, and not to embarrass me, but when he arrives to pick me up, Grace slaps her hand over her mouth.

"I remember you! You tripped over a chair during the wedding scene."

"Grace," I say warningly. He's nervous enough about seeing his parents. He doesn't need to be reminded of an onstage blunder.

"You've got sharp eyes," he says, not minding at all. "I thought I was pretty enough that people wouldn't have noticed."

It is Grace's turn to be embarrassed. "I just—um, I shouldn't have—"

"It's fine," Connie says. "It's why they didn't give me any lines. I can't be trusted to walk and talk at the same time."

She grins at him. "But you *are* pretty."

He turns to me. "Can we bring this one along to dinner? She might be a good distraction."

I shake my head, imagining my loose cannon of a sister turned loose in a situation already so fraught with so much potential drama. "Let's hope I'm distraction enough."

A cab takes us across town to a small restaurant with a flickering neon sign above the door. The Brauhaus.

"Not your usual style." Connie's taste runs more toward plush banquettes and champagne bottles in shining silver buckets.

"It's for my parents." His face is white, and his Adam's apple bobs nervously. "I need to tell you about them, Thelma."

"You've left it a little late." For days, I've been asking him to give me enough information to prepare; all he's told me is I can't mention that I work in theater. "What's wrong with them?"

"Nothing wrong. Only they're—" He breaks off, swallowing hard. "Never mind, they're here."

The restaurant is small, no more than a dozen tables set out on a tiled floor. All are occupied but only one group turns to look at us. Four men, all with beards, all wearing black. A soft-faced older woman with a black bonnet and a dark gray caped dress. They look like the Pennsylvania Germans who sell food at the Reading Terminal.

I turn to look at Connie. "You're *Amish*?"

"Not currently," he says in a voice totally lacking his regular gaiety. "I haven't been home in two years, and they've come to find out why."

We approach the table. When his father rises, Connie drops my hand.

"Conrad," he says in a booming voice. "It has been a long time."

"Yes, Vater." Connie shakes his hand, then leans down to kiss the woman on the cheek. "Mutter, this is my friend, Thelma Kimber. Thelma, these are my parents, Mr. and Mrs. Stoltzfus. And my brothers, Aaron, Benjamin, and Daniel."

I stifle an absurd urge to curtsy. "I'm very pleased to meet you."

Connie sits next to his mother, while I am seated between the brothers. They're larger than my friend, with the same thick brown hair—badly cut—and plain dark clothes. They don't say a word.

Mrs. Stoltzfus speaks. "How did you come to know my son, Miss Kimber?"

I meet Connie's eyes across the table. We haven't discussed what I should say, so I wing it. "At a diner. Near where I work."

"What is your job?" The father interrupts before I can explain that Connie saved me from an ill-intentioned customer.

"I work part-time for my uncle's firm," I tell him. "And I'm in my last year of college."

"Our daughters were all married by your age," Mr. Stoltzfus says. "Every one of them."

"How many daughters do you have?" I can't believe he's never told me any of this.

"Four. Anna, Ruth, Lotte, and Miriam."

"But Conrad is our youngest son." Mrs. Stoltzfus gazes at him fondly. "The last to leave the nest. And, I hope, to return to us from his time among the English."

Connie stares down at the menu on the table.

"Conrad?"

"We should order," he says brusquely, signaling to the waiter. "I chose this place because I thought you'd be more comfortable with the food."

"We don't eat often in restaurants." His mother turns to me. "Our Ordnung doesn't forbid it. It simply isn't something we do."

Ordnung sounds like ordinance; I assume it's some kind of rule they follow. Instead of asking her to explain, which she might find offensive, I say, "What do you recommend?"

We order sauerbraten, some sort of potato dumplings, and sauerkraut, and Mr. Stoltzfus asks for a pitcher of beer. After I finish telling them about how Connie and I met, the conversation is stilted. For the most part Connie remains silent, staring at his mother.

"You have not answered, Conrad," his father says, after our plates are put in front of us. "When will you be coming home? It has been two years."

"I'm sorry, Vater." Connie smiles benignly. "I'm going to stay in Philadelphia and marry Thelma."

"You asked me to play your girlfriend. You didn't say anything about getting married."

Broad Street Station is vast, and at this hour, nearly empty. We'd put his family—silent, stunned, hurt—on the late train back to Lancaster, where they would drive home to their farm in a horse and buggy, to a world a hundred years distant from their son's chosen life.

"I'm sorry." Connie's blue eyes, which are normally filled with light and humor, like he is about to break into laughter, shine with tears. "I didn't plan it. It slipped out when he asked when I was coming home."

Apparently, Amish boys are allowed a year or two to try out the wider world before committing to growing their beards and their families. His mother called it rum spring or something like that. Connie knew from the moment he set foot on the train that he wouldn't be returning; after a month in Philadelphia, he was a city boy to his core. After his first time at a theater—as the escort of a much older man—he'd fallen in love. With theater, not the man, though that had been when his inclinations had become clear to him.

His family's reaction mirrored the shock I felt; his mother pretended to be pleased that her son had found someone, but even as a respectable secretary/college student, I was an English girl—non-Amish, modern. Very far from the girl she would have chosen for him. If we'd told her I was a dancer, I'm not sure how she would have responded.

"Did your sisters get to take time away to decide how they wanted to live?" If they're all married, they couldn't have.

"Miriam tried," he says. "Vater told her it was not permitted, but she left anyway."

"And?"

Connie shakes his head. The anguish in his eyes tells me Miriam didn't achieve her freedom.

"He and my brothers and two of my uncles went to fetch her. She'd walked nearly ten miles to the train station, in her bare feet, because they locked up her shoes at bedtime."

"Why?"

"So she couldn't leave." He shrugs defeatedly. "It's easier for a man to live out in the world. Miriam didn't know how to do anything—she wouldn't have been able to buy a train ticket."

Any girl capable of walking barefoot for ten miles would have found a way to buy a train ticket; that she was brought home and married off makes my heart hurt for her and for Connie, who would have undoubtedly supported her if he'd been allowed. It strikes me how much courage it took for him to refuse to go back.

"Did you ever have a beard?" I've only ever seen beards like those on the Stoltzfus men in the costume department and they required adhesive.

"Beards are for married men." Connie strokes his smooth jaw. "I never wanted a beard. Or, as you may have figured, a wife."

I reach down and take his hand. It is icy cold, more from nerves, I think, than the temperature. "Does that mean I'm being jilted before I even get to the altar? Because I'm not sure if I like that."

His laugh is shaky but genuine. "I adore you, you know."

"Then take me home. It's not every day a girl gets engaged and dumped in the space of two hours."

It took all my strength not to tell Viv about that strange night when we met a few days later at the Durang for the audition. But it wasn't my secret to share, and she was full of details about her whirlwind romance with Joe Dexter.

"He really is a jerk," she says, almost fondly. "But he knows how to show a girl a good time. We took the train to Atlantic City on Tuesday and walked the boardwalk. It was so cold! But he held my hand and then he took me to dinner and a show."

I'd like to do things like that, but not enough to do them with him. Connie would take me out if he could, but he has no more money than

I do. He spent the bulk of his savings on that ridiculous dinner—most of which had gone uneaten once he told them he wasn't coming back.

"I'm glad you're having fun." Viv's curls bob with enthusiasm as she talks. "Have you been practicing for today, or have you been too busy?"

"Don't you worry about me." She flutters her eyelashes. "I'm going to charm their socks off."

I don't count on charm. I've gone to class every day this week, ballet twice, tap once, and extra hours of studio time to work up a new audition routine, which I paid for with the very last of my money from *Trials*.

I was as prepared as I could be. I was also so tired that my muscles quivered. As I've had no time to rest, the pain in my hip has come back with a vengeance. Mama caught me limping the other day and I lied and told her I'd twisted my ankle getting off the streetcar. I didn't like lying to her, but the truth was dangerous.

Many of the girls on the stage are familiar, and there are some faces I recognize from class. They make their way to my side, though we've barely exchanged words before. Any port in a storm is a good thing. I smile and make room for them. Viv huffs and shifts to one side.

The casting director is a thin man with a strong New York accent who pushes us around as if we're dolls, arranging us first by height and then by coloring before we're even asked to dance a step. Two girls are dismissed without having had a chance to try.

"He's tough," Viv murmurs. "I'm going to enjoy impressing him."

I hope we get the opportunity.

Finally, we are told to line up, and one by one, we're called forward to perform our audition piece. Mr. Barnet is in the front row with several other men, and he gives me a quick wink as I come forward.

Love Letters is an unfamiliar show, so I'm not certain whether to give them something more classical or to stick with a combination of modern and tap that I know they'll appreciate, but the choreographer's wink decides it. I tell the pianist what to play and begin my routine, letting my body do what it does best. It sometimes surprises me the things I can do—even with all my training, something deep inside remembers not being able to move easily, much less with grace—and it pushes me forward.

The music stops and I stop with it, trying to slow my breathing. I drop a curtsy, not looking at the casting director. "Stay in line," is all he says, but it is enough. For now.

Viv is cut on the second pass. Her shoulders stiffen and she ducks past me without a word, her eyes bright with tears of rage at being rejected. She won't wait around for me; I'll call her later to tell her what happened—hopefully that I got the job. I don't know how she'll handle the news if she reacted so badly to being cut.

Having a friend is harder than I expected.

By the end of the afternoon, the casting director, director, and choreographer have made their selections. Several of us linger in the wings, straining our ears to hear their discussion. At one point, Mr. Barnet says, "I want the blonde. Byrne. She's a worker."

When my name is called, I step forward calmly to stand with the others, though every nerve in my body is singing with excitement.

Mr. Barnet looks us up and down. "You know the drill by now," he says, clasping his hands in front of him. His jacket is plum-colored velvet and he's wearing a polka-dotted ascot. Connie would look divine in this outfit, but it doesn't suit our middle-aged choreographer at all. "Nine o'clock tomorrow in the practice room. Be prepared to work."

One of the girls from my ballet class was also chosen and she attaches herself to me as we get changed. "Have you worked with him before?" she asks anxiously, stuffing her practice clothes into her bag. "How hard is he?"

"He's like Madame," I tell her, and watch her face fall. "He's not bad, so long as you're willing to work. He knows what he likes."

Her name is Nora, I remember. Nora Kelly.

"I didn't know you wanted to be on stage," I say, trying to recall if I've ever heard her voice opinions other than the names of her favorite movie stars. "Have you auditioned before?"

"Once or twice. My family doesn't approve. They think we're above all this." She lowers her voice. "Do you know my cousin Grace? John Kelly's daughter?"

I hadn't realized she was related to the same Mr. Kelly who ran for mayor when I was a little girl. My uncle Harry worked on his campaign, and I came along once or twice, playing with the candidate's daughter while the men talked politics and made speeches, mostly to each other.

"I knew her," I say. "But it's been a long time since I've seen her."

My family doesn't exactly run in those circles; even Aunt Claire prefers to stay away from politics these days

"She's in New York," Nora confides. "Modeling and trying to become an actress. If my parents are upset, hers are frantic. Being a dancer is one step above being a streetwalker, according to them."

I've run across that opinion before, though thankfully not expressed by anyone in my family. I can't imagine being judged by the people who are supposed to love me best. Mama isn't thrilled about what I do, but that's because she's a worrier, not because she disapproves.

"But you've been dancing for years." I zip my dress and reach for my jacket. "Didn't they mind then?"

"Ballet is different." Nora looks utterly miserable but also determined. "That was to make me graceful and attract a good husband. Ballet was for them. This is for me."

When I call Viv later, her landlady tells me she's not in, which is patently untrue; I can hear her voice in the background.

"That's a shame," I say. "Please tell her I got the job and I'm sorry she didn't."

"I'll do that." Her voice drops. "She came home in a mood. If I had a cat, she'd have kicked it."

Perhaps it's just as well she's keeping her distance, whatever the reason. I'm thrilled to have work again so soon. I don't want my balloon punctured because my friend is unable to be glad for me. This business is filled with rejection; we have to bounce back or we'll never survive.

Connie gave me the celebration I needed, taking me out for coffee and a dizzying afternoon at Bonwit Teller, where we resurrected our pretend engagement and I tried on a full trousseau for his doting approval, dresses and gowns and beach pajamas, even a scandalous black silk nightdress and peignoir set that made him blush like a boy.'

"Most gentlemen would be champing at the bit to see such a vision," the salesclerk says as he hides his face in his hands. "She looks lovely."

"I'm not most gentlemen," he says in a strangled voice. "I think it's a touch... obvious, darling. If you know what I mean."

I lean over, one hand to the plunging neckline, and give him my most seductive smile. "But darling, we're allowed to be obvious on our honeymoon."

The salesclerk, a well-built woman in her fifties, looks at him with disappointment. "Where are you going on your honeymoon?"

"Venice," I say, as he says, "Atlantic City."

"Well, which is it?"

"Atlantic City," I tell her with a shake of my head. "A girl can dream, can't she? If we never open the curtains, we could be anywhere."

The rehearsal situation is different this time. Because we're not filling in for missing cast members and getting used to being on stage quickly, our routines are learned in a stuffy practice room next door to where the actors rehearse their lines. I can hear them whenever our music stops and within two weeks, I have both my steps down and a passing familiarity with the script.

Love Letters has no more substance than *Trials and Tribulations*, but I've learned not to judge a show by its substance. Audiences will come to see almost anything and shows beloved by critics frequently have the smallest crowds. Still, I would like to be in a show that, when I said the name, people congratulated me, rather than admitting they'd never heard of it.

But as I tell Connie when he meets me at the stage door in the late afternoon, I'm in back-to-back shows. It feels like a big step forward in my career.

"I'd like a step forward myself." He's looking for his next role, haunting the callboards, reading the newspapers, and catching up with anyone he's ever worked with in the hopes of finding something. "I've burned my bridges. This has to work."

"You wanted to burn those bridges, didn't you?" I can't imagine my friend in the repressive environment he's described. "That's not your world anymore."

"They're still my family. I love them." Connie sighs. "My mother wrote to me last week. My father told everyone I died."

"I'm so sorry." I squeeze his hand, uncertain how to comfort him. My family isn't perfect, but they would never reject me for being who I am. Then I think of something. "Would you like to come for dinner? My mother never minds if we bring people home."

She prefers it, in fact; I don't think she's entirely adjusted to her children leaving home. It's not that she doesn't want us to go out into the world, but living in a nearly empty house must be disorienting.

"You don't think they'd mind?" He perks up. "Should I bring wine? Flowers?"

"Just yourself." I brush off his shoulder and straighten the carnation in his lapel. "You dress well. She'll appreciate that."

During the third week of rehearsals, I've finished for the day and am about to head back to the dressing area when Mr. Barnet calls me over. "Mr. Hartley wants to see you."

I look at myself in the full-length mirror. I'm in a wrinkled knee-length skirt, dance tights, and a sweater tied around my shoulders. Not an outfit to make an impression, certainly. "Should I change?"

He shrugs. "I wouldn't bother. Apparently, there's been some sort of calamity with Rose Petrie. Your name came up as a replacement. I said you're a quick study and knew the lines already."

We'd heard sobbing and shouting in the hall earlier in the afternoon, but I'd been catching a breath of air in the alley a short while later when Rose Petrie stormed out the stage door, her face blotched with tears. Calvin Owens, her dance partner, followed on her heels, entreating in a low voice.

"Don't you dare!" Her delicate fist connected with Mr. Owens's chin, and he fell backward through the door.

My giggle was stifled too late. Miss Petrie's fiery gaze lit on my face, and for a moment I thought I was next. Then she exhaled and shrugged. "You're welcome to them, toots. Just don't let them in your pants."

After shocking Mr. Barnet by hugging him, I make my way up to the manager's office on the second floor. The door is partway open, and I knock before entering, wishing I'd taken the time to put on street clothes.

"Mr. Hartley?"

"Come in!"

Pushing the door wide, I step into the office. It's a small space, filled with furniture: a large desk and chair, where the theater manager is seated, a couch along one wall, a metal file cabinet between the narrow windows. The radiator in the corner is working overtime; the room is almost tropical. Beads of sweat immediately form along my hairline.

"Miss Byrne." Mr. Hartley doesn't bother to stand. His sweat-glazed face lights up as he stares at my legs. "Thank you for coming so quickly. You may have heard Miss Petrie will be leaving the show?"

"Yes, sir." My chest tightens and I force my hands to remain at my sides.

Mr. Hartley licks his lips, his eyes never rising above the level of my chest. "I've discussed the matter with the director, and we think you'd do nicely as her replacement. She has a few lines, so you'll have to attend rehearsals with the actors in addition to working with the dancers. Can you handle that?"

Part of me wants to spin around, shrieking with joy—so much for that girl in her clanking braces—but I keep a bland expression and ask, "What about Katie Bridger? She's Miss Petrie's understudy."

He looks up, apparently surprised there is a head on my body and that it makes words. "Alas, she has also abandoned our fair ship. You're a relative unknown, it's true, but Ollie says you're a quick study. If he says you can do it, that's enough for me."

Do what, is the question. *Just don't let them in your pants.*

"That's very kind," I say, stalling as I hunt for the right words. "What do I have to do?"

Because I want this job. It's all I've wanted since I was ten years old. Rose Petrie be damned, I'll even let him in my pants if it will seal the deal.

It's one more toll to be paid on the road to my future. It won't be the first time, and it won't be the last. I was lucky enough to be born with a face and a figure that make men want to give me things, while they take other things from me. The price is always calculated in small humiliations; I learned young not to place too much value on what they want—only on what I want.

He stands and takes my hand in both of his. "Just be a good girl, Miss Byrne."

I want to pull away from his moist, clammy paws—slap him or, better yet, punch him in his round, absurdly dimpled chin, but instead I smile sweetly. My eyes remain limpid with promise, but my voice goes hard. "I'll be a good girl once the contract is signed."

Mr. Hartley gapes and the tent in his baggy pants deflates with shock. "Miss Byrne!"

Smiling again, I remove my hand and cross the room to stand by the door. "No contract for me, no good girl for you." I raise my skirt until I feel a breeze. "Do we have a deal?"

"We do," he huffs, dropping into the wheeled chair behind his desk. It groans and rolls backward, almost depositing him on the floor. "Come back tomorrow afternoon at three."

It's ten after three when I finally knock on his door. I've spent the better part of an hour hiding out backstage, working up the nerve to do what I'm about to do. One of the stagehands took pity on me—I told him I'd broken up with my boyfriend—and gave me a slug from the flask in his pocket. Whiskey. It burned all the way down and lit a fire in my brain.

There are other ways to advance in the theater, but none of them have worked so far. It will be five minutes of unpleasantness. I can do that. I have to.

The door opens and Mr. Hartley waves me in.

"I thought you got cold feet." He's wearing another baggy suit, and the muggy office is wreathed in cigar smoke. Memory strikes at the scent. I want to turn and run but I walk calmly up to the desk.

"Where's the contract?"

"Aren't you a cold little bitch?" He sounds amused. "Right here. Sign on the line, sweetheart, and then sit down here. Drink?"

"Sure." I skim over the printed sheet. It certainly *looks* like a contract: Kimber Byrne, to play the role of Evelyn for the duration of *Love Letters*. There's a raise in salary, although not as much as I would like for a speaking role.

I sign my name, then turn around to face the music.

Mr. Hartley is sitting on the old green damask sofa, a glass of amber liquid in each hand. It looks like a prop couch that outlived its usefulness and made its way upstairs. I take one of the glasses and sit down, leaving a foot of space between us.

"Thank you." I raise the glass and take a sip. It's even stronger than the stuff the stagehand gave me; my throat burns, and I want to cough, but I won't give him the satisfaction.

"All you little girls drink like fish, I know that." He reaches over and pats my knee. His hand lingers, thick fingers tracing along my thigh. "Now about what we discussed yesterday..."

I go very still as his hand slips under my skirt. This one apparently doesn't want me to do anything but let him go exploring. It's not that I like the other stuff, but it's over quickly and I'm the one doing the touching. Feeling like I'm in control is important.

When his fingers slide under my garter, I squirm away. "That's enough."

"I beg to differ." The grip on my leg is harder now, pinning me to the slippery green cushion. "You promised to be good, Miss Byrne, and we haven't reached good yet."

He launches himself at me and I slide backward under his weight. The glass flies out of my hand and shatters. One of his hands is on my thigh, trying to pull down my pants, while the other presses my shoulder to the sofa.

There is a knock and the door opens. "Lou, do you have a mo—Jesus Christ!"

Mr. Hartley freezes and I take the opportunity to scramble out from underneath him. A man is framed in the doorway, his silhouette stark against brightly-lit hall. He steps in and slams the door, and I retreat behind the desk, realizing I'm now trapped in here with two men. I wasn't doing well fending off one of them.

"Miss Byrne."

It's Stan Arkright, the director from *Trials and Tribulations*. Oh, God. What must he think?

"You should go," he says. "You were done, weren't you, Lou?"

"No, if you must know," the theater manager says sullenly. "We were having a nice little conversation."

The director looks from him to the broken glass. "One that involves whiskey and flattening unsuspecting chorus girls?"

"She came in to sign a contract," he mutters. "We were celebrating."

Mr. Arkright advances to the desk. I stay well on the other side. He picks up the contract, looks at it, and waves it at Mr. Hartley. "You haven't signed yet, Lou. Let me get you a pen."

I sidle around the far side of the desk. Mr. Arkright nods and mouths, "Go on now," and I bolt out the door, wondering if I'll have a job in the morning.

8

Connie takes one look at my face, puts up his umbrella, and hauls me down the alley to the tiny luncheonette at the corner. A handful of theater people are sitting at scattered tables, but he pushes me into a seat in the far corner and places himself so I can't be seen.

"What is it?" He raises a hand to the waitress. "You look like death."

"I feel even worse." I cover my face and through my fingers tell him of my new role and the price I nearly paid to achieve it.

"What an absolute shit." I smother a laugh; he is not yet accustomed to swearing, and the word leaves his mouth with the glee of a small boy getting away with something. "Did he think you would do that?"

"I would have," I interrupted. "He wasn't going to give me the part any other way. You're the one who said never to turn down a job. Work is work. But when it came right down to it—his hands—"

Viv would understand, but we're still not speaking. Maybe I should call again and tell her she's lucky to have missed out on this particular show.

"It's probably why Katie Bridger walked out after Rose quit." Our coffees arrive and he spoons sugar into his like it's about to be rationed. "That absolute shit," he says again. "How did you escape?"

I can't think about that part, because it makes my skin crawl with shame. Viv would find a way to make me laugh, but telling Connie somehow makes it more embarrassing.

"You remember Mr. Arkright?"

"Our dashing director?" His eyes go distant and his lips curve into a smile. "I'm not likely to forget him."

"Well, he's not likely to forget me," I say. "He walked in and found me underneath that repulsive man."

I don't tell him Mr. Arkright made certain the contract was signed, nor that he sent me away without looking me in the face—for which I am nearly as grateful as I am for the rescue itself.

"I've never been so mortified in my life. What can he possibly think of me?" I take a sip of coffee, gag, and reach for the sugar bowl. "God, this is awful."

Connie puts his hand over mine. "He thinks you're another in a long line of girls Hartley has tried this with. He probably feels like a hero, Thelma, for saving you."

"Knowing my luck, he'll expect a reward in his turn someday." I shake my head. "It's so much easier for men."

"Not for me." He turns so I can admire his profile. Beyond the glass, the streets are dark; car headlights momentarily illuminate the rainy sidewalks. "Barnet is one of the few of my tribe around—in the open. I'd offer my virtue to the highest bidder if it wouldn't get me a beating in an alley rather than a part. Take it as the compliment it is."

He's right. It just doesn't feel like much of a compliment.

The next day, instead of joining the dancers, I go to the room next door, where Rex Malone, the director, introduces me to everyone.

"Apparently, we should be grateful Miss Byrne was willing to step in after not one but two actresses quit the production."

Most of them look at me curiously, this oddity sprung from the chorus. I look down to hide my discomfort, wondering what Mr. Hartley has told the director about me. There was a copy of the signed contract waiting when I arrived today, but I'm not convinced he won't appear at any time to exact his revenge.

"Miss Byrne, come and sit by me," Calvin Owens says. "We have two scenes together, as well as the dance."

"At least we know you *can* dance," the director says, acid in his voice. My taking the role of Evelyn was clearly not his idea.

I sit beside Mr. Owens and pick up the bound copy of the script. Seeing Rose Petrie's name crossed out and mine written beneath makes me break into a cold sweat.

I'm not an actress. My talent lies in my body, in movement, not in becoming another person in front of an audience. Just because Evelyn has a significant dance number doesn't mean I can handle the rest of the part. What foolhardy ambition made me agree to go onstage and say lines and convince people I know what I'm doing?

My fingertips go numb, but I open the script and page through it, looking for Evelyn's name. Rose considerately underlined all her dialogue, and I try to focus on the words as the room spins gently around me.

They go through an entire reading that morning. I speak when it is time, listen to Mr. Malone's suggestions—couched in sarcasm—and do my best to follow his direction. Several times I see surprise on the faces of the other actors; if I'm not good, I'm not a complete disaster, either.

When we break for lunch, Calvin Owens turns to me. "Come along," he says. "I need food. We'll work on our scene over lunch."

My packed lunch remains in my bag. He doesn't want to eat in the theater, so instead we go to the luncheonette Connie took me to yesterday and sit in the same corner booth.

"You've got decent timing," he says straight off. "That comes from the dancing, huh?"

"I guess." I glance at the menu and decide swiftly on grilled cheese and tomato soup: tasty, filling, and in my budget. "You can tell me, Mr. Owens. Am I awful?"

I want very badly for him to tell me I'm good, but I wouldn't believe him if he did.

"Not awful," he says with a crooked smile. "Just not good yet. But you'll get there, come hell or high water."

We place our order, then Mr. Owens tells me in detail everything I did wrong in the morning. "You're too quick," he says. "There's a pace to a show. You'll feel it, when you've had more time."

Now that's a critique I can understand; he's speaking like a dancer.

"What about the dance?" I ask around a mouthful of grilled cheese. "When do we start on the dance?"

"Not before the weekend," he says. "Malone wants you to get your lines down. The show is blocked, and we've been rehearsing in the theater—we're back in the hotbox today for your benefit. Barnet told us you're a quick study."

"I am, but I'd also like to feel like I'm good at something." I tell him a version of the truth. "Plus, if I don't dance, I'll start to stiffen up."

Mr. Owens laughs and takes a drink of Coke. "I don't dance enough. My last two shows I didn't dance a step."

"Which do you prefer?" The tomato soup is rich and smooth, almost as good as Mama's. "I can't imagine not dancing."

"I prefer acting, but work is work." He shrugs. "I was in the Pacific for three years. Getting to act feels like a reward for surviving."

"Two of my brothers were there." While Toby and George came home in one piece, they've never been quite the same. Compared to them, Calvin Owens is almost childlike. I shouldn't judge; it's almost impossible to know what's going on inside a person, and he's an actor, better at concealing his feelings than most.

He pulls the rolled-up script from inside his pocket and spreads it open on the table, anchoring it with the sugar dispenser. "Now," he says, "here's what I mean about pacing. When Evelyn says, 'You mean it was me... all along?' you need to lean into the pause before 'all along.' Let us hear her thinking about all the times she might have misinterpreted my behavior."

"I wish there were notes like that in the script instead of stage directions." I think of Pearl's novels—all those emotional bits are written down, so we can't misinterpret what she means.

"Theater is about interpretation," he proclaims, as if reading my mind. "But instead of writing it all down, we lead the audience to those conclusions. We know how the story ends. They don't. The way you're playing it, you're giving it away."

I'll try to think of it that way as I say Evelyn's lines: she doesn't know yet that she'll have a happy ending. "May I ask a question?"

"Of course."

"Why did Miss Petrie hit you?" At his horrified look, I clarify, "I was in the alley. I saw it."

I wish you hadn't." He ceases to look boyish. "That was between Rose and me. It was a personal disagreement."

"I don't care what was between you and Miss Petrie." I gather my courage. "For better or worse, Evelyn is my part now and I want to do the best job I can."

He takes another pull of soda and stares over my shoulder toward the front window. Finally, he says, "You're here because Hartley wants you here. You could walk on stage and speak in tongues, and it wouldn't hurt your credit with him one bit."

Dinner is long over by the time I get home. The family is in the living room, listening to the radio, but Mama puts down her knitting when I come in and pats Pop's shoulder. "I put a dish in the oven for you," she says, following me to the kitchen. "You work harder putting these shows together than you do once they're running."

"It sure feels like it." I drop down into the hard chair and let her bustle around getting my food; she would anyway, and I'm too tired to argue. "I'm completely lost. It's so different from chorus work. We haven't even started working on the dance routines yet."

She slides the plate in front of me: meatloaf, gravy, potatoes. I attack it like I'm starving. Which I am.

"I know you get tired of hearing me say I worry about you, but I do. It's not something a mother can turn off."

I've always thought she worried more about me than the others because I started out as her broken child. Pearl once told me Mama felt guilty, as if she'd done something wrong when she was pregnant with me. When I get impatient, I remember those words and squash my feelings down.

"It's okay." I carry a fork full of mashed potatoes to my mouth. "This is what I want, Mama. This work. It's not easy, but that's part of what I love about it."

She sighs. "I thought you'd get over wanting to be a performer."

"I'm not fit to do anything else," I tell her. "Apparently I'm not fit to be an actress—just ask the director."

"Do you want tea?" She's already moving to the stove. "How did you end up with a speaking part, then, if you're not a good actress?"

My plate is nearly clear and I don't remember eating half of it. Lunch with Calvin Owens was more than eight hours ago and it feels like several days.

"The original actress and her understudy both quit." When I say it aloud, I hear how odd it sounds.

"Does that happen often?" Mama leans against the counter as the water heats. "Or is there something wrong there?"

"The director is a bit of a jerk, and the theater manager is awful, but that's the case in a lot of theaters." I hesitate before mentioning my suspicions about Calvin Owens. "I think she might have been dating her co-star, and something went wrong."

Mama is silent, mulling this over. The kettle begins to shriek. She wraps a dish towel around the handle and pours water into waiting mugs.

"Now that," she says quietly, "is another thing I worry about. You hear about casting couches and… well, we all know what men can be like. You haven't had much experience with men like that in your life, Thel. That's all."

When she puts the mug down in front of me, I catch her hand and squeeze it. "You taught me well," I say. "I can handle myself. I can handle them, if it comes down to it."

By Friday evening, Mr. Malone pronounces himself satisfied that I will not make a fool of myself and ruin his entire production. "As an actress, Miss Byrne, you're a good dancer. Barnet and Owens will meet you here at nine tomorrow to start on your routine."

I had hoped, naively, to have the weekend off. Madame Duchay is going to forget my name if I don't come to class soon. "I'll be there."

When I arrive at the practice room in the morning, Mr. Barnet gives me the eye. "Out late, dear? You look like something the cat dragged in."

"I'm fine." My practice clothes feel unfamiliar, and my legs and back are stiff from a week of sitting around. On the plus side, my hip feels better.

"I hope so. You girls need to take better care of yourselves."

I bite my tongue, wanting to tell him it wasn't my fault Mr. Malone didn't let us go until after ten. By the time I got home and ate dinner and had a hot bath, it was after midnight, and I was so over-tired that my eyes refused to stay closed.

Mr. Owens looks no more well rested, but the choreographer doesn't address the bags under his eyes—or the faint smell of alcohol that lingers around his person. He drops his jacket on a chair and bounces up to stand beside me.

"Ready, Miss Byrne?"

"Aren't you going to change?" He's in flannel trousers and shirt and tie, and his leather-soled shoes aren't suitable for dancing.

"Nah." He shakes his head. "I already know the routine."

Mr. Barnet wakes from his daze. "You may know the routine, but you're dancing it with a new partner. I do hope you have other shoes in that bag."

He grumbles but goes off to change his footwear and I allow myself a small inward smile.

It is my last smile for several hours. Mr. Barnet goes over the routine, dancing the female part with Mr. Owens, and then walks me through it several times, snapping when I don't get the steps quickly enough. I keep a placid expression for all that I'm ready to scream, damned if I'll buckle before the men drop from exhaustion. This is not how I like learning, with an expectation that I'll know everything before leaving for the day.

Dancing with a partner onstage isn't the same as dancing with a man on a dance floor. We hold ourselves differently, and each gesture is calculated to be seen from the back row. In the beginning, as I absorb the steps, my movements are smaller; I want to learn everything before I try to match his movements. It's not enough for Mr. Barnet.

"Larger, Byrne. Larger."

"I'm trying." I clench my teeth to keep from shouting at the annoying little man.

"It's about eye contact," Mr. Barnet says sharply. "Look at him, Byrne. You're in love with him. Don't you know what that feels like?"

"Of course." I can fake it well enough for his purposes.

At five, he says, "Now the lift. If you can get that right, we'll call it a day."

My partner nods. "She's a little thing, anyway. Rosie had some bottom weight."

"Miss Petrie had equally complimentary things to say about you." Mr. Barnet tuts at him.

The music begins. We do the steps leading up to the lift, an intricate back-and-forth routine—part tap, part ballroom, wholly lifted from every Rogers and Astaire movie that thrilled me as a girl—which is supposed to mirror the relationship of the characters, their misunderstandings, and the final realization of their feelings. When that happens, we stop and look at each other, and then I run toward my partner. Mr.

Owens is supposed to sweep me up over his head and then lower me slowly into an embrace.

I've never done a lift. Being in the chorus, there'd been no reason to learn. If I'd known about the lift, I wouldn't have slept at all.

"Are you sure you won't drop me?" I whisper to Mr. Owens as the choreographer bends to speak to the piano player.

"You saw me lift him. You weigh half what that little—"

Mr. Barnet returns. "I'm assuming, Miss Byrne, that you are unfamiliar with lifts?"

"I've never done one," I confess. "But I can learn."

We go through it slowly, the step sequence, the pause, the meaningful look. Then I flutter toward Mr. Owens, and we count along with the music until it's time for the embrace. When Mr. Barnet decides we have it down well enough, he leaves us alone to work.

"Two more hours," he calls, as he and the piano player don their coats. "If you do well tonight, you don't have to come in until noon tomorrow."

"We need to get this down," Mr. Owens says. "I'm meeting a girl at eight. I don't want to be late because I was making love to another woman."

I suck in a deep breath. "Well, heaven forbid your plans are disrupted by your job. Let's try it."

We start again. It goes more smoothly without the choreographer's watchful eye, even though it takes time to get comfortable. The first time Mr. Owens attempts the lift, I have a brief flash of Mr. Hartley's hands on my body, and I lose my balance. I apologize and we try it again. The first half dozen attempts fail, but eventually I launch at the right time, and he catches me at the right angle, lifting me up and changing his grip so my hips are resting on his open palms. Both of us are so thrilled by the result that our embrace is almost genuine.

Once we have it, time flies by. Now that my body understands the assignment, it wants to do it until I drop. I'm so excited by our achievement that I can focus on nothing else, until Mr. Owens reminds me of the choreographer's instructions, "Look at me," he says, pointing at his face. "Remember, you're in love with me."

"I don't fall in love," I say airily. The only thing I've ever loved, outside of my family, is dancing.

"You will, cupcake," he tells me, backing away so we can repeat the lift once more. "I just hope I'm around to see it."

9

Mr. Barnet is pleased with our progress. Mr. Malone is pleased to have us back for the bulk of the day, as I now need to practice saying my lines while moving about onstage, avoiding props or taped lines meant to represent pieces of scenery or furniture.

It appears I have a facility for learning dialogue, if not delivering it. When I hear a scene several times through, it begins to stick. Over the weekend, I persuaded Grace to run lines with me in exchange for a new lipstick and I got the bulk of Evelyn's lines down. Now I need to get better at saying them.

Our calls remain early. Connie appears at the theater one day at noon and strong-arms me into walking to Chinatown with him. He drags me into a tiny, delicious-smelling hole in the wall, and we sit at a rickety table. Connie orders chow mein and egg drop soup while I make do with a bowl of wonton soup—we're doing the dance routine as part of the afternoon rehearsal, and I don't want my nervous stomach too full for the lift.

"You're playing hard to get," he says. "Can't you see I'm pining away for want of your lovely face?"

"You look perfectly fine."

He beams. "But doesn't it feel nice to be wanted?"

"It does. But tell me what's going on with you, because you already know everything that's happening in my life."

Over the soup—which is as delicious as the place smells—he tells me about two auditions and a date that didn't end well.

"I thought we'd hit it off nicely," he confides. "But apparently, he thought I was another pretty face. If there'd been a sofa in evidence, I would have been you, flattened by an overeager man."

"Eww." I don't like thinking about that day for many reasons, not least of which is I'm petrified I'll run into Mr. Hartley and he'll fire me before I even get onstage.

"I know." He twirls the noodles on his fork. "Men are so disappointing. It almost makes me wish I liked girls."

The waiter comes with the check and puts down a small plate with two fortune cookies. When I don't break mine right away, Connie takes it and cracks it open. "*Don't hold onto things that require a tight grip,*" he reads. "What does that even mean?"

"It's my fortune." I tuck the slip of paper into my bag. "Maybe it's not for you to understand. What does yours say?"

"*Good luck will come to you next Thursday.*" He smiles triumphantly. "I have an audition next Thursday. That means I'll get the part."

I prefer cryptic fortunes to something this specific, which will have him holding onto hope until next Friday morning.

"Have you seen Viv lately?" Eventually, she'll get over being mad at me. Cutting me off because I got a job and she didn't isn't fair. After all, she befriended me first.

"I ran into her at the callboard at the Shubert last week." He knows how much I miss her. "I told her you were doing well and she snorted."

"When you see her again, tell her I said hello." I'd call her myself, but I'm afraid she won't talk to me and I don't want to find out how much that will hurt.

"Will do." We part company at the stage door. Connie kisses my cheek and squeezes the air out of me. "Knock 'em dead, dollface."

On Sunday, we have an afternoon call. I sleep late instead of going to church, coming downstairs in time to help Pop prepare lunch. It's easier now there are so few of us, but it feels strange to have only four or five at the table.

My mother and sister return from church with Teddy, who is deep in conversation with Grace. He stops to acknowledge my presence, but she leads him into the kitchen, still talking.

"Those two," I say. "Do they ever stop for breath?"

Mama sees my bag on the step and peers in, wrinkling her nose. "Good lord, your laundry," she says. "It's like having boys in the house again."

"I'm sorry." My practice clothes are stiff with sweat when I take them off and I haven't remembered to put them in the basket. "I'll do my wash."

"When?" she asks practically. "By the time you drag yourself in here, supper's been and gone. You don't sleep enough as it is, except on Sundays, and you'll be out the door like a shot again tomorrow morning."

I try not to think about my schedule. When I do, it makes me tired and I'm tired enough already. My stamina, of which I've always been so proud, is beginning to flag.

"Once the show opens, it will get easier," I tell her, hoping I'm right. "I'll be late, but I won't be there all day."

"No, you'll go back to your dance classes every day instead."

But I won't, not until I recover from the last few weeks. At this point, I don't care what Madame Duchay says about my absence; the pain in my hip is almost constant lately, varying from a dull ache to a sharp, grinding pain that stops me in my tracks. I'm beginning to fear I've actually hurt myself.

Thankfully, no one else has caught on yet, but it's a matter of time before Mr. Barnet's sharp eyes detect that something is wrong. It's likely even less time before my mother figures it out.

Monday's rehearsal goes smoothly and we are released early, for once. Nora Kelly asks if I'll walk with her. I put her off, saying I have a call to make and I'll meet her at the luncheonette in fifteen minutes. Once she is gone, I walk quickly in the other direction. A nearby hotel offers a private lobby phone booth. I shut myself in, drop my nickel in the slot and dial a familiar number.

"Dr. Byrne's office, how may I help you?"

I bite my lower lip. "I'd like to make an appointment, please."

"Very good. Has the doctor seen you before or are you a new patient?"

"A new patient." I wrap the phone cord around my wrist until it cuts into my flesh. "My name is Vivian Collins."

A pen scratches as she writes down my name. "Doctor doesn't have any openings this week. Do you have a time preference?"

"I work during the day," I say, "but I can be late, if necessary. Does Dr. Byrne have any early morning appointments?"

We settle on next Wednesday at eight. When I hang up the phone, I'm sweating like I've finished a three-hour ballet class.

The next week, I fib and tell Mr. Malone I have a dentist appointment. When he objects, I ask if he would like me to appear on opening night with a swollen face. He subsides, muttering, "Just get here as soon as you can."

No one at home knows. I leave earlier than usual and have a cup of coffee down the street from Pop's Chestnut Street office. He works part-time at my aunt's charity clinic in South Philadelphia, but I chose not to go there; it is farther away and most of the staff have known me since I was a child. I couldn't count on them not to tell my mother or my aunt.

At ten minutes to eight, I present myself at the office. There are already several people seated in the colorless waiting room. I give Viv's name and take a seat, opening a dated copy of McCall's.

After fifteen minutes, the nurse calls, "Miss Collins?"

I make my way through the now crowded space. "I'm Miss Collins."

"Come along." She leads me down a short hall and opens the door to a small room, furnished with an exam table, a file cabinet, and a stool. "Doctor will be with you shortly. Take a seat."

I haven't met this nurse before, or I'd have a heck of a time explaining why I made an appointment under a false name. I don't know myself, except I feel like if I asked Pop at home, I'd be his daughter; here, I'm a patient, and he can't tell Mama what I say.

More than a few minutes pass before there is a quick knock on the door, followed by a turning of the knob. Pop enters, looking down at a clipboard in his hand. His multi-colored tie is barely visible at the neck of his white coat but it adds life to the bland room.

"Miss Collins." He leans against the cabinet, looking at his notes. "What brings you in today?"

"Hiya, Pop."

He looks up from his chart, momentarily confused, and then his face breaks into an easy grin. "Thelma! What have you done with Miss Collins?"

"She's at home," I confess. "I used her name to make the appointment."

"You don't need an appointment. I always have time for you." He tosses the chart aside and takes a seat, not minding that it puts him lower than me. Most men I know wouldn't willingly put themselves in a position where a woman is above them.

I cross my ankles and lean forward, my fingers tight on the edge of the padded table. "It's not something I can talk about at home."

"Oh." His brows draw together. "Are you… all right?"

"I'm not in trouble, if that's what you mean." Laughter takes some of the tension from the air. "But I don't want Mama knowing about this, and she knows everything that happens, even when she's not there."

Pop nods acknowledgement of my mother's powers. "What's the problem?"

"It's my legs." I slide off the table with a crackle of paper. "Or my hips, to be more exact. Mostly the right one. On days when rehearsals go long, they've been hurting." I give him a warning look. "And before you ask, I won't stop, or dance less. I need it to *hurt* less."

"So you're where all the aspirin has been disappearing to." He pushes back his chair. "I'll have to examine you."

"Okay." I'd expected that. I reach behind to unfasten my skirt.

"It's not like when you were a kid," he says hastily, making for the door. "I have to call a nurse to be in here with us. While I'm gone, take off your skirt and sit back on the table."

He returns with a different nurse. I don't know her either.

"Vivian Collins," he says tersely. "Twenty-two-year-old dancer. Childhood history of rickets. Treated with braces and exercise." He pauses. "Treated by me, actually. She's been experiencing pain in her hips. For how long, Miss Collins?"

"About six months," I say sheepishly. "Sometimes before that, but it wasn't frequent, so I didn't pay much attention."

"Okay." He is choosing not to lecture me in front of his nurse, which I appreciate. "Can you show me where it hurts?"

I put my hand on my right hip, pressing until I feel the round head of the bone at the top of my thigh. "Right in here."

He places his hand in the same location, and I rotate my leg until the pain stabs at me. "It's worse on this side, but it's beginning to hurt on the left, as well."

"Does the pain feel like it's on the surface, or deeper?" Pop moves to my other side and asks me to repeat the movements. I do, with less discomfort, though there is still a wrongness there.

"Deeper." I try to describe something I have no words for. "Almost like something's rubbing, if that makes sense. There are times when it's fine, and then it's not. There's no in-between."

"Hmm." He steps back and makes a note on Viv's chart. "Interesting."

"Can you fix me?"

"It's not that easy, I'm afraid." His eyes are rueful. "I'm going to send you for x-rays."

"Why?" I want a miracle cure, preferably one that will go into effect before I get to the Durang later this morning.

"Because we need to see what's going on in there. X-rays will give me a much clearer idea than a physical examination." He paces the tile floor, running one hand distractedly through his hair. "You responded well to the braces and exercises you were given when you were young."

"I still do the exercises," I interrupt. "They help, sometimes. But right now, they hurt."

"That's good to know." Pop rubs his chin. "And dancing certainly strengthened your legs, once the braces came off. But I'm concerned that perhaps there's some residual weakness which is being exacerbated by how *much* you're dancing."

"I can't stop." Ever since the braces were removed and he convinced Aunt Claire to send me for dance lessons, it's the only thing I've wanted to do. "I'm just starting to get somewhere. I can't waltz in and tell the director I don't want to rehearse because I'll have to go home and sit in a hot tub all night if I do."

A lot of the girls talk about hot baths and stretching; one gets massages from her boyfriend, so she's limber enough to go to bed with him after.

"I know how important it is." He pats my shoulder, and I understand he's worried; normally Pop would be much more affectionate—even in front of the starchy nurse, who hasn't said a word this entire time. "The x-rays will tell us more. Once they're done, we'll take it from there. Miss Hampel will schedule an appointment on your way out."

Why had I thought he would be able to pull a solution out of the pocket of his white coat? Just because he'd done it once before didn't mean he had an infinite supply of answers.

"I'll wait until after the show opens," I tell him. "I'll have Mondays off. And maybe it'll stop hurting before then."

"And maybe it won't," he says. "As your doctor, I would advise finding out."

"I think I've found out enough for now." I meet his sympathetic gaze and look away. I don't want him to feel sorry for me.

They step out so I can resume my skirt. When Pop comes back in, alone, I throw my arms around him, hugging him the way I did years ago, when he was the unknown Dr. Max who told me he could straighten my legs.

"I'll be grateful all my life for everything you've done," I say against his neck. "For me and the family."

"Don't be silly." He holds me off and smiles. I can see tears in the corners of his eyes. "You know I'll do everything I can, princess. I'm just not sure what that will be."

"Just try," I say, ignoring the tears pricking my eyes. "Just try."

Before I go to the theater, I find a phone booth and make another call. "Is Vivian there?" I ask when the landlady picks up. "Vivian Collins?"

"She's gone out," the woman says. "Another audition, if you'll believe it."

"I believe it." I'm glad she's auditioning; I've been imagining her sitting at home and brooding or spending too much time with Joe Dexter. "Do you know when she'll be back?"

"She said by dinner time, if she got lucky." A beat. "I'd guess she'll be in by two."

That doesn't sound promising, but then again, landladies aren't fond of tenants who keep late hours, receive inconsistent paychecks, and use too much hot water.

"I'll try her later." I hang up, look at my watch, and sprint toward Market Street. If I rush, I'll be no more than an hour late. Mr. Malone will undoubtedly shout, but maybe he'll stop before he reaches the point of calling me a dumb blonde.

10

I pull on a second sweater and lean back against the headboard, going over my lines one last time. From the moment I opened my eyes today, I've been freezing. Even after a hot bath and wrapping myself in a towel warm from the radiator, I shivered like I was outdoors. The cold is inside, a part of me, nothing to do with the temperature—which is finally beginning to feel like spring.

Nerves. No matter how prepared I am, it never changes. Fifteen years are gone in a heartbeat, and I am a small, scared girl with satin bows on her tap shoes, waiting to go on at her very first recital.

My layers are peeled away at the last possible moment, and I dress in trousers and another, nicer sweater, my gown for the after party already waiting in a bag downstairs. The trip to the theater passes in a blur, as does the bedlam of getting ready. As I wait in the wings with the other girls, the fear in my gut turns to something else, something more urgent. I wave frantically at the nearest stagehand.

He interprets my expression correctly and comes running with a bucket. Nora holds my hair as I vomit. When I straighten, I feel remarkably better, especially when I remember I won't have to embrace Calvin Owens until after intermission and I will have an opportunity to rinse my mouth first.

I remember almost nothing after that, just the sound of my voice, strange in my ears as I speak my first lines. The stage is beneath my feet, the sets are the same as they have been for weeks, the other actors and dancers are all familiar, but I feel like I'm floating somewhere above the stage, unable to clearly see or hear what's going on.

The applause at the end of the first half sounds genuine. I retreat to the dressing room allotted to me and the other principal dancers—although

I have lines and am a small part of the main plot, I'm not considered an actress.

That's fine by me; I don't consider myself an actress either. But that makes thoughts about my future as a dancer even more fraught; until I finally face up to those x-rays, my entire future is uncertain.

Dress rehearsal was a disaster. Mr. Malone, clutching his head, told us it was a good harbinger for opening night. Several actors missed their marks or spoke out of turn, one of the dancers tripped over her feet, and when Mr. Owens lifted me, his fingers dug into my hip. I couldn't restrain a cry.

"What happened?" he asked when I was on solid ground again.

"It felt off when you grabbed me," I said, trying not to think about how it felt to be up in the air, unsure if my legs would bear my weight when I came down. "I thought I was going to fall."

I haven't told anyone about my appointment with Pop. When I'm in the house, I avoid him for fear he'll ask when I'm going to schedule the x-rays.

Mama has asked several times if everything is all right and I lie straight to her face—convincingly, I hope—and say I'm tired and overworked.

I'll make the appointment as soon as the show is under way, once I feel more settled in the role and am less likely to be called in on a Monday for an extra rehearsal or some last-minute change that occurred to Mr. Barnet or Mr. Malone.

The second half goes smoothly, and this time I am present in my body and feel myself moving and speaking, feel Mr. Owens's hands grip mine as we dance, feel gravity as I leave the ground and hover over the stage to scattered clapping.

When the curtain comes down, I join the rest of the cast to stand hand-in-hand before the audience and take our bows. Mr. Owens and I are second, but there is genuine applause, though not of the scale received by the show's stars, which is thunderous. My heart thumps in time with it—what if that were for me? It's the closest I've come to that sort of ovation, and I want it for myself.

A boy brings an armload of roses back to the dressing room and tells me my family is waiting.

"Tell them I'll be along as soon as I can." I bury my face in the roses—pure white—and know whichever family member paid for them, they were Aunt Claire's choice.

When I appear, wearing another one of my aunt's cast-off gowns, my family is holding down a corner of the shabby, enormous lounge. I cross a wide expanse of floor, my heels clacking on the green-and-white marble, to the circular velvet couch where they are uncomfortably perched. Those things look so cunning but they're pointless when trying to have a conversation.

They all stand at once, their voices layering over one another. It sounds like the beginning of the show, when the orchestra is tuning up in the pit and each instrument is talking to itself. In addition to my parents, Aunt Claire, Grace and Teddy, Pearl and her husband took the train down from New York, and George and Ruthie are there, as well.

I accept their congratulations and hugs, wipe my tears and my mother's, and thrill in Pearl's arms when she whispers, "I didn't know you had a speaking part. You did wonderfully!"

Pearl and Julian have offered to take us out to celebrate at their hotel. They're staying overnight on Broad Street and heading back to New York tomorrow.

As I throw a wrap over my shoulders, a flash of red catches my eye. Someone is standing, mostly concealed, by one of the marble pillars.

"Viv?"

She sidles into view, wearing the same red dress she'd worn to the closing party. "Congratulations," she says, her voice quiet. Her chin is tucked, so I can't see her eyes. "You looked great up there."

I throw my arms around her, happy beyond reason to see my friend. "I've missed you."

"I've missed you too." Viv looks up at me with tear-stained cheeks. "I'm sorry. I'm an idiot."

"You are," I say with affection, "but I don't want to talk about that now. Come and meet my family."

"Connie's here somewhere," she says. "We didn't sit together because I didn't tell him I was coming, but I saw him at intermission. It's difficult to miss that hair."

If anything, the swoop has become more aggressive since his break with his family.

"I hope he finds us." I would like my family to know both my friends—a strange state of affairs, because I've never been one to bring people home. Is this how other people feel all the time? I grab Viv's hand and drag her over to the group.

"Everyone, this is my very good friend Vivian Collins." I wave a hand at them. "These are my parents, Dr. and Mrs. Byrne; my sister Pearl and her husband, Julian Armitage; my aunt, Claire Warriner; my cousin Teddy; my little sister Grace; and my brother George and his wife, Ruth."

"There are a lot of you," Viv says, her green eyes wide with amazement.

"There are more," Mama tells her. "It's hard to get everyone together, no matter how special the occasion. I'm very pleased to meet you."

Pop steps forward to take her hands, not looking at me. "Miss Collins," he says. "I feel like we've met somewhere before."

Mama looks at him; they've met Connie, but I haven't mentioned Viv very often. Having a girlfriend is a new and uncomfortable thing. Having a male friend—whether or not he likes women—is easier to explain.

We fit her into the group and exit through the theater's massive front doors. It's dark now, so the flickering of the gas lamps is more noticeable than the cherubs themselves. Grace sees them, however, and pats the nearest one on the bottom as she passes.

"Grace!" Teddy sounds scandalized; his upbringing with my aunt and uncle was very different from ours.

"Babies' bottoms are cute," she points out. "You looked like that once upon a time. Didn't he, Aunt Claire?"

"Much pinker and smoother," she says, trying not to laugh. "And with the sweetest dimples."

Teddy blushes easily; I'm sure he's blessing the darkness that hides his red face.

"There's Connie." Viv points toward the corner, where he is lingering, looking hopefully back at the theater.

I glance at Julian. "Is there room for one more?"

Why not?" He shrugs, patiently amused as always by my family and our numbers. "We're already going to fill three taxis."

Julian's British manners get us a large velvet banquette in the hotel restaurant. He requests two bottles of champagne to start and tells us to order whatever else we'd like. Mama orders tea and George and his wife both ask for beer; I don't think he has much use for champagne, and Ruthie follows his lead in most things.

One bottle is opened and set down at my end of the table. Julian gestures to share it with my friends. I blow him a kiss, and the waiter fills our glasses.

Under the general hum of the restaurant, Viv snugs up against me. "I don't know what came over me. I didn't even want that show—you remember I was going to take some time before my next audition. If you'd been cut, too, we could have cried on each other's shoulders and that would have been the end of it. But you weren't, and it felt like a sign that you were too good for me."

Someday I will get Viv to tell me about whatever it was in her past that made her this way, but for now I'm just happy to have my friend back and to have somewhat of a key to her behavior.

"It would have helped if I'd known that." I lean against her, thinking what a picture we make with her vivid coloring and red dress and my pallor and black satin.

She nods, and her voice grows thick. "I knew I was being stupid, but I didn't know how to say sorry. The longer I left it, the worse it got."

"We're okay now." I include Connie in my words, and raise my glass, holding it aloft until they join me. "We're here, together, and we're going to stick together in this business. It's hard enough. We shouldn't do it alone."

"To us!" Connie shouts, and once the rest of the table hears him, they all lift their glasses and toast us, as well.

After a whispered conversation, Viv goes to phone her landlady. She returns to the table smiling, despite having called at such a late hour. "Are you sure your parents won't mind me staying over?"

"We don't mind," Pop says helpfully. "The house feels empty with only Thelma and Grace around anyway."

"Thanks!" Grace sticks out her tongue at him, then ruins the effect by blowing a kiss. "I thought there was enough of me to make up for at least two?"

"Sometimes three." Mama smiles at her, then focuses on Pearl, across the table. "Are you going back first thing in the morning?"

"Not until after lunch," my sister says. "I thought you could show me what you're working on down at the shop."

"You don't want to waste your visit with that," she says, as if Pearl didn't have an interest in fashion as deep as my aunt's and hadn't helped with the dressmaking business until she left home. "Come over once you've had breakfast. We can catch up until lunch time. Then I'll feed you and you can go to the station."

The party breaks up after this. Aunt Claire and Teddy take a cab toward Rittenhouse Square, while my parents and Grace get in one heading in the opposite direction. George and Ruthie, who hardly spoke all night, congratulate me again and disappear down the steps to the subway.

Viv, Connie, and I had announced our decision to walk home while in the restaurant. Connie's rooms are on the other side of Market Street, but he insists on escorting us, even though it's obvious he's had too much to drink. When we reach the house a good twenty minutes behind the others, I tell him to come in.

"There's room for you, too. The sofa, if not an actual bed."

"Sofa is fine by me. I've slept in a barn." Connie yawns dramatically. "I could fall asleep now, if you two want to continue making up in private."

We kiss him goodnight and climb the stairs to my room. My parents' door is closed, but Grace's is open, and she comes out of the bathroom, braiding her hair.

"G'night," she says. "You were swell, Thelma. And your partner is so handsome. Lucky!"

"He's not as handsome as me." Connie's voice drifts up from the living room. "I can hear you, you know."

"Go to sleep," Viv calls. "Let the champagne sing you a lullaby."

While she uses the bathroom, I dig an extra pair of pajamas from the drawer and toss them on the bed, then set about removing my gown, which has tiny invisible snaps down one side, one of Mama's hallmarks. I'm almost finished when Viv returns.

"I'd kill for a dress like that," she says matter-of-factly, peeling off the red gown and throwing it over the chair. "I look like a tart in this."

"My mother would make one for you." I shouldn't volunteer; Mama rarely sews for pleasure anymore, and Viv can't afford her prices.

"But I wouldn't look like you in it." She comes to stand beside me before the full-length mirror. Several inches separate us in height, and in Viv's case, those inches are added into her bust and hips. "You're elegant. I'm... busty."

"Sexy," I say. "And funny. I'm an ornament, but people meet you and think you're fun."

Slip, bra, and stockings follow the dress, and she pulls my pajama top over her head.

"So I look like what I want to be." She throws herself back on the bed. "Why won't anyone give me a chance to be funny, then?"

There it is: the reason she has avoided me for the last six weeks. My good fortune and her lack of it. If she'd known at the time I would take over for Rose Petrie, she'd still not be talking to me.

"Someone will," I tell her. "Better that it's the right situation."

"How often does that happen? I obviously don't come across well at auditions. Or in real life."

"You know absolutely everyone. They all like you." Compared to me, she's the picture of charm.

"Superficially, yes. It's easy to have a laugh or drink or even to go to bed with someone. But should I become friends with them"—she makes a pained face—"that's letting someone inside."

"And that's bad?"

"The way I grew up, it's dangerous." When I begin to speak, she says, "I don't want to talk about it, Thelma. Just understand how hard this is for me and give me a little slack if I go wrong again. Remind me that we're not competing for anything."

To raise her spirits and distract her from the demons of her past, I begin to tell her, with several stops and starts, of my close call with Lou Hartley—and whose timely interruption saved me.

"That bastard." Viv bestows several more colorful names on the lecherous theater manager before asking, "And did you want to crawl through the floorboards when Arkright walked in?"

"Oh, God." Even now, the thought makes my skin crawl with shame. "He—I—he told me to get out, but he also made Hartley sign my contract."

"That was swell of him." Viv scratches her head, tumbling her curls into a bird's nest around her pert face. "Arkright scared me a little, but he seemed like a straight arrow. For a director."

"Definitely better than Mr. Malone." I regale her with rehearsal stories, imitating his spats with the choreographer, until she is weeping with laughter.

"Now I'm glad I didn't get cast," she wheezes. "I wouldn't have been able to keep a straight face."

I flip back the sheet and crawl in beside her. "I've missed you," I say again. "If I tell you something, will you promise not to repeat it?"

"Of course." Viv's merriment drains away; whatever this is, she understands it's serious. "Tell me."

"I mentioned once or twice during *Trials* that my hip hurt, do you remember?"

She nods. "Is it bothering you?"

"Almost all the time." I tell her about the pain, and the time I thought my leg would give out after the lift. Finally, feeling almost sick from holding back my secret for so long, I tell her about the visit with Pop. "He thinks I should get x-rays," I conclude. "To see what's really going on."

"He's right, obviously." She sits up straight. "I'm coming with you. When can you make the appointment?"

"You don't have to come with me." I don't tell her she was with me in spirit for that first appointment. "I'll have to do it on a Monday. That's my only day off until the end of June."

"Then you'll call tomorrow and make the appointment." Her tone brooks no argument, and I wouldn't dare—I'm too happy to have her back.

"Yes, Mother." I stretch over and turn off the bedside lamp, the tightness in my chest easing for the first time in weeks. I have family. I have friends; with their help, I can do this.

11

"Have you made the appointment yet?" The words are out of Viv's mouth as soon as I'm close enough to hear her. We've spent most of our time since opening night together and she hasn't let up on me for a moment. I'm grateful we're heading into a dance class so she'll have to be quiet. "You could have gone today."

I could have, but I haven't even made the appointment; the thought of committing to a date and time makes it hard to breathe. It's too early in the show's run to receive the kind of news I'm dreading.

"Leave me be, will you?" No matter what they tell me, I won't back out of the show and let someone else have this part. "It's too soon."

For two weeks, I've done everything possible to distract myself from thinking about those damned x-rays. Long classes on Mondays, morning classes or extra rehearsals the rest of the week. I've even welcomed matinees, which are generally my least favorite part of working in theater, because two shows a day limits my time to think. By the time I get home, it's bedtime; if anyone is awake, I claim exhaustion, unwilling to risk conversation. Pop hasn't said anything, but he's working up the nerve to talk to me, and I don't think I can bear that.

"We need to know what's going on." She puts her leg up on the bar and stretches over it in a way that, had we been at ballet, would have gotten her a reprimand for bad form, if not a crack on the shin with Madame's stick. "I'm not sure what you're waiting for."

"We?"

While I am glad down to my toes Viv is back in my life, it's my body we're talking about, my career that might be affected. When my fear takes over, I question whether she is jealous and hopes I'll be told to stop dancing. Then I remember her tearful confession and know I'm being ridiculous.

"I'll call tomorrow morning," I say heavily. "Mama has an early fitting, so I can use the phone at the house. I'll ask for an appointment for next Monday, if there's one available."

"About time." She swings her leg down and reverses position. "Do you want me to come with you?"

I'd like to think I have the courage to do this alone—and I would have done it, eventually—but something about Viv makes me feel bolder, more capable.

"Would you?"

"I'll hold your hand in the waiting room." She gives me a wide smile and for a moment, the tightness in my chest eases. "If they let me come in with you, I'll hold your hand there, too. They can x-ray our hands together."

I laugh. "I hope that's not necessary, but I'll let you know when the time comes."

I make the call the next morning and spend the rest of the week alternately worrying myself sick and pretending to all the world that nothing is wrong. Saturday night was a packed house, with a loud and enthusiastic crowd. I went out afterward with Connie as an early birthday treat and let him feed me daiquiris at a new little bar on Thirteenth Street to keep my good mood afloat.

He delivers me, via taxi, well after midnight. The house is dark when I let myself in, all but a single lamp on the end table that stays lit until the last of us are home. I turn it off and remove my shoes, moving silently up the stairs.

When I open the door to my room, Mama is sitting on my bed in her nightgown, engrossed in one of the neglected books from the stack on my bedside table. She looks up at my entrance, light glinting off the pins in her hair.

"Mama!"

"Thelma." She closes the book, marking the page with her finger. "I was beginning to wonder if you were coming home."

I drop my bag and shoes and unpin my hat. "I said I'd be late."

"One in the morning is beyond late." She pats the space next to her. "Come and sit."

"I'm tired." Mama has a near-supernatural ability to weasel secrets from her children, even when we're at our sharpest, and I am dull-witted from exhaustion and birthday daiquiris. "Can we talk tomorrow?"

She makes a face. "Tomorrow you'll sleep in, then you'll go out with your friends, and in the evening, we'll have a cake and there will be no time to talk properly." Putting her hand over mine, she says, "Don't misunderstand. I'm glad you have friends. I like them, both of them. It just feels like between them and your job, we never see you anymore."

"It's a busy time right now." I blame the show for my avoidance of the family, but she's not having it. "It'll be better soon."

"What will be better? I know something's going on. I tried asking Max—"

"He's got nothing to do with it." Pop knows I don't want her to worry before there's a reason. "Let him alone."

"He's got something to do with it," she says grimly, pushing up from the bed. "He told me to mind my business."

I pull my pajamas out from under my pillow. "Mama, I'm tired. Pop is right. I'll talk about it when I'm ready. It's nothing bad, I promise."

She pauses, her hand on the doorknob. "I'm not used to you keeping secrets. You were always such an open child."

My patience, rubbed raw by weeks of worry, shatters. "I'm not your broken little girl anymore. I'm a grown woman and I would love some privacy in this house. Is that too much to ask?"

The flicker of pain is gone from her face before I even take it in, but I know my mother; I've hurt her in a way that will take a while to heal. "I'm sorry, Mama."

"No," she says stiffly. "You're right. You're a grown woman. You pay rent like your brothers and sisters did before you. I shouldn't badger you."

On Sunday, Pop is reading the paper at the table when I finally creep downstairs. He shakes his head at the sight of me.

"We're both in the doghouse, birthday girl."

"I know." I pour a cup of coffee and sit across from him, propping my bare feet on an empty chair, something that wouldn't be permitted if

Mama were home. She does her best to civilize us, and we pretend she's succeeded. "Did you get an earful this morning?"

"No." He folds the paper and puts it aside. "I got it last night, after she came to bed steaming like a tea kettle."

"Sorry." I debate whether I want anything for breakfast and decide lunch will come soon enough; I'll help prepare sandwiches as penance because he took the brunt of Mama's temper. "She wasn't being reasonable."

"Your mother is always reasonable." He may be on my side, but he'll never speak a word against her. "She's just worried."

"Well, so am I!" I turn away so he can't see my face. "But she ambushed me, and I was too tired to be careful with my words."

He reaches across to take my hand. "They'll be in from church soon. I suggested she ask Claire to come for lunch, to blunt the impact. If you apologize and they spend the afternoon together, you'll be able to avoid any real conversation until tomorrow."

"My appointment is tomorrow." I'm not going to be able to keep this to myself forever. "Can you keep her occupied until I'm out of the house? I promise I'll talk to you both when I get home."

The doctor's office is close to Pop's digs. When we arrive, I give my name to the nurse at the desk and sit down to wait. As promised, Viv is holding my hand. It isn't long before my name is called. I say to the nurse, a thickset woman with a starched cap, "Can my friend come back with me?"

"No." Looking at my stricken expression, she adds, "There's nothing to it. I'll be with you the entire time."

Viv squeezes my hand and drops it, and I am left to follow in the nurse's wake, down a tiled hallway and through an open door through which comes a wall of frigid air. The impression of cold isn't helped by the drab green paint on the walls. Light fixtures hang from the ceiling, casting an indirect glow on a contraption of wires and metal. I hug myself, as much from the chill as from nerves—though they have certainly spiked without Viv's calming presence.

"All right, Miss Kimber, come over here." The nurse gestures to a long table in the center of the room. Just looking at it makes me stiffen all over. There is no cushion, only an unyielding dark surface. I hesitate for a moment, then climb on, trying to make myself as comfortable as possible. My light rayon dress offers neither warmth nor padding.

"I know it's uncomfortable in here," she says in a strong South Philadelphia accent. "That's how the machine likes it."

I fold my arms across my chest to keep from shivering. "Does it take long?"

"Not if you don't move. According to the chart, we're taking pictures of your hips and legs today, so I'm going to move your skirt to get the best angle." She adjusts my position, shifting my legs until they are perfectly straight. It's awkward, lying exposed, especially with the chill seeping into my bones.

The nurse produces a dark blanket and spreads it over my upper body, leaving my lower abdomen and legs exposed. The blanket is surprisingly heavy. "It's lead," she says by way of explanation. "For your protection. It keeps the rays from touching anything we don't need to look at."

I know x-rays are dangerous, and this covering, though reassuring, makes the whole procedure feel even more serious.

After a brief wait, a man in a white coat enters. He's about Pop's age, with a trim, dark beard and mustache. He nods to me, then the nurse. "I'm Dr. Jessup, the radiologist. Max Byrne is your physician?"

"Yes." I'm hoping Pop's name brings its usual warm reception, but he gives no sign that they know each other. The doctor moves a large piece of equipment into place above me. It is connected to a box on the wall by thick cables. A low hum emanates from it, like a very faint dentist's drill or the sound of a radio searching for a station.

Dr. Jessup comes closer, moving my right leg slightly. His hands are cold, and I try not to flinch. He shifts from me to the machine, peering at the dials, which cast greenish light on his face.

"Just a moment, Miss Kimber." He pulls a large, dark panel into place between us. The nurse smiles encouragingly at me, then follows him behind the panel. I am alone with the humming machine. The lead blanket on my torso makes it hard to breathe.

There is a sharp, crackling sound, like radio static. A flash, very brief, illuminates the room. It is over almost as soon as it begins. I blink, my eyes adjusting again to the dim light.

"All right, stay still for another," he says from behind the screen.

Again, the crackle, again the flash. I'm ready for it this time, but it's startling. The table trembles beneath me—or is it that I'm shivering again? I force myself to remain motionless; I don't want him to have to take more pictures because I've inadvertently moved.

He rolls the machine lower. "Just a couple more of your knees and ankles."

Two more sets of images are taken, then he disappears behind the screen again, saying something quietly to the nurse.

"Is everything all right?" Can he really see right through to my bones? And can he tell what's causing the pain?

"Nothing for you to worry about," he says. "Dr. Byrne will be able to answer all your questions. He'll call you as soon as the results are in."

I'm sure he will, but whether they will be the answers I want to hear is another thing entirely.

The nurse removes the blanket and helps me to sit up. The relief is immediate, both from the weight and the chill. I swing my legs over the side of the table and the room shifts. I should have eaten something before coming in.

I'm cold and a bit wobbly, but the examination is over: I'm free to go. I pull my dress into place, eager to feel the sun on my skin. Maybe Viv and I can go to Horn & Hardart before our afternoon class. At some point during the day, I'll have to figure out exactly what I'm going to tell Mama when I don't have an answer yet myself.

12

As I balance on the front step, pawing through my bag in search of my key, the phone begins to ring. Letting myself in, I zigzag around the sofa to snatch up the receiver, wondering why no one else has answered.

"Hello?"

"Thelma, thank goodness you're home." Aunt Claire's voice has an unfamiliar brittle quality.

"I just got in. Has something happened?"

"Grace and Teddy," she says with a rueful laugh. "Isn't it always? They were doing something this afternoon—I couldn't get out of either of them exactly what—and Grace broke her wrist. We took her to the hospital. Ava and Max met us there. Do you want to eat with us tonight? They won't be home for another hour or two."

I sink down into a chair, wrapping the phone cord around my wrist until it hurts.

"I'll be fine," I tell her. "I'd rather be here when they get home."

Teddy's voice intrudes, muffled, as if Aunt Claire has put her hand over the receiver.

"If you're sure, dear."

Unwinding the cord again, I say, "I'm sure. Is Teddy all right?"

"As far as I can tell, he was the instigator." A pause and she says, not to me, "Honestly, I thought you two had outgrown these capers."

Teddy tries to defend himself, but Aunt Claire is having none of it, running roughshod over him in a way that would make Mama proud.

"I'll leave you to it," I say, and hang up while my cousin is protesting. I put my things away, change into a pair of lightweight trousers and an old blouse, and go back downstairs to put the kettle on. They'll need tea when they get in.

Whatever happened, there is no doubt in my mind that my sister was the instigator and Teddy is taking the blame. Still, a broken wrist is a considerable punishment; it's not even summer vacation and she'll likely be in a cast until school starts.

They are home within the hour. Grace has a raw mark on her chin that will scab over soon enough. She looks drawn but waves her cast triumphantly. "I want your autograph, Thelma!"

"Oh, do be quiet." Mama is about five minutes from shouting at someone; she's dealt with injuries to the boys for years, but her daughters have stayed intact, until now.

Pop kisses me and says, "Go and put the kettle on, kid. It's your lucky night."

For a moment, I don't understand, and then I do. For better or worse, my sister's accident has distracted Mama. I won't have to talk to her until tomorrow.

We have tea and a late supper of sandwiches. Grace eats heartily, commenting that she's glad it isn't her right wrist.

I ask what happened. Mama cuts me a glance across the table. "Apparently, she and Teddy were out joyriding in Claire's car, and they had an accident."

"Grace!" The two of them are incorrigible, and young for their ages until they are startlingly adult.

"What? We weren't out robbing a bank or drinking or hanging on a street corner."

Pop tips his chair back. "Leave yourself something for next year."

"Max." Mama looks exhausted. "Everything isn't a joke."

"I know that, love." He leans over and kisses the side of her face. "But she's in one piece and it's not a bad break. You can be as angry as you want tomorrow, when we all have more energy."

I stand. "Do you need help getting changed?"

Grace looks from me to our parents. "Thanks, sis. I'd appreciate that. This cast is going to take some getting used to."

When we get upstairs, she shuts her bedroom door and says, "I don't need help, but you were driving the getaway car, so I got in."

"Understandable." I sit at her desk, watching as she gets changed. "You're lucky to have been wearing short sleeves."

"I know. Ruining my top would have been one more thing to make Mama mad." Grace stares at her pajamas, eyeballing the size of the sleeve opening against her cast, and chooses a sleeveless nightgown instead.

"She's more worried than mad." I round my back and stretch my arms in front of me, feeling my spine crackle. "Raising us can't be easy."

"You're the one she's worried about lately," she says, "so I think you owe me."

"What do you mean?"

She rolls her eyes and flops back on the bed, the cast thumping against the mattress. "Ow. She knows you're hiding something."

Whatever the x-rays reveal, I hope the results come in quickly, so I can face them and have all this subterfuge over with.

"I'm not hiding anything," I say. "Not exactly. I've got something on my mind, and if I tell her, she'll worry."

"And then you'll have to worry about her. And your own worry is enough."

"That's it." My sister has a lot more common sense than she generally lets on. "You're a pretty smart kid."

"Except when I do dumb things with Teddy." She grins; despite the pain of a broken bone, she knows, as the youngest, that she'll get off lightly.

"What exactly did you do? I know it wasn't as simple as joyriding."

Grace rolls over onto her stomach, working out how to cross her arms under her head. "It wasn't. But as I was told today, I've learned my lesson."

"Have you?"

"Probably not." Her eyes widen with a sudden realization. "My hair! What am I going to do?"

Her hair is my sister's sole vanity. Black and shining, it reaches almost to her waist. She wears it in coronet braids that make her look like a young queen.

"You'll have to ask one of us to braid it for you."

Her face falls. "The heck with that."

"Maybe we could teach Pop?" The thought of him sitting still long enough to braid her hair makes me laugh, and Grace joins in.

"No," she says decisively. "We're going to have to cut it."

"Mama will hate that." She rarely fusses about our looks beyond asking us to be clean and presentable, but she taught Grace how to put her hair up like that, saying it reminded her of Granny.

"Then she can grow *her* hair out," she says grumpily. "Will you cut it, Thel, or should I get Teddy to do it?"

"I don't think you'll be seeing Teddy for a while. Aunt Claire was mad."

Grace snorts and dissolves into inexplicable laughter. "If she's mad now..." is all I can understand.

"I don't want to know." I shake my head. "I'll get the scissors, but you'll have to make the first cut and then tell them I stepped in after you butchered it."

"Deal." She sticks out her right hand. "As sisters go, you're not half bad."

Pop calls not long after Mama leaves for the shop. I pretended to sleep in, missing my little sister's dramatic entrance at breakfast sporting a severe flapper-style bob, the only haircut I could manage with any degree of success. She looks adorable, but it's a drastic change.

"What time are you due at the theater?" Pop asks directly. "I have your films and the radiology report."

"Can't it wait until tonight?" I'm pretty sure he's going to tell me I need to cut back, and I don't want to hear it right before going into work.

He hesitates. "I'd rather you were here, so I can show you the films. If you can get here in the next hour, I'll push my appointments back."

I make it there before ten, and the nurse leads me to his office, rather than an exam room. She knocks, opens the door, and leaves.

"You didn't have to run." Pop stands and comes over to give me a kiss. "I know mornings aren't your favorite."

I had run, or nearly so—his office is close enough to the house that waiting for the streetcar is a waste of time, but the walk made me over-warm. The headache that's been lurking since I woke up is threatening to crash into my skull.

"Miss Collins is better at mornings than I am." I give him a half-hearted smile. "Well? What's the verdict?"

He gestures for me to take a seat. There is a gray metal screen behind him with what look like photo negatives pinned to it: my x-rays. "Not a lot, unfortunately," he says. "Dr. Jessup confirmed there are no avulsion fractures, which is good news. But that doesn't tell us why you're in pain."

"I thought the x-rays would tell you what was wrong?"

"In some cases, they do." He flips a switch and the screen lights up. I marvel at the sight of my bones, the pelvis like a bow, the long bones of my thighs, jutting out at the top. "Your bones, for the most part, appear normal."

"Then what hurts?"

"I said 'for the most part'." He points at my right hip. "X-rays are excellent for visualizing bones, but not so good at things like muscles, tendons, and ligaments—the connective tissue that holds them in place."

"Why not?" What's the point of all this modern technology if it can't tell what's wrong with me?

"Bones are dense. They absorb the rays and appear white on the film. Soft tissues are less dense, so the x-ray passes through them, which results in the gray areas you see." His finger dances over the film, pointing out the differences in color. "Rickets can affect more than your bones."

"I thought I was okay." It is a credit to my self-control that my voice doesn't tremble. "I thought you fixed me."

Pop's face crumples and he drops back into his chair. "Aww, baby," he says. "*I* thought I fixed you. But even with successful treatment, rickets can leave behind imperceptible deformities. It can also weaken the tendons and ligaments, which appears to be what's happened with you."

It's disorienting to think of these things happening under my smooth skin.

"What do I have to do?" I can handle more exercises. They'll hurt, but they have always hurt; I never told anyone because they might have made me stop.

"Taking it easy would be a good start." His hands drop to his thighs. "I know it's not what you want to hear, but your body isn't causing the pain, Thelma. Dancing is causing the pain."

"No." I refuse to hear it. "There has to be something you can do. You're a doctor."

Pop comes out from behind the desk and starts pacing, which is never a good sign. "The weakness in your soft tissues and any subtle misalignments they have caused can make your joints more vulnerable to wear and tear over time."

I grasp at the straw before me. "Over how much time?"

"Hard to tell," he answers. "But I know you. If you've admitted to being in pain, it's already pretty significant." He puts his hands on my shoulders and rests his forehead against the top of my head. "This isn't good, kid. You're looking at something like osteoarthritis in your future."

"Granny had arthritis." I remember her hands, gnarled but capable of almost anything. "She managed."

"It's no picnic," he says. "And yes, you're as tough as every other woman in your family. But since the arthritis would be in your knees and hips, you would not only continue to experience pain, it would severely limit your mobility when you get older."

Another straw. "How much older? Your age?"

His laughter is soothing, even as I suspect I won't like the words that follow.

"I'm only fifty-five. I'd like for Grace not to have to push me around in a chair before I'm a doddering old fool." He sobers. "I know how much your career means to you. I do. But is it worth destroying your body?"

I don't remember leaving the office. According to the clock on City Hall's tower, which I can see in the distance from where I stand on the Chestnut Street bridge, it is after twelve. For nearly two hours, I have walked and walked in the humid spring air with no destination, hearing Pop's words in my head.

Is it worth destroying your body?

What else am I, if not my body? I have always been my body: trapped in it, then released, and now, finally, thriving. Dancing.

Dancing brings me to life. Dancing causes me pain. The question is: which pain will be worse—giving up or continuing on?

I can't give up. After years of throwing myself at closed doors, I'm finally beginning to get somewhere. *Love Letters* has had good reviews;

I was even mentioned in one, albeit in a throwaway line praising the ensemble of dancers holding up the myriad subplots.

The only way forward for me is on my feet. I don't know how to do anything else. I have almost no interests outside my career; it's because of the theater that I have friends.

Friends! Connie and Viv will know what to do. I should be thinking about how to tell my family, but my friends, who understand my drive and my passion, will be the ones I can lean on as I'm cast adrift in a sea of uncertainty.

With a deep breath, I push Pop's news firmly out of my mind. However I decide to move forward—and it will involve more conversations with him, as well as letting Mama in on the secret—I will do nothing until the show is over. The damage to my body is already done. How much worse can it be if I continue on for another month?

Because the long walk has made me sweat through my dress, I treat myself to a cab back to the Durang. When I push through the doors into the cool, dark theater, I enter another world, one where everything makes sense, where there are steps and lines and marks to memorize, and all I have to do is my job.

That night I give my best performance of the entire run. Cal Owens and I strike sparks off each other—we both know it—and when he lifts me into the air, I feel as if I could float right off his palms and keep going, out over the audience in the red plush seats and up to the painted ceiling.

"You've known this for how long?" Mama's voice is steely. "Max?"

Pop's shoulders hunch reflexively. "For a while now. But she came to me as a patient, not as my daughter. I promised to keep quiet about this until we knew more."

I watch their conversation like a tennis match; at some point I'll be invited to participate in this conversation about my future. When lunch is over, I ask them both to stay at the table. Grace leaves without objection, having already been told she would hear all later; she's undoubtedly on the landing where she can hear every word anyway.

"And now you know more?" Two sharp ridges have formed between her brows; she's been more worried than she let on, and the truth is as bad as she feared. "What is it?"

"We don't know everything yet," I interrupt. "And we won't, until the show's over. Pop says I need more tests, but I won't have them until the show is over."

"But you're in pain!" Her palms press against the tablecloth. "I don't understand you, Thelma. You want us to treat you like an adult when you won't even look after yourself."

"I am looking after myself." I draw in a steadying breath. "But that involves looking after my career, as well. I can't quit in the middle of a show. And it's not as bad right now, when I'm not rehearsing constantly. I've cut down on my dance classes."

"And that's supposed to make me feel better?" Her words are addressed to me, but she's looking at Pop, her eyes pleading for him to do something that will make me see sense.

"It makes me feel better." I push my chair away from the table. "I can't have this conversation now if you won't talk to me, Mama. I told Pop something was wrong. He sent me for tests. We have the results, and we know the next step. It's now a matter of taking it."

"And that will be—"

"When the show closes," I say with finality. "I'll see you both later."

Grace is on the landing, as expected. I walk around her and she follows me into my room.

"That didn't go well." She bounces onto my bed, cradling the cast in her lap. "Did she look as mad as she sounded?"

"Pretty much." I sit in front of my mirror. I don't look good myself. Pan-Stik will cover the circle under my eyes, but I don't have any at home; I'll have to go to work looking like this.

She continues to talk as I get ready—tales of her latest exploits with Teddy, whose leash was extended by Aunt Claire in a matter of days—and then she asks a question that stops me in my tracks.

"What will you do if you can't dance?"

The answer exists in a big blank space in my mind. Every time I try to think about it, I have trouble breathing.

"I don't know," I tell her. "I've never been good at anything else."

Part Two

A New Rhythm

13

"Labor Day is next weekend," Aunt Claire says from the lounge chair next to mine. "Are you ready to go home?"

"I suppose." I try to sound enthusiastic about going back to Philadelphia. I've had my fill of lying on the beach doing nothing. "Have you had enough of babysitting me after two months?"

Despite steady ticket sales and positive reviews, *Love Letters* closed at the end of June. I was standing with Nora and two other girls at the closing party when Mr. Hartley approached.

"Miss Byrne." He glared at me with his little piggy eyes. "I see you made it through the production without embarrassing yourself."

"It's been a wonderful experience." A whiff of cigar smoke lingered in the air around him. He wasn't a pleasant man to begin with; embarrassment made him worse. "I do enjoy working at the Durang."

He smiled thinly. "You'll never get another opportunity, girlie. Your boyfriend Arkright can say whatever he wants, but you're barred from here on out, do you hear me?"

My heart pounded in my ears. For a moment I was back on that green couch with his hand up my skirt.

"Don't worry, Mr. Hartley," I said smoothly, doing my best to hold it together in front of the girls. "I have bigger plans than anything the Durang can give me."

After he walked away, I drank two glasses of champagne in quick succession, got sick in the washroom, and took a cab home to cry myself to sleep.

The very next day, Mama started in on me about the next round of tests. In my weakened condition, she was hard to resist. Still distraught that I'd kept something so important from her, it took some talking on Pop's part to get her to see it from my point of view.

"Why didn't you tell me?" she asked again. "You know you can tell me anything."

Anticipating the test results had been difficult enough; I hadn't had the strength to bear her worry as well, nor did I have the energy to explain myself. Pop intervened, understanding how close I was to my breaking point, and told us he'd found another doctor, a specialist, who was willing to take me as a patient.

Dr. Hendricks did further tests, including some very uncomfortable x-rays where he pressed on and manipulated my joints. Afterward, he recommended a course of treatment involving rest and careful exercise and absolutely no dancing.

"None at all?" I asked, stricken. "Not even a little?"

He shook his head. "None at all, for the time being. You've been dancing a minimum of five hours a day, six days a week. It's too much. Dancing through pain isn't brave, it's dangerous." A stifled sound escaped me, and he looked up. "I'm not saying you'll never dance again, Miss Kimber, but for the time being—at least the next six months—I want you to limit your movement to the absolute minimum."

"Will she have to stay in bed?" I could see Mama calculating how to rearrange the household around an invalid.

"I don't want to stay in bed." It was hard enough to take in the doctor's advice without the added strain of turning the house—and my life—upside down.

"Going from constant activity to bed rest would be a trial for a young woman such as yourself, I can see that." He folded his hands on the desk. "But it would be extremely beneficial for you to be still. If not in bed, then not walking or running about all the time. The only other option would be a cast."

The thought of being immobilized in plaster was terrifying. Enforced inactivity was nearly as bad. Both felt like a death sentence.

How would I manage without working? And how would I live without dancing?

A tear slipped down my cheek, and I tried to wipe it without anyone noticing. Mama saw it; after failing to see something right under her nose, she was watching me like a hawk.

"I have an idea," she said slowly. "What would you think about spending the summer at the shore?"

"We can't afford that," I said, sounding for the first time in my life like her.

"But Claire can." She tapped her upper lip, thinking. "Irene Warriner inherited her sister's house down in Cape May. Since the old woman is getting frail, she rarely goes there."

"Aunt Claire hates her mother-in-law." Irene Warriner had, I'd learned a few years ago, interfered in her son's marriage to the point where Uncle Harry—the most patient of men—had nearly cut her off.

"True enough," Pop said, his eyes glinting. "But remember, in the last year or two, the old bat has decided that Teddy is a credit to the Warriner name. If Claire says Teddy wants to spend some time down the shore, she'll have the house key dipped in gold and delivered by carrier pigeon."

And that is what happened. While I hid in my room or cried my heart out on Connie and Viv's shoulders, Mama and Aunt Claire organized everything.

For the month of July, the Cape May house—a lovely white Victorian blocks from the beach—was full of women. Mama, my aunt, Grace, and even Pearl came together to support and distract me in equal measure.

In the mornings, Mama would make breakfast and then we would take a gentle stroll along the boardwalk while the sea breezes did their best to blow my cares away. They didn't succeed, any more than my family succeeded in distracting me, but it was better than being in sticky Philadelphia, confined to my room with nothing more than a palm fan.

I'm sure I tried their patience. Lack of activity and movement made me both sullen and occasionally snappish. For over ten years, I had done nothing but dance—had thought of myself only as a dancer. If I couldn't dance, who was I?

It was not a question any of us could answer.

Pearl, whose life revolved around words, brought stacks of plays for me to read as I lay pointlessly in a cushioned lounger outside.

"You were good in that awful show," she said. "Acting isn't dancing, but it's still theater. Maybe you could..."

"I'm not an actress," I said roughly. "I managed all right, but the director spent all his time shouting at me for having no emotion in my voice."

"So instead of dance lessons, maybe you take acting classes." She rubbed her temples in frustration. "Elocution lessons. There's bound to be someone in the city you could study with."

I didn't tell her that Connie, trying to prove his family wrong, had taken a night job so he could attend acting classes during the day.

Grace joined in the conversation from her towel at the exposed end of the upper porch. "It's either that or you'll have to get a real job," she said, sitting up and blocking the sun with her cast. "A drab nine-to-five in an office or maybe back at Woolworths."

A fate worse than death, and they all knew it.

"I've only ever auditioned as a dancer," I muttered, not willing to give in to Pearl's idea so easily.

"You acted in high school," Grace pointed out. "Was it Shake-speare?"

"Yes, *A Midsummer Night's Dream*. I was the Queen of the Fairies."

I'd been given the role because I looked like a fairy queen, not be-cause of any particular talent. The director, our senior English teacher, spent most of the production telling me to stay put, but if she had wanted a motionless fairy, she cast the wrong girl. My Titania floated across the stage, sprang from behind painted trees to surprise Oberon, and danced her affections for Bottom like a burlesque girl from the Troc, garnering so much applause she finally gave up.

"It didn't take much to impress a school audience," I said. "All those doting relatives. Real theater is different. I don't know if I can even act."

"Read these over and pick out a few scenes that strike you," Pearl suggested. "Characters you think you could play. You're a quick study."

"Quick for a lousy student." I had never been able to memorize in school, but I'd learned the lines of every show I'd been in, just from hearing them repeated. I'd never tried to memorize them deliberately.

Mama and my sisters returned to the city after a month. Pearl didn't like being away from Julian for long and it was almost time for Grace's cast to come off. Their departure left me alone with my aunt.

It is a peaceful existence; Aunt Claire sleeps late and requires very little from me, and I return the favor. We spend our time either at the beach or on the front porch, separately or together. Both of us have turned a lovely golden brown and our hair has lightened from the sun.

"Don't you miss Teddy?" I ask, as we sit outside later with wine, cheese and crackers in lieu of dinner. Now that Mama is gone, our housekeeping is haphazard, as neither of us are particularly domestic.

"I do," she says, staring off down the street toward the beach. "But he wanted to stay home and log some hours at the office before going back to school."

Although too young to inherit his father's mantle as a captain of industry, Teddy works at the office during his vacations to get practical experience for later. He started out waxing floors and delivering mail; after this many years, he should be permitted to sharpen pencils and put papers in folders.

"He has his work and his friends and keeping out of Irene's way," she continues. "With Grace back, he won't miss me at all."

"But you miss him." Aunt Claire's relationship with Teddy is more than mother-son. Ever since Uncle Harry died, right after the war ended, Teddy has stepped up to take his place. She, in turn, has tried to loosen her grip, knowing that first college and then business and marriage will take him from her.

"Of course." She takes a contemplative sip of wine, her delicate profile turned toward the dying light. In her late forties, most of the time she looks ten years younger. "But I haven't lost him. Not like I lost Harry."

I don't know what to say to her; my father is dead, but Mama grieved him privately, only mentioning him when she thought we needed comforting.

"I'm sorry."

"Don't be. We had nearly thirty years together." She places her glass on the rail. "I always knew he'd go first—he was more than twenty years older than me. I just thought we'd have more time." With a sigh, she stands, her silk robe falling in shining folds around her bare feet. "I'm going to bed."

I remain on the porch, wondering what will happen when we return to the city. I've missed my family, and even more, I've missed my friends. Viv took the train down for a long weekend but couldn't be induced to stay longer. It was difficult to be around her firecracker personality when I was feeling like such a damp rag.

The last window on the house across the street goes dark. The sky is black, the kind of darkness we don't get in the city. I approach the rail, placing Claire's glass carefully on the floor. Gripping the smooth painted wood with one hand, I raise the other over my head and extend one leg behind me. Not a full arabesque—my hip would surely object—but a test, to see how it feels.

As if to remind me of what I cannot do, my sleep has been filled with nightmares of missing costumes and falls onstage, interspersed with Madame's vicious critiques as she calls me out in class. Occasionally, there are fantasies of triumphant returns with flowers and standing ovations, but more often my dreams make me question whether I'll ever dance again.

I raise my leg further, my entire focus tuned to the inside of my body. My muscles flex and stretch, greedy for more, but the movement feels stiff and unfamiliar; it would be easy to injure myself simply from lack of practice.

Returning my foot to the ground, I try the other leg, letting my traitorous body know who's in charge. It says nothing. I stretch again, tendu to the front, back, and side, before going to bed. If my face is wet with tears of joy, there is no one to see.

There is no peace to be found in Philadelphia. Almost immediately, I have an appointment with Dr. Hendricks, who does another round of poking and prodding and declares himself, for the most part, pleased with my progress.

"Before you ask," he says, holding up a finger, "that doesn't mean you can go out and take a job in the chorus of the next big musical. I said six months of rest and I meant it."

My heart sinks. I had hoped, after two months of inactivity, to be released back into my life like a prisoner who'd served his sentence.

"Can she dance at all, doctor?" Mama leans forward, intent on his response.

I hadn't wanted her to come with me, but I apparently had no choice in the matter.

"She can," he says, and now it's my turn to lean forward. "Not in the way she was before, though. Even with the progress she's made this summer, it would be far too easy to regress."

"Can you please talk like I'm in the room?" I'm far too old for Mama to be taking over my doctor's appointments.

Dr. Hendricks accepts my reproof. "I'm sorry, Miss Kimber. I should be addressing you." He straightens his cuffs. "What I mean to say is that you can dance in a social setting or in a situation where you wouldn't be practicing for several hours each day."

That eliminates stage work, as I certainly can't waltz up to the choreographer and tell him I'm allowed to dance but not to rehearse.

"What about classes?"

"Once a week, no more." His tone manages to sound as if I've twisted his arm. "If you feel any pain, stop immediately. In any case, take it easy the next day."

"Would it be better if she didn't dance at all?" Mama has that fixed look on her face, where she's going to get to the bottom of my problems, come hell or high water.

"I've sat all summer long," I say, my voice rising. "If I'm allowed to take a class, I'm going to take the class."

"I would ask one thing," Dr. Hendricks says. "Keep a log. Write down what you do in each class, and how you feel the next day and the days after. Make note of any discomfort, at the time or afterward. The more information we have about your activities and any after-effects, the better we can determine how to move forward."

"I could do that." I've always kept a notebook for classes and shows, routines I've learned, recitals I've been in, any particular praise or criticism I've received. *Trials and Tribulations* took several pages; *Love Letters* filled half the book.

"Then I think it might be all right." Dr. Hendricks looks at Mama for permission. "Let's set another appointment for this time next month and see how it goes."

"I'd rather you didn't start back up with those classes immediately," she says as we make our way outside to the sunlit grounds of Pennsylvania Hospital. "Don't you like feeling better?"

I sigh and pick up my pace, making her chase me to the streetcar stop. "I don't feel *better*, Mama. I'm just not in pain. When I can dance again, then I'll feel better."

She fishes in her pocket for the fare. "It means that much to you?"

I turn to stare at her. "Yes."

"I didn't mean it that way." She reddens. "I've never wanted anything the way you want this. It's hard for me to understand."

"Didn't you want your shop?" I look at her sideways. "I remember how excited you were when that happened."

"Not because making dresses for rich women gives meaning to my life," she says. "It allowed me to feed my kids while doing something I was good at. I couldn't take a job too far from home if I wanted to be available for you all. The shop gave me the work I needed, with the flexibility to be with you kids."

As far as I can remember, she'd worked all the hours there were. Before the shop, when she'd had a space in the basement of our old house, she was there from right after breakfast until bedtime, with time off to prepare meals, while Pearl and I were burdened with the cleanup.

"What about being a mother?"

A screech of brakes announces the streetcar's arrival. We climb on and take seats by an open window. I think she's forgotten my question until she turns and says, "Motherhood has been the joy of my life, Thelma, but it wasn't something I set out to do. I set out to marry your father. Babies were the result of loving each other."

Considering how many of us there are, they must have loved each other a lot.

"Did you ever think about having fewer kids?"

Her mouth quirks. "Not until after I'd had them. There were more than a few times I thought about marking your brothers 'return to sender'."

"I would have appreciated that."

The streetcar stops and we all jolt forward. Mama takes my arm. "I'm glad it's a different world for you, even if I don't understand it. You weren't expected to marry right out of school, and you don't have to have babies if you don't want them."

I feel bad. She'll be an amazing grandmother, but so far, the only one of us to behave properly and give her a grandchild is George. Dan won't; Pearl certainly doesn't want to; and with the life I've always wanted, I don't see babies in my future, either.

A man would want a woman who stayed home, like Mama. Even if he didn't mind me working, I couldn't take a show with a long run or go on tour. And what if I got knocked up? After Mama had babies, her figure was never the same. Pop loves her as she is, but I'd prefer to be loved, if I must be, as I am.

Slender. Unpregnant. Dancing.

I return to ballet on Monday. Madame Duchay's plucked eyebrows raise to her hairline when she sees me. She softens when I tell her the story I've decided on—that I suffered an injury and am slowly returning. I won't be attending daily classes for the foreseeable future.

"Your body is an instrument," she says. "It would be foolish to damage it." She rakes me with her dark eyes. "You look soft. You should take the eleven o'clock class with the younger girls."

"I'm sure I'll be fine." My stealthy practice at home should be enough preparation; I can't possibly dance with the schoolgirls.

We've barely passed the warm-up when I understand how wrong I am.

> *"Ballet: 2 hours. Legs: like jelly. Shaky but no hip pain. Arms: heavy. Stamina: none. It's going to take forever to get back to where I was just in the spring."*

I stare at the page. What I didn't write for Dr. Hendricks was how *wrong* everything felt. It's not only that my legs were weak: I was sweating and out of breath before the other dancers finished their warm-up. I'm out of practice, physically and mentally. Madame's classes aren't for the faint of heart, and after a summer of doing nothing but pampering myself, her critique of my efforts hit hard.

"Your line, it is a disaster," she told me at the end. I stood with my head bowed, trying to get my breathing under control. "Your extension is sloppy. You will work with the younger girls from now on." She taps my shoulder with her pointer. "When you are ready for this class again, I will tell you."

14

Connie, Viv and I made plans to meet for lunch. It will be the first time I've seen them since my return. I arrive early to prolong the pleasure of waiting for them. When I tell the waitress who I'm meeting, she seats me at a window table. Connie must be a regular; this never happens to girls dining alone or with other women.

My friends come up Chestnut Street shoulder-to-shoulder, expressions animated. Viv's arm is linked through his. My heart leaps at the sight of them, but their casual familiarity causes a simultaneous stab of jealousy. Have I lost them to each other? Is there room for me?

When Viv catches sight of me through the window, she breaks away, pressing her hands to her heart, pantomiming joy in over-large gestures. With her vivid makeup and poppy-print dress, she looks like she escaped in the middle of a performance. Connie is less of a showboater, tossing his head so his hair falls forward and blowing me a discreet kiss.

The door flies open, and they pile on me in a huddle of embracing arms and cheeks to be kissed, all of us talking at once until the waitress steps in.

"There's no floor show here," she says with an air of having said it before. "No one is going to clap or throw flowers, so you might as well sit down and order something."

Once she hands out the menus, takes our order, and stomps off to terrify other customers, we dissolve into giggles. After everything I've been through lately, it feels good to know that we haven't changed.

"Look at your tan!" He squeezes my hand. "This one here is a poor substitute. You look absolutely glorious."

"Maybe you should have written to me more than once," I say, as Viv snaps, "Speak for yourself. If he tries any harder, Thelma, he'll be prettier than both of us."

"That's my intention, darling." Connie strikes a pose, batting his lashes in my direction. "If they can't appreciate my talent, I'll have to get by on looks."

I shake my head. "I've missed you two so much."

Spending all those weeks with Aunt Claire was lovely—we haven't had that much time together since I was a little girl—but she doesn't have the electricity of my friends. I don't know if it's her age, losing Uncle Harry, or a difference in personality; for all that I love her, with them I feel like the lights have been turned on after a long time in the dark.

"We've missed you. I've been auditioning like a fiend. Without a single callback, mind you. I need someone to complain to"—she glares at Connie—"who doesn't constantly make it about himself."

Three plates arrive—grilled cheese, club sandwich, Waldorf salad—and we dig in. Between bites, I say, "I went to ballet yesterday."

"I thought you weren't allowed—"

"Was it awful?"

I put down my sandwich. "I'm allowed, within reason, so long as I pay attention to how I feel. And it was honestly the most awful experience. Madame put me back in the kids' class because I couldn't keep up."

Connie points his fork at me. "You didn't injure yourself, did you?"

"No, I'm stiff and sore from playing statues all summer." I have a vision of my childhood doll, Flora, motionless on her shelf. "It's made me realize something."

"What's that?" Viv signals the waitress for more coffee.

"I need a job."

The *Inquirer's* "Help Wanted - Female" page is open before me. I've circled several possibilities but I'm not sure which, if any, I want to try. Before making any decisions, I call to ask Dr. Hendricks's opinion on what sort of work I should attempt.

"I'm not qualified for much," I tell him. "Especially if I can't be onstage. Ushering, waitressing, counter work at a store. That kind of thing."

"Before we get to all that," he says, "tell me how you're feeling. Did you go back to dance class?"

"Once." I tell him how it felt, and how long it took me to recover. "I wasn't in pain, only stiff. And so tired."

He chuckles. "Your body isn't used to working hard anymore. Let's keep to a weekly class for another month. I'll want to see you again before you do anything more strenuous."

I don't have it in me to deal with Madame's kiddie class more than once a week, so that is fine.

"What about work, though? Is there anything you think I shouldn't do?"

What I want is to dance, and to dance the way I had before my hip started bothering me. According to Madame—and my body—that isn't going to happen anytime soon. I have resigned myself to regular work.

"I assume ushering might be difficult," he says, with unexpected empathy. "Being in a theater without being able to do what you love."

"Yes." I'd thought of that. I can't go back to the Durang—Mr. Hartley made that clear—and applying at another theater would mean starting over.

"As long as you're not in some greasy spoon where you're on your feet twelve hours a day, I have no objection to waitress work. It certainly pays better than cashiering."

Spoken like a man. Behind a counter, no one is likely to try to touch me. If I tie on an apron, a man's hand will be on my backside before the end of the day.

I decide to try for a job at one of the nicer stores: Bonwit Teller or Wanamaker's. They have a better class of customers, and I could stay behind a counter most of the time instead of swishing around between tightly packed tables dodging pinching fingers.

"Your blue dress would be nice for an interview," Mama says when I tell her where I'm going.

"I was thinking of wearing it." I will pair it with my caramel-colored straw hat trimmed with forget-me-nots.

"I'll freshen it up so you'll look like you stepped out of one of Claire's magazines."

That's exactly what I do look like, I think, turning in front of the full-length mirror. My sedentary summer has added a layer of softness to my normally slender build, but the dress fits beautifully thanks to

Mama's last-minute tweaks. I settle my hat over one eye, tuck my bag under my arm, and take a pair of short white gloves from the top drawer.

I should be able to manage, but in my desperation to get out of the house, I am willing to call in reinforcements; my aunt's account with Wanamaker's is of sufficient balance and duration that they would hire me on her word alone.

As it turns out, mentioning her name is unnecessary. Miss Violet Coffey, head of the ladies' sales force, takes one look at me and her eyes light up. "You're certain you want a sales job?" she asks. "With your figure, you could easily be taken on to model dresses."

"I'm not interested in modeling." I modeled briefly in high school to make money for ballet classes and learned that I hated being a walking coat hanger.

"Then you're exactly who I need in accessories. Gloves and bags and scarves. You have the kind of face that sells convincingly, without making the customer feel pressured."

I didn't know my face had those kinds of powers, but I let her explain the job. When she asked if I would be full or part-time, I said, "I'd prefer part-time at first. I'm recovering from an injury, and I have doctors' appointments and dance classes to rebuild my strength."

"An interesting method." She peers over her half glasses, which are attached to a beaded chain around her neck. "You are obviously very presentable, Miss Kimber, but if you're going to be on the sales floor, you'll need a black skirt and a white blouse. Can you manage that?"

"I can." Having worked as an usherette means I have two good skirts and a selection of appropriate blouses.

"Excellent." She stands and offers her hand. "Well, then. We'll start you on afternoon shifts. Tuesday through Friday, noon to six, and Saturday from ten until four."

Such a schedule leaves only Sunday and Monday to dance and see my friends. But beggars can't be choosers. "When do I start?"

The job is easy enough. My years of listening and watching Mama and Aunt Claire stand me in good stead; I like helping women understand what suits them. Miss Coffey stops by at the end of my first week to congratulate me.

"If you keep going at this level, you'll soon start earning commissions."

That would certainly be a help. Connie's acting classes aren't cheap and I'm making a point of paying my board before anything else. It's the least I can do after all my parents have done for me. Once I would have put every penny toward classes. Am I becoming a better person or am I simply so disoriented by the turns my life has taken that I'm holding fast to what matters most?

When the discreet bell sounds six, I wish my co-worker, Janet, a good evening and take the elevator to the staff area. Many of the girls wear their black-and-whites home, but I don't see the point; as soon as I'm off the clock, I want to be myself again.

Today's vivid pink print dress is an antidote to the weather, which has been in the mid-eighties all week, with intermittent rain. Emerging from the elevator, I dodge a clutch of customers carrying furled umbrellas and head for the Market Street doors. It is faster to leave via Chestnut Street, but I would be more likely to run into Miss Coffey on that side of the store, and I don't want to be delayed any further.

"Miss Byrne!"

I turn. My smile fades when I recognize the voice's owner and recall the last time we saw each other—and the circumstances in which he found me. It's enough to make me want to dive under the nearest counter.

"Mr. Arkright, how are you?"

"Very well. And you?"

"Well enough." I shift my focus on the bag in his hand. "Have you been shopping?"

"A gift for my mother. It's her birthday." He tilts his head and looks at me with frank appreciation. "Where are you working now?"

"Here." At his surprised expression, I clarify, "I just got off work. Obviously, you didn't buy your mother anything from the fine accessories department or I would have been the one to sell it to you."

"I'll remember that next time. I buy her a bottle of Chanel No. 5 every year, which I suppose shows a lack of imagination on my part." He falls into step beside me. "Are you no longer working in the theater?"

"I had... an accident in the spring. I'm supposed to lay off the dancing for a while. I'll be back soon, I hope."

"I'm sorry to hear that. You're well otherwise?"

"Better every day." He has a nice enough face, rather like Pop's in that his attractiveness is somehow *because of* the ordinariness of his features. "What about you?"

"Well enough," he says. "But I'm never doing another musical. *Trials and Tribulations* scarred me for life."

My smile is unforced. "Why did you do it, if it was so awful?"

"As a favor." He shrugs. "A producer I wanted to work with. I thought if I directed *Trials*, it might lead to something better."

"And has it?"

"Not so far." Mr. Arkright gives me a crooked smile. "Directing a musical is like herding cats. Too many personalities, all wanting the spotlight."

We pass through the doors into a solid wall of humid air. People walk swiftly along Market Street, despite the heat, arrowing toward the nearest subway station or streetcar stop.

"Aren't actors as bad?" I discreetly mop my neck. From everything I've experienced, actors are needy and demanding and would happily climb over each other for even a sliver of spotlight.

"They are," he concedes. "There just aren't as many of them." He pauses at the light and looks up at City Hall. "Do you act at all, Miss Byrne?"

The light changes and we cross the street, carried along by the tide of workers heading home. I will have to turn around if I don't want to be late for dinner, but I enjoy talking theater with someone who isn't Viv or Connie.

"Some," I say. "My last role—at the Durang—was a speaking part."

Mr. Arkright's expression changes. He hasn't forgotten seeing me sprawled on the couch with that disgusting man's hand up my skirt. He'd rescued me, but from what Mr. Hartley had later said—*your boyfriend Arkright*—I imagine he is no different. Men seldom are.

"I have a show coming up," he says. "Auditions aren't for a while yet, but if you're interested..."

"I am!"

The passage through City Hall to the interior courtyard is shadowed and cool. A line at the newsstand blocks our way for a moment. When we emerge, squinting, into the bright early evening light, Mr. Arkright says, "I can't guarantee anything, you understand. It would be a small part. I'm not even sure if you'd be right for it."

"All right." Which of us is he trying to talk out of the idea? "Then I shouldn't try out for it—whatever it is?"

"No, you should. Here, take this." Abruptly, he holds out a small white card. "Have your agent or manager call me next week. If I'm not there, they can leave a message with my girl."

"I'll be the one calling." The thought of being successful enough to have a manager makes me laugh. "And the number will be for my family's house, so if you call, be very clear. My younger sister doesn't take good messages."

"Understood," he says. "It was a pleasure running into you, Miss Byrne."

"Likewise." If he has a part for me, the pleasure will be entirely mine.

The possibility of auditioning for Stan Arkright hurls me into a frenzy of preparation. Unlike an audition for a spot in the chorus, I can't walk onto the stage and dance. He and the casting director will expect me to have a scene prepared. I dig out Pearl's box of scripts and look at them with fresh eyes. While there are a few Shakespeare plays, more than half the scripts are contemporary work—*A Streetcar Named Desire*, which I saw on its opening night at the Walnut Street Theatre, *Glass Menagerie*, *Born Yesterday*, and two Noël Coward plays, including *Blithe Spirit*.

While all of the scripts are excellent, I doubt my ability to play dramatic roles. Even if what Mr. Arkright is offering is a tiny part, I need to prepare like a serious actress trying for a serious part.

"I thought you didn't want to act," Grace says when I beg her to run lines with me. "I thought you were all dance, dance, dance."

"I'd rather dance, but it's not in the cards right now." I lean back against the headboard and flatten the script on the bedspread between us. "And even if they let me start again, being a half decent actress could lead to more roles. And it's better than working at Wanamaker's."

"Are you going to quit?" Grace asks. "Because I'd love that job."

"Helping rich women spend their money?" I ruffle her cropped hair. Even though I was the one to cut it, her appearance surprises me. She looks more like a young lady and less like the mischievous child she still is. "You'd hate it. You'd have to be tactful and polite all the time."

She falls over on the bed with a thud. "That means you're already a good actress."

It hadn't occurred to me to think of it that way. I begin reading *Blithe Spirit* with renewed interest.

I manage to hold off for two days before calling Mr. Arkright's office, leaving my name and telephone number with his secretary. I don't expect to hear back. He was being polite to someone he'd once worked with; he has no real reason to consider me for a part.

As the days pass, I think about the audition less and less. My schedule is packed with acting classes, weekly ballet, afternoons at Wanamaker's, and the occasional visit to Dr. Hendricks. He is satisfied with my progress, but after I couldn't hide a flinch when he manipulated my leg, he refused to allow a second dance class.

I wouldn't have time, anyway. Connie and I are taking acting classes twice a week and then spend a third morning practicing what we've learned. He drills me until I have my audition pieces down pat. In return, I work on love scenes with him, so he'll have a modicum of comfort if he's ever cast in a romantic role.

"Nothing personal," he says, pushing back his hair and looking straight in my face. "You look like an angel, but you're not my flavor."

"Too vanilla?" My traditional prettiness has always gotten me noticed, but I long to be more exotic than a blue-eyed blonde.

"Too female." He grins like a naughty child. "But I'll find my Prince Charming around the same time as I land a leading role on Broadway."

There's nothing wrong with dreaming big. I've thought plenty about moving to New York over the years. As many of those dreams involved being a Rockette, I try not to think about them now. And with my limited funds, even the idea of moving is impractical.

"I'll settle for a starring role in Philadelphia." Until Dr. Hendricks clears me to dance, if I want to be in the theater, it will either be as an actress or an usherette. And I'm done showing patrons to their seats and watching other people perform. "Heck, I'd settle for any role."

"Does it bother you?" Connie asks, dropping back into the sofa and swinging his long legs up to rest his feet in my lap.

"Does what bother me?" I shift so his heels aren't digging into my thigh.

"Having to try acting because you can't dance."

I shrug, trying not to show how much it does bother me. "I wouldn't know what to do otherwise. I'm not good at anything else."

The phone jangles and I jump up, spilling him sideways. "Ow!" he complains, rubbing his head.

"Shut up," I say, lifting the receiver. "Hello?"

"Miss Byrne?" It's the voice of Stan Arkright's secretary.

"This is Kimber Byrne." *It's her!* I mouth to Connie. He scrambles to his feet and comes to my side so we can both hear.

"Mr. Arkright wanted me to let you know that auditions are being held on Monday at the Fitler."

"Thank you," I manage to say, holding back the shriek building inside me. "What time should I be there?"

"The role he's considering you for will be read in the afternoon, but he thought you might want to come in the morning, to get a feel for the play."

I'll have to miss ballet. But if I get cast, I'll miss Madame's classes anyway.

"I'll be there at nine," I say. "Please thank Mr. Arkright for me."

I place the receiver back in its cradle and turn to Connie. "I have an audition."

"You wonderful girl!" he cries, swinging me up into his arms and kissing me almost convincingly.

15

Despite the early hour, a jostling crowd is already waiting for the doors of the Fitler Theater to open. There are familiar faces, but no one I know well. Once we are allowed inside, I find a quiet spot against a wall, pull *Blithe Spirit* from my bag and go over my scene for what must be the hundredth time.

I've chosen to read the part of Ruth. Even though Elvira, the first wife, is the more interesting role, I don't believe I have what it takes to be a sexy, petulant ghost.

Auditions for the lead roles go on all morning. I listen with half an ear, wrapped up in my own concerns. When we break for lunch, I've worked out a new way to deliver Ruth's speech and I'm practicing it under my breath when I run smack into Viv.

She's wearing a red beret on her curly hair and one of her more costume-like outfits, with a neckline that dips questionably low. Although our styles are completely different, I immediately question if my dark blue dress is too staid and mature for the role I want.

"I didn't know you were auditioning for this show." The sight of her quells my nerves. "You never said."

She shrugs. "There aren't a lot of parts going right now for girls our age. I felt like I had to."

Her statement is patently untrue; one of the best things about the theater is the abundance of roles for girls in their twenties. But if she wasn't here earlier, when they were testing for Amelia, that means...

"Are you trying for Caroline?"

"Of course." She pulls a folder from her bag. "Did you see my new head shots? Aren't they divine?"

I flip through them, pierced by envy. She looks dewy and wide-eyed, completely incapable of the language which regularly comes from her mouth.

"Davis did them," she says. "I didn't know I could look this good."

"Isn't Davis expensive?" Dan took my head shots against a backdrop in our garden; despite his skill, they don't hold up against professional photos like these.

"He is, but he also has a thing for busty girls. I let him take me to lunch and feel me up under the table." Viv laughs as if such behavior is nothing unusual. "We worked out a nice discount."

The men are called next: an uncle, a brother, and some minor players. Soon only twenty girls remain in the backstage area. We gradually drift toward the wings where we can observe what's happening.

There is one light on the stage. Unless I'm in the exact right spot, the powerful men out front making judgments on my meager abilities won't be able to see my face—the only asset, at the moment, in which I have any confidence whatsoever. I watch as other girls go out and do their scenes. Some are dismissed immediately, while others are asked to read from the script.

I try to determine the difference between their auditions. Are they looking for a specific type or is there something else? Each girl's reading is equally adept. Half are thanked and sent away, while half are asked to stay. I can't see any difference between their auditions.

My own prepared scene in the back of my mind, I strain to pick up the script dialogue and puzzle out what is going on. I didn't realize I would be expected to read from the script without having had time to prepare or understand the story. The fluttering in my stomach grows worse. Just to be safe, I locate the nearest trash can. Knowing there is a place to safely throw up makes it less likely I will need to.

"One of us has got this," Viv whispers at my side.

I want it to be me. Though if she's sent off and I get a call back, I hope it won't hurt our friendship this time.

"Vivian Collins!"

She squeezes my hand and saunters out onto the stage, head high, brimming with confidence. She stops shy of where I think she should to be fully seen. Lifting her chin, she announces the scene she's chosen.

It's the same scene I've prepared from *Blithe Spirit*—the one we've worked on together over the past week.

My heart sinks. Viv knows how hard I've been working! She has to have done it on purpose. But why?

I will deal later with her betrayal; at present I have to come up with something else to do out there. I can't perform the same scene, even though from the sound of it our interpretations are very different.

Think, Thelma, think!

I not only want this role; now, I want to take it from my friend.

Viv comes off in a swirl of skirts. "Good luck, kid!" she says with a broad smile. "I warmed 'em up for you."

"Is that what you did?"

There is no time for more; my name is called next.

Twenty steps to the center of the stage, where a metal stool sits under the light. A small table alongside holds a copy of the script. My heels echo hollowly on the wood, and I stop short from where Viv was. Using my hand to block the light, I address the faceless men. "Can you see me?"

"A little to your right, if you will."

It's Mr. Arkright. I take strength from his voice—someone wants me here—and smile as I shift position. I direct my next words to him.

"I had a scene prepared," I say, somehow keeping my voice from shaking. "But you've already heard it from someone else. Would you mind if I went straight to the script?"

There is a moment of silence, then another voice says, "Go ahead, Miss Byrne."

I pick up the open script and scan the lines. It seems impossible to read them—to know *who* this character is on the strength of listening to a half dozen other girls reading the same words.

She is a sister; I know that much. She is pleading with her brother not to make a mistake that could break up their family. I've never done that, but I could, in the right circumstances. Certainly, Pearl would plead. Grace would blow something up to prevent something like that from happening.

I take a breath and cast my gaze once more over the darkened theater.

"Rob." I let my voice wobble. "Don't you see? If you go with her, Father will never forgive you. And Mother will be heartbroken." I pause and look downstage. "I know you love Emily. I love her, too—she's a wonderful girl. But they'll never allow it. No one is good enough for us in their eyes." The next lines strike me, and I give them everything I have. "We must stick together, you and I. Brothers and sisters against the world. Or our parents, if need be. You can't leave, Rob. What will I do without you?"

They are words I could fully see myself using with my siblings if the situation warranted.

The scene continues for a few more lines. When it ends, I stand with my hand resting on the table. My heart is beating in my ears and my stomach is in knots.

"Thank you, Miss Byrne," Mr. Arkright says. "Can you tell us about yourself? What else have you done?"

Oh, God. I hadn't expected to have to give them a biography.

"I started out as a dancer," I say. "Four shows in the last three years. I was in the chorus for three of them. In my last show I had a small speaking part in addition to being a featured dancer."

"And now you want to be an actress?" It's someone else, a thinner, older voice.

I smile in the voice's direction. "I'm a performer. Just because I started as a dancer doesn't mean that's where I want to end up."

I pretend not to hear the quiet laughter from the seats; is it positive or negative?

"Thank you, that will do." Mr. Arkright again. "Please wait with the others. We'll be seeing some of you at the end."

I've done it! I survived my first proper dramatic audition without crying or getting sick, although I feel a need to reach around to pull Viv's knife from between my shoulder blades.

Backstage, she rushes up, her face all concern. "I can't believe you went right to the script. You should never do that!"

I take a deep breath, swallow my fury. "I didn't have much choice, since you did my scene."

"You know more than one scene," she says dismissively. "And honestly, you're more of an Elvira anyway."

Biting my lip, I turn away and hide in the bathroom for fifteen minutes while the remaining girls audition. When I come out to join the chosen four, I stand as far as possible from Viv.

Mr. Arkright is onstage now, with several of the young men who tested for Rob. He swiftly pairs us up and tells us we will be doing the same scene again, then rejoins the other auditors out front.

Jack Kenney is the Rob I've been assigned. He's sandy blond and hulking, more football player than actor, but his crooked, boyish smile will charm an audience. "Hell of a business, isn't it?"

"We do it because it's so much fun, right?" My sweaty fingers leave marks on the script.

"And because the asylums don't have enough room for all of us."

I watch jealously as Viv reads with her partner, a lanky young man who looks the part. When his nerves get the better of him, Viv takes over. Her interpretation is completely different from mine, her voice more strident, demanding that her brother listen. She's good, but I think it's the wrong way to play it.

What do I know? Maybe she's right, maybe I should ape what she's doing. Viv has had speaking parts before. I've only had one because they needed a dancer who wouldn't trip over her words or her feet, and because Mr. Hartley wanted to go to bed with me. Those aren't exactly qualifications.

"Thank you." The words are clipped. "We'll see the next couple now."

They turn, and then Viv turns back. "That's it?"

"What would you like us to say, Miss Collins?" This time it's Mr. Arkright, with an edge I remember from rehearsals for *Trials and Tribulations*.

Her bluster fades. "I thought..."

"There are three couples left to see. Could we have Mr. Kenney and Miss Byrne next?

I give my friend a private smile as we pass. I don't know much about how all this works but letting her nerves get the better of her and challenging the director can't be good.

Mr. Kenney and I take the stage. The spot is the same, not large enough for two people. Neither of us is willing to give up the light, so we stand close together.

"We're leaving tonight," he says, going right into the scene. His delivery tells me we're on the same track. "I don't care what Father wants. It's my life!"

"Rob, don't you see?" I put my hand on his arm, feel the tension coursing through him. "If you go with her, Father will never forgive you. And Mother will be heartbroken." Saying the words with someone else feels different. I pause and look away, as if worried we might be overheard. "I know you love Emily. I love her, too—she's a wonderful girl. But they'll never allow it. No one is good enough for us in their eyes."

"But she is." He tears himself away and paces back and forth, darkness into light. "You let them run your life, drive away any fellow who's ever shown an interest in you. Well, I won't. I *can't*."

It's not difficult to let desperation creep into my voice. "We must stick together, you and I. Brothers and sisters against the world. Or our parents, if need be. You can't leave, Rob. What will I do without you?"

He stops pacing and stares at me. "If you're lucky, Caroline, you'll figure out how to live. That's what I intend to do."

After the last two couples read, another break is called. I follow Mr. Kenney out into the alley where he lights a cigarette and wipes his brow theatrically.

"You're good," he says and offers me a drag, which I refuse. "I think we've got a shot."

I do, too, but I'm afraid to jinx us by saying so.

Backstage, Viv is probably letting someone cop a feel to make up for her earlier hostility. It was understandable; performing and being spoken to by men we can't see feels very confrontational. But Mama raised us to have manners, and they are helpful in a situation such as this.

Four people are sent home after the break. Viv is one of them. She looks at no one as she gathers her things. I don't have time to wonder what will happen next or how much I care, because Mr. Arkright calls up for us to change partners and try the scene again.

Mr. Arkright stays onstage, watching closely, occasionally offering direction. I notice he asks different things from each of us, and from me in each pairing. I try to understand what he wants and give it to him; one time he catches my eye and gives a tiny nod, and I warm down to my toes.

Eventually I test with all three men. Jack Kenney is my favorite. His energy complements mine, and he's the easiest to work with.

"That's enough," comes a voice as we're standing together, very nearly holding each other up at this point. "You'll hear from us tomorrow after we've discussed it further."

It is anticlimactic to be dismissed so easily after so many hours of work. I can almost understand Viv's reaction but simply nod toward the darkness as if spending time in their invisible presence has been the highlight of my week.

"Thank you all," Mr. Arkright says, coming forward into the lights. "Good work."

It's nearly six when we emerge onto Pine Street. If I hurry, I can catch the streetcar and be home in time for dinner. Then I see a snatch of red—Viv's beret—in the crowd lingering at the corner. I spin around, stepping out into traffic, one arm upraised.

"Taxi!"

16

Connie responds to my distress call and is on the doorstep by eight.

"We're going out for a walk," I tell the family. Grace is reading in her favorite armchair and Mama and Pop are on the couch, talking quietly while Mama knits. The radio is on in the background.

"You've been out all day." Mama's needles stop clicking. "Don't forget you have work tomorrow."

"I won't." As the door closes behind us, I say, "She treats me like I'm twelve."

"I wish I had someone to worry that I was getting enough rest." Connie takes my hand. "Where to, princess?"

"Anywhere that isn't a theater." I survived dinner with the family by telling them I was too tired to talk about the audition. I'm not, really; I just want to talk about it with someone who understands. And I *need* to talk about Viv.

The night is warm, so we walk up Spruce Street, pausing at Broad Street, both of us automatically looking at the cluster of theaters between us and City Hall.

"Viv called last night," he says. "She wanted me to—"

"No," I interrupt. "I've had enough of her excuses. Did she *tell* you what she did?"

"Not in so many words."

"Well, she's good at words. Ask her to use them next time. While you're at it, explain to her that she stabbed me in the back." I tell him how she stole my audition piece and it all comes flooding back. For a moment, rage makes me dizzy. "She can't expect me to forgive her."

"That's awful." He stops. "I understand why you're upset. I do."

"Then why do I feel like you're about to defend her?" The suspicion I'd had when I returned from Cape May—that my friends had moved on without me—is back. "Can you imagine what it felt like when she went out there and read the scene she knew I'd prepared?"

"Not good." He puts an arm around my shoulders as we cross the street. "She's very upset."

"She should be." I'm not in a forgiving mood. "Did she tell you I went straight to the script?"

The blare of a horn cuts off his response, and we are silent until we reach Eighteenth Street. Turning down past the Curtis Institute, we find an empty bench near the entrance so we can listen to the students practice. Mozart, I think they're playing.

Connie dusts the wood with his handkerchief and gestures for me to sit. "She said you were fearless. For all her bravado, Viv is terrified up there."

"So that's a reason to sabotage me?" It's hard to tell how the audition went from the point of view of the men who watched and judged. Other than an occasional question, and the persistent crackling of sandwich wrappers, they were mostly silent.

"I know. But she's jealous of you, Thelma." He stretches one arm along the back of the bench. "You're drop-dead gorgeous, you dress like something from a magazine, and you have this wonderful family who loves you. She's got none of that. If you cut her off, she'll be completely alone."

The streetlights blink on, golden through the autumn leaves. People are out and about; some couples are waiting for the darkness to deepen to give them privacy.

"That makes no sense." I don't discount my looks—they serve me well—but I'm more traditionally pretty. Viv has confidence and an ebullient personality; no one who meets her will forget her.

"Honey, Viv looks like a tart next to you and she knows it. She doesn't talk about her family. Did you know she has a kid?"

"No!" How could I have believed us to be close? "Where is it?"

"With her parents. They threw her out after it was born. Considering what little she's told me, it was the nicest thing they could have done." He leans his shoulder against mine. "You have everything she wants. Including that part."

"I don't even know if I got it." I have a decent chance, but it's impossible to predict what a casting director wants.

"You didn't get eliminated. She did."

I remember her badly calculated words at the end of her audition and understand the fear that was likely behind them. There is more to Viv than I knew, but it's hard to forgive her actions.

"Connie, a friend who deliberately hurts me isn't a friend." He needs to understand how I feel, and how much worse he's making it by defending her. "For all my close family, I'm used to being on my own. It can be hard sometimes, but it's better than how she made me feel today."

He takes my hand. "I know. And I'm not on her side here, whatever it may look like. I love my girls, and I don't want to lose either of you. But if you want me to, I'll cut her loose."

"You won't lose me." Having a man in my life without the added pressure of being a boyfriend is wonderful. "And I can't tell you who to be friends with."

It would serve Viv right if Connie dropped her, but it isn't my place to direct his behavior—although it makes me very happy that, given the choice, he would choose me.

"Let's get ice cream." He bounds off the bench. "There's a place over on Walnut Street, do you know it?"

"I've been going there for years." As we cross the park, I tell him my stepfather took me and my mother there for ice cream the day we met. "I think he fell in love with her right then and there. I was more interested in the ice cream."

Over a shared banana split, we finally talk him about the audition—the script, how I thought I did, the other actors.

"When will you know?"

There is a line of whipped cream on his upper lip. I take his chin in my fingers and wipe his face. "Tomorrow, they said. I'm hoping to hear before I go into work."

"You'll get it." He runs his spoon around the inside of the dish. "How could they choose anyone else?"

But they do choose someone else. When I put the phone down in the morning, Mr. Arkright's secretary's words ring in my ears. "I'm sorry, but they've decided to go in a different direction."

"Do you know why?" My stomach drops; I'd wanted the part of Caroline more than I realized. And now I am without a part *and* without Viv. It isn't fair.

"No, I don't. I'm sorry. I was given a list of names to call."

I return to the kitchen, where Mama is coming in from hanging laundry in the tiny back yard. "Did I hear the phone?"

"Yep." I drop into a chair and rest my chin in my hands. "I didn't get the part."

"Oh, I'm sorry." Her hands rest lightly on my shoulders. "When is your next audition?"

I look up. "Aren't you going to tell me it's too hard and I should give up?"

"Why would I do that?" She pulls up a chair. "I know you think I worry too much, but that's part of being a parent. One minute you're bursting with pride at something your kid has done, and the next you're scared they'll be hurt. I've worried more about you than the others because you had a rough start and I felt responsible."

This is the longest speech I've ever heard Mama make, and the most personal. "But I'm fine now."

"I don't know if I should tell you this," she continues, as if I haven't spoken. "Your father was angry when I left you with Claire. I told him it was so Max could help with your legs, but he didn't want his little girl so far away. He said there was nothing wrong with you."

"But there was." Life as the wheelbarrow girl would have been unbearable.

"I think sometimes we've gone too far in the other direction. If Max hadn't straightened your legs, you'd still be Thelma."

"No, I wouldn't." Thelma is the girl who dances. Thelma hasn't stopped moving since her braces came off. The sad little girl I was before that day rarely stirred from her chair because she didn't want people to look at her. "It would have been irresponsible," I say, "for you to have taken me home when there was even a chance he could fix me."

"Max *helped* you," she says. "He didn't fix you. Both of us—you and I—have looked at you as if you were broken. You weren't. Only seeing value in yourself after your legs were straightened is unfair to the young woman you have become. It says your value is in walking and running and dancing. What if Dr. Hendricks says you can no longer dance?"

"Then I'll try harder to get acting jobs."

"You can go from one to the other so easily?" She takes a sip from the mug on the table, then makes a face; the coffee has grown cold while she's been working.

"It's not easy. And I'd rather be dancing. I understand what I'm doing there, even when it's hard. Acting is a mystery."

"Then why keep doing theater work at all?" Mama sounds genuinely curious. "If you don't like it."

"I don't dislike it, I just don't know if I'm good at it yet." I run my fingers through my curls, then immediately smooth any damage I've done. "But I *know* I'm not good at anything else. I've never wanted to be and I wouldn't know where to even start."

Mama gets up and pours the cold coffee down the drain. "You're stronger than I've given you credit for being," she says. "I can put on a fresh pot, if you have time for a cup before you go to work."

By Friday, my disappointment has begun to fade. I'd even gone with Connie in the morning to look at the call boards at several theaters, writing down possible auditions for which I might be suited.

"I think Viv is trying for that one," Connie said at the third stop.

"I don't care." He won't give up trying to get me to accept her apology—or at least talk to her—but I wasn't ready yet.

"Do you have to go to Wanamaker's?" he asked. "I'll treat you to lunch at the Oyster Bar."

Reading Terminal was tempting, but it was after eleven and I already didn't have time to go home to change. I was glad I'd left my work clothes in my locker.

"Another day," I said, giving him a quick kiss on the cheek. "I'm almost late as it is."

I arrive at the store bang on time, change rapidly, and am at the accessories counter by two minutes after twelve. Business is brisk. Women come in from the suburbs for lunch at the Crystal Tea Room and are unable to leave the store without one or two little treats. I sell gloves and scarves and a particularly lovely alligator bag before my break at three.

"See you in fifteen minutes." I slip out from behind the counter. "I need some air."

Technically, we're supposed to use the employee entrance, but it's busy enough that I manage to escape through the men's department unnoticed.

On Market Street, I lean against an enormous pillar and fill my lungs with exhaust fumes and cigar smoke and all the smells of the city, so different from the perfumed precincts of the store.

Should I tell Viv how hurt I was by her behavior? Angry as I am, I do miss her. Being with Connie isn't the same as having a girlfriend.

By the time I go back in—through the proper entrance this time—I have come to no conclusion, but I've had a breather and will be able to make it through to six o'clock without snapping at any customers.

There are several people lingering at the counter when I return. Janet gives me a relieved smile. "Here she is, sir."

Coming around behind the glass enclosure filled with luxury items, I say, "How can I help you?" before looking up at the customer.

"Miss Byrne." Mr. Arkright seems uncomfortable in this deeply feminine space. "I'd like a word."

"I'm working." Janet is talking to two women who smell like money even from a distance; I don't want her to rake in both those commissions.

"Then I'll buy something." He scans the selection between us. "Those gloves, the brown calfskin. I'll have those."

"What size are her hands?" I remove several flat boxes from beneath the counter and fan them out on the glass surface.

"I don't know."

"Small? Large?" I'm enjoying this. How dare he turn me down and then show up at my job expecting a friendly chat?

"About your size, I suppose." He offers a half-smile. "Would you try them on?"

"Fine." I slip on a size seven, tugging them into place. The soft leather is lovely. I fan my fingers with pleasure. "There. How do they look?"

"Very well. Would you like them if someone gave them to you?" He's leaning against the counter now. "I mean, theoretically."

"I might," I say, playing along. "Though I'd prefer the gray suede with the squirrel lining. Theoretically."

The gloves are a lovely pearl gray with stitching on the backs. They cost almost two dollars more than the brown gloves. If Mr. Arkright is going to spend money because he feels guilty, then let him spend more.

"I trust your taste. I'll take the gray ones." He follows me along the counter as I wrap them and put them in a bag. "Can I talk to you now?"

"We are talking," I say, writing up the receipt. "We're conducting a business transaction."

He follows me farther along. "I was wondering, Miss Byrne, if you could be persuaded to have dinner with me."

"No, thank you." If Miss Coffey hears him asking me out, I'll be reprimanded. "My supervisor doesn't approve of fraternizing with customers."

"Just a drink, then?" He opens his billfold and produces a twenty-dollar bill from what looks like a considerable number. "I'd like to talk to you about your audition."

I give him his change. "What is there to say? I didn't get the part. You told me you weren't sure if I was suitable, and I obviously wasn't."

A stocky older woman in a fur wrap approaches. "Can I see one of those scarves, please? The floral ones?"

"Of course." I turn my back on Mr. Arkright. "Is it for you, or is it a gift?"

"For me." She titters. "It's not as if I need it, but..."

"But it's a pretty day and the sun is shining," I say encouragingly. "So you deserve a little treat."

"Exactly." She runs her fingers, adorned with several rings, over the selection of scarves I place before her. "Do you know, I think I'll have two."

When she has tottered off with two scarves and a new wallet, Mr. Arkright is still there.

"Can I help you with something else?" My tone is crisp; his transaction is complete. I no longer need to be polite.

"I'm simply admiring your performance." It's the same frank gaze as before. I respond to it without intending to. "I've never conflated sales with acting before."

There's a compliment in there somewhere. I look over my shoulder. Other than the customer Janet is currently dealing with, we are alone.

Miss Coffey is nowhere in sight. "Why do you want to have dinner with me?"

He looks startled, as if he didn't expect me to speak up for myself. "Because you had a very good audition, Miss Byrne. While you weren't right for the production, I don't want you to think you did badly. You should keep going. Keep auditioning. I thought you might appreciate a few suggestions."

Ah, there we are: the price. He's smoother than Mr. Hartley, but the intention is the same.

Even so. Could I manage a wrestling match in exchange for advice that might serve me in future auditions? He doesn't strike me as the type to leap; I might actually get something from talking to him.

"I didn't have lunch." That truth is making my stomach rumble. "But I don't get off until six."

His smile makes him look much younger. "Then I'll meet you at the Chestnut Street doors at—what, six-thirty?"

"Six-twenty," I say. "I'm a quick change."

Mr. Arkright hails a taxi as soon as my feet touch the pavement. "Still up for a meal?" he asks.

"Unless you've changed your mind." He'd better not have; I called home and told Grace I wouldn't be in until eight at the earliest.

"Not at all." A cab slews into the curb and he hands me in. "How do you feel about Italian?"

"I love it." Also, Italian restaurants aren't as likely to have a dress code; I'm wearing the same clothes I'd worn while visiting theaters in the morning and I'm uncomfortable with being taken to a nice restaurant and looking out of place.

The cab stops in front of a tiny storefront restaurant in South Philadelphia not far from the market. Mr. Arkright opens the door, and we are met with a wall of warm, garlic-scented air.

"Stanley!" An older woman hustles over from a table and kisses him on both cheeks. "I am so glad you called—we have saved you a table."

She leads us to a small table and lights a candle wedged into an old wine bottle, then disappears after handing us menus.

"They know you here." It's a homey sort of place, with smells of food and familiar service, but it feels like a stage set of an Italian restaurant.

He nods. "I've been coming here for years when I work in the city."

"Don't you live in the city?" The number he'd given me was a local exchange.

"No, I live in Delaware. When I have a show in production, I stay in the city and treat myself to dinner here when I need to feel nourished." He peers over his glasses. "I don't often have such charming company."

I ignore his comment and peruse the menu, deciding swiftly on cheese ravioli in fresh tomato sauce. Dan's Tommy made ravioli for us once and I liked them. Despite what I told Mr. Arkright, I haven't had much Italian food.

We place our order. He suggests a bowl of minestrone to precede the ravioli and I accept, hungry enough to eat his food and mine.

"What did you want to tell me about my audition?" I ask as the waiter arrives with soup and a bottle of red wine.

He pauses with the spoon halfway to his lips. "I thought we could talk after dinner, Miss Byrne."

"You don't get me all night," I say sharply, imagining the discussion beginning in another cab and continuing until it stops, not at my house, but his. "I've got work tomorrow."

"Very well." He puts down his spoon. "I suppose you want to know why you weren't chosen for *The Devil's Been Busy*?"

I do, but what I want to know even more is why he came looking for me, why he's paying for my meal when there's nothing in it for him that couldn't be had more easily from another girl.

"I knew when I told you about Caroline that you likely weren't right for the part," he says, choosing his words deliberately. "You're too pretty, for one thing. You'd take away from the leading lady. That's not good for such a small part."

He pauses, and I think he's waiting for me to blush or protest at being called pretty.

"I also wasn't sure you'd be good enough." He takes a sip of wine, as if for courage. "I didn't see *Love Letters*, but I know the script. It's hardly challenging stuff. Your audition surprised me, though."

Finally, something that requires a response! "Why? Was I so awful?"

"On the contrary, you were quite good." Mr. Arkright stops talking as our bowls are cleared away and the main courses are placed in front of us. The waiter refills my glass; I hadn't realized I'd emptied it.

For a moment, we address our attention to the food. The ravioli are soft and filled with rich cheese; the tomato sauce is bright and summery. Mr. Arkright ordered something with veal, and he's attacking it like a man who hasn't eaten in days. After we've made decent inroads to our plates, he speaks again.

"You haven't acted much, you said?"

"Not much, no." The wine is made better by the food. I take another mouthful while I wait for him to tell me what I did wrong.

"At the end, when we were trying different pairings, you took direction well, which can be hard for a more seasoned actress, much less a novice. And you adjusted your performance depending on who you were paired with."

"That comes from dancing, I suppose. I'm used to being told what to do. Working with other dancers, you have to be able to anticipate their moves, whether it's a partner or an ensemble."

The candle flares, lighting his face. It's a nice face, but I don't understand what Connie sees in him.

"Being able to listen is rare for such an inexperienced actress. It's not just hearing, you understand. It's taking in what you hear and letting it affect you. Your reaction makes a difference."

I don't understand exactly what he means, but there's another compliment buried in those words and I let it warm me. "I'm glad I passed muster, even if you didn't want me."

"It was also unusual," he says, "that you went straight to the script."

I explain that the girl before me had done my prepared scene. "I didn't think it would be helpful—even if I was better than her, you'd be making comparisons, not necessarily listening to what I was saying."

"You think on your feet." He polishes off the veal. "You responded well when asked about yourself. Was that also something you'd prepared?"

"Not at all." I laugh. "I've never been asked about myself before. All they care about with dancers is whether we can keep time."

"You did well. I don't suppose you've ever thought about auditions from our point of view?"

"I can't say that I have." The last ravioli is gone; I place my knife and fork regretfully across the plate. "Why?"

"You're one person up there, performing to a faceless audience, but we see actor after actor, hoping we'll find someone that makes the process worthwhile. Sometimes it never happens. Sometimes it does." He brushes the back of my hand with his fingertips. "I saw something worthwhile in you, Miss Byrne."

17

Over the next two weeks, I have three auditions and each time I return to Stan Arkright's words. Perhaps they weren't flattery, intended to warm me up, but actual advice. I direct my performance to the invisible men, imagining him in one of those seats. Although I am not chosen, each time I am given more positive feedback to consider.

At the last audition, Viv walks up to me, her expression pleading. "Thelma, I'm sorry—"

"Go away." I cut her off. "If I talk to you at all, it will be after. Not now."

I have worked up a new rehearsal piece, a scene from *Born Yesterday*. Billie Dawn is no more like me than the ladies from *Blithe Spirit*, but I understand it isn't about my resemblance to the character, only what my emotional experience can bring to the role.

Billie would be an excellent role for Viv, but I won't be the one to tell her. Seeing her again makes me want to speak to her, though, if only to tell her how much she hurt me. The depth of my pain proves our closeness. She's the first real girlfriend I've had since I was in grade school. With my sisters either far away or deep into their own interests, there is no one to spend time with except Connie. Even though he's not my boyfriend, he's a man. There are certain things I'm not comfortable discussing with him.

My name is called next. The audition goes smoothly enough, but I'm dismissed almost immediately. I thank the faceless men before heading backstage to pick up my things.

As I pass, Viv reaches out and grabs my wrist. "Please wait," she says. "I've worked harder on my groveling apology than on any audition I've ever prepared for."

"Harder than the scene you stole from me?" I pull away. "Why should I? You'll do it again."

Her eyes filled with tears. "I won't, I promise. I'm so stupid—"

"Miss Collins!"

She freezes, the color draining from her face. After this, she'll give an impossibly bad reading. She scuttles past and gives an impossibly bad reading. Before she's finished, someone cuts her off and thanks her for her time.

When she appears, angrily wiping her eyes, I hold out her jacket. "Come on."

Viv stuffs her headshots into her bag, creasing them badly. "You've decided to talk to me?"

"I'm not sure, but since I ruined your audition, I'll give you ten minutes."

We head to Horn and Hardart as it's not far from Wanamaker's and I'm due at work in a little more than an hour.

"I'm sorry," Viv says again as we walk. "I don't know why I did it."

"Because you wanted the part," I say. "And you didn't want me to have it."

"It's not the part." She turns to look at me. Her eyes are bright with tears. "I get scared, and I do stupid, desperate things. I told you before. I'm not good with people. I push them away before they have the chance to leave."

I don't ask why she gets scared; we all do, and for a multitude of reasons. What's important is whether I can trust her.

"If I forgive you," I begin, "and I'm not saying I do, will you promise to never to do anything like that again? Even if it means I get a part, and you don't? Because this is your last chance, Viv, I swear to God."

Pushing through the door into the muted clamor of the automat, we take our trays and get in line.

"I promise," she says miserably. "I... I get jealous. You have so much."

I feed my coins into the slot and retrieve a slice of lemon meringue pie, then move along to the coffee station.

"I haven't had you,' I say tightly, not wanting to admit how much it has hurt to be without her. "I can't talk to my family about my life. That's what friends are for."

She throws her arms around me, almost tipping the contents of my tray onto the floor. "I swear, I swear, I swear I will never be such an idiot ever again."

"You might be stretching the truth there." I set my tray down and hug her back. "Are you capable of being good for the rest of your life?"

Viv puts her coffee on my tray and carries it all to a table. "I never said I'd be good, just good to you."

"I suppose that's a start." I sip my coffee. "Are you still seeing Joe Dexter?"

"No, he's done and over with." She removes her hat and fluffs her curls. "All he wanted was to get me into bed."

"I thought you *had* gone to bed with him." I take a forkful of pie and push the plate toward her.

"Oh, I did," she says with an unrepentant smile. "But it was all he ever wanted to do. And we both live in boarding houses, so it's not like either of us can waltz in with a date and our landladies will turn a blind eye."

We alternate bites of pie until it is gone. I debate telling her about my dinner with Stan Arkright when she says, "So, Connie told me you're dating a director."

Damn him! If we hadn't made up, that is information she could absolutely use against me.

"We had one meal," I say. "Weeks ago. He wanted to give me some audition pointers."

"I'll bet that's not all he wanted to give you." She smirks. I can't help but grin back. "Connie thinks he's dishy. I'm not a fan of older men myself."

"Does that mean you won't try to steal him away?"

I turn it into a joke, though I'm tempted to tell her that dinner lasted for three hours. Then, while we were in the taxi, he gave me the gray suede gloves he'd purchased that afternoon. They are tucked into my coat pockets, the nicest gloves I've ever owned that didn't first belong to Aunt Claire.

Viv crosses her eyes. "I solemnly swear I will never try to steal your man, even if you get one who's young and handsome."

"If you promise not to steal my parts or my boyfriends, I think I can forgive you."

It was one evening. Not even a date, though I felt certain, in the taxi, that he wanted to kiss me. I'd never been out with a man who talked about so many things other than himself and baseball, but Mr. Arkright's dinner conversation ranged from city politics to shows he'd seen in Philadelphia and New York, and his dream of starting a repertory company someday that could compete with the older, established theaters. He asked about my family, how long I'd been dancing, and whether I'd given it up in favor of acting.

"Don't you have to be in at noon?" Viv points at the clock.

"Miss Coffey won't care if it's your fault I'm late." I stand and brush crumbs from my skirt. "Come on. If I have to run, you're running with me."

I'm on my bed reading scripts when Grace knocks on the door. "Phone for you," she said, making a face. "It's a man!"

Connie, as usual, calling too late. I roll over and say, "Tell him I'm in the tub or something."

"It's not Connie," she whispers, eyes wide. "It's someone asking for Miss Byrne."

I bound up, smoothing my hair as if the caller is in the room. "Didn't you think to ask his name?"

She shrugs. "How many men do you have calling you?"

"Hello?" I'm breathless from my headlong dash down the stairs.

"Miss Byrne. I'm not calling too late, am I?"

Judging from the looks coming from the sofa—curious (Pop) and annoyed (Mama)—he is, but I assure Mr. Arkright that it's not late at all.

"I assume you've already had your dinner," he says, "since you come from civilized people. Would you be willing to come out for a drink? I just got out of a two-hour meeting with the money people for my next show and I can't bear the thought of my bleak hotel room."

"Well..." It's after nine and I'm already in my pajamas.

"I'm sorry." His voice goes formal. "I don't know what I was thinking. I needed a little brightening up and you came to mind."

Had he said his *next* show?

"No, it's perfectly fine. What time?"

"Twenty minutes?" he hazards.

"I'll be ready."

Mama stands as I hang up the phone. "And who was that?"

"The director from one of my shows." My mind races: what can I possibly change into so quickly? "The one I had dinner. He's asked me to go for a drink."

"At this time of night?" Her acid tone tells me she's going to be waiting by the front door to meet him.

"He just got out of a meeting." It sounds like an excuse, so I add, "He's working on a new show. It can't hurt to be nice."

Shaking her head, she says, "Just don't be *too* nice." Pop snorts. She turns on him. "And not a peep out of you."

When she follows me upstairs, I say, "Mama, it's not a date."

"Well, whatever it is, I assume you need help getting ready." She riffles through my closet, rattling hangers, and holds out my midnight blue cocktail dress. "No, he doesn't deserve it, calling at this time of night. How about this?"

The dress in her hand is one I "borrowed" from the depths of Aunt Claire's closet over a year ago, a slim black crepe with a stark white collar and cuffs. Mama tapered the skirt into a sheath. I think it makes me look sophisticated.

"Do you remember this dress?"

"No." It's familiar, but a lot of my aunt's things feel familiar because she dresses like a movie star and I spent much of my childhood staring at a flickering screen.

"She wore it to your granny's funeral, back in '31. The first time you met her."

I touch up my makeup while Mama removes it from the hanger and lays it, along with a pair of black stockings, on the bedspread.

"I'll leave you to it." Mama doesn't realize whatever modesty I ever had was lost long ago in a communal dressing room. "Call me if you need help with the zipper."

Face freshened, hair pinned into place, the doorbell rings as I'm doing up the zip. My heart rises to my throat. I feel no older than Grace—though Mama's always been civil to my sister's boyfriend.

Stan Arkright isn't my boyfriend! There's no reason for her to treat him one way or another, except that he called too late and expected me to be ready at a moment's notice. But hadn't I said yes? If there's fault to be had, it's equally mine.

I tear off my earrings, deeming them too dressy, and pin my hair back with rhinestone combs. They, too, are dressy, but more appropriate than the earrings.

A murmur of voices reaches me from the living room: male voices and what sounds like Mama's laugh. Except that isn't possible.

I come down slowly, to get a look at what's going on. Mr. Arkright is by the fireplace with Pop. Grace and Mama are on the sofa, listening to them. At the sound of my heels, Grace turns and gives me a stealthy thumbs-up.

"You look lovely," Once again, the appreciation in his gaze warms me. "Please let me apologize again. I hadn't realized how late it was when I called."

"She was in her pajamas," Grace says.

I slap the back of her head as I pass. "I did say I was a quick change."

"You weren't lying." He holds my coat for me and then turns back to my parents. "Thank you again for being so gracious."

Pop shakes his hand. "Don't keep her out all night. She's got another one of those auditions tomorrow morning."

"No, it's a dance class." Mama meets my eyes. Somehow, he's won her over. "Have a good time."

The taxi is waiting in the street. I climb in, tucking my skirt around my legs. "Where are we going?"

"What about The Downbeat? Are you up for that?"

"I'd love it."

The Downbeat is a small, second-story jazz club on Eleventh Street, located above a bar. It's been closed down several times, ostensibly for underage drinking, but more likely because the club attracts a mixed crowd. Philadelphia may not be the south, but there are few establishments where white and colored people can drink and dance together.

He gives the driver our destination and sits back. "Have you ever been there?"

"Once or twice." I don't mention that both occasions were spectacularly unsatisfying dates.

The club's windows glow with warm light. The music is audible in the street. It feels like New York, and it looks like a movie set. I am underdressed and say so.

"Nonsense," Mr. Arkright says. "I'm wearing an ordinary suit. No one will look twice."

"You're a man." I open the front of my coat, exposing the clean lines of my black dress. "I look like I'm going to a very stylish funeral."

He offers his arm. "With your face, Miss Byrne, no one will notice your clothes unless you draw attention to them."

My lips twitch. His unorthodox compliments are growing on me.

Inside, the packed bar stretches the length of the dimly lit room. Mr. Arkright has a quiet word with the maître d and he escorts us to a small table off to the side. We are close enough to see the musicians but can hold a conversation.

"Champagne?" he asks. "Or would you prefer something else?"

"I make it a policy never to say no to champagne." When I go out with Connie and Viv, it's not in the budget, so I've only ever drunk it at cast parties and my aunt and uncle's house.

"A wise policy." He places the order and then turns his focus to me. "Thank you again for coming out on such short notice."

"I don't understand why you wanted to see me." I cross my legs. His eyes drift down and then back to my face.

"An indulgence on my part," he admits. "When you spend half your life begging unlikeable men for money, you occasionally have to do something for pleasure. I don't want their faces to be the last thing I think of before going to sleep."

"Buying me champagne gives you pleasure?"

The waiter appears with the bottle and a bucket of ice. He draws the cork neatly, fills two glasses, and departs without a word.

"It does." Mr. Arkright waits until I lift my glass before touching his drink to mine. "Here's to simple pleasures."

I close my eyes and let the champagne and music work their magic. This isn't jazz but bebop, faster and more danceable. If he heard this, Connie would take me out on the floor and swing me around like a rag doll.

"Miss Byrne."

"Yes?" While I was dreaming, he'd lit a cigarette and polished off half his drink.

"Cigarette?"

"No, thank you. I don't smoke."

"I thought all dancers smoked."

"Not this one." I've never wanted to make it harder to breathe while dancing. "How are your rehearsals going?"

"Well enough." His expression is pained. "For a high school production."

I look at him through lowered lashes. "You should have cast me."

He sets his glass down. "You know how to hurt a man."

"You know how to hurt an actress." It tickles me that I've hit a nerve. "You know I'm willing to put in the work."

"Miss Byrne." He pauses. "May I call you Kimber? It feels awkward to keep calling you miss."

"Of course." I don't know if I'm comfortable calling him by his first name, however; he's twice my age and in a position of authority—or he would be, if he'd hired me. "I don't mind."

"Kimber." He scoots his chair closer, so he doesn't have to raise his voice. "Believe me, I regret not casting you. But you weren't right for this particular show. When I have something that suits you better—and where there's no issue of you being prettier than the leading lady—I'll give your audition my utmost consideration."

I will have to accept that. Taking another swallow of champagne, I gather my courage and say, "I don't understand. Why me? Don't you have actresses throwing themselves at your feet? Ones who'd even pay for the champagne to have your ear?"

He leans back in his chair, his laughter audible over the music. "What if I want to spend time with someone who doesn't have an agenda?"

If Stan Arkright thinks I don't have an agenda, he's not as sharp as he appears. "And that's me?"

"I'd like to think so."

There is a sudden burst of activity by the rear door. A woman strides into the club, followed by several men. She has warm brown skin, a lavish fur coat, and a very recognizable face.

"Isn't that Ella Fitzgerald?"

"She's playing at the Earle this week," he says. "Quite often the musicians will come around the corner to do a set here." One corner of his mouth turns up. "Are you happy you came out now?"

"I was already happy I came out. Now I'm ecstatic."

We drink in silence after that, listening as Miss Fitzgerald does a short set of her hits: *Black Code*, *Summertime*, and *Cheek to Cheek*, sung with a man who does a credible imitation of Louis Armstrong.

When she steps back to loud applause, hoots, and whistles, the band is replaced with an energetic young trio. The tables empty rapidly, bodies filling the dance floor below the stage.

"I don't suppose you'd like to dance?" His brows lift questioningly.

I'm out of my chair before he's finished speaking. "I'd love to."

He's not as smooth as Connie or my brothers—who were taught by me and Pearl—but the floor is too crowded for any kind of showmanship. He holds me respectfully and does his best with the space we've been allotted.

"I'm going to get run over if you leave me all the way out there." I shift to one side as an energetic couple nearly collides with us.

"Again, simple pleasures." He draws me closer. "Thank you, Kimber."

It's well after midnight when the cab draws up out front. A lamp burns in the living room window, but I'm grateful the family has gone to bed. There will be no scene, no discussion of what I've been doing all this time. I'll be able to creep upstairs and go over the evening in peace, and decide what, if anything, to tell Viv and Connie in the morning.

"Thank you again." He's only touched me while we are dancing—a light hand on the small of my back, a respectful distance between our bodies—yet I'm certain he wants to kiss me. I reach for the door handle. "I had a lovely time."

"So did I." Mr. Arkright puts his hand on my wrist. "Would it be unwelcome if I asked for a kiss goodnight?"

I feel a pang of disappointment, mixed with curiosity.

"You don't have to ask."

I tilt my face in his direction, expecting him to swarm over me. Instead, he cups my chin in one hand and gives me a quick kiss on the mouth. There is no more passion in it than Connie has shown during our rehearsed love scenes.

"Good night, Kimber."

18

Stan Arkright gave me two tickets to the opening night performance of *The Devil's Been Busy*. After much consideration, I decide to go with Viv. We watch the show with a critical eye and go out afterward and tear it to pieces. Both of us have strong opinions on the leading lady, and neither of us liked the actress playing Caroline. Jack Kenney did well as Rob, and I am pleased for him.

I've been out twice more with Mr. Arkright. If he were any other man, I would have classed neither occasion as a date. Even though we went to the Palm Room one night and back to the Downbeat to see John Coltrane perform on the other, his demands have consisted of nothing more than a goodnight kiss in the taxi.

As I've come to know him better, I would almost welcome something more. The fact that he hasn't asked—much less taken without asking—is unsettling. From the way he looks at me, I can tell he likes women. Am I somehow the problem? Connie suggested Stan might be uncomfortable dating an actress, but he knew what I was from the day we met. Perhaps his uncertainty stems from walking in on me with Mr. Hartley. I know for a fact he wouldn't want to be put in the same category as that gross theater manager.

When he calls and asks me to dinner on Monday night, I decide it's time to find out. Even if I somehow ruin things, the weeks of uncertainty are starting to wear on me.

He suggests a place in South Philadelphia I've heard about for years but have never visited. Palumbo's isn't the kind of Italian restaurant he took me to the first time—this place is as much about seeing and being seen and mingling with the powerful people and celebrities as it is about the food.

This is absolutely the occasion to wear my blue cocktail dress. When I tell Mama where we're going, she spruces it up with beads and some discreet sequins around the sweetheart neckline.

"This way, you don't have to wear jewelry if you don't want to." She holds the dress against me with a satisfied smile. "Personally, I'd stick to earrings."

"You like him, don't you?"

"He's very nice." She reaches out to touch my hair, which is styled in loose curls to my shoulders. "Why does he call you Kimber?"

"He only knows my stage name." Each time he's taken me out, Mr. Arkright has come in to speak to my parents. It's like Mama to notice such a thing. "It would feel strange to ask him to call me something different after all this time."

"I would feel strange, if someone who I went out with didn't know my name." She shrugs. "But you're used to being called Kimber, so maybe it doesn't bother you."

It does bother me, though, more than I care to admit. Stan Arkright only knows the carefully curated details I have shared with him. Without my name, how much of me does he know? But then, what do I know about him? When we're together, we talk all the time, but very little about our lives outside the theater or the little bubble we've constructed.

The phone rings at quarter to eight. Pop answers and hands the receiver to me.

"Kimber," he says immediately. "I'm so sorry."

"You can't make it?" The depth of my disappointment surprises me.

"No, I can. But I'm running late." His voice is tight with frustration. "Would you object if I sent a car? I don't want to miss our reservation, and I swear I'll be no more than twenty minutes behind you."

Having a car sent for me sounds like something from *Stage Door*. Am I Ginger Rogers or Katharine Hepburn?

"That will be fine," I tell him. "I'm about ready."

His sigh of relief is audible. "You wonderful girl. I'll get away from this lot if I have to bludgeon them. If I show up at Palumbo's with blood on my cuffs, no one will look twice."

I explain to the family what's happened. Grace's reaction is the same as mine, but more expansive. She claps a hand to her forehead and falls over in a mock faint. "La di da, look at you. *He'll send a car.*"

Mama is more restrained, but I can see she's impressed. "Should I assume this will be another late night?"

Within minutes, a long black car pulls up outside. Curtains twitch across the street and Pop cracks, "You've elevated our status with the neighbors."

Grace has already opened the door and is peering out while Mama chides her about letting in the cold air. I put on my good coat with the Persian lamb collar, kiss everyone quickly, and run outside.

"Evening, miss." The driver opens the door and hands me in. Once he's back in the front seat, he says, "Palumbo's, is it?"

"Yes, please." I rub my hands together; even in gloves, they're cold. Temperature or nerves?

"Great place," the driver says. "My sister, she got married last year. Had the dinner at Frank's."

It takes a moment to realize he's referring to the owner, Frank Palumbo. "I've never been there."

He turns onto Thirteenth Street and heads south. "It's a great place," he says again. "You going for dinner and a show?"

"I guess so." I slide my compact out of my bag and check my lipstick, then bring my wrist to my nose to see if I remembered perfume. "Is there anything you'd recommend?"

For the rest of the short ride, the driver gives me a treatise on his favorite dishes, his opinions on the house band— "swell!"—and his thoughts on Frank Palumbo—"a great guy, should be mayor." When we stop, he comes around to let me out.

Once inside the restaurant, the doorman hands me over to the hostess, who smiles when I tell her I'm meeting Stan Arkright. She passes me to the coat check, where I reluctantly surrender my coat. Being alone in this place gives me the shivers.

"Come along, I'll take you to your table." An older man with slicked-back, graying hair leads me through an arch and into the dining room. I look across the acres of tables and wonder how the waitstaff ever find their stations, and how often the waitresses get pinched.

"Whoa, hold on there!" A familiar voice intrudes, and the waiter stops. "Yes?"

"This pretty lady can't be here by herself."

I look up into startlingly blue, startlingly familiar eyes. "I'm meeting someone, Mr. Sinatra," I murmur as all the blood in my body mounts to my chest. Far from being cold, now I feel like I'm radiating heat.

"Is he here yet?" He looks from me to the waiter. "Tell the truth, Benny."

"Not yet," the waiter admits. "But I'm taking the young lady to wait at the table."

"No, you're not." Mr. Sinatra takes my elbow in a possessive grip. "You hold that table, Benny. I'll send her back when her date gets here."

Heads raise all over the room as I am escorted out by possibly the most famous man in America. Mr. Sinatra leads me back through the entrance area and into the bar, walking me up to a crowd of men seated at a large, round table. "Gentlemen, look what I found in the dining room, sitting all alone."

"You grabbed me before I even reached my table!" I protest. The men laugh. Several of them are familiar, as well, but I can put a name to only one: Phil Silvers, who had been in several pictures with Gene Kelly. As has my erstwhile kidnapper, who looks far more dapper—and substantial—in a tuxedo than he did in a sailor suit.

Mr. Sinatra grabs an empty chair from a nearby table and waves me toward it. "You can wait here with us, dollface. Benny will come get you if your date shows up."

"He will." I accept a glass of champagne someone puts in my hand. "But this is rather pleasant."

"Here he comes!" one of the men says. "Left or right, Phil?"

"Ten bucks it's left," he responds, then whirls around. "Left!"

I look from them to Mr. Sinatra. "What are they talking about?"

"Phil will gamble on anything," he explains, sinking down beside me in a boneless movement. "I think that one was whether the waiter would have the napkin over his left or right arm."

The men continue their conversation as if I weren't there, making comments about other women in the saloon bar and urging Mr. Silvers on to more and more ridiculous bets. Even though I could sit and look at Frank Sinatra all night, I begin to worry that Stan will never appear. Or worse, he will, and he'll see me sitting here with these men and think I'm not interested in having dinner with him.

"So, kid," Mr. Sinatra says, startling me. "What kind of man leaves his girl sitting alone in a restaurant?"

"He's a director," I say, straightening. "He was delayed but sent a car so I could meet him here."

I don't know why I said that; Frank Sinatra is hardly going to be impressed by a man who sends a car. He likely has an entire fleet of them at his disposal, driven by cousins of the man who delivered me to the restaurant.

"A likely story," he scoffs. "He may not be out with another blonde, but he's out with another dame."

"I don't think so." I get up, tucking my bag under my arm. "I'm going back to my table."

He blocks my exit. "You'll wait here. If he's worth anything, he'll come find you. Benny knows you're with me."

"You say that like it's something special." I can't believe I'm being rude to Frank Sinatra. Grace will never recover; I'm pretty sure she prays to her signed photo of him every night. "Maybe I'd rather sit alone than be surrounded by men who drink too much and make silly bets about things that don't matter."

"Touchy," one of the men says. "You got a live one, Frank."

I don't think he appreciates my liveliness. Something dark moves over his face, replaced quickly by a devastating smile. "Do I need to get you more champagne?"

"You need to let me go. My date is here." This time, Mr. Sinatra lets me stand unimpeded.

"Kimber," Stan says, cutting between the men as if they were no one. "I'm sorry I'm late."

"Don't worry," I say, wrapping my arms around his neck. "These gentlemen were amusing enough, but I'll be leaving now that you're here."

Three of the men, including Phil Silvers, kiss my hand. Mr. Sinatra does not.

"You better take care," he says roughly. "If you'd been much later, she'd be going home with me."

"I don't think so," I say, my arms locked around Stan's neck. "I like a man with manners."

Stan shifts toward the door, but I haven't released him yet. Instead, I lean forward and kiss him on the mouth. It's mostly for the benefit of Sinatra and his friends, but there's a healthy dose of curiosity behind it, as well.

His shocked inhale parts his lips. I take the opportunity to kiss him properly. There's a moment when everything in the bar stops and I wonder if I have made the worst miscalculation of my life. Then he begins to kiss me back. When his tongue sweeps into my mouth, I make a small sound of surprise and hear the cat calls and applause from Sinatra's group.

Breaking away, I say, with more composure than I feel, "I forgive you for being late. Now let's have dinner."

Sinatra puts out his hand and Stan shakes it awkwardly. "The meal's on me," he says. 'I gave your girl a hard time."

The same gray-haired waiter escorts us to our table. As he pulls out the chair and settles the napkin on my lap, he gives me a wink.

The meal that follows is the longest period Stan and I have ever gone without speaking. I'm grateful for the floor show, which, in addition to providing a distraction, makes conversation impossible. When the waiter comes to clear our table and asks if we want dessert, I say no.

Stan looks surprised. "You always want dessert."

"It's been a long evening," I respond. "I'd rather go home."

It has begun to rain. As we wait under the awning for the car to be brought around, he says, "I'm sorry if you didn't have a good time."

"It was fine," I say, although it wasn't. "I'm sorry about what happened in the bar."

"With Frank or with me?" he asks. "Because one wasn't your fault and I appreciated the other."

I turn on him, my eyes filling with angry tears. "Then why have you never kissed me? Those chaste kisses in the cab, after spending all this time and money on me? Don't you want anything more?"

"It's not that I haven't wanted to."

"Well, then?"

He sighs. I haven't been honest with you, Kimber."

"In what way?" I haven't been honest with him, either, but I'll let him go first.

The car stops in front of us. We continue to stand under the awning as rain patters on the canvas. I pull my collar up around my ears.

His lips press together as if he's gathering strength. "I'm married."

While I hadn't expected his answer, I'm also not surprised. "Why didn't you tell me sooner?"

"Because you would have backed away," he says, as if it were obvious. "You can do better than a forty-six-year-old man who's spent the last weeks trying to convince himself that so long as all I do with you is have dinner and listen to music and talk theater, I'm not being unfaithful."

"I don't want to get married." I wrap my fingers around his upper arm. "I want to be known for what *I* accomplish, not because I'm Mrs. So and So. Whether you're married or not doesn't matter to me."

The driver rolls down the window. "Am I taking the lady back or both of you?"

Stan ignores him. "You're not upset?'

"I wish you'd told me straight away, but other than that, no." My grip tightens. "Now that I know the truth, does that mean I don't have to kiss you first?"

"It definitely means that."

He lowers his face to mine. The kiss is filled with promise. A tingle runs through me all the way to my toes.

"I don't have to go home yet," I suggest. "You could offer me a nightcap."

"I'm in a hotel."

"Does that mean you're not allowed visitors?"

"No." His eyes crinkle. "It's just not particularly nice and I don't want you to feel uncomfortable."

"When I'm uncomfortable," I say over my shoulder, getting into the car, "I'll let you know."

"Deal." He slides in behind me. "Clinton Hotel."

The black car is long gone, back to the producer from whom it was borrowed. Stan escorts me home in a taxi, one arm around my shoulders, his other hand holding mine, as if he can't get enough of me.

I feel the same, though I'm not willing to show it. The last thing I want, after an hour in his bed, is to get dressed and go out in the cold rain. But it wouldn't be right to stay overnight, and anyway, swanning in at breakfast would push Mama's patience too far.

"All right?" he asks quietly as we cruise through the empty streets.

"Very much so." I wasn't a virgin by any means, but I've never had a man pay such dedicated attention to my body and its responses.

I'm tired, but I feel as if I've taken the best dance class in the world. Once I understood that intercourse was another form of dance and figured out the steps, I could work at it. Get better. Add some personal flourishes. There weren't many boys who deserved the effort. Maybe I hadn't put in the work; maybe it was because they thought their presence was enough.

But Stan Arkright isn't a boy. Despite his age, his body is trim and lightly muscled, his chest covered with a mat of brown hair that draws my fingers. He brought the same focused attention to making love as he did to blocking a play. Everything felt spontaneous and yet perfectly timed. He took so long to enter me that I felt like a firework ready to explode. My response delighted him. His pleasure was secondary; he made sure everything was good for me first.

"Good night," Stan says when the taxi stops. "Sleep well."

"Sweet dreams." I put everything into my good night kiss that I don't know how to say.

"You needn't worry about that." The look he gives me is ardent. I almost tell him to take me back to the hotel, but the lamp is lit in the window, and my mother is listening for the taxi's motor from the front bedroom. "I'll call you soon."

I turn off the lamp, remove my shoes, and go quietly upstairs. I will clean my face in the morning. Right now, I just want to think about what happened and what it might mean for the future.

When I wake up, the house is empty. The clock tells me I have less than an hour before I'm due at work, so I take a shower instead of the leisurely bath I want, throw on clothes, and go downstairs to find an enormous arrangement of roses on the dining room table. Parchment-pale and tipped with pink, they fill the room with their glorious fragrance. I close my eyes and bury my face in them, inhaling deeply.

An envelope is tucked deep into the stems. I open it and read the words, my cheeks burning at his comparison of the roses to my breasts. Afraid the note will fall into Grace's hands, I tuck it into my bag and go. I will be of little use to Mr. Wanamaker's retail empire today.

On my break, I call Connie. "Find Viv and meet me at the store at six," I tell him. "I have to be home for dinner, but there's something that can't wait."

We decamp to a local coffee shop where I tell them, discreetly, about my evening. Connie is at first more interested in Frank Sinatra, until he realizes my date did not, in fact, end on the doorstep.

"You little trollop!" He beams. "Still a shame I'm not his type, but I give him points for good taste."

Viv nods her approval. "And I give you points for good sense. With a man like that on your side, you'll go far."

"That's not why I did it." I can't explain my sudden feelings or hear my friends attempt to justify what I did last night.

"Even so, even if he doesn't cast you in his next show, he can lean on a friend to give you a part." She raises her coffee cup. "And when you're rich and famous because of your relationship with Stan Arkright, I hope you remember the friends who supported you way back when."

19

I call in at Pop's office on my way to work. After my diagnosis, the nurses were let in on my identity, so they greet me with smiles and hustle me into an exam room to wait for him.

"You again?" he says when he comes in. "Didn't I see you at breakfast?"

"I have another question," I say. "Of a medical nature."

"What's that, princess?" He makes a note on the chart in his hand.

"Before you ask, I'm not in trouble," I say bluntly. "But I don't want to be, either. Can you give me a Dutch cap?"

Pop lowers the chart, his cheeks bright red. "I can't."

"I thought you'd understand."

"That's not the problem." He makes a face. "You need to be examined to get a diaphragm. On the inside."

Now it's my turn to blush. In all the conversations I've overheard, none of the girls have ever mentioned anything beyond their doctors giving them the thing.

"Can you recommend someone?" No matter what the exam is like, I'd rather be in charge of my body. Expecting Stan to wear a rubber every time we're together and then worrying about getting pregnant doesn't add anything to my enjoyment of our time together.

"That I can do," he says with evident relief. "They're not meant to be prescribed to unmarried women, but I have friends who understand it's our place to provide care, not make judgments."

Not long after, Mama sits me down and asks how things are going with Stan. "It's becoming a regular thing," she says. "You've always been so focused on your dancing, and now you have friends and a proper boyfriend. I'm glad for you."

"He's not a proper boyfriend." I'm ashamed to tell her about him, but I also know she'll figure it out eventually.

"What do you mean?" She leans her elbows on the worn kitchen table.

"He's married." I stare into my mug. "He told me the night I met Frank Sinatra. He wasn't trying to put anything over on me."

"Okay." The word is said on an exhale. "So you're all right with the situation?"

I nod. "You said I'm only getting used to having friends. I don't want a demanding boyfriend who will turn into a fiancé and then a husband and then a father. This is... pleasant. I can learn a lot from him. And I like him."

"I like him, too," she says. "But maybe I like him a little less than I did. A married man may suit the two of you, Thelma, but there are other people involved. Do they have children?"

I tell her I don't know. "We've never talked about his wife, other than that she exists."

Mama gets up to start dinner, and I follow her, taking plates down from the shelf to set the table. Her voice follows me into the dining room.

"You should ask if there are children," she says. "What adults do among themselves is one thing. I can feel for his wife, but she's a grown woman. If there are kids who can be harmed, you should think if you want to be involved in that."

"I will." It surprises me that she has no harsher judgment, but Mama often surprises me. We're so different that it's hard to anticipate each other's reactions; Pearl could have told me, down to the words, what Mama would have said.

Stan comes for me after dinner and Mama is perfectly civil. Pop is more standoffish, which means they've spoken and he's not as pleased with my boyfriend as he was.

After we walk to the Downbeat for a drink and some music. I tell Stan that I have a question.

"Ask away. I'll tell you anything you want."

"You may not want to tell me this." I put my hands in my pockets. "It's about your wife."

"Oh." We pass beneath a streetlight, and I see how his expression has tightened. "What about her?"

I stop, wanting to get this over with before we step into the club, in case it blows up in my face. "What's her name?"

"Susan," he says curtly. "She was a teacher before we married. She's recently gone back to teaching math at a private school in Wilmington." He makes a sound that is almost a laugh. "She grows roses."

It is very little, as biographies go, but more than I want to know.

"Do you have children?"

"A son," he says slowly. "Phillip is twenty-two. He graduated college last year. He lives in Delaware, not far from where we live."

"Where in Delaware?" I start walking again. A son who's a college graduate is not the same as a child.

"Just south of Wilmington. It's a hell of a commute when I'm working. And if you're worried, she rarely comes into the city." He takes my arm. "I've stayed at the Clinton on and off for years."

"Have you been bringing girls to the Clinton on and off for years?" The words are out before I finish the thought. My face heats. I sound like a silly, jealous girl. "I'm sorry, I don't need to know that."

"You're well within your rights." He keeps my arm, and we turn on to Eleventh Street. "There was another girl, once, years ago. It was a mistake. I never did it again."

"Why are you doing it now?" If Stan hasn't brought anyone back to his rooms, that means he either has a couch in his office—I've not been there yet—or his previous girls didn't live at home.

"Because you're not like other girls," he says. "I don't know what else to tell you, Kimber."

After the show, he walks me home again. He doesn't invite me back to the hotel and there is no suggestion of meeting later in the week. He kisses my cheek and heads back toward Spruce Street, moving as if he's exhausted.

I let myself in, feeling no better myself. Why did I have to listen to Mama? I've obviously ruined everything by inserting myself into his personal life where I don't belong.

He doesn't call. Not the next day, not for the next week. I sit at home on Halloween night, listening to Grace gripe about her scavenger hunt being rained out, and understand what I've done.

But how to fix it? I do want to fix it, I realize. I don't just miss going out or making love. I miss *him*, which I hadn't expected. This was supposed to be something casual; feelings don't need to be brought into it.

"You in again tonight?" Grace asks, propping her chin on her hand. She's sprawled on the carpet in front of the fireplace. "You've been home a lot."

"I know."

I tuck my legs under the skirt of my bathrobe and tip my head back. My parents are out, for goodness' sake, while I'm at home with my sister, prepared to hand out candy to trick-or-treaters who never came.

"Did you break up with Mr. Arkright?"

"I'm not sure."

I'm pretty sure we have, but talking about it will make it real. My heart leaps whenever the phone rings, but it's never him.

Is he in the city tonight, or did he go home for the weekend? It's Monday night, he could be at Palumbo's. Maybe Frank Sinatra will be there. It pleases me that the city is haunted for him, as well as me. So many places we've been together. Even if he can't forgive me for invading his privacy, he can't erase all those memories.

"You look like crud." Grace hops to her feet. "I'm going to make cocoa. That makes everything better."

I throw myself into my job at Wanamaker's and spend time with my friends. Connie has been cast in a show but manages to make time for me around rehearsals and Viv sticks to me like glue, even staying over once or twice a week.

We talk about our ambitions, our dreams of show business and about moving to New York, which we both want and can't conceive how to manage.

Slowly Viv opens up. She doesn't tell me about her baby, but that knowledge informs what little she does share. Her father, she says, was violent; her mother blamed Viv for provoking him.

"No wonder you like my family so much."

She looks up from her ice cream. "Your mom is great, but your dad? Honestly, I could eat that man with a spoon, he's so sweet."

"He's exactly what my mother needs to dull her sharp edges." I don't remember my father very clearly now, just that he was as unlike Pop as it was possible for a man to be. Mama loved him, though, and I always assumed she took to Pop because he was so very different.

"No word from your man yet?" she asks, tripping me up. I'm not ready to talk about him.

"Not yet." I need to talk to someone before I burst. Mama is sympathetic but I can't tell her everything, and Connie is too much of a romantic. "I think I made a mistake."

"You asked about his wife?" When I tell her, she is shocked. "Are you crazy? You have a director eating out of the palm of your hand and you make him think about what he's doing?"

"He's not just a director." I understand what she means, but it's the loss of the man I feel, not the potential benefit to my career.

"What else could it be?" Viv opens her eyes wide. "He's nearly fifty, isn't he? He's not particularly good-looking. I can't imagine he'd be anything to write home about in bed."

I'm not going to tell her about how it was between us in bed. It's one of the things I miss most. That and talking shop, learning about the theater from his perspective. I could lie there and listen to him all night.

"I enjoyed spending time with him." At her skeptical smirk, I elaborate. "He took me places I could never afford otherwise. And I've never dated anyone who could afford them either."

"So, you like the old man because he takes you to nice restaurants but not because he could give you a starring role in his next play."

I've been uncomfortable with that idea ever since he asked me out. Casting couch rumors spread quickly; I don't want any success I might achieve to be credited to anything other than talent and hard work.

"I would never ask him for a part."

"Well, then, you're an idiot." Viv sees my stricken expression and difference. "Fine, Thel, you like him. But it was never going to be more than what it was. You have to look out for yourself in this world. Find a new boyfriend, that'll distract you."

"Absolutely not." I hadn't been looking for someone before and I'm certainly not going to try to find someone now, heading into the holiday season. "I'm going to keep going to acting class and take all the hours Miss Coffey will give me. I need to start putting money aside for New York."

"Oh, me, too!" Her bright eyes grow brighter, and she squeezes my hand. "Viv and Thelma take Manhattan. How does that sound?"

I shrug. "Thelma and Viv sound better, but I get your drift."

Thanksgiving comes, with its family gatherings and food. Mama scolds me for working Black Friday, but we are shorthanded and I don't mind.

If Stan is in Philadelphia—and why would he be, with his family in Delaware?—he will know where to find me.

But while the counter is inundated by men all day, buying gifts for wives and mothers and daughters, he doesn't come. I smile and write out receipts and send my customers along to the gift wrap station, calculating my commissions and wondering how much it will cost to move to New York.

I need a change. I need to be somewhere else, with more opportunities and where no one looks at me with sympathy because of what I can no longer do. I'll be Kimber Byrne in New York, not Thelma the failed dancer.

The more I talk about it with Viv, the more excited she grows.

"I told Connie. We're going to need a bigger apartment."

"He wants to come with us?" Having him there would make it perfect. Being away from my family will be hard, but with my friends and Pearl and Julian in the same city, I will be all right.

"He says he'll hold onto our ankles and make us drag him if he's not invited." We laugh at the thought. "I don't think it will come to that."

"No," I agree. "We need him."

The lights dim, the signal to take our seats, and we enter the auditorium to see Connie in his first show since *Trials and Tribulations*.

"He wasn't bad," I say afterward as we shiver by the stage door. After a warm October, November turned brisk. Now, in December, the air is frosty, although there's no sign of snow.

"But the show is terrible." Viv's cheeks are red, and she hunches her shoulders against the cold. "It can't last through Christmas."

I think the cast will be lucky to be employed through next weekend. Knowing what goes into a show—the weeks of rehearsals, the effort put into costumes and sets—always makes an early closure more tragic.

Connie appears a few minutes later, blazing like a light bulb in the dark street. "How was I?"

"You were wonderful." I wrap my arms around his middle. He's boiling hot, his coat open and his habitual scarf flapping.

"Those lessons have paid off." Viv takes his scarf and wraps it around her neck.

His laughter fills the alley and bounces off the walls. "It's a terrible show and you know it. But I agree with you—I am rather wonderful. It's a stepping stone, girls. We need every one of those we can get if we're going to be rich and famous someday."

20

All I want for Christmas is something to distract me from thoughts of Stan. Sensing my mood, my parents invite my friends to stay for the holiday. With Pearl arriving on the twenty-third and Julian the next morning, the house is crowded and loud enough to dull the ache in my heart, if not eliminate it entirely.

"How are you?" Pearl asks as we tidy the living room for the arrival of the rest of the family. It is tradition that we host Christmas Eve dinner and Aunt Claire takes Christmas Day.

"Okay." I put more cheer into my voice. "Just tired. I've been working a lot. You'd be surprised how many people leave their shopping to the very last minute."

"I cut through Macy's the other day," she responds. "It looked like a wrestling match."

I rub at a stubborn scuff mark with my dustcloth, wondering how it got there on the fireplace. "It must be Grace. What does she do?"

"Whatever she wants." Pearl shakes her head at how lenient Mama is with our youngest sister. "You weren't as chaotic as she is when you were in your Ginger Rogers phase."

"Except for the time she caught me tap dancing on the dining room table." She'd shouted at me while Pop covered his face to hide his laughter.

The front door bangs open and Toby strolls in, dropping his coat on the sofa and sitting down like it hasn't been three months since we've last seen him.

"Hey," he says. "What time's supper?"

"Hello to you, too." Pearl shoves his feet off the coffee table, then kisses him. "We eat at six. You're early enough that we can put you to work."

He scrambles up. "Umm, no. Pop around?"

"Still at the clinic." I note his frayed cuffs when I hang up his coat. Toby lives in a rented room and visits when it suits him. He didn't come for Thanksgiving, but Mama sent word via George that he was expected for Christmas or she would drag him out with her bare hands. "Grace and Mama ran out to the store for some last-minute things."

He stretches and a button pops off his shirt. Unselfconsciously, he picks it up and slips it into his pocket, tucking his tie into his pants to hide the gap.

"Fine. What do you need me to do?"

Dinner is a long, drawn-out affair with everyone talking at once, voices rising and competing for attention until Pop finally bangs his knife and fork on the table and asks for two minutes of peace. The final number is seventeen, with George and Ruthie's baby and the surprise addition of Sofie. Connie does his best to draw her out, but her walls are as high as ever.

Viv, across the table from me, is fizzing with some private secret. When at last we've finished eating, she jumps to her feet and volunteers to do the dishes—volunteering me, as well. Connie tags along to lift heavy things and pretend to be helpful.

"Put the coffee on," Mama directs. "And start the dishes. There's dessert yet to come."

Connie looks down at himself, as flat as he is long. "Where do you expect me to put it, Mrs. Byrne? I'm stuffed fatter than the turkey!"

When we are in the kitchen, I put my stack of plates on the counter and look at Viv. "What's going on? You look like you're about to pop."

She puts the wash basin in the sink and turns on the hot water. "Reach in my pocket," she says. "The left one. I figured you hadn't seen it, or you'd be more excited than I am."

What I retrieve is a scrap of newsprint, folded several times, with a casting call for a show opening in the new year. *You Can't Take It With You*, by George Kaufman and Moss Hart—a play I know as well as my name, and with a part expressly made for me.

"Oh, my God."

"Look at the small print." She starts in on the glassware. "Connie, make yourself useful and go fetch the rest of the glasses."

Under the name of the play, the theater, and the date of the audition, it says "Director: Stanley Arkright."

Something turns over in my chest. Stan, putting on my dream show? It must be a sign from the universe—except I don't believe in signs. Still, I can either ignore this opportunity, or I can face it—and him. If I ignore it, I'll never forgive myself.

Connie comes back in with a scant handful of glasses. "Did you tell her?"

"I did." She plunges them into the hot water. "I think she's speechless."

"I'm not." I rapidly sort the silver and put it to one side. "I'm surprised, that's all. Who are you going for?"

I hope she won't say Essie; I can't bear the thought of competing with her again, nor how it might feel if she got the part over me.

"Tony Kirby," Connie says. "Unless I get sent straight to Broadway before then."

We ignore him.

"I'm not good enough for a lead," Viv says with a matter-of-fact shrug. "I thought I'd try for Gay Wellington or the Grand Duchess."

"Oh, I like you as Gay." It's not a big part, but there's a good bit of comedy in the role until she falls asleep. "It's a shame you're not older. You'd be an amazing Penelope."

"I will *not* play your mother, Thelma Kimber. I'm two years older than you." She pulls a face. "But I would be an excellent Penelope."

I think of Connie's recent remark about roles as stepping stones. But Essie Carmichael is more than a stepping stone. I can't let her get away. How do I tell Stan that? How do I tell Stan anything, after more than two months of silence? He's probably moved on and forgotten all about me by now. Showing up at an audition would be an abrupt, possibly unpleasant, reminder. Nevertheless, I'm going to have to find a way. Could I go to his office? Or linger in the Clinton's lobby until he comes in?

"Which is better, do you think?" I ask, interrupting a conversation I've completely missed. "Calling him or showing up at his office?"

"Don't just show up," Connie says, appalled. "Especially not where he works. That would embarrass him."

The hotel is a worse idea, Viv says. What if he came in with a woman? If that happened, I'd have to throw myself on my sister's mercy and move to New York early. I could never face Stan again, and he would never consider me for a part for the rest of my life.

I could call the hotel, but again, I might be interrupting something I can visualize all too well.

"You're no help," I say at last. "I'll think of something."

The serving of coffee and cake breaks up our discussion. I sit on the ottoman near my aunt, listening to George and Toby bicker as if they were ten years old. My mind wanders back to Stan. If I could get him alone, I'm sure I could persuade him to give me an audition, even if he didn't want to see me again. It's the getting him alone part that's difficult.

"Aunt Claire," I say. "Can I talk to you upstairs for a moment?"

She arranges herself on my bed, and I close the door before coming to sit beside her. "I need some advice."

"Have you already asked Ava?" She never wants to get on Mama's bad side, much less during the holidays.

"This isn't something I can ask her," I say. "I know you weren't with anyone but Uncle Harry, but your experience of the world is broader than hers."

"Don't bet on it." She laughs lightly, then sobers. "I'm happy to help. What do you need?"

"I need to know how to seduce a man," I say bluntly. "I did something stupid and made a mess of my relationship with Stan, and I want him back."

"Even though he's married?"

I knew she and Mama shared everything.

"Even though he's married." I don't tell her that I wake up from dreams where he's looking at me with his head cocked, like I've said something clever and he doesn't know whether to chuckle or kiss me. Instead, I give an easier answer. "He's got a show coming up and I want a part in it. The way things are right now, he won't even take the audition."

Aunt Claire slips off the bed and goes to look at the cluster of programs pinned around the mirror. "Is ambition better than love?" she asks. "Your sister managed both."

"I don't want love. Neither does he." I want what we had *and* I want to play Essie Carmichael. If forced to choose, I would take the role, but if I handle it properly, maybe there's a way to have both. If we keep our relationship quiet—as quiet as we can in such an incestuous community—no one could accuse me of sleeping my way into the part.

Except I think Aunt Claire just did.

"I do like him," I say quietly. "But he's married. I'll take what I can have."

"Even though it's not enough." She looks sad all of a sudden. I wonder if our conversation is making her think of my uncle, dead before his time.

"Yes. Even if it's not enough."

"All right." She nods decisively. "How well does he know you?"

I wonder where she's going with this. "Pretty well, I'd say."

"Does he know you or Kimber?"

I stand, smoothing the bedspread, and join her at the mirror. The dresser top is cluttered with makeup and perfume. I begin to straighten the bottles while I get my words in order. "Mostly he knows Kimber." I've never known how to introduce him to the other parts of me, and once I realized I wanted him to know me as Thelma, it was too late. "Why?"

"Because he's never seen you be vulnerable. Let him see that part of you. Tell him you've missed him. Then show him."

I describe the plan that came to me downstairs: I'll contact the night desk clerk at the Clinton and promise to pay him if he calls me when Stan comes in alone. "Then I'll call a cab," I conclude, "and knock on his door."

"The direct approach." She smiles. "You have grown up, Thelma."

"I'm glad someone in this family notices." When I hug her, her bones are as light as a bird's. "Now the next question. What do I wear?"

"That, at least, I'm qualified to answer."

The day after Christmas, I make the excuse of going to visit Sofie and call the Clinton from my aunt's phone. When the clerk informs me Stan hasn't been there since November, my stomach knots.

"He's coming back," he says, after a long pause. "A few days after the new year."

Relief floods through me. "Do you know what day?"

"Not before the fifth. The book says he'll be checking into his standard room."

"Thank you." I mention what I want him to do and, as expected, it comes at a price—five dollars, not two. I agree and hang up, wondering where I'm going to get the money. He wants payment in advance, and my paycheck won't arrive until the sixth.

I corner Pop before dinner and ask if I can be late with my board.

"You know you don't have to give us anything, baby," he says. "You're hardly ever here."

"I wasn't brought up to be a freeloader." I lean over the back of his chair and press my cheek to his. "But this once I feel okay about it."

The lobby of the Clinton Hotel is well-lit but has an abandoned air; by this time of night, most of the patrons have retired. When I approach the desk, the clerk tips me a wink and points to the ceiling. "He's up there."

The elevator takes me to the third floor. I step out, holding my coat close around me. Room 304 is at the far end of a hallway that has doubled in length since my last visit. I reach the door and stand there, my hand raised, unable to bring myself to knock.

This is ridiculous. He's going to take one look at me and throw me out. Then I'll have to face the clerk again as I slink away in disgrace. I could use the fire stairs—though descending three flights in my highest heels isn't appealing. Maybe I'll linger in the hallway for half an hour and then leave.

Footsteps from inside the room make me freeze. I step back as the door opens.

"Kimber." He's wearing his coat and hat—he's going to meet someone.

I am an idiot.

"I'm sorry, you're going out." I'll have to share the elevator with him. Is it possible to drop through the carpet?

"I can't sleep. I was going to go for a drink." Stan catches my arm and turns me around. "Why are you here?"

I remember my aunt's advice and find it's easy enough to tell the truth when I'm face-to-face with him. "Because I missed you."

Before I've finished speaking, I'm inside and the door is closing. Stan removes my coat and stops for a moment to take in the silvery gown Aunt Claire lent me. It's French and clings to every curve; she told me it had to be worn without underwear.

"It's hard to find words when you look like that."

I turn so the light shimmers off the fabric. "Then just listen instead. I'm sorry. I shouldn't have asked about things that weren't my business. I won't do it again."

He runs one hand slowly along my hip, turning my insides to liquid. "It wasn't anything you did," he says. "I... I couldn't look at myself in the mirror and go on with what I was doing—to you or to Susan. You deserve more, Kimber. More than this"—his arm encompasses the shabby room, but also himself—"and I won't be the one to keep you from having it."

I put my hand over his and press it to my hip, so his warmth burns through to my flesh. "I loved what we had together," I remind him, stepping closer. "I've missed it. I've missed *you*."

"Damn it." Stan makes a defeated sound and gathers me into his arms. He lowers his mouth to mine and kisses me in a way that is almost savage. My desire surges to meet his. I raise his hand to my breast, the nipple hard beneath the satin. He brushes it with his thumb, and I stifle a moan against his neck.

The bedroom is beyond the couch and the small kitchen area, through another door. We move unsteadily past the furniture and stumble into the room. Stan reaches out blindly and snaps on the lamp.

"I want to look at you," he says hoarsely, dropping to the edge of the bed and leaving me standing in the center of the room. "My God, you're lovely."

I meet his gaze and hold it as I run my hands down my body. If he doesn't make love to me soon, I might burst into flames. "Looking is fine, but isn't touching better?"

We lay in the faint glow of the streetlight outside, our heart rates slowly returning to normal. Stan tips his head up to check the alarm clock. "It's after two," he says. "I should get you home while your mother still likes me."

I shake my head and snuggle closer. "They think I'm staying with a friend. You have me until morning, if you want me."

"I want you." He gets up and walks naked into the other room. I watch him, wondering why a man's hairy legs are attractive and yet mine must be perfectly smooth. Stan returns with a bottle of whiskey and two small glasses. "Can I interest you in a nightcap?"

As I sit up against the headboard to admire him, the sheet falls away, exposing my upper body. Instead of handing me the drink, he sits on the edge of the bed and runs the cold glass along the curve of my breast, leaving a cold, wet trail that he follows with his lips. By the time we come up for air, the whiskey is room temperature, and I am glowing from his attentions.

"We can't go again," he says. "I don't have another—"

I roll over and put one leg across his body. "You don't need to worry about that anymore. I went to the doctor."

He goes very still. "You did what?"

"I want to enjoy the time we have together." Leaning down, I rub my cheek on his chest. Faint traces of a spicy cologne remain. "I don't want us to worry about anything."

21

Waking up in Stan's bed is something new. I lie there quietly, trying not to move, so I can watch him sleep. His rough brown hair, threaded with gray, is flattened like a dog's coat. The morning light strikes the bristles on his chin, turning them to bronze.

I've never spent an entire night with a man before. Despite the hours I've lingered in this man's bed, sleeping beside him is different. I feel as though I've been allowed to witness something special by seeing him asleep and unguarded.

Abruptly his eyes open and he stares back at me. "Do I snore?"

I smile, embarrassed to be caught watching him. "A little."

"Do you have time for breakfast?" he asks. "There's a little spot around the corner with good French toast."

"I don't have anything to wear." My gown is over the back of a chair and my shoes are nowhere to be seen.

Stan lifts the sheet and smiles down at me. "You could stay this way all day, as far as I'm concerned."

I slide out of bed and put on his shirt, closing the buttons. "I'm going to look ridiculous going home in this."

"In my shirt or your gown?" He puts his arms around me from behind and pulls me back against him. I wriggle against him to feel his response. "I'm not going to let you go at this rate."

"Don't you have work to do?" Ever since Christmas, I haven't been able to get that audition notice out of my mind. Even as we made love, I was thinking about Essie and how I would play her.

"I do, but that's the best part about being the man in charge," he says. "I make my own hours."

There's an intense focus in the way he looks at me. It cracks me open deep inside and makes me want to take his blunt-fingered hand and lead him back to the tumbled bed. How can the look in a man's eyes make me feel naked and seen at the same time?

The tiny kitchenette boasts an electric coffee pot. I fill it with water and add coffee, hoping I'm doing it correctly; at home, we have a glass stovetop pot. Stan doesn't even have a stove in this room, only a sink and a hot plate.

"What's your next show going to be?" When we were last together, he was talking to producers and money men. He never mentioned the name of the play and I am uncomfortable knowing something he hasn't told me.

"*You Can't Take It With You*." Stan reaches past me to retrieve two mugs from a shelf. "Ever seen it?"

"Oh, yes." I squeeze my eyes shut tight, then turn to face him. "Have you cast it yet?"

"Not yet." He crosses the room and opens a drawer, removing a pair of blue boxer shorts. "You weren't thinking of auditioning, were you?"

The coffee drips in the silent room as I take in the fact that he doesn't want me to try for a part in his show.

"I am now that I know what play you're doing." I put my hand on his chest, scratching my nails lightly through the mat of brown hair. "Do you not want me to?"

Stan leans in and kisses my neck. "Wouldn't it be uncomfortable for us to be working together, considering?"

"No." I move away, feeling a sudden chill. "We've worked together before. I can take direction from you without letting it affect this."

He pours the coffee and puts the mugs on the table, then hooks a chair out with his foot and gestures for me to sit.

"I don't know." He rubs his forehead, the creases evident. "If word got out…"

I thought we'd decided not to speak about his wife.

"Delaware is a long way away," I say sharply. "If we're careful, there's no reason she'll find out anything."

He looks at me. "I'm not worried about Susan. I'm worried about your reputation. For that matter, I'm worried about my reputation as a director."

Lou Hartley's face flashes before my eyes. My skin breaks out in goose-flesh.

"Are you talking about what you saw at the Durang?" He doesn't want to be seen in the same way, even though he's had more of me than Mr. Hartley could have dreamed of.

"Not entirely." Stan sounds uncomfortable. "But yes, if you must know. I've never been involved with an actress, much less in one of my shows."

"There's a first time for everything." I put my mug down a little harder than I intended. "Stan, I really want Essie. Let me audition."

"I thought you'd ask for Alice." He catches my chin in his fingers. "She's the lead. The beauty."

"I'm not good enough to play Alice." I take heart that he thinks I want the ingenue role. "And that's not the point. I *am* Essie Carmichael."

"You're too pretty." It doesn't sound like a compliment.

"You can't keep using that as an excuse not to cast me."

"Essie is a figure of fun."

"But she's not funny on purpose." I want this part in a way that is almost carnal, the same way I want Stan when we are apart. "She takes herself seriously. It's not her fault she's not very good."

"You're an excellent dancer," he points out, turning his mug in a circle. "Can you be *not very good*?"

I remember being Essie: dancing all over the house because I couldn't *not* dance. "Stan, this role means a lot to me."

"This role means a lot to the thirty other girls who will show up for the audition." He reaches for a crumpled pack of cigarettes on the counter and offers one to me.

"No, thanks." I look at him, make a quick decision to be vulnerable—Aunt Claire's word again—and share something I've never told him. "It's not just the role, it's the entire show."

I tell him about how my aunt and uncle took me to the premiere at the Chestnut Street Opera House. I'd fallen in love with the whole quirky Sycamore clan, but especially Essie, who, despite her years of ballet training, flung herself about the stage with more enthusiasm than skill. When the movie came out two years later, I must have seen it half a dozen times, although Ann Miller is so spectacularly talented that her Essie was a very different character.

"I want to play Essie more than anything." Showing this much of myself makes me feel naked in a way I've never been before. Taking off my clothes is one thing; taking off my mask and showing him who I am is much harder. "I've been her, all my life."

"Well." Stan leans forward and gives me that close look of his. I can't tell if he doesn't see well without his glasses or if he sees better than most. "It's a compelling argument, Kimber. I'll keep that in mind—when you audition."

I throw myself across the table, knocking my mug onto the floor in the process. "You won't regret it."

The promise of an audition makes me giddy, until it leads to the first fight of my life with Mama. When I step out of the cab, wearing a crumpled satin dress and my winter coat, with Stan's scarf around my neck—the weather turned icy overnight—the front door opens. My mother's horrified expression tells me I should have gone to my aunt's and borrowed something suitable to wear home.

"Look at you!" She drags me into the house and kicks the door shut, leaving a mark on the wood.

"Mama, I—"

I don't finish because she's spitting words at me like pebbles: that she didn't bring me up to stay out all night with men, that I was setting no kind of example for Grace by coming home wearing last night's clothes.

"And where did you get that?" She points at my dress. "You can see absolutely everything."

"It's Aunt Claire's," I say, glad to get a word in edgewise. "She—"

"Of course it's Claire's." Mama whirls on her heel. "I'll deal with her later. Go upstairs and change your clothes. Do you remember you have to go to work today?"

"I called out sick," I mutter as I stamp up the stairs. "And I'll dress however I want. I'm a grown woman."

"You will not behave like a tramp under my roof."

The word stops me in my tracks. Is that how she sees me? She didn't call me names when I told her Stan was married. Was she lying then or did my staying out all night push her over the edge? I'd told her I was staying with Viv. Because I'd never lied to her before, it hadn't occurred to me that I should have taken a change of clothes.

I shut my door quietly and put a chair under the knob. I'll talk to her again when I'm ready, but this way she can't barge in while I'm getting changed.

The silver dress drops to the floor and I step out of it, turning to the full-length mirror. I look the same, but I'm not. The Thelma of yesterday hadn't shown up at a man's hotel room uninvited, hadn't seduced him into making love to her, hadn't wrangled an audition because he doesn't want to have to find another girl to warm his bed.

My body doesn't even look the same because not dancing has added unfamiliar curves to my figure. Stan's appreciation has also made me see myself in a new way. I've always defined myself by what my body is capable of; now I have new capabilities.

I yank underwear and a pullover out of my drawers, letting my clothes scatter every which way, and take a skirt from the closet. Dressed, I look like what Mama wants: a bland and boring daughter who works in a department store and has no goals beyond earning her next commission.

"That's not the daughter you've got," I say under my breath, pulling a comb through my tangled hair and wiping away my spoiled makeup with spit and a handkerchief. "You don't want me under your roof, I won't stay here."

I fetch my suitcase down from the third-floor storage room, moving quietly in case Mama is listening. Into it goes underwear, stockings, two pairs of shoes, practice clothes, my Wanamaker's skirt and blouse, and two dresses that I think will serve as audition outfits for Essie. At the last minute, I cram in an evening gown and a pair of dressy sandals in case the opportunity arises to see Stan.

The crash of angry dishwashing is audible when I tiptoe down the stairs. I pause for a moment, then slip out the front door.

22

Aunt Claire is shocked when I announce my intention to stay with her.

"Your mother will kill me."

"Doesn't anyone outgrow being scared of her?" I drop my suitcase on the hall floor, then feel guilty because Cecie will have to polish the mark away. "She treats everyone like they're children and she's the only one who's right."

"Well, she's had a lot of practice with children, and she's right more often than not." Leaving my bag in the hall, she takes me to her sitting room and rings for Cecie to bring tea. "My niece left a suitcase in the front hall," she says when the maid arrives. "Please take it up to the guest room next to Sofie's bedroom."

She's going to let me stay! I bounce in my chair with glee at getting over on Mama. Aunt Claire sees and her expression goes even more serious.

"This is only until you both calm down," she cautions. "I love you, Thelma, and I know Ava can have a rough tongue sometimes, but she wants what's best for you."

I wait until I hear Cecie's footsteps in the hall to say, "She called me a tramp," and watch my aunt's mouth fall open.

After she goes out to meet a friend, I take over the telephone and call Viv and Connie's respective boarding houses, leaving them my new number.

More important is letting Stan know where I am. Do I call his office or wait until tonight to reach him at his hotel? I decide on a middle ground and leave a message at the Clinton's front desk, to be given to him on his return. I don't want to tell him straight off that I've left home, in case he takes it badly.

I'm not sure why he would, but something tells me he might feel guilty for causing difficulties for me, even if they are all of my mother's making.

As if Grace could be influenced by anyone's example! That girl came out of the womb with a will of iron and a head as hard as granite. She's not going to start staying out all night because I did.

I settle into the spacious guest room, decorated in my aunt's understated, elegant colors—pink, in this case—with French pictures on the walls and pretty, polished furniture.

My clothes, unpacked by Cecie and nicely pressed, take up a small corner of the closet. It occurs to me that I now reside in the same house as my favorite source of wardrobe. If only Aunt Claire's feet were larger! Shoes are my weakness and, for a dancer, very important. She has an amazing collection but they're all too small for me.

After a quiet dinner with my aunt and cousin, Cecie comes into the living room. "Miss Thelma, there's a telephone call for you."

I don't bother asking who it is: it's too early for Stan, so it's probably Connie and Viv, huddled together in a phone booth, wanting to hear what happened.

"Hello?"

"Thelma."

"Who called you, Mama or Aunt Claire?"

Pearl sighs. "Mama. She's upset."

As if I need her to tell me that; I was the one who'd been hit with that firehose of bitterness.

"So am I." I sit on the edge of the delicate chair in the phone alcove. "You didn't hear what she said."

"She's turned her temper on me before," she says with a soft laugh. "Remember when she wouldn't let me go to Paris?"

"Yes, but you were fifteen." Pearl was the good child, and the months where she and Mama barely spoke stands out in my memory. "I'm twenty-three and I'm entitled to live my life. This is more like what happened between Daddy and Dan."

The same year Mama brought me to Philadelphia, my father and brother had a blowup that had barely healed when Daddy died. Dan moved out, Daddy went silent, and Mama snapped out of the funk she'd been in after Teddy's birth to try and make peace.

"Well, then, let me play peacemaker," Pearl says. "I can take the train down tomorrow if you'd like."

"I'm preparing for an audition tomorrow," I tell her. "And it won't help. I'm not talking to her until she apologizes for what she called me."

From the way the silence stretches, I know Mama told her what I'd done, and possibly what she'd said. That proves she's embarrassed, but until she admits she was wrong, I won't let myself care.

"You know what she can be like." Pearl tries again. "She wants us to have easier lives than she did, and she thinks you're opening yourself up to being hurt."

It's not for her to say! I want to howl the house down, but instead I say quietly, "I know what I'm doing. So does he. No one is going to get hurt except Mama. Because I won't see her until she says she's sorry."

The next day, I get up early and rehearse before work, keeping Cecie from her chores after Aunt Claire goes out.

Miss Coffey looks me over when I clock in. "You don't look unwell, Miss Kimber."

"Female trouble." I grin at her. "I'm much better now, but I have a doctor's appointment on Thursday afternoon. I can work extra shifts on Friday and Saturday to make up for it."

Her eyes narrow. "You can't make your own schedule. If you don't come in on Thursday, you'll be docked a day's pay. I can't have you girls rearranging the calendar for your convenience."

If I get this part, I'll quit anyway.

My friends meet me at six and we walk back to my aunt's house on Delancey Place, talking a mile a minute. They want to hear what happened with Mama, but as they're also both auditioning for *You Can't Take It With You*, we trade lines and ideas, our excitement building until we're as rambunctious as a trio of toddlers.

Aunt Claire raises her eyebrows at two unexpected dinner guests, and it strikes me that her household, for all its comfort, is too well-regulated to accommodate spontaneity. Mama would have shrugged and added more potatoes to the pot, then set someone to slicing more bread.

She darts away to the kitchen and returns a few minutes later, looking mollified. "Dinner will be a little late," she says smoothly. "Why don't we all sit in the living room?"

Viv is silent, snugged into a corner of the couch, taking everything in, but Connie charms away any lingering tension as we have cocktails. After ten minutes, the front door bangs and Teddy jogs past with a bag in his hand.

Aunt Claire visibly relaxes. "It shouldn't be long now," she murmurs. "Mrs. Hedges is doing fried chicken tonight."

Fried chicken is something that would be served at home, not in my aunt's highly civilized house. I hadn't realized two extra mouths would throw off her menu plans.

"I'm sorry," I say, breaking into one of Connie's amusing stories. "I didn't think."

"It's fine," she says with a pretty little shrug. "Ava's more accustomed to chaos than I am."

The doorbell rings as we're sitting down to dinner. Teddy bounces up to get it and returns with Grace, who smiles widely and says, "I hear you have extra."

Aunt Claire laughs in defeat. "Sit down. Does your mother know you're here?"

"She told me to go away." She slides in next to Teddy. "I'm surprised Pearl isn't here, too."

Despite being unplanned, the fried chicken is delicious. It's not hard to imagine that this is what Mrs. Hedges makes for Cecie and her husband while upstairs eats roast chicken or broiled fish. A fluffy mountain of mashed potatoes causes a discreet shoving match between Grace and Teddy. Connie fits right in by removing the bowl from their grip and passing it to my aunt.

Grace turns to me, her mouth full, and says, "You've really done it, you know? Pop can't do anything with her."

"That's not my problem," I say. "Mama's in the wrong and I intend to stay here until she apologizes."

Aunt Claire speaks up. "I love having you here, Thelma, but you can't stay indefinitely. You and Ava need to sort this out."

If I stay too long, Mama won't forgive her. But how can Aunt Claire expect me to go home after what's been said?

"You can stay with me," Viv pipes up. "It's cramped, and the food is terrible, but one of the girls is going to New York next week, so we could get her double room."

Now there's a thought. True independence. I could see Stan whenever I wanted with no one to call me names or ask what time I'd be home.

"Let's get through tomorrow first,' I say. "But that sounds like a good idea."

Grace and Teddy snicker. Aunt Claire covers her face with her hands.

The waiting area of the Franklin Grand is already crowded when we arrive. We sign in and hand over our resumes and head shots to a disinterested woman with a cigarette. She looks at my sheet and then up at me

"You're here for Alice, right?"

"No. Essie."

She looks doubtful but points me to a cluster on the left-hand side. "That's your group, then. We're doing Alice first, that's why I asked."

I tried hard not to look like Alice today, wearing a bright dress with a sailor collar and carrying both tap shoes and ballet slippers in my bag. Better to be overprepared. I also know three of her speeches off by heart, though I wouldn't be so stupid as to not use the script.

Connie is sorted into the group trying for Tony Kirby and Viv is with a knot of women who have come prepared to be alcoholic actresses and grand duchesses.

Then we wait. Connie's is the first group to be called out. He returns quickly, but gives a bright smile and says, "They suggested I stick around to try for Ed Carmichael."

Ed is Essie's husband. It would be too perfect if we were cast as a married couple.

"Alices!" comes the next call. At least thirty conventionally pretty girls surge forward, hope written all over their faces.

Their auditions take a long time and are followed by Penelope, the mother.

Lunch is called, and although Connie runs out to get sandwiches, I won't be able to eat anything until we're released. Viv and I huddle together during the brief break. Her hands, when she grips mine, are icy. Knowing how terrifying she finds the audition process, it's easier to comprehend what she did to me.

"You'll be fine," I say, rubbing her hands to warm them. "It's not a big part, but I think you'll be great."

She nods, her red lips tight. "Will you move in with me?" she asks. "When your aunt gets tired of you?"

"If I can afford it." The day of Aunt Claire getting tired of me might come sooner than anticipated; I heard her on the phone with Mama this morning, promising to make me see sense. I have no intention of seeing sense until she finds her manners.

"Essie!"

Connie gives me a kiss, and I sail out onto the stage with the others, doing my best to present myself as confident. Inside I'm shaking. Out there in the darkness sits my lover, giving me this chance against his better judgment. I have to prove to Stan, even more than to myself, that I can handle this role.

When my turn comes, I step forward, smile out at the invisible men, and do my reading. I finish and wait, hope shivering through my veins.

"Thank you, Miss Byrne," says an unfamiliar voice. "Now could you try the script? Scene one. The director's assistant will read Penelope."

I pick up the script from the table and find my place. "Just read? I ask, wishing I'd changed my shoes.

"Just read." It's Stan. His voice is cool and impersonal. He's as good an actor as anyone in this theater.

The woman who took our paperwork comes out from the wings on the opposite side. She's lost her cigarette, but her bored attitude is firmly in place. "Ready?" She sounds as if she'd sooner take a nap than read the part of a flighty author of racy plays.

Instead of responding, I say Essie's first line, and we toss the brisk mother/daughter conversation back and forth. I've never enjoyed an audition more. Even the assistant gets in on the fun eventually. Her Penelope ends with more emotion than she'd begun with.

We finish and she steps back. I look out at the audience, not shading my eyes to see their faces, waiting for them to speak.

"Very nice," comes the first voice. "The next question is, can you dance?"

"Yes, I can." He obviously hasn't read my resume. "I've taken ballet since I was twelve and tap since I was six. Most of my experience until recently has been in musicals. I've even worked with Mr. Arkright be-fore."

There is a rumble of conversation from the seats. I can't make out a word of it, no matter how I try, but I'm told to go in the back and wait to be called.

Connie wraps his arms around me as I stumble backstage. "You were wonderful," he whispers, rubbing my back. "You've got this."

"There are ten girls to go." My stomach lurches and I run for the bathroom, losing what little breakfast I'd been able to eat.

The auditions run late, and at five those of us who remain are told to come back in the morning to do further readings. All three of us are still in the running and we leave together, wilted but triumphant, to have a celebratory meal at Horn and Hardart. I stop at a phone booth and call Aunt Claire to let her know I won't be home for dinner.

Teddy answers. "Again?" he asks. "Yesterday I had to run out and buy food and today you decide not to come home?"

"Don't be an old woman," I say. "Aren't leftovers better than not enough? Maybe you can invite Grace over again."

It's after ten when I get in. No one is downstairs but there is a message for me on the telephone table to call Stan.

My heart in my throat, I dial the hotel and ask for his room. He picks up on the first ring.

"Stan?"

"Congratulations," he says. "You need to come in tomorrow morning to read again, but it's a formality. You convinced me. Just as importantly, you convinced the casting director. The part is yours."

Part Three
Turning Point

23

First thing in the morning, I call Wanamaker's and give my notice. Miss Coffey is less than amused, even after I tell her I have a part in a major show.

"These theatrics are all well and good," she sniffs, "but they won't keep a roof over your head, Miss Kimber. And the kind of man who will want to put a roof over your head is never going to find you in the chorus."

I don't point out that I'm no longer in the chorus, and that, for the moment, I have a man. Stan will get tired of me at some point—working together will be the final nail in the coffin—but I have vowed to enjoy this relationship while it lasts.

The second audition feels as pressured as the first; if I didn't know I already had the part, I would be backstage vomiting. But after the final three girls read and follow some choreography created for Essie, I am the one told to remain.

Eventually, while the other actors are being cast, I slip down into the seats, sitting off to one side so I can watch Stan and the other men make their decisions. From the stage, they are little more than a cloud of smoke and crackling sandwich wrappers. It is amazing to see them and know they wield so much power.

Connie doesn't make it through and departs with good grace. Viv, however, gets the part of Gay Wellington, the alcoholic actress. I'm glad for her. I'm also glad for me; having her in the same show means we can travel to and from work together once we begin living in the same house.

Aunt Claire's patience will last for no more than a week. It's all right; I don't want to damage our relationship and I'm more than ready to move in with Viv. I've never lived away from my family before. The experience of boarding house life will be something new and different, even though Viv warns me repeatedly about the quality of her landlady's cooking.

Before we leave the theater, the director's assistant hands each of us a contract to sign. Mine has a slip of paper clipped to the last page.

"Be ready at 8."

I stuff the note into my pocket and sign the contract, catching up to Viv outside. "Sorry," I tell her, "I can't meet you and Connie tonight."

She gives me a wicked grin. "Is lover boy taking you out to celebrate?"

"He is." I take her arm. "Viv, you do understand you can't talk about him in the theater, right? He agreed to take my audition if we pretended not to know each other."

"Don't worry," she says. "My lips are sealed. I'm going to enjoy watching him watch you kiss your stage husband."

"I wish it had been Connie." The actor cast as Ed is perfectly nice, but it will feel strange to behave like a wife in front of my lover.

Lover. I savor the word. It feels so adult. I don't have a boyfriend; I have a lover. It should feel scandalous, because he's married, and yet there is nothing scandalous about Stan. If I didn't understand the transaction underpinning our relationship, I would think he genuinely cared for me.

I've certainly begun to care about him. Falling for a man wasn't on my agenda and I'm fighting as hard as I can to keep from falling farther. It's a good thing rehearsals are bound to set us at odds; if all our time together was spent either in bed or at some fancy place I couldn't afford without him, I'd be thoroughly in love and totally lost.

"Did you see Tony Kirby?" Viv fans herself. "I've never run across him before. You don't forget a face like that."

Lee Miles is a lithe, beautiful man, taller than me, with black curls so crisp they look like they would crunch under my fingers. He has the kind of chiseled lips that make you wonder what it would be like to kiss him.

"Maybe I should have tried out for Alice after all."

Laughing, we part ways and I go home to tell Aunt Claire the good news.

"In that play? How perfect!" she exclaims. "Will you call your mother? Please? I know she'd be happy for you."

I'm not so sure. I somehow doubt her liking for Stan is at the same level as before he kept me out all night.

"You can tell her," I say carelessly. "I've got a date, and I'm dying for a bath."

She steps back out of my way. "Don't let me stop you. The Hotel Warriner is fully stocked to meet all your needs."

As I submerge myself in fragrant bubbles, my hair tied up in a silk scarf, I think about her words. I am treating her home like a hotel, but I won't be here much longer. Once I'm gone, she'll be able to face Mama again.

I would like to call and give them the news—Pop and Grace, at least. Maybe I'll tell Teddy to have Grace call me. That way I can arrange to pick up the rest of my things when Mama isn't around.

Stan takes me somewhere new—a jazz club called The Click at Sixteenth and Market Streets. The bar—the longest in the world—runs the length of the block-long building and is lined three deep with people. On the revolving stage at the center of the room, a small jazz band is fronted by a female singer. Despite the noise of the crowds, her voice rises above it. The day falls away as the music enters my bones.

"This is lovely." I cling to Stan's arm as we are led to our table. "You know the best places."

The smile he gives me feels like a caress. "I have to keep my girl amused or she'll leave me for someone younger and better looking."

I slide into my seat and shrug off my wrap. "Like who?"

"Like our Tony Kirby, for one," he says. "I saw the girls twittering about him."

Thank goodness he hadn't overheard my conversation with Viv!

"He's too pretty." I curl my fingers through his. "What girl wants to share her mirror with a pretty boy?"

He looks up when the waiter arrives and orders a bottle of champagne.

"Lee Miles is the kind of man you should be with, Kimber. Someone young and talented and going somewhere in this business."

"Did you give me a part to get rid of me?" I lower my lashes and pout. "Because that's not why I auditioned. I'm happy with the way things are between us. I've told you."

"And I'm happy with you." He takes off his glasses and polishes them on his tie, looking at me with a slightly unfocused gaze that nevertheless sees deep inside me, all the way to Thelma. "A little too happy, I sometimes think. I never intended for this to happen."

The champagne arrives and I accept a brimming glass. "Neither did I," I tell him. "Let's drink to things we never intended to happen."

We go back to his hotel and make love, and afterward he insists on returning me to the Delancey Place house in a cab. "I've caused enough trouble with your mother," he explains. "I'm not getting on your aunt's bad side as well."

"She's not likely to be up this late." I slide over to rest my head on his shoulder, slipping my fingers inside his shirt. We dressed hastily, and his undershirt is hanging over a lamp. "You could have kept me tonight and met her some other time."

He extracts my fingers from his chest hair and kisses the back of my hand. "Staying over is a bad habit to get into. I might grow to like it too much."

Once rehearsals begin early next week, my free time will become limited. With Teddy as intermediary, I set a time to meet my sister when Mama will be at the shop. Aunt Claire agreed to send Hedges with the car whenever I'm ready, so I spend the afternoon packing a lifetime of possessions into two suitcases and a half-dozen boxes.

"I don't see why you and Mama don't make up," Grace says for the third time. "It's stupid to stay mad. I miss you and I don't like being the only one left at home. Too much attention."

"It would have happened sooner or later—the moving out, anyway." I set another pile of clothes on the bed and marvel at the contents of my closet. It's a wonder there's anything left in my aunt's attic with the way I've plundered her wardrobe over the years.

"Someday when I'm rich and famous, I'll buy all new clothes." I hold up the beaded dress, which, because of its weight, lives in a flat box rather than on a hanger. "Though I do love this."

"I love all your clothes." Grace picks up another gown, dark blue satin with a back drape. Still daring even now, it must have been something in the early thirties. "It's who you are to me, my sister in all her funny clothes."

"Thanks." I fill the suitcases and close them, then turn to the empty cartons. "Can you take the stuff down off the mirror? Gently?"

As I load my remaining clothes into boxes, Grace carefully removes movie star photos and theater programs, being particularly careful of my precious signed Vera Ellen. I look up at a high shelf. "I guess you can finally have her."

The 'her' in question is a large, porcelain-headed doll given to me by Aunt Claire when I was little. Grace has been campaigning for Flora since she could speak.

"I don't want her now," she says, pausing with a picture of Vera Ellen in one hand. "I'd rather have you."

"Well, it's either you or I'll put her in the garbage."

Grace quickly drags a chair over to the shelf and lifts the doll down. "I would rather you gave her to me because I wanted her instead of because you were moving out."

"You finally got what you wanted," I say sharply. "Don't complain about how."

It hurts to see Flora in Grace's arms. I didn't refuse to give her the doll for all those years because I was being selfish; she belonged to the wheelbarrow girl, one last vestige of that time when my legs didn't work and my father was alive. But she is large and fragile; there will be no safe place for her in my new life. It's better she stays with someone who will care for her, even if that means I don't have her painted face gazing benevolently down at me every morning.

Once everything is packed, I call Aunt Claire. Grace and I sit in the living room, drinking tea while we wait. She's strangely jittery, bouncing from the sofa to the footstool and then to the window.

"You've got ants in your pants," I say when she nearly trips over my feet. "What's wrong?"

She stops and stares at me. "Other than my sister abandoning me? Other than Mama being too stiff-necked to come home and have it out with you? And let's not even get into poor Pop. She's barely talking to him."

I feel bad that he's stuck in the middle. For all that he adores Mama, he's never hesitated to tell her when he thinks she's wrong. Their arguments last no more than fifteen minutes because he can always make her laugh.

"You told her I was coming?"

Grace crosses her arms belligerently. "Of course, I did."

But she doesn't come. Until Hedges appears with the car, ten minutes later, Camac Street remains empty but for the elderly lady down the block directing her granddaughter in how to scrub the marble stoop.

While he loads my things into the back of the Packard, Grace hugs me like I'm going to the other side of the world, not just the other side of South Street.

"Can I come visit?" she asks. "Me and Teddy, we'll come down and take you out for coffee."

"Any time you want." I hug her again. "Let me get settled and find out my rehearsal schedule."

"I'll bet you'll find time for your fellow before us." Grace smirks. "Is he really married, Thel?"

"How do you know that?" I'm embarrassed to be talking about my personal life with my little sister.

"I listen to them when they think I'm in bed," she says. "I hear all sorts of things."

I'll bet she does. Mama and Pop always end the night with a cup of tea before going upstairs.

"They keep going once the door's shut. But I usually stop listening then because they're not always talking." Grace cocks her head. "So, what's it like, anyway? Sex, I mean."

She pins me with her eyes. I try to avoid answering by asking Hedges if he needs help with my largest bag. When I turn around, Grace's arms are crossed and her chin is out, a pose familiar since she was a toddler. She doesn't back down. It's a family trait, I guess.

"It's nice," I say swiftly. "Especially when the man knows what he's doing."

She leans back against the doorframe. "You're able to make comparisons, so that means you've done it with more than one."

Hedges has gone strategically deaf. He waits by the open door, his eyes on the cobbles.

"Don't you have a boyfriend?" She does, I know for a fact: a blandly nice boy named Mitchell who bores the socks off me, and probably her.

"Well, yes, but..." She scrunches up her face. "I can't imagine taking off my clothes with him."

Hedges looks discreetly at his watch. I snatch the lifeline he's thrown. "Don't rush into it," I tell her. "You're young, he's young. Take your time."

Grace leans through the car window. "Maybe I'll follow your example and find a talented geriatric. See how Mama likes that."

24

Viv is waiting on the sidewalk when we pull up. "You're here!" She drags me out of the car. "Come on, let me introduce you to Mrs. Morrissey."

Mrs. Morrissey is a stout, middle-aged woman with dyed red hair and full theatrical makeup. She wears a floridly embroidered satin kimono.

"Nice to meet you," the landlady says around a wad of chewing gum. "Viv's been so excited." Looking from my friend to me, she adds, "I think she wants a room with a bigger closet."

"You haven't seen Thelma's wardrobe yet," Viv cracks, as Hedges brings in the first load. "I'll be lucky to get a drawer and a couple of hangers."

Our second-floor room has a single window overlooking the back alley. There are two narrow beds, one on either side, two rickety, unmatched dressers, and a small closet. Viv isn't wrong. I could fill every corner of the room without trying; I'll have to keep my off-season things in suitcases under the bed.

I look out the window, taking a hesitant sniff of the faded chintz curtains. They reek of cigarettes, while the rest of the house smells like cabbage. This place won't remind me of home, that's for sure. And it definitely isn't the Hotel Warriner.

"So, is Mrs. Morrissey going to have a problem if I stay out late? Or all night?"

Viv bursts into laughter and falls back on her bed. "Did you see her? She's one of us. Or she was, way back whenever. She'll give you an extra helping for having the sense to advance your career by sleeping with a director."

No matter how often I've said it, she and Connie refuse to believe I'm with Stan for any reasons beyond ambition. I'm a convenience for him, I know that, but the return he's given me, in conversation and coaching and allowing me to absorb everything he knows about the theater, is invaluable. I'm grateful for every moment, no matter the basis of our relationship.

I don't want to think about my other feelings, which have progressed to an uncomfortable point. I can't be in love with this man. It's not just that he's married—if Viv and I move to New York, I'll have to leave him behind. And I don't want to fall in love.

"You keep telling yourself that." Viv bounces up—as much as she can bounce from the sagging mattress—and heads for the nearest suitcase. "Let's get started or we'll be hanging up dresses at midnight."

We've finished long before then, making it downstairs for dinner at six. I meet the other women who live here, though their names disappear instantly from my mind. For the most part, they are my age or younger, though there are two women well into their forties who have the double room on the third floor. Viv whispers to me that they are a couple, one an actress and the other a costumer at the Walnut Street Theatre.

The theatrical community's acceptance of such relationships makes me proud of us. Now if only I could get the same understanding of my relationship.

I left a message at the Clinton with my new phone number. Not long after dinner, when we are all seated in the living room, the phone rings. Mrs. Morrissey answers and calls me from the hall.

"Stan?"

"How are the new digs? Are you okay?"

"I'm fine." I sink down on the bottom step. "You don't need to worry about me."

"Well, I am." His lighter flicks and I hear an indrawn breath. "It's my fault you're living in some shabby boarding house instead of at home with your family."

I look around for the landlady, but she's nowhere in sight. "Other than the fact that it smells like an ashtray, it's not bad. Honestly. And it was time I left home."

He sighs. "I'd have rather it not been because of me. Are you in for the night or would you like to go out?"

"I'd like to see you," I say. "But nowhere fancy. A quiet drink or a walk—unless I can come down to visit?"

"I'll be there in a half hour." He doesn't take the hint, only confirms the address of the boarding house and hangs up.

Viv teases me for moving in and immediately going out. "I thought I was going to have a roommate, but you're the amazing disappearing girl."

I yank off my tired dress and put on something nicer. "I won't be out long. I'm tired."

"But not too tired for Stanley!" she singsongs. "Admit it, you like him."

"I never said I didn't." I comb my hair and touch up my makeup, then add a fresh spritz of perfume. He loves how I smell; maybe he'll change his mind and take me back to his place after all.

The cab draws up promptly thirty minutes later, and the driver opens the door for me.

"Fancy meeting you here," I say, sliding across the seat and into his arms.

His kiss is most satisfactory and lasts long enough for the door to close and the cabbie to walk around the vehicle, let himself in, and tactfully wait for us to come up for air.

"Where to?" he asks as we separate, both breathing hard.

"Drive up toward the art museum." Stan turns to me. "If we're outside, you can't follow up on the promise you gave me."

"But I want to." My hand is on his thigh and slips higher, to check the response to our kiss. He catches my wrist and returns it to my lap. "What's wrong?"

"Nothing's wrong," he says. "We need to talk."

The driver clears his throat, and we fall silent for the duration of the drive. When the car reaches the Swann Fountain, Stan tells him to stop. "We'll get out here," he says.

Despite the cold and the darkness, people linger in the square. We walk around the dry fountain until we find a bench whose location behind a bush blocks us from the wind.

"What did you want to say?" He sits beside me and I shift so my leg rests against his. I could use the temperature as an excuse, but I just want to be near him.

Stan moves enough so there's cold air between us. "I thought we should talk about what's going to happen, once rehearsals start."

"Not much is going to happen once rehearsals start," I say. "I know you'll be working late and will probably be very tired. But I'll be around when you want to see me. And we've got all this weekend."

"We don't have this weekend, actually." He takes my hand in his, absently stroking my gray suede glove. "I have to go home before spending such a long stretch in the city."

"Oh." My fantasy of two whole days together, in bed and out, eating and talking and preparing for the show, vanishes like a popped soap bubble. "I suppose they deserve to see you. I've had so much of you lately."

His eyes close briefly, as if in pain. "Don't think that hasn't occurred to me. I feel guilty as it is, but wanting to stay here with you—do you realize how it makes me feel? I've always thought of myself as a good husband, before you."

He's obviously not a good husband if he's with me, but I want to argue the point. Because he *is* a good man, otherwise what we're doing wouldn't bother him at all.

"You're not a bad husband." I lean against his shoulder, as the wind whips my hair into tangles. "Maybe a bit inattentive. Aren't you cold?"

"I hate myself for my lack of originality," he says, as if he hadn't heard my question. "An aging man who reassures himself of his virility by seducing a woman young enough to be his daughter."

"You didn't seduce me, if you recall. I kissed you first."

"After how many dinners and nights on the town?" His expression is bleak. "I knew what I wanted."

"So did I." I kiss him, catching his lower lip in my teeth. "I didn't trade my body for dinner at Palumbo's."

"You don't know." His voice is low. "You don't know how often I think about you, Kimber. How I wish I'd met you first."

That sounds like every unfaithful man in every novel I've ever bothered to read, but this is Stan: I wouldn't' say something so cruel, even if I wanted to.

"If you'd met me at the age you got married, I'd have barely been out of the cradle." For all the objections he has to our relationship, sometimes I think he forgets our more than twenty-year age difference.

"Don't remind me. I'm not just a bad husband. I'm a dirty old man." He raises my gloved hand and kisses my wrist, sending sparks all over my body. "Susan has done nothing to deserve this."

I don't want to talk about his wife. It's enough to know she exists and would be hurt if she learned about me. Thinking about her makes me complicit in what we're doing.

"If I'm not going to see you for a few days," I murmur, "don't you think this time would be better spent elsewhere?" I move closer and whisper into his ear, using words that would ordinarily make me blush but that he likes to hear when we're in his bed. "If you do that to me, then I'll let you leave."

25

I don't see Stan again until the morning of the table read. Despite having a minor part, Viv drags me out of bed at six so we can shower ahead of the other girls.

"Let them find out how it is to take a cold shower," she says. "We deserve this."

"Don't they?" Having spent my life in a crowded house, I'm used to occasional cold water.

She wrinkles her nose. "I suppose so, but we're heading off to *real jobs*, not waitressing or standing behind a counter. So we deserve the hot water."

For now, rehearsals aren't being held at the theater but at a rehearsal space closer to where we live, which means we can walk to work, and it will be for Stan to come for me after his day is done.

The building is nondescript, with a small sign near the door announcing its purpose. We enter and are presented with two signs bearing arrows and the names of shows. We turn left down a short hall and enter the rehearsal space. It's a large room, but we're a ensemble cast. Just inside the door, someone has pinned our headshots on the wall with our character names beneath.

There are several people already sitting around a big table with paper cups of coffee. A bakery box of sticky buns rests in the center, but no one has touched them yet. Tablets and pencils wait at each place.

Mr. Carter, the stage manager, introduces himself and tells us where to sit. I'm between the actress playing Penelope, my mother, and Jim Gorey, who has the role of Ed Carmichael. The devastating Lee Miles is almost directly across from me, sitting with Carrie Docherty, who plays Alice, the normal member of the family.

I've seen her before; she's very good. Her somewhat ordinary looks come to life when she speaks, making her a worthy foil for him.

"You're a fresh face," Margaret Richardson says. "I've been around long enough that I would have seen you."

"I've mostly danced before this," I tell her. "But I have acted."

"I hope so." She smiles disarmingly. "Don't mind me. I'm always a bitch before my third coffee."

The actor who plays her husband is seated on her other side. He pokes her and says, "It all depends on the amount of whiskey you had the night before, eh, Madge?"

She sniffs. "Gin, darling, not whiskey. Get your details straight."

While we've been talking, the rest of the cast has entered, filling the empty seats. Two chairs remain. Mr. Carter takes one of them.

The door opens and Stan enters. There is a collective breath and everyone at the table sits a little straighter.

"Good morning," he says without preamble. "Welcome, everyone. We'll start by going around the table so everyone can introduce themselves. Give your name, your part, and a little something about yourself. I'm Stan Arkright, your director. I'll be keeping this happy little ship afloat, so if you have any issues, bring them to me or the stage manager."

The actor who plays Grandpa Vanderhof introduces himself. He's got a deep, rolling voice, and I can already imagine him in the role.

The man and woman playing Paul and Penelope Sycamore go next, and then it's my turn.

"I'm Kimber Byrne," I say. "I play Essie and I feel like I know her because I grew up wanting to be a dancer and annoyed my family by dancing all over the house."

There is a ripple of laughter. Stan nods without meeting my eyes, and Mr. Gorey goes on to introduce himself.

I make mental notes on each person, casting them in this play I know so well. When it is Lee Miles's turn to speak, I pay close attention.

"I'm Lee Miles," he says. "Leland, if you listen to my mother, which I don't. I'm playing Tony Kirby. I've recently moved here from Chicago, so I'm looking forward to getting to know everyone."

Carrie Docherty beams; she will have more opportunity to get to know him than the rest of us.

When the introductions are complete, Stan taps his pencil on the table. "I know you've had ample time to read through the script, so nothing I say here should come as a surprise. This play was a hit when it premiered, and the Capra movie solidified its popularity. While we're no longer in the midst of a depression, much of the show is still relevant.

"There are several themes at play here. The inequality—and other differences—between the two families. Liberating oneself from societal expectations and doing what makes you happy. Living life in the moment." He looks around the table. "Because you *can't* take it with you. I want our audience to feel that joie de vivre."

"Joy de who?" cracks one of the men playing an FBI agent. "Never met her."

Stan ignores his comment. "Mr. Carter will read the stage directions. Let's dive in."

The stage manager reads the beginning of the script, describing the Sycamore living room and Penelope at her typewriter. Beside me, Margaret's fingers begin to dance over the table top.

Suddenly, it's my turn. I give Essie's first line, then fall into dialogue with Penelope, who is as sharp in her role as she is as herself.

The actress playing Rheba adds her lines, playing the maid not as comic, but as convinced of the rightness of her unique housekeeping style as the rest of the family are of their own passions.

We finish the first scene. Stan rises to his feet. "Not bad," he says. "Miss Byrne, I'll start with you, because you're fortunate enough to have the opening line. What were you doing before you carried the candy into the living room?"

What is he talking about? Essie says exactly what she was doing. "I was making candy."

"Yes," he says, with a touch of impatience. "In the hot kitchen. We *know* that. What was Essie doing in the kitchen besides making candy? The first line of this play is yours, and it's nothing earthshaking, so you have to make it count."

"I'm... talking to Rheba?" I hazard. "And probably doing stretches with a kitchen chair."

"That's better." He grinds out his cigarette in a glass ashtray. "You can't come onstage like you've walked out of the dressing room. *You* might have done that, but Essie's been slaving away in a hot kitchen, making candy and dancing and talking to the maid. The audience has to believe Essie exists before they ever see her."

He is no easier on the actress playing Penelope, telling her she's too sharp. "Even if her dialogue is fast-paced, part of Penny is off with the fairies, in one of her many imaginary worlds. She's a firecracker, but she's not always paying attention to what's going on around her."

Each actor comes in for their share of commentary and criticism before we move on to the next scene. It's exhausting and exhilarating. Though Stan's tone is crisp, I take comfort that everyone is treated the same.

At lunchtime, sandwiches are delivered, and we're given fifteen minutes after we've eaten to stretch our legs and get some fresh air. I linger for a moment, hoping for a moment of Stan's attention, but he carries the remains of his corned beef sandwich out of the room. Deflated, I look around for Viv.

"You were good," she says. "I'll be worn out before I ever get to say a word."

It felt strange reading the play aloud. I put effort and characterization into the lines, but only enough to give a sense of how I would play Essie. Glenda Pigeon, one of the older women at the boarding house, told me that was the way to go for a first reading. "Don't overact," she said. "Save something for later. The table read is so you get a feel for each other."

Because of all the discussion involved, it takes nearly eight hours to read a two-hour play. By the time we're done, it is after six.

Part of me wants to hear Stan's thoughts on my performance and on the production overall, but a larger part wants dinner, a bath, and an early bedtime. By half-past nine, I give up waiting for the phone to ring and go to bed. The lumps in the mattress can't compete with my exhaustion. I fall asleep while Viv is putting cream on her face.

The next few days are taken up with rehearsals. The table read was the only time we were all together; now, the call sheet lists the groups of actors required each day, which means Viv, with her small part, goes back to waitressing until the end of the week. Although Essie isn't a starring role, she's onstage most of the time. I miss Viv, but walking alone to rehearsals gives me time to get into my role and to think about how the day will proceed.

As a director, Stan is very different from the man I have come to know. Rehearsals for *Trials* had been so intense—so rushed—I hadn't paid attention to him beyond following his instructions. I watch him closely now. When things go wrong, he is patient; when someone doesn't try, he is sharp. When an actor who's been stuck finally gets it, his joy is as vivid as theirs. Warmth spreads in my chest when I see how much it all matters to him.

Stan is determined to get the opening scene just right. He drives me, Margaret, and Della, who plays Rheba, to the point where the three of us sit down over lunch and laughingly plot his demise.

"It's going to get worse when we start blocking." Margaret lights a cigarette with a weary gesture. "Then it will be perfection down to the half inch."

Della stretches and rolls her neck. "He spoken to you yet about your dancing? Only there's no choreographer."

"He hasn't." Essie's dancing shouldn't put much strain on my body—it won't require hours of rehearsal to be not very good—but I'm out of practice at learning routines and would like to get started as quickly as possible.

I bring it up at the end of the day when Stan asks, as usual, if anyone has any questions.

"For now, I'd like you to follow the notes in the script and do what comes naturally. What you think Essie would do based on what's on the page."

"What?" When I told him about dancing around the house as a girl, I didn't expect to have choreograph my part. Everyone else will be blocked within an inch of their lives, and I'll be up all night trying to remember how my character moved in the stage and screen productions

"I'll have someone come on in a week or so to work with you," he says when I continue to stare at him in disbelief. "You're a quick study, Miss Byrne."

It is well after eight when I'm called to the phone. I go slowly downstairs, not sure if I want to speak to Stan. It's been a week since we've been in a room without a dozen other people.

"Stan?"

"I've missed you."

Two girls pass in the hall and head up the steps. I pause until they are out of earshot. "You haven't even looked at me this week. I didn't think you were going to call."

There is a long silence. "I told you that working together would strain things."

"You can't vanish to Delaware and come back and act like there's nothing between us."

"I do have to go home sometimes." He sighs. "I suppose it's too late to see you?"

"The call sheet doesn't have me in until after lunch." The need in his voice makes me forget my ambivalence. "I'll cook you breakfast and catch up on my sleep afterward."

"Do you not intend to get any sleep?" He sounds younger, a pulse of energy in his voice that I feel in my low belly.

"As little as possible," I say. "I've missed you, too."

That evening is about more than food and music and pleasure: it's an abbreviated version of the dream weekend lost to his family. When we get back to his hotel, we sit and talk for hours, not getting to bed until the sky begins to lighten.

Stan tells me things he thinks will make me a better actress. He talks about what he looks for as a director and different ways to find my way into a characterization.

It's fascinating. I recently purchased a fresh notebook for this new life, and faithfully transcribe every conversation with him, every note I'm given in rehearsals, and my thoughts on my performance and those of my fellow actors. Between my own work in becoming Essie and what he teaches me, I've come to see it on a deeper level. Acting becomes something I want to be good at, the way I wanted to be a good dancer.

"This is harder than dancing," I tell him, after he's had me read a part three different ways and critiqued each reading.

"Is that good or bad?"

I stop and think. "It's good, just not something I ever expected?" I turn the statement into a question. "I never assumed acting was easy, but this is as draining as dancing ever was. When we work like this, I go home exhausted, but I can't sleep because my brain won't stop."

"Because you get it." He puts the script down and beckons me to him. "It's early days yet, Kimber, but you have the potential to be a very good actress."

"Really?" I'm not fishing for compliments; I trust him not to flatter me.

"It's because you're open." He absently strokes my shoulder. "And you'll get better with time."

"What do you mean, open?" Sometimes his thoughts on the craft of acting go over my head.

"You're willing to receive," he explains. "You want to know other people. It serves you well in life, but it will also serve you on stage."

I don't tell him my openness is new, that he, Viv, and Connie have fundamentally changed me. "I think that's enough talking for one night, don't you?"

I put my hands on his chest, let him kiss me, and feel his response. "What a wonderful idea."

A night with Stan does much to improve my mood, as does Mrs. Morrissey's understanding smile when I let myself in at eight. I sleep for a few hours, then treat myself to a scented bath before heading to rehearsal.

Even though he said it was killing him to keep his distance, when I walk into the rehearsal space, he looks up, says my name as if checking me off on a list, and goes right back to his conversation with Mr. Carter.

We work on the second scene of the first act, when Alice and Tony come in from the ballet and are inundated with members of her family as they try desperately to be alone. As Essie, I get to throw my arms around Tony's neck and ask him to be Fred Astaire to my Ginger Rogers. It is only a moment, but instead of being shocked, as Tony would be, Lee Miles pushes himself against me. A jolt goes through my body. I stop myself from jerking away, knowing it would look ridiculous.

"That's not it. Try it again." I follow Stan's direction, watching from outside myself as Essie throws her arms around Tony twice more. It's clear Stan can't see what Lee is doing, but surely Carrie has noticed.

Tony speaks, but I'm so distracted I can't remember my line. He repeats the words and the correct response arrives on my lips, but it takes an effort to pull myself back to the play. As the scene continues, I look anywhere but at him, wondering how he dares to rub himself on me, and why I didn't break character and tell him to stop.

The few times I've gone to Atlantic City, one of my favorite things is to wade into the ocean with Pop. We keep going until we're up to our chests, hold hands and let the waves roll over us and wash us into shore. That's how I feel now; I'm shivering and struggling to right myself.

When Stan calls a break, Lee walks abruptly away from Carrie. "Kimber, you're looking lovely today."

"Thank you," I say shortly. "Shouldn't you be talking to Carrie?"

"Why? Every single one of my scenes is with her. You're the one I don't see enough of." He does a few steps. "Want to try that dance again? I'm no Fred Astaire, but I'll do my best."

My eyes flick up. Stan is looking at us over his clipboard.

"I don't like the way you dance." I head for the hallway, hoping someone will be there to get between us.

"What about a coffee?" he asks, catching up to me. "We've got ten minutes."

"No, thank you. I'm going outside to talk to Margaret."

"We're going to be together a lot." He keeps pace with me all the way to the door. "We should get to know each other better."

I take a breath and stare right into his eyes. They're hazel, with green flecks and a darker ring around the iris. He disgusts me and yet I want to keep staring at him until one of us stops breathing.

"Or we could ignore each other and act," I say. "Isn't that what we're being paid to do?"

At the end of the day, Lee follows me outside. I climb into a cab to get him to leave me alone. When I ask to be let out a block later, I get such a blistering look from the driver that I give him an extra quarter.

Stan takes me back to the Italian restaurant where we first had dinner. I am included now in the owner's familiar greeting, and he tucks us into a corner table and dotes on us like family, bringing wine and small bites from the kitchen before our meal.

"Did you see Lee Miles had his hands all over me this afternoon?" I've had time to cool down, but I'm annoyed and I want Stan to know it. "How did you not see?"

"Carrie Docherty would kill to be in your position."

"What, with someone who touches without asking? No, thank you. She's welcome to him."

Our plates arrive—pasta with a fragrant seafood sauce—and the waiter leaves.

"You think I'm a big deal, Kimber, but I'm in Philadelphia because I couldn't survive New York." Stan takes a swallow of wine. "You're not doing yourself any favors."

"I'm with you because I want to be." I can't put my arms around his neck, not in a public place, so I content myself with stroking his rough hair with my fingertips. "I'm living in the moment, like a proper Sycamore."

"If you were with someone your age, someone single, you could go out whenever you wanted." Stan spears a shrimp with his fork. "A beautiful girl like you should be seen."

"We've been out. I've been seen."

"Yes," he says bitterly, "at the kind of places that keep secrets. It's not the same."

"I wish you'd stop telling me what's best for me. You sound like my mother."

"I've never thought she was wrong." He puts his fork down and looks at me directly. "Her daughter deserves more than I can give her."

"Mama didn't call me a tramp because of you." My meal is equally neglected as I try to get him to understand. "She didn't like that I stayed out all night and the neighbors saw me coming home in evening dress. That's what upset her."

He shakes his head. "She wasn't being unreasonable. You're her daughter, and she has to live there among her neighbors."

I don't want to see it from Mama's point of view; I've been avoiding that for too long. And I hate it when Stan is like this, focusing on the differences between us, instead of what we have in common.

26

Connie and I have an established ritual: come what may, one night each week we eat dinner together. Otherwise, because of our schedules—both personal and work—we wouldn't see each other for weeks at a time. His living on the other side of Market Street complicates things, and his new theater so inconveniently located I've only ever been there once.

"It's a good part, so it's worth it," he insists when I question him. "The director has worked in Hollywood. He's got some new ideas and ways of doing things. It's really something, Thelma."

"What does a Hollywood director know about putting on a play?"

"Enough." Connie tilts his head, then straightens self-consciously. He's cut his hair for this role and doesn't know what to do without his favorite prop. "And he's had a lot to say about my performance. Including that he thinks I'd do well on film."

"I thought you wanted to move to New York." We've talked about it since the beginning, the three of us saving up to get a place to share and split expenses. It seems impossible. We don't make enough to put much aside, and now that I'm paying rent to Mrs. Morrissey, my meager savings are being rapidly depleted.

"I do." He stares into his cup. "But I'd be as happy in the movies. It's the same as what you're going through. You've been a dancer all your life and now you're an actress. It's not the same, but it can be equally good."

It surprises me how much I've come to enjoy acting—the challenge of finding my way into a character, the parts of myself I bring in, as well as the parts I leave out. It makes me think and feel and uses more of my brain than dancing ever did.

Not to mention the fact that it doesn't hurt.

"If I decided on California instead of New York, would you come with me?" His gaze is earnest. "I wouldn't want to do it without you."

"And I wouldn't want to do it without you." I take his hands across the table. "We're a team, Con. Where you go, I go. Whichever one of us gets a break first, the other goes with."

The waitress comes to clear the table and Connie asks if she might have a slice of lemon meringue pie.

"I do," she says. "Growing boy, are you?"

"That's me." He gives her his most charming smile. "Can we have two forks, please?"

Later in the week, Stan calls me aside at the end of the day and dismisses the rest of the ensemble. He's done it before with other cast members, so no one will think anything of our being alone. I follow him into the tiny office he's claimed now that we're in the theater and wait for him to take me in his arms.

Instead, he stands behind the desk. "What were you doing out there today?"

"What do you mean?" I expected him to lock the door and kiss me, not talk about work.

"You're dancing like Ann Miller," he says. "You're nothing like Ann Miller."

Blindsided by his sharpest criticism to date, my eyes fill with tears. I'm not doing anything different since I worked with the choreographer Stan brought in. He and I went over the script and worked out the steps together. That collaborative process reminded me how much I love to dance, even as ballet, even badly done, caused the ache in my hip to reappear.

"I've always seen Essie as a bit sad." He paces back and forth, thinking aloud. "There are two sides to every performance, even if the script shows just one. Essie's confidence works because deep inside she's afraid she's a terrible dancer. Still, she won't give up because she loves it. Your job is to show the audience that duality without saying a word. Do you understand?"

I do, I'm just not sure I'm good enough to know how to convey it. What appeals to me about Essie is her physicality, her determination; while I always knew I had talent, she doesn't have the same certainty. Even her dance teacher can't convince her, because he knows the truth.

"Yes, but—"

Did I always know I had talent? I remember, in the beginning, those first dance classes where my brain understood the teacher's instructions, but my legs couldn't follow them. I thought I'd never learn, never be any good. After years trapped in a chair, I wanted so, so much to be good.

"I... I do understand," I say. "I'm trying to convince myself I have talent, but inside I know the truth as surely as the rest of my family?"

"That's it," he says. "Your acting is fine—more than fine. But your dancing is *dancing*, not acting. It doesn't convey what Essie is feeling. She's doing this thing that lights her up inside, and her family, these odd people who love her so much, support her because they believe everyone should do what makes them happy."

Stan's insight into Essie and the supportive Sycamore clan makes me think of Mama. If we were speaking, I would go right home and tell her about how he's made me rethink my character and even some things about myself.

But since we're not speaking, I can't. Viv, who would otherwise listen, has a date tonight. Connie is in rehearsals. It makes me wish I was more like Pearl and kept a diary for when there's no one to talk to.

He sits down beside me at last. "You look sad. Have you spoken to your family lately?"

"My aunt called yesterday," I say. "And I had lunch with my stepfather on Tuesday."

Although the food was good, Pop wasn't his usual live-wire self. When I asked what was wrong, he shook his head and asked for the check. Aunt Claire is much the same. There's something bruised about her, the same as in the days after Uncle Harry's death.

All these good people, hurt by my fight with Mama.

"Not your mother?"

"No."

"Don't you miss them?" His arm is heavy on my shoulders. I want him to sink into me and stop talking. That is another reason for sex, I've learned; it postpones difficult conversations. While he could kiss me in his office, we can't risk anything more, not when someone's always around.

"Of course. But I haven't done anything wrong."

He takes breath so deep that my body moves with the rise and fall of his chest. "Is being right so important? Can't you tell her what she wants to hear?"

Hot tears spill over and run down my face. "I won't apologize," I say. "And I won't be judged, not by her or by you."

"Shh." Stan pulls me up against his chest. "I'm sorry, Kimber. I won't talk about it if it upsets you."

"No, I'm sorry." I wipe my eyes with the heels of my hands and put on my best smile. "You don't keep me around to watch me fall apart. I'm better now."

"You don't have to be better." His expression is dismayed. "I don't keep you around, as you say, because you're beautiful. It's every part of you. Don't you understand?"

I don't, because no one has ever wanted every part of me. Girls think I'm too pretty. Boys think I'm standoffish. My family loves me, but finds me confusing. How can he possibly see—much less want—all of me?

Viv sits up when I creep in at dawn. "Another late night?" She yawns. "You hussy."

"We were working," I say, unbuckling my shoes and kicking them under the bed. I've stopped worrying about my things with the hours I've been keeping. "I'm sorry I woke you."

"I hadn't been asleep long enough to not hear you come in." She turns on the lamp between our beds. "I was up late making a list."

"A list of what?" I sit down on the other side of the bed and pretend to take off my stockings, not wanting her to know they're balled up in my bag. "Handsome actors in the Delaware Valley?"

"Reasons to stay in Philadelphia." Viv pulls a folded paper from beneath her pillow and hands it to me. "There aren't many."

The list reads:

Thelma
Connie
Fear

"Are you thinking about New York again?" I throw my slip over the chair and pull on my pajamas over my underwear.

"Or Hollywood." Viv tried New York before but returned when her money ran out.

"You'd need a car in California." It's another thing we've discussed. "You don't even know how to drive."

"I could learn." She gets up and stands at the window. "My life is trickling away, Thelma. I'll get little parts like Gay Wellington now and again, but they'll get me nowhere. I'll end up sleeping with photographers and stage managers in the hopes of achieving something better and waitressing until my arches fall. I'm not lucky like you."

"That's all it is," I tell her. "Luck. I'll never get a better part than Essie."

"You will. Stan will make sure of it."

I both want and don't want that to be true. I'd like anything I achieve to be because of my talent, but I'm always going to wonder: if something good happens, is he behind it?

"He likes you," Viv says. "I have nothing to do at rehearsals, so I watch him watch you."

"He doesn't." I don't know why it's important to deny it. "I mean, he likes me well enough, but this is... convenient for both of us. He likes having a girl in the city, and I like having someone to go out with."

"You could have someone taking you out every night," she points out. "Your head is in the clouds most of the time. You don't understand how pretty you are."

"I understand it well enough," I snap, too tired to be kind. "People have pointed it out since I was a kid. I'm pretty and I can dance."

Stan has noticed more, though. He talks to me, the way my friends and family do; in all my life, I've never had a boyfriend who asked what I thought about anything. They were always too busy telling me what they thought.

"You're wrong." She shakes her head impatiently. "He's got it bad. You don't see it."

"Men want one thing, isn't that what you're always telling me?" Why would Stan Arkright—married, successful—need anything from me beyond what he's already getting? "I'm learning so much from him. Isn't that enough?"

"No." Viv makes it sound like I should know better. "Don't you want to be in love?"

"It would hurt my career." With this play, I'm finally getting somewhere. I've begun to feel a connection to acting, to becoming someone else, if only for a little while. I'm not going to derail the progress I've made by opening my heart, especially when my feelings won't be reciprocated. Even if Stan were in love with me, neither of us wants our relationship out in the open for fear of what it would make people think.

"Everything isn't about your career, dummy." She drops her list on the bed and looks at me with something akin to pity. "If I had a man like him, I'd be kissing his feet. I certainly wouldn't be letting Lee Miles drool all over me."

"I don't let him drool," I say. "I just can't always make him stop. And what ever happened to 'Lee Miles is so attractive?'"

She shrugs. "I didn't say he isn't attractive. But he's trying to get you purely for his amusement. Is that worth risking what you have?"

"What do I have?"

I mean the question in all sincerity. I don't know how to define what Stan and I have together. I care deeply for him, but I don't want to call it love. Loving people hurts: I've learned that much from my family. I'm not giving someone that kind of power over me.

"You're beautiful and talented, but my God, you're stupid." Viv yanks on her robe. "I'm going down and make tea. Mrs. Morrissey's chipped teacups have more self-awareness than you do."

The door closes quietly but it feels like a slam. I don't want to be alone with my thoughts right now. There have been times when I've almost let myself believe Stan's feelings are genuine, but even if they are, nothing will come of it. He's not going to leave his wife for a girl the same age as his son. Looking at it like that, I'm surprised he can bring himself to touch me.

The last week of rehearsals, we go through the entire play each day. When we're not onstage, we're being fitted for costumes, trying on wigs, and doing makeup tests. Essie's clothes are girlish and brightly colored. Her one ballet costume is a child's dream of *Swan Lake*, with tulle skirts and spangles on the bodice. Since they're already broken in, the wardrobe mistress allowed me to use my own pointe shoes.

"One less thing for me to cope with," she says wearily, tightening a button on the front of my act one costume. "Ballet skirts and business suits and evening gowns and Roman togas, all in one play. My Lord."

"I like the toga." Fully dressed, the actor who plays Mr. DePinna is stout; swathed in yards of fabric, with his abundant chest hair on display, he doesn't have to utter a word to be funny.

"It does its job," she concedes. "It's a pleasure to dress you and Miss Docherty, though. Pretty girls with pretty figures. I like a challenge, but sometimes you want to make a pretty girl look prettier."

"You do beautiful work." I fluff the tulle skirt, letting the fabric settle against my fingers. "I would have loved this when I was dancing ballet."

I share a dressing room with Carrie and Margaret, the other two actresses with the most stage time. After all of our costumes are loaded in, the space becomes snug and airless. When the dresser arrives to help us change, it will be impossible to move around.

The first dress rehearsal goes off without a hitch. When Stan calls us together afterward to give us notes, he is pacing the way he does when something has him worked up. When the cigarette in his hand burns down too far, he stubs it out and lights another without bringing it to his lips.

"I hope to God you screw it up tomorrow night," he says. "That was entirely too good for dress."

"The lighting was off," ventures Jim Gorey. "In the second act. At least I thought it was."

"It was," he concedes. "And Mr. Carter will speak to the stagehands. I'm talking about you lot. You're good, but not *that* good. You should have done something wrong."

"I could get *actually* drunk?" Viv grins cheekily and breaks the spell of his bad mood. "Would that help, Mr. Arkright?"

He laughs at her. "Miss Collins, that might do it."

When we made plans earlier, Stan suggested I have dinner with my friends and then come to the hotel. If he's not there yet, the desk clerk will let me in.

Viv and I meet Connie at his theater and go to a diner close by. The food isn't that good but it isn't boarding house bad, either. Connie brings a bag of slightly squashed doughnuts from the Reading Terminal and distributes them under the table.

I look at him, eyebrows raised. The doughnut seller is Amish and occasionally passes on news of his family. He shrugs; nothing to tell.

"I've been thinking," Viv says lazily. "I was trying to tell Thelma the other morning, but she was being thick. Philadelphia isn't big enough for the three of us anymore."

When it became apparent I'd never be able to become a Rockette, I put my dream of New York away, but I've never stopped thinking about it.

"Then you should go," Connie says. "But not by yourself. *We* should go. Together, all three of us."

"What happened to Hollywood?" I ask. "And how would we manage?"

When I turn twenty-five, I'll inherit some money from my uncle. Not enough to live on, but enough to give me a solid cushion in case of emergencies. My family history proves emergencies happen, and Aunt Claire won't always be around to bail me out. I've never mentioned the money to my friends; I don't want to count on it.

"It's not a sure thing," Connie says. "Anyway, I can't let you girls go alone. Not to the big, bad city."

"Every city needs waitresses and usherettes." Viv speaks with her eyes closed. "We can find jobs and go to auditions and live on next to nothing."

"Cheap in New York isn't the same as cheap in Philadelphia." The last time I visited Pearl, I looked at apartment listings in the newspaper, then checked the cost to rent a room in areas of the city where I'd feel safe on my own. In both cases, it was prohibitive; even my inheritance wouldn't last for long in New York.

We would be better off sharing a small apartment, except what landlord would rent to the three of us? They would immediately suspect something immoral. If they realized Connie was homosexual, they would assume something even worse.

"We'll figure something out." Connie slides down in the booth. I give in and lean against him. "There's too much beauty and talent here to stay in Philadelphia all our lives."

"If we were younger," Viv says, "we'd be pulling out a pen knife to become blood brothers."

"I don't like blood." Connie shudders. "But I take your point. Can we do it without the knives?"

"We're already blood." I look between them—as different as they are, they are more precious to me than my siblings. "And you're right. We'll figure something out. Once our shows are done, let's sit down and make a proper plan."

Viv takes my hand. I reach for Connie and he links his hands with ours. "All for one," he says. "And one for all."

27

When Stan finally arrives, I'm fast asleep. I don't wake until he slides into the bed and fits himself against me under the blankets.

"What time is it?"

"After midnight." His breath tickles my neck. "Go back to sleep."

I shift against him, feeling the coolness of his skin against my warmth. "I wanted to celebrate. I bought champagne and everything."

"We'll have it in the morning, with breakfast." He kisses my shoulder and loops his arm over me, cradling my breast. "I couldn't do justice to champagne right now, and I certainly can't do justice to you."

In the morning, justice is followed by orange juice and champagne in bed.

"I should run out and get something," I say, not moving. Everything will begin to change when we leave the bed.

"Later," he responds. "Today is going to be hell. I want to keep you here as long as possible."

We remain, drowsing and talking, for another hour. I pepper him with questions about acting, as if I can learn everything I need to bring Essie to full and vibrant life in one last morning.

"In real life, we feel guilty for pretending to be someone else. In acting, it's perfectly fine."

I prop myself up on my elbows and smile as he glances down at my breasts. "Don't get distracted," I warn. "What do you mean?"

Stan turns his gaze resolutely toward the ceiling and I settle onto the pillow, my head on my crossed arms. "You're not the same girl in every aspect of your life," he says. "Are you?"

"I think I am."

"You're the same person with me as you are with your parents or your friends?" He shakes his head slowly. "You show a facet of yourself to each of us, but I doubt anyone knows all of you. You are your parents' daughter, but you don't play that role with me; I don't want a daughter."

He's right. My mother's daughter wouldn't lounge naked in a man's bed all morning; Stan's lover wouldn't walk on eggshells so as not to upset her mother. Viv and Connie see neither of these people, but they don't know all of me, either—though they know more than I've revealed to Stan.

"I understand." I get up and fetch the champagne from the kitchen. "More?"

"How can I say no?" He smiles and pats the place beside him. "Come back before I have to start sharing you with everyone else."

We drink champagne and spend a long time kissing and touching, a leisurely and pleasurable way to spend the last hour of the morning. Finally, we roll apart, breathless. After a few minutes, he speaks again.

"When the show is over, are you going to stick with acting or go back to dancing?" Stan runs a finger along my rib cage, making my skin prickle. "You almost have me convinced you're not as good as I know you are."

"I can't go back to dancing." I managed to fit in an appointment with Dr. Hendricks a week ago. After a painful examination, he asked what I'd been doing lately to strain myself, because there was new inflammation in my right hip. I didn't need to be told; I'd felt the dull ache, which I tried to explain away as simply being out of practice, all through rehearsals.

"Why not?" He rolls over so he can see me. "You love it."

"I do. But it doesn't love me."

Once again, I realize how much I haven't told him. My friends know nearly everything about me, but this man—who has seen parts of me never seen by anyone—knows almost nothing about my past. Does that even matter? Once the show opens, we won't be seeing much of each other anyway. He's mentioned going home once rehearsals end. Stan's recent distance and heavier drinking lead me to believe he doesn't know how to bring up parting company.

With a sigh, I explain it all: being born crippled, the braces, the exercises. How dance saved me and gave me a new life. And then how my body betrayed me. "Dancing hurts," I say. "And not dancing hurts. But if I go back to dancing full-time, I could injure myself permanently."

"Then you shouldn't be doing it at all." Stan sits up, turning immediately into the authoritative director. "I can't believe you would take on a role that could maim you just to get ahead."

"I'm not in pain now," I lie. "I just can't put in the hours of practice I need to dance professionally. This little bit won't hurt me."

He slides out of bed and pulls on his boxers. "I don't understand you, Kimber. First you let our relationship come between you and your family and now you're risking your health for a part in a show. You can be such a child."

"Don't call me a child." I throw his undershirt across the room. "I know what I can and can't do."

"But you've made me part of it—made me a part of hurting yourself in all sorts of ways."

"You don't get to say that." I *am* a stupid child, because I gave him a weapon and showed him how to hurt me with it. "It's my body. My health. My family, for that matter. This is my career, Stan. It's the most important thing in the world to me."

He puts his hands on my shoulders before I throw any more of his clothes. "And you have become the most important thing in my world," he says unsteadily. "I'm going to leave Susan. I'll tell her once the show's open."

The chill that runs over me has nothing to do with being naked. I thought he was planning to break up with me. "Why would you do that?"

"Because I want to be with you." He shakes me gently. "How do you not see that?"

I bow my head, look down at the space between us and understand that I'm about to break his heart, as well as mine.

"I'm not the kind of girl you leave your wife for." I rest my forehead on his chest and fill my nostrils with his familiar, spicy scent. "I'm not saying we haven't had a good time, Stan. You're a wonderful man and I've learned so much from you. But I don't want to stay in Philadelphia. Once the show's over, my friends and I are going to New York."

He makes a sound like I've struck him and pushes me away.

"What exactly did you think we were doing these last months?" He turns his face away, but his feelings are evident in his voice. "Did you think I was like Hartley, just out for what I could get? If that were the case, I wouldn't have spent all this time with you—I would have fucked you on my couch and thrown you a bit part to make you go away quietly." I gasp and he puts a hand on my cheek. "It's never been like that for me. Kimber, I love you."

The buzzing in my head almost drowns out his words. I want *him*, but I don't want *this*.

"It was never going to be love for me." It takes all my strength not to reach for him and tell him how I feel. "I have plans for my life and they don't include us."

If I let myself love him, all my plans will be gone. The door will close, and I'll never get away. He'll leave his wife and marry me, and I'll be stuck in Philadelphia—or worse, Delaware. With a husband and possibly a baby. I'll have Stan, but I'll never find out what I'm capable of, never become a proper actress.

My plan to go to New York with Viv and Connie, tentative as it is, is weighed against my feelings for Stan Arkright. He has to come down on the losing side, otherwise, what have I done with my entire life?

"So, you just let me fall in love with you."

I bend to pick up my slip, so he can't see my face. "I didn't think you would. It's not my fault."

"You're a better actress than you give yourself credit for," he says drily, buttoning his shirt like it's done him wrong. "Do you know, Kimber, I thought you cared."

Rather than give in to tears, I summon the skills he's honed over the past weeks. "I could never love a man who doesn't call me by my real name."

Stan's face undergoes a series of transformations, finally settling on anger. "You've never told me what the hell it is!" he bursts out. "Am I supposed to read your mind?"

"You could have asked." I shove my stockings into my bag and pull my dress over my head. "Can you call the front desk and ask them to hail a cab? I should go."

Walking through the lobby, I keep my eyes lowered. It's not that I'm in yesterday's clothes again. I feel so brittle that if the desk clerk stopped me to chat, I might shatter all over the scuffed parquet floor.

The curb in front of the hotel is empty. A cab will be along soon, but I decide to walk. I don't want Stan to come down and find me there.

But again, what does it matter if he sees me? He'll be gone soon, back to Delaware. Back to Susan. Will he leave or stay? It doesn't matter. If I can't have him—and I won't allow myself to consider that again—then she might as well. He should have someone who cares for him; obviously she's better than I am, because I can let him go.

I keep walking. The streets pass in a blur until I find myself on a block of small, mismatched brick rowhouses. Instead of walking south, to Mrs. Morrissey's, instinct has taken me west, to my parents' house.

And suddenly that is all I want: my parents. My mother, especially. If I have to go on my knees and apologize, I'll do it, so I can cry on her shoulder. No matter how angry she's been, she'll see I'm hurting and find a way to make it better.

I dig into my bag for the key. The door swings wide into the living room, where I am greeted by the familiar blue sofa and chairs, but also a new crocheted throw folded over the arm. The room smells of polish and trapped sunlight. It is also empty.

The kitchen, too, is uninhabited, as are the bedrooms. Flora, wearing a ruffled gown, has pride of place on Grace's dresser.

"Mama?" I call uncertainly. "Are you here?"

I walk through the house which no longer feels like home, tears running down my face.

She's at the shop. I could go there, but I won't. It's too public and I need some time to get myself together before going to the theater. Going back to the living room, I pick up the phone and dial Connie. His landlady has to roust him out of bed, but when he hears my voice, he is instantly alert.

"Con," I say, not hiding anything. "Can you come? It's bad."

"I'll be right there," he says. "Where am I going?"

"Mrs. Morrissey's." I can't let anyone find me here. They can never know I broke down and came crawling back because I needed my mother.

28

Mrs. Morrissey takes one look at my tear-stained face and hustles me into her private room. "Let me get a compress for your eyes, lovey," she says. "And a nice cup of tea with some whiskey. What's happened?"

Sniffling, I tell her I've broken up with my boyfriend. Stan was never a boyfriend, but my landlady doesn't knows only that I had a man who kept me out all night. I can't tell her I deliberately shattered the love between us to save my own life.

"Oh, you poor dear. And tonight's your opening." She pats me distractedly and goes off to fetch the tea.

Connie is with her when she returns. He gathers me into his arms and lets me cry, then turns into a mother hen with a cool rag and a mug of tea.

"Tell me." He pushes me back onto the couch. "Rest your eyes. Whatever happened, you can't go on tonight looking like you've been crying."

I don't want to go on tonight, but I will. How can I walk into the theater and look at Stan, knowing that—somehow—he was in love with me the whole time. He is willing to leave his wife for me, and I can't even tell him my name, much less that I'm in love with him.

Of course I love him. All the shows and movies I've seen where the heroine floats around in a rose-colored trance because of her man—I feel that for Stan. I would give up my career to be with him except I know that, eventually, I would hate myself for it, and then I would hate him for letting me quit. I love him too much to ever allow that to happen.

I make up an excuse about the relationship ending because of the show, because I can't bear to tell him what Stan said. It will do well enough. Viv won't get the truth either; it would be too embarrassing to tell her she was right. Their role is to comfort me, and thankfully, comfort only requires the outlines of truth.

"The bastard," he says predictably. "How could he do that to you?"

"It's not his fault," I say tiredly from under the towel. "It's no one's fault."

"Oh, honey." He sits on the floor so we're at the same level. "It was all over your face, how you felt about him. And I'll bet my virtue, such as it is, that it was mutual."

I thought I'd hidden it better. I'd certainly managed to hide it from myself. Is it possible I still don't understand how people work?

"Well, whatever, it's over now." I shift so I can take another sip of the spiked tea. "And I'll go on tonight, no matter what I look like, and I'll do well. This is a new beginning, Con. It's the next step. It has to be."

"There's my brave girl." He takes my hand. "So will it be New York next?"

It will. Somehow. The show doesn't pay so much that I can afford to put money aside, but I have some decent pieces jewelry that my aunt and uncle have given me at Christmas over the years. They must be worth something.

We fall into a discussion of New York: where to live, which theater marquee would look best with our names in lights. It is a good distraction. When Viv comes in, I'm over the worst of it and tell her I'll explain everything later.

We leave at four, handing over tickets to Connie and Mrs. Morrissey so they can come to the show.

"You look like hell," she says in the back of the taxi. "Your eyes are all puffy."

"Spoken like a true best friend." Makeup will take care of the worst of it.

"I care, but I won't lie to you." The vehicle bounces over a pothole, and she leans against me. "Was it bad?"

"Bad enough that I don't want to talk about it until after we're done," I tell her. "Connie and I were talking before you came in. New York before the end of the year, what do you think?"

"Unless his Hollywood director lures him west. I think there's something going on that Con's not talking about. Honestly," she says, wrinkling her nose. "The pair of you. Am I going to have to find my own director to show you how to do this properly?"

As the cast straggles in, Mr. Carter calls us together backstage. "Before you go off to your dressing rooms," he says, "I want to say a few words—and a few more from your director, who will be in the audience tonight. He didn't want to throw you off by coming backstage to speak to you himself.

"Yesterday's dress was good. There's no denying it. But you can do better. And you *will* do better tonight." He paces in a way that reminds me painfully of Stan. "I know most of you have plans to go out after the show. It's opening night, I understand wanting to celebrate. But be here an hour early tomorrow. No matter how well you do tonight, we'll have notes for you."

I escape to the dressing room, weak with relief. He'll be in the audience, but I won't be able to see him.

"You ready?" Margaret is already daubing Pan Stik on her face. Her short dark hair is held back with a band, in preparation for Penelope's wig.

"As I'll ever be." A wig on a stand waits on my dressing table. Stan and the wardrobe mistress agreed my light hair would be distracting when Carrie should be the focus.

I don't mind. Alice is the lead, and I don't want to take that from her. While I was talking to Connie, I dampened my hair and set it with clips. After the show, when I take off Essie's auburn curls, I'll have finger waves to suit Aunt Claire's blue satin gown.

As time grows closer, the tightness in my chest increases. At least that has nothing to do with Stan; I always feel this way before going on. There is a wastebasket under my dressing table. I nudge it closer with my foot.

In any case, there's nothing to bring up. All I've had all day is champagne, orange juice, and Mrs. Morrissey's tea. I think of her kindness, and the reason for it, and start shaking again.

I've made such an unholy mess of my life. When we move to New York, I want it to be because it's time, not because I'm running away. Connie and Viv, not having family, can leave whenever they have the funds. I'm the one leaving people behind but it feels like I'm in the same boat as my friends.

Alone.

When the ten-minute call comes, I make my way to the wings, wanting to see the Sycamore living room the way the audience will see it. The set designer somehow constructed a space that resembles an entire house. An old Victorian sofa anchors the main room, with chairs and lamps at various intervals to make it more homelike. Penelope's small table with her typewriter is prominently placed, along with the dining set. Doors lead offstage to the kitchen, the front hall, and the basement. A partial stairwell ends in a landing—a platform just big enough for us to climb back down on the other side.

A stagehand smiles and nods his head toward a nearby trash can. "You all right, missy?"

"I am." I swallow again. "I will be."

It's nearly time. Swallowing hard, I pick up my tray of prop candy and wait to hear Penelope start typing so I can make my entrance from the kitchen door.

Like a child letting go of a balloon, I let Thelma drift away. When it is my cue, I'll enter the room as Essie Carmichael, having spent the morning in the hot kitchen, making candy and talking to the maid.

My performance is the last gift I can give Stan.

Applause comes in waves as the curtain falls. The ensemble bows first—Viv and the Grand Duchess, flanked by the IRS and FBI men—and then the actor and actress playing the Tony Kirby's parents. Mr. dePinna, Boris Kolenkhov, Rheba, and Donald are next. The sound grows.

Jim Gorey grins and holds out his hand. We go out to center stage together. Someone gives me a bunch of roses, and I channel Essie one last time and drop into a deep ballet curtsy.

Paul and Penelope and Grandpa are next, followed at last by Alice and Tony Kirby. There are cheers and an armload of roses for Carrie, which she presses to her chest with an enormous grin.

We bow together several times before splitting and going off stage.

I lean against the wall for a moment, overtaken by trembling, though this time for different reasons. It went well. It went, I think, very well.

Viv barrels into me from behind. "You were fabulous!" she shouts. "And look at your flowers!"

I look at them for the first time, and my heart turns over in my chest. They are the same parchment-pale, pink-tipped roses he sent before. I bury my face in them to hide my tears and inhale their sweetness.

"I need to get out of all this," I say. "Connie's meeting us in the lobby. He says he has a surprise."

"He'd better not spend our traveling money on something extravagant." Viv makes a face, then says, "You know what, tonight I'd let him. This is special."

The dressing room looks like a florist's shop, with multiple bouquets for Carrie, who is sobbing like a child, and a stiff bunch of red roses for Margaret.

"From my husband," she explains. "He's up in the balcony, the same seats we sat in when we were courting twenty years ago."

I place Stan's roses on the dressing table and slide my fingers inside the wrapping to see if there's a note, but there is nothing but a card with my name. I don't need words to tell me what they mean. What is broken between us can't be mended. This is simply an acknowledgment of what has been.

My hair survived the wig cap with minimal damage. I touch up my waves carefully with a comb, adding a few discreet pins, and slip into the navy satin gown. It zips up the side, from my hip to my underarm, while the draped back extends almost to my buttocks. It's one of Mama's best efforts, and I chose it tonight so she would be with me.

"Stop admiring yourself." Viv leans in the door and meets my eyes in the mirror. "Come on. Gay Wellington needs a drink, and so do I."

I catch up my small bag and Stan's roses, leaving my street clothes for tomorrow. We follow a roundabout path behind the scenes to a set of doors opening into the lobby.

"Connie said he'd be front and center." She pushes the door open. "Do you see him?"

I step out, holding the roses, and am immediately surrounded by hoots and cheers and clapping.

Connie is there, but he's flanked by Pop, my aunt, Grace, and Teddy. Behind them are two tall, thin, dark men: Dan and Tommy. Pearl and Julian are there, too, along with Toby, George, and Ruthie.

My mouth drops open at the sight of them—my precious, longed-for family—and then Mama comes from behind a pillar, her arms outstretched. There are tears on her face. Her mouth trembles as she says, "I'm so proud of you, baby. And I've missed you so much."

Viv plants her hands on my bare back and shoves me forward. Mama catches me before I fall, and we both begin to sob.

29

Aunt Claire has reserved a table at one of her fancy restaurants, the sort of place I love going to, but as we pile into the room and are led to a table long enough to accommodate our party, I see no one but Mama. Clinging to her hand like a little girl, I try to tell her everything that's happened in the last months while she does the same.

"Enough, my girls." Pop shoulders his way between us. "You have all the time in the world to make up. Tonight is about celebrating Thelma's achievement."

There is champagne and loud, joyous conversation. Pearl and her husband have paired off with Dan and Tom, while Viv and Connie are talking a mile a minute with Grace. Teddy looks on, amused, putting in an occasional word and trying unsuccessfully to draw Toby and George into their conversation.

Despite Pop's order, Mama and I sit together and keep a quiet, running conversation going under the din.

"I didn't think you would come," I say. "I didn't know any of you were coming."

"We'd never miss an opening night," she says, with a touch of her old crispness. "I'm hard-headed enough to keep a fight going, but not so stupid I'd miss something like this."

"It was good, wasn't it?" I don't mean my performance, or not entirely. The show took on a life around me until it felt entirely real.

"It was good," she says bluntly. "But you were excellent. You were meant to play that girl."

"That's what I said to—" I don't want to say Stan's name and bring up memories that will have to be ironed out in the coming days. "That's what I thought."

Mama covers her glass when the waiter tries to refill her champagne. I, on the other hand, hold mine up to make sure he sees it.

"Your man called me, you know." She meets my eyes and the noise of the party fades away. "Yesterday. He wanted to make sure we were coming tonight."

"He did?" After everything that was said and left unsaid. My eyes burn. "Why would he do that?"

She puts her hand on my wrist. "He might have done something he shouldn't have, Thelma, but he's not a monster."

I lean close so she can hear my whispered words. "I love him, Mama. I didn't plan it. I didn't think he loved me, either, but he does."

"What are you going to do about it?" There's no judgment on her face, only an understanding that people can't always predict their hearts.

"Nothing." All the sadness I feel is loaded onto that word. "He offered to leave his wife. But I never wanted that. When I told him Connie and Viv and I were talking about New York, he was shocked."

"No man wants to be second best."

There is no choice: after the party, I go home with my family. Viv promises to thank Mrs. Morrissey for coming to the show. "Are you sure you're coming back?" she asks. "Living with them would save money."

"It would," I concede. "But we're a team."

Pop overhears our conversation. As we cram ourselves into our assorted vehicles—his, Aunt Claire's, and Teddy's—he says, "You know, Thel, I'm sure we have room for your friend, if you'd prefer to live at home."

It never occurred to me that they would welcome Viv into the house, although one of Pearl's friends lived with us for years.

"Really?" I look from him to Mama. She nods agreement. "I think she'd love that."

I certainly would—and it will make our escape from Philadelphia happen all the sooner, even though now I have less reason to go.

When I arrive at the theater the next day, the *Inquirer*'s review is pinned up on the call board. I shoulder my way through the crowd, hoping my name is mentioned in the ensemble.

Sycamore Family Charms Audiences in Delightful Revival

Last night's opening of the perennial favorite, *You Can't Take It With You*, at the Franklin Grand Theatre proved a thoroughly enjoyable evening, transporting the audience into the eccentric yet endearing world of the Sycamore family. Under the always-steady hand of director Stan Arkright, this latest rendition of the Pulitzer Prize-winning comedy sparkles with genuine warmth.

The play, a showcase to the enduring appeal of unconventional living, found strong footing in its capable cast. Lee Miles delivered a commendable performance as the earnest Tony Kirby, navigating the delightful chaos of the Sycamore household with a believable blend of exasperation and affection. His scenes with Carrie Docherty, playing the charming Alice, were well-handled, showcasing a sweet and genuine chemistry. Ralph Carpenter embodied the quirky Grandpa Vanderhof with a relaxed charm, providing the philosophical backbone to the family's joyous disarray.

However, the evening's true revelation came in the form of newcomer Kimber Byrne's portrayal of Essie Carmichael. Often a role that can fade into the background, Miss Byrne brought wide-eyed enthusiasm to the aspiring ballerina, managing to make Essie not merely a caricature, but a living, breathing, and hilariously endearing young woman.

The production is a testament to the play's timeless humor and heart. The sets perfectly capture the home's cluttered charm, and the costumes are suitably fitting for the era and the characters' distinct personalities.

You Can't Take It With You continues its run nightly through April 15, and we highly recommend an evening spent in the company of the Sycamore clan.

As I read, spots swim before my eyes. I put out my hand to hold myself up.

"Look at her!" says Margaret. "She's so enthralled with her review she has to touch it."

"I can't believe it." I'd known it was a good performance; sitting up late with Mama and my sisters, they assured me over and over it was the best thing I'd ever done. But I hadn't expected to be singled out! "I need a copy of this in case it never happens again."

"There's one on your dressing table," Lee Miles says, putting his hands on my shoulders and drawing me back against him. "We all got a copy."

"Thank you." I shake him off and move away, but he follows.

"Now that the show's open and we're not rehearsing all the hours of the day, how about a date?"

I turn a withering glance on him. "Does that work? Asking nicely after doing everything short of rubbing yourself on me like a dog in heat?"

His laughter is shocked; he didn't expect me to come back at him. "You're the prettiest girl in this place, Kimber. I've been thinking about you since auditions." He lowers his voice. "I think about you a *lot*."

My skin crawls at the entitlement of this man who believes he deserves me because I'm pretty. I open my mouth to tell him what I think, then I see Stan at the end of the hall. He's talking to Mr. Carter, but he's looking at us.

"Well," I say, "I'm not sure how I feel about that. A girl has to have standards, you know."

Lee's fingers circle my arm. "I'll meet every standard you have, and then some."

My gaze flicks toward Stan. He's there, still watching.

I tip my head back and look into Lee's face. "I'll let you buy me one drink after tonight's show, but if you get fresh, Tony Kirby will need Pan-Stik for his black eye."

He smiles broadly. "I'll take my chances. We're off for two days. I'm a fast healer."

"Thanks for the warning. I'll have to hit you twice as hard, then." I detach his fingers from my sleeve. "See you after curtain call."

I shut the door and lean against it, my heart pounding. What was I thinking, to encourage him? Stan doesn't need to see me with Lee to know that things are over between us.

But it was his idea. How many times had he said I should be with Lee or someone like him? I'd always argued that I didn't want someone who only saw me as a pretty face, yet now I've committed to having a drink with him.

"I should know better," I grumble, turning toward my dressing table. A copy of the *Inquirer* review awaits, almost completely covered by another sheaf of Stan's roses. The sight of them causes me to groan aloud. Last night was one thing, but today? Is he trying to torture me?

There's a card this time, a small envelope tucked into the long stems. I pull it out, breaking the seal with my fingernail.

Thelma,

Your Essie is beyond reproach, as are you. If there is any way I can help when you get to NY, you have only to ask. S

It sounds as if he's both accepted my plan and forgiven me, which is more than I deserve. I read the note again and am struck by one word.

Thelma.

Despite my misgivings, when the curtain falls and we retreat from another wave of applause, I change into a nice dress and meet Lee in the common area where the call board is posted.

"Ready?" He offers his arm, but I shake my head.

"I need to wait for Viv."

"Who's Viv?" He leans against the wall, his body a long, elegant, unappealing line.

"Vivian Collins?" At his blank expression, I say, "She plays Gay Wellington, in this play? We live together, and I want her to know I'll be a little late."

We don't live together at the moment, but she'll be moving in on Monday. When I told her about Pop's offer, she jumped at it. Even though he said they could afford to let us live there for free, so we could save for New York, neither of us feel comfortable not paying our way.

A raucous laugh warns me of Viv's arrival. "Here she is."

Her face registers shock when she sees me with Lee. "I guess we're not traveling together?"

"Not unless you're going my way." He tries to put his arm around me and I move to the side. "Kimber and I are going out for drinks to celebrate that review."

"One drink." I squeeze Viv's hand and watch as she walks out the back door. This late, we should be sharing a cab; if she's on her own, she'll take the subway. "Maybe this isn't a good idea."

"It's an excellent idea." Lee takes my hand and draws me close. Where would you like to go, Kimber? There's a good bar in the lobby of my hotel."

"I don't think so." What gall to think I would go to his hotel with him, even the lobby bar. "I'd prefer someplace more public, if you don't mind."

"Really? His voice drops. "I thought you were a hole-in-the-wall kind of gal. What about the Downbeat? Or would you prefer The Click?"

He knows. Somehow, he knows about me and Stan—maybe not the extent of our relationship, but he must have seen us.

"The Click would be lovely," I say with a calm I don't feel. The Click is familiar; if I decide to abandon him, I can go to the ladies' room and duck out by another exit.

He leads me to a cab and opens the door. "We're not dressed for it, but what the hell. We're both too attractive for them not to let us in."

As we are led to a table, I wonder again what I am even doing here. I only spoke to him in the hall so Stan would see us. If I'd known about his note, I would never have given Lee Miles the time of day.

"Carrie is a perfectly good actress." He raises a finger to catch the waiter's attention. "But as far as looks? It was criminal to put you in that frumpy wig. No one can see you."

"I'm not me in that wig, I'm Essie." I don't want to be myself on stage; part of the reason I've always loved performing was it allowed me to be someone else, or no one at all.

He gives me a skeptical look. "It's a waste. Looking like that, you could go far."

The drinks arrive. He's ordered martinis, which I don't particularly like. It will be easy to leave after one drink.

"Thank you for being so concerned about my career," I say. "I'm going to try my luck in New York by the end of the year."

"I was thinking of that myself," he says, raising his glass. "Philadelphia is better than Chicago, but New York is where it's at. Unless I try for Hollywood."

"I think you would do well there." His sort of looks would translate well on film, and I don't want him dogging my footsteps in New York.

"We'll see." He shifts his chair so he can put his arm over the back of mine. "I want to rack up some good reviews here first."

"That's understandable." I lean forward so he's not touching me.

"You girls have it easier."

I'm trying to listen to the music, but he keeps talking. "What do you mean?"

"You can always find someone to give you a part. Men have to work harder. You girls, you just lean over a desk or hike up your skirt and you get whatever you want."

"Is that what you think?" The gin burns the back of my throat.

"I saw you with Arkright." His beautiful eyes narrow. "You should have tried a little harder. You could have got Alice if you'd given him more."

For the second time in a day, my vision swims, but this time, instead of disbelief, it's fury. "Is that what Carrie told you?"

"She won't tell me anything. She thinks I take her out because I like her, but being seen together will help both our careers."

"I'll be right back." I pick up my bag. "Just going to powder my nose."

"Thought you did all that back at the theater." As I scoot past, he raises his hand and pats my bottom. I've never wanted to hurt someone so badly in my life.

The bathroom attendant takes my ticket and, for an ample tip, retrieves my coat and points me to the staff exit. I sigh with relief and head for the corner of Market Street to find a cab.

Across the street, the Click's garish neon sign reflects off a phone booth. I take a deep breath and dash through traffic, fishing in my bag for a nickel.

"Clinton Hotel."

"Room 304, please."

There is a pause. "If you're looking for Mr. Arkright," the desk clerk says, "he checked out this afternoon."

30

Sunday is for sleeping in and reconsidering every choice I've ever made, from wanting to be a dancer to my open-eyed decision to be with Stan to walking out on Lee Miles the night before. The rest of the run will be uncomfortable because of my decision, but I couldn't have lived with myself if I had stayed.

Because Pop took a last-minute shift at the clinic, which shifted our weekly lunch to my aunt's house, I also have time to sit down with Mama and Aunt Claire to tell them about the plans we've been making.

My aunt's living room is a haven of peace compared to our house, but even so, as we curl up on her comfortable sofa, Teddy's music—and Grace's voice—filter down the stairs.

"Those two," Aunt Claire says. "Ava, how did you manage with six? I've got one and a half and they're going to make me climb into the gin bottle!"

Mama shakes her head. "It's only noise, Claire. When Teddy steals a Wanamaker's delivery van, then you can tell me about having sons."

I remember Toby's shame at being caught. Pop's focused attention on the boys after that did them both a world of good.

"You're a stronger woman than I am." Aunt Claire reaches for one of Mrs. Hedges's delicious coconut cookies. Covered in a drizzle of sugar icing, they are impossible to resist. "Now, Thelma, tell us more about this scheme of yours."

There is no judgment in either of them; they understand this is going to happen. They just want to help.

"Right now, we're trying to save up enough to move and get a place together. It's the getting there that's complicated,' I say. "Between the three of us, we should be all right once we're there. Even if we don't get cast right away, there's always other work."

I've been thinking about Grace Kelly, Nora's cousin. She did a lot of modeling while trying to break into acting. It might be easier to get a modeling contract than a theatrical agent, and it could put me in front of powerful people. Or people with money, which is often the same thing. For the last few years, I've avoided modeling because it felt too much like relying on looks instead of talent, but to survive in New York, I might have to be a little less proud.

"Your money will be coming soon," Aunt Claire says. "I can't change the terms of Harry's trust, but I could advance it personally if you don't want to wait."

"We want to do this on our own." I appreciate her offer, and while it would give us a faster start, I don't want my friends to feel like they're living off my money. "Not that I won't accept when the time comes, because I will. But we're ready now."

"You've given up so much," Mama says. "I'm proud of you for finding a new way forward."

"It's not what I grew up wanting to do, but I think I can be good at this."

After so many years of a singular focus on dance, it shocks me how quickly I have left it behind—although the discipline and understanding of my body's capabilities continue to serve me. While I have less experience than many actresses my age, I've learned that my facility for learning lines and the ability to translate a stage direction into movement doesn't come easily to everyone.

"You already are." Aunt Claire speaks decisively. "You, of all people, Thelma, know how many plays I've sat through over the years, both good and bad. What I saw on opening night was impressive. I'm not saying that because I love you. I mean it."

Her praise is gratifying precisely because I do know. "Connie and Viv both have talent, as well. We just need a bigger stage—the best shows in Philadelphia are tryouts for Broadway, so we can't get into them. And the local theaters... there's nothing wrong with most of them, but no one will see us there. No one," I amend, "who can give us the kind of roles we want."

My ambition has only grown since parting with Stan. I have to make something of myself to justify turning my back on love.

"I wish you'd chosen an easier path." Mama pushes the tempting plate toward my aunt. "But you kids have never chosen easy. God knows what Grace will do when it's her turn."

It's hard to speculate about Grace. She's charming and willful but not driven in the way Pearl and I are; she will, I think, end up as normal as George and Toby, solidly if blandly married, with a nice house and a couple of children.

"Let's not get started on Grace," Aunt Claire says. "That makes me think about Teddy and whatever those two will come up with next to make me pull out my hair." She opens a small notebook and holds her pen above the blank page. "Now, I've been looking at the papers, the apartment ads, to see what sort of budget you'll need."

"Take whatever number you've come up with and divide it in half." Her idea of thrift is well-intentioned but laughable. "And then half again."

She shrugs. "Then between the three of you, you should be able to get by."

"We know how to be poor." While I like my comforts, I can already see this new life. It's as real to me as Essie's ballet dreams, except the people who love me push me to improve, not revel in my delusions.

"Then you'll be fine," Mama says. "And Claire, I know you want to help, but if Thelma needs money before the trust comes in, Max and I will be the ones to give it to her."

Viv arrives late Monday morning, all her belongings crammed into the back seat of a yellow cab. Mama gives her the spare bedroom even though we offer to share a room.

"I'm used to having three girls," she says. "And there's enough space that you don't have to share."

"Then I thank you kindly, Mrs. Byrne." Viv is particularly bubbly today, no doubt thrilled to be away from Mrs. Morrissey's terrible cooking. "I'll earn my keep, too. I might not be a very good cook, but I'm a good cleaner."

"I'll take you up on that." Mama gives her shoulder a squeeze before turning serious. "We need to talk before Grace gets in."

"What about?" I carry three cups of coffee to the table and point to the sugar bowl on the shelf above the sink. Viv grabs it and finds the cream pitcher in the icebox.

Mama places her palms on the table. "You two keep late hours because of your work. I understand that. And you're young women with personal lives. I'm not going to tell you that you can't date, because that's none of my concern, but this isn't a boarding house, either."

I open my mouth to object. Viv says smoothly, "It's also not a good example for Grace."

"Exactly." She looks pleased that we don't argue. "Thank you for understanding."

"How do you want us to handle it?" I dump a spoonful of sugar into my cup and stir. "If we do stay out?"

She purses her lips. "I've been thinking. I don't want you to feel like you're being treated like children, but there need to be some rules, so we know where we stand."

"We'll be at work five nights a week," I say. "So there'll be no issue of holding dinner. And I think I can safely say that I won't be going out after the show."

Viv snickers; I've filled her in on my date with Lee. "Except for closing, Thelma. We have to go to the closing party."

Do we? Stan will undoubtedly be there and I'm not sure I'll be ready to see him, even in two months.

"There can be exceptions, of course." Mama looks pleased that this is going so well. "I don't want you to feel like you're in prison."

"We're not in prison," Viv says. "But we're working toward a goal and staying out gallivanting into the wee hours won't add to our savings."

I suggest we help Pop with Sunday lunches and eat as a family, which leaves us Sunday night and Monday to do as we please—likely acting classes and time with Connie. No matter that Mama didn't discourage us from dating, I can't imagine wanting to anytime soon.

"Do we have to go to the closing party?" I ask Viv when we go up to unpack her things.

"Yes, we do. Get back on that horse." Her lip curls as she registers her double entendre. "You miss him?"

"More than I expected. But it will fade."

I didn't tell her that Stan offered to leave his wife because I don't expect her to let me off easily as Mama. For all her ambition, Viv is as much of a romantic as Connie. It isn't fair the only one of us not looking for love was the one to find it.

"He was that good?" She makes a rude gesture. "I wouldn't have thought he had it in him."

"Shut up." I don't have the words to talk about the physical aspect of our relationship; I miss it desperately, the same as I miss his conversation. Stan is as obsessed with the theater as I am. I think I could give up the rest just to talk to him for the rest of my life.

Mama knocks lightly on the doorframe. "Do you need me to set up the ironing board, Vivian?"

Viv looks over her shoulder at the jumble of clothes on the bed. "Maybe a garbage can would be more appropriate," she says. "None of it looks very good on me."

It's the first time she's acknowledged the limitations of her wardrobe. Viv is petite and curvaceous; personally, I think her tight clothes cause people not to take her seriously.

"Nonsense." Mama picks up a brightly flowered dress, rubbing the fabric between her fingers. "This is... well, it's cheerful. I understand why you like it."

Viv holds up the red dress she wears on dates. "This one makes me look like a prostitute."

Mama's mouth falls open. She is stock still for a moment, then she starts to laugh, bending at the middle, and finally sitting on the bed with a thump. Tears leak from the corners of her eyes. She wipes them with her fingers.

It's rare to see her lose control. Even when our lives became easier, she's always tightly wound. Only Pop can make her laugh like this. And now, apparently, Viv. I feel a tiny sliver of jealousy, but mostly I'm thrilled my friend has penetrated her shell.

"Lord." She wipes her eyes one last time. "That felt good."

"I knew I was funny," Viv says. "But if everyone reacted like that when I spoke, my name would be in lights."

"When that happens, we can't have you looking like a prostitute." My mother gets up and puts her hands on Viv's shoulders, looking her over critically. "You need a new dress."

"I can't afford a dress." Viv spins away, executing a complicated tap sequence between the bed and the dresser. "Unless I *become* a prostitute." She stops. "But then I wouldn't need clothes."

Mama's lips twitch but she doesn't laugh this time. "I have some fabric at the shop from a canceled order." She lifts Viv's hair. "You've got very pretty shoulders, you should show those off and keep that bosom under wraps."

"It took me years to grow these!" Viv hitches her breasts up and they wobble with a life of their own. "They're my best asset."

"Leave something to the imagination." She's got that look in her eyes, where I know she's seeing a dress come together in her head. "Thelma, go and find a measuring tape. It should be in the basket by the couch. We have work to do."

On Tuesday, we travel to the Franklin Grand together. Viv is chattering nonstop, thrilled beyond measure with her new living situation. "Your family is amazing," she says. "They're so *nice*. I mean, your mom is making me a dress? And your stepdad is adorable. I love how much he loves your mom. And Grace! I always wanted a sister."

"You don't have sisters and brothers?" Whenever I've asked about her family, she's deflected my questions. Connie told me what little he knew but I don't know how he found out; she's as tight as a clam when talking about her past.

"An older brother." She bites her lip. "If there were any justice in the world, Hitler would have got him, but I don't have that kind of luck."

That tells me uncomfortably more about her situation than I wanted to know.

"Well, you're an honorary member of my family now. Mama's the hardest nut to crack, and she likes you, so you're in." She told me last night she'd originally been doubtful about letting Viv move in. I'm not sure if it's Viv's smart mouth—acceptable in a child not her own—or her terrible clothes and the need they represent that changed her mind. She likes to fix things, and people.

Viv tucks her arm through mine. "You're so lucky. If I came from people like them, I don't think I could bear to leave."

"That's what my sister thought," I tell her. "Then she went to Paris for a year and got married. New York isn't far. We see Pearl once a month and she calls every Sunday night."

We arrive at the theater and part ways. Before I go to the dressing room, I like to find a quiet place where I can breathe and get myself back into Essie's head. When I emerge from my hiding spot half an hour later, the first person I run into is Lee. He's got Carrie backed up against the wall. They kiss with a great show of suction and passion. Her fingers are tangled in his black curls, and he's pasted against her.

"Evening," I say as I pass. Carrie moans but they don't break their kiss.

"Thank God one of you is here." Margaret brandishes a brush in my direction. Her makeup is almost done. "Have you seen Carrie?"

"Lee is eating her face." I take off my street clothes and shrug into my robe so I can start my makeup. "He should be done soon."

"I hope he's left enough for her to go on. The understudy has the sniffles." She puts her brush down and looks closely at herself, coming close to the mirror because she refuses to wear her glasses. "I thought he was after you."

"He was." I tell her that I left him in the club and she cackles until she chokes. I'm fetching her a cup of water when Carrie comes in.

"I'm not late, am I?" She looks panicked to see us so far ahead.

"You don't need much." Margaret wipes her streaming eyes and swears when the napkin comes away black. "But your mouth is swollen and there's a red mark on your neck."

"This is terrible!" Tears spring to her eyes and she grips the back of the chair like she doesn't know what to do next. Margaret meets my eyes and tosses me a stick of concealer.

"Sit," I say. "It needs to dry, or it will come off on the neck of your second act costume."

As we work, Carrie tells us how she thought Lee no longer cared because he stood her up on Saturday night. "But it's okay," she concludes. "He told me he fell right to sleep and didn't wake up until it was time for church on Sunday."

Considering it was nearly Sunday when I abandoned him at The Click, that would have been an impressive feat of time management. I make sympathetic noises and continue fixing her face. By the time the dressers arrive, we are ready.

31

You Can't Take It With You continues its run to appreciative audiences and solid reviews, though none as good as that first one. I hear nothing from Stan, but I don't expect to. He's back in Delaware with his family, planning his next show. If he thinks about me at all, it's to be grateful that he didn't blow up his life for so little reason.

Because I've been dancing regularly, my hip has begun to hurt. Although it's not as bad as before, I don't want it to grow any worse and I begin, almost imperceptibly, to adapt Essie's routines. To the uninitiated, I'm still doing ballet, but I no longer attempt a perfect turnout. On nights when I'm in pain, I vary her stretches or change legs. I can feel the difference almost immediately.

One Monday, in a fit of experimentation, I take a tap class. While it is a strain due to lack of practice, it doesn't hurt otherwise. It comforts me to know that tap, my first love, is still possible. Only ballet, the bête noire of my life, has it in for me.

I explain to Viv and Connie that I'm able to dance, but they both counsel against continuing with it.

"It may hurt less than ballet," Connie says. "But you don't know if it will last."

"And you're too good an actress to go back to the chorus." Viv shakes her head. "Can you imagine how jealous I would have been if we'd met now?"

All that drama feels so long ago; it feels as if I've known the two of them forever. The things that have gone wrong add to that sense of history. I trust Viv now to know our paths are separate but run side-by-side, so we can support each other. If we are true to the kind of actresses we want to be, we will rarely be in line for the same parts.

"That's over now," Connie says, always the one to smooth things over. "It's time to talk about me."

We straighten in our seats; it's rare that Connie demands attention instead of showering us with it.

"What's going on?" I ask.

"Well," he says, drawing the word out like a rubber band, "you're not the only one who can snag a director, Miss Byrne."

"I knew it!" Viv shouts.

I sometimes wish I hadn't told them about Stan. Just when I begin to forget, one of them mentions him and I remember why I needed to.

"Because now the show's closed, he asked me to lunch the other day." His smile widens, cat-like. "At the Palm Court, if you will."

"And?" she demands. "If your timing was this bad on stage, they'd throw rotten tomatoes at you."

"He agrees New York is the place for me—unless I want to go to Hollywood. As his special guest."

"Are you two...?" I don't know what's more surprising: that the director has invited him or that something is going on Connie hasn't shared with us. "I didn't think you were."

"We weren't," he says. "But *now* we are. And he wants me to go with him." His blazing smile fades. "I told him no, of course."

"Why?" we say at the same time.

"Because we're the Three Musketeers." He throws his arms around our shoulders. "All for one, one for all, remember?"

"Yes, but if this is an actual opportunity," Viv says, "you'd be an idiot to turn it down."

"We're in this together," he insists. "I'm not flying off to California because Victor whispers sweet nothings about screen tests. It might never happen. I might end up as a kept boy. As attractive a proposition as that is, I want to be an actor."

"You are an actor," I tell him. "And you can be one in either place." I lean into him. "We're not going anywhere yet. See how it goes, if he genuinely means it."

He looks stricken. "But what'll I do without you?"

"If you make it in Hollywood, you can fly us out," Viv says. "We'll lie by the pool, turning gloriously brown, while you line up screen tests and devastating men."

She makes him laugh and the moment passes, but that night, as we sit on my bed rehashing the day, she says, "It feels like it's all coming apart, Thel. Connie finds someone and gets this opportunity to go to Hollywood, and now we're down to two. What if Stan crooks his finger and offers you another part?"

"First of all, that won't happen." Much as it would hurt to turn it down, Stan is in my past. He has to be. "And second of all, we have a plan. I'm sticking to it. Are you?"

"Of course." She wrinkles her nose. "You're stuck with me."

"And you're stuck with me." I put my feet against her thigh and push. "Now go back to your room. I need my beauty sleep."

Closing comes long before I am ready for it. Other than Lee, who hasn't uttered a word to me offstage since our date, the cast has begun to feel like family. On matinee days, Ralph Carpenter, who plays Grandpa, takes us all to lunch at a grimy bar around the corner. Despite appearing not to have been cleaned since before the war, their kitchen turns out tasty sandwiches. I've even gone there with Connie on my day off.

There is an aura of sadness in the dressing room when I arrive. Carrie is already at the mirror. Her reflection is big-eyed and fragile.

"Are you all right?" I hang my gown on the hook for later and come up behind her.

"I'm fine." Her voice wobbles.

"What did he do?" It's clear who caused her distress.

"How did you know?" She lifts red-rimmed eyes. "He said I was shallow. Being with me wouldn't do anything to his career."

I envision my fingers around his neck. "He says you're shallow because he is, Carrie. All he can do is accuse you of being like him."

"I thought he was in love with me."

She sounds so sad that I want to sit down and explain life to her. I don't know much more myself; for all my heartache, I was simply luckier in my choice of man.

A light knock breaks the moment. One of the boys who calls time pops his head in. "Flowers for you, Miss Byrne."

"Now?" I expected flowers from my family, but they shouldn't arrive until after the performance.

"The instructions said to bring them now." He hands me a long, white cardboard box, tips an invisible cap, and disappears, whistling.

I know before I open the box what I will find inside: a dozen pink-tipped roses.

"They're beautiful," Carrie breathes. "Who are they from?"

"Someone who's no longer in my life." I drop the box on the dressing table and close my eyes.

"Don't you want to read the note?" She fishes out a small square envelope with my name on it. "Or is it too much before the show?"

"Can you give me a minute?"

Carrie obligingly puts on her robe and ducks out into the hall. When the door closes behind her, I take a deep breath and open the envelope. It's not a card, but a note.

Thelma,

I hope you know how talented you are. I hope you know how much you mean to me. I hope you know I'll always be here. I hope you know.

When Carrie returns, Margaret is with her. They look at my tear-stained face and kiss me, one on either cheek.

"Well, kids," Margaret says, "it's been a pleasure. Let's make this one to remember, shall we?"

The dress I selected for tonight's party is one that Mama made for Aunt Claire's trip to Paris. A bias-cut column of navy-blue silk organza with angel sleeves, it is both devastatingly simple and extremely sexy due to the sheerness of the fabric. The matching slip was long gone, so in addition to concocting an entire dress for Viv, Mama threw together a low-backed slip with narrow straps which allows the embroidered organza to be the star.

I take trouble over my makeup and hair. I'm almost certain Stan will be at the party and I can't be seen as anything less than my best. Viv knocks and puts her head around the door.

"Are you ready for this?" Her grin is enormous.

I can't believe how good she looks. When Mama has an idea for a dress, there's no stopping her. Viv's pretty shoulders are on display and her ample bust is contained by a boned, whiskey-colored satin that has been on the shelf in the shop for over a year.

"You look beautiful." I tuck my compact and lipstick into my bag

She twirls, the calf-length skirt belling out to fill the doorway. "I do, don't I?"

We gather the rest of my things—taking down the bits and pieces that have accumulated on my dressing table over the weeks of the run—and pack them into a bag. After the taxi driver drops us at the party, he will continue on to deliver our things to the house.

"Are you ready?" she asks as we walk into the already crowded space. "What should I do?"

"I'll be fine." I hope I'll be fine. "He's not likely to talk to me, and if he does, I'll walk away."

She snickers, then tosses her head and sashays into the room. I watch the reactions to this new version of Viv. I can't wait to tell Mama about the success of her transformation.

Carrie appears at my side, wearing a severe black dress that accentuates her sadness. "I'm so glad you're here," she says. "Do you mind if I stand with you? Everybody knows he dumped me."

"And they're all congratulating you on your good fortune." I take her elbow. "I'll stand with you, but not here. I need champagne."

A waiter with a tray passes before we reach the bar, and we snag two glasses, retiring to a small table at the side of the room where we can watch everyone.

"Your friend is having a good time," Carrie says. "Men like her."

I shrug. "She likes men. But she doesn't expect much from them, so she's never disappointed."

Despite having shared a dressing room, Carrie and I have never spoken in depth. She tells me now of her ambitions—she wants to do Shakespeare—and her eyes widen when I tell her Viv and I are off to New York as soon as we have sufficient funds.

"That's so brave. I could never."

"You'd be surprised what you can do." Was I ever that young? "I wanted to be a Rockette, but I've got something wrong with my hip so I'm not allowed to dance that much anymore."

It's best to say it out loud, so I start to believe it.

"You'll be a big success, whatever you do." She smiles brightly, and I see the beginning of the mask that will improve over time. "You're so much prettier than they let you be as Essie."

"Alice wasn't just the only normal family member, she was the beauty." I knew from the start that I couldn't look like myself.

"You're prettier than I am." Her head lowers. "Lee told me that several times."

"And the one time I went out with him, he told me things I wouldn't even bother to repeat." I want her to get it into her head that he is no loss.

He's brought a date to the party, a young, dark-haired woman in a lavender sequined gown. She is hanging on his arm and his every word.

I turn to point her out to Carrie and see, through the crush of people, Stan Arkright staring at me from across the room. My throat tightens and my mouth goes dry. I gulp the last of my drink.

"Are you all right?"

Sound is suddenly muffled. The room spins in a way that has nothing to do with champagne. As I stand, I feel like I'm watching myself from a great distance.

"I'm going to the ladies. I'll be right back."

Carrie picks up her bag. "I'll go with you."

"Please don't." Somehow my voice sounds normal. "I need a moment alone."

I make my way through the space, smiling and exchanging greetings with half a dozen people before I reach the door. The hall outside is cool, not so packed with humanity. Hearing laughter behind the ladies' room door, I turn away and instead open a door at the end of the hall, stepping into the dimly lit stairwell and breathing a sigh of relief.

I didn't think it would hurt so much to see him. Just one look at his face made me revisit our entire relationship, like a sped-up filmstrip—the dinners, the music, conversation, the bed.

Our departure can't come soon enough. I draw in a shaky breath, wondering how I'm going to get through the rest of this evening without making a fool of myself.

The door opens a few inches. Stan appears in the bar of light from the hall.

"I thought you'd be here." His voice is quiet, assuming nothing. "I don't know if you even want to see me, but our first words shouldn't be in front of a crowd."

"Thank you for the flowers." My palms burn with the urge to touch his skin. "They were beautiful."

He leans against the door. "They were a vehicle to get a message to you, that's all. Did you read it?"

"Yes." I back a little farther away, so the light from the bare bulb doesn't touch my face.

"I meant every word." He sighs. "I'm not saying I wasn't hurt, but I understand. You're young. You're ambitious. I can't keep you here, it would be too selfish."

A single tear slips down my cheek.

"I'd stay, if I could." My voice trembles. "I didn't tell you the truth, that last day. I love you. I wouldn't admit it to myself because I didn't think you could."

He's beside me in an instant, those warm, familiar hands on my upper arms. "How could you think that? You're beautiful. You're talented. You're smart." His grip tightens. "I miss talking to you as much as I miss having you in my bed."

"Oh, God," I say as he pulls me against him. "I've made such a mess of things."

"You haven't." Stan puts a gentle hand on my hair. "You've done what you always intended to do. You've become a successful actress, and now you're going to take New York by storm."

"In New York, I'll just be one more pretty girl." I sniffle. "This was the best role I'll ever have."

"You're wrong." He tilts my face up to look into my eyes. "There is something in you, something any director with sense will see. You'll find what you're looking for."

I exhale and it turns into a sob. "I don't want to leave you. I don't care... I don't care if it's meetings at hotels and dinners at places where no one will ever see us. I don't want to leave you." His lips brush my neck and my body turns to liquid. "Stan…"

"I can't touch you." He steps back, breaking the contact between us. "I can't touch you because I can't stop wanting you."

"I don't want you to stop wanting me." I place his hand on my breast. Two layers of silk fade away; it's as if our skins are touching. My nipple hardens when he brushes his palm across it.

"Thelma." There is a world in that word, the name I've never heard him say before. "I couldn't live with myself if you gave up this opportunity for me."

"But—"

"Maybe it's not what either of us want, but it's for the best." He takes a handkerchief from his breast pocket. "Dry your face. We have to go back."

"I don't want to." We're in a hotel; I want to go downstairs to a room where we can disappear until the world is easier.

"Neither do I." His smile is resigned. "But Susan's here. I can't abandon her."

"No, you can't." Tears rise again and I swallow them. "Will you introduce me?"

"Do you want me to?" He gestures for me to keep the mascara-smeared handkerchief.

I nod. "Maybe if I meet her, I'll accept that I can't have you."

He leaves first. Afterward, I go to the ladies' room to check my face and repair the damage wrought by tears.

Before I can even make my way back to the table, Stan approaches with a woman in tow.

"Kimber," he says. "I'd like you to meet my wife, Susan. She was particularly struck by your performance."

We shake hands. I try not to think about her with him, this pleasant, ordinary woman who reminds me somewhat of Pearl.

"Congratulations," she says. "The whole cast was wonderful, but I've always had a soft spot for Essie."

"I'm glad you enjoyed the play." How can I speak so calmly to his wife, in his presence, as if I hadn't offered myself to him on the stairs?

Carrie walks past and I call her over so Stan can introduce them. My heart is pounding in my ears. All I can think about is being alone with him again. Whenever.

"Can we see each other?" I murmur as Susan compliments Carrie on her performance. "When I come home?"

"Call the office." He raises his voice. "Keep in touch, Kimber. I want to know how you get on in New York."

"I will." I include his wife in my smile. "Thank you so much for everything you've done for me. This has been the most wonderful experience of my life."

Part Four

Her Own Encore

32

Without Connie to share expenses, it will cost far more than we anticipated to move to New York. Now that the show is over, we need to find
new ways to make money. Almost immediately, Viv finds a place in the
chorus of another show, while keeping her waitress job for mornings and
days off. I warn that she's going to work herself into a rag, but she insists
it's for a good purpose—and her hours give her no opportunity to spend
money.

Savoring my triumph, I ignore the call boards and audition notices;
another part holds no allure. Instead, I call in a favor from Aunt Claire,
who never needs to be asked. Wanamaker's takes me on again, this time
as a model in ladies' finer dresses. Relying on my looks doesn't feel the
same when they earn me a better income than I would have earned on
the sales floor—or on the stage.

Not to mention not having to deal with the likes of Miss Coffey.

Connie decides to go to California. Two days later, he changes
his mind. Finally, after being given an ultimatum by his gentleman
friend—whom Viv and I still haven't met—he chooses love and the
vague promise of a screen test. At Mama's invitation, he comes to dinner.
By the end of the evening, all three of us are in floods of tears.

"I can't leave my girls," he says, wiping his face with a paper napkin.
"How will you manage without me?"

"We'll have the pick of all the men," Viv says smartly, "without you
making eyes at them."

I can't take his defection lightly. "We'll have to delay. Or share a room.
We won't be able to afford an apartment now."

Not an apartment, nor the savings of cooking for ourselves. We'll be
stuck with boarding house food, which is good for the figure but not
very good otherwise.

"I'm a terrible person." Connie drops his head into his hands. "My family thinks so, and now so do you."

"We don't think you're terrible," I assure him. "It just alters our plan, that's all."

Grace's voice reaches us from the kitchen, where she's doing dishes. "I think you're wonderful, Con. I want my sister to stay here. I'm even okay with Viv."

"Thanks, kid." Viv rolls her eyes. "Good thing I like you."

"Everybody likes me." This is followed by a crash and quiet swearing. "Don't worry about me, it's nothing."

We return to our conversation. I pull out the list we made months ago, divided into thirds. A sound escapes him as I draw a line through his portion.

"Are you sure?" I ask. "Not because of us, but for you. Is he good enough?"

Neither of my friends ever questioned my relationship, but that was perhaps because I had never truly questioned it. From the beginning, Connie's relationship with Victor has been a roller coaster.

"I'd feel better if we could meet him."

His eyes widen. "You'd scare him to death, Viv."

Ruffled, she says, "Well, the sight of Thelma could resurrect him. You're not getting off that easily."

"She's not his type, remember?" He leans back in the chair. When it creaks, he looks guiltily at the living room, as if Mama can see through walls, and sits up straight. "Trust me on this."

"I agree with Viv. We should meet him."

Before the meeting can be arranged, I hunt down a phone number for Nora Kelly; re-establishing my connection with her cousin might be useful. As my aunt is famously casual about long distance charges, I make the call from her house.

"Of course, I remember you." Grace's voice has clarified somehow, steel beneath the silk. "Nora told me you're going to try your luck in the city."

"It's time." I tell her I'm coming with a friend, to share expenses. "I was hoping we could meet for lunch once I'm there."

"That would be lovely." A long pause. "I won't be here much longer, though. I just finished shooting a movie. My fingers are crossed so tightly I can barely hold the phone."

"That's wonderful!" I'm truly glad for her, but also sorry I might not be able to make use of our acquaintance. "Did you go to Hollywood?"

"No, the movie was filmed in New York, but that's where I'm going next."

I recount my many auditions and few parts, while Grace tells me about the film, called *Fourteen Hours*, and gives me the number of her agent.

"I can't promise anything," she says. "Because we never know what they're looking for, do we? But we're very similar. Maybe he'll have room on the books for another cool blonde."

It takes repeated nagging, but Connie finally arranges a Saturday lunch with Victor at the Brauhaus. The location mystifies Viv, while I wonder if he's missing his family.

"Ah, the place where you asked me to marry you," I tease, to watch him turn red. "Don't worry, I won't tell Victor that we're engaged—unless I don't like him."

"Please don't!" His puppy dog eyes show how serious he is about this man. "Victor doesn't understand why I'm so close to the two of you."

"Now I really don't like him." Viv squirms in her seat. "First, he's late and now he doesn't understand why you have female friends? Tell me again what's so good about him?"

The waiter fills our water glasses, leaving the fourth one empty. Connie stares fixedly at the far wall until he departs.

"He sees me," he says softly. "He knows what I am, and he doesn't think I'm a freak."

"You're not a freak! And everyone who knows you sees you."

"I mean as I am." He shakes his head. "It's not easy, Thelma."

"My brother has someone who sees him," I argue. "And Tommy doesn't question who Dan's friends are, or why he spends time with them."

We're all entitled to our mistakes. I've spent the last weeks wondering about mine, and whether the mistake was being with Stan, breaking up with him, or telling him I wanted to see him again. But he never gave the slightest impression that he cared who I spent my time with when we were apart. I don't believe it's because he's married; for all his flaws, he's not controlling.

"He doesn't own you." Viv's whisper is spiky with anger. "Only *we* own you."

"I hope no one owns anyone," a voice says from behind us. "It's not the done thing anymore."

Connie turns ashen. Viv's mouth opens, making her look like a goldfish. As the only one not paralyzed by the situation, I take a breath and hold out my hand to the tall, solidly built man to my left. "You must be Victor. I'm Thelma Kimber."

Victor shakes my hand, then moves to Viv, and finally to Connie, dropping both hands on his shoulders. "I'm sorry I'm late," he says smoothly. He has a precisely trimmed mustache and a silver-threaded goatee. "The cab got stuck in traffic and it took forever to find this hole-in-the-wall. Couldn't you have chosen someplace more central, Con?"

"I like it." His tone is unexpectedly stubborn.

"It's my fault." I try to smooth things over. "We came here once when we first met. Connie thought it would put me more at ease."

"You should have been thinking of me, darling," he says. "After all, I'm the one being thrown to the lions... lionesses. Do I pass inspection?"

Viv cocks her head. "It's too early to tell. You can't expect us to be happy that you're taking our friend so far away."

"It's his decision." Victor nods and the waiter appears with a fan of menus. "Great Gods, this food. I'll have indigestion for a week."

"It's very good." Connie already told us the meal will be on Victor, so I order schnitzel with a mushroom cream sauce, potato dumplings, and sauerkraut. "I'm going to eat every bite."

He looks at me critically. "You eat like that all the time, no one will have trouble seeing you on stage. They'll have trouble seeing *past* you."

"Victor!" Connie's face is red, but his embarrassment is different this time; after all his fine words, Victor isn't showing himself to his best advantage. "I'll have you know Thelma is a goddess."

"If you say so, darling." He orders a beer and a plate of potato pancakes. "I'm looking out for her best interests."

"Thelma can do that for herself," Viv says sharply. "I'll have the rouladen and the potato dumplings."

Connie asks for bratwurst and spätzle and orders a pitcher of beer for the table. "I told you, Victor, these girls can take care of themselves."

"Hmm." He tilts the knife as if checking his reflection. "So, you're off to conquer Broadway, is that the plan? After how many shows in Philadelphia?"

The entire meal goes that way, a constant drip of negativity. No matter what any of us say, Victor knows better or has seen something different, and is happy to tell us about it. He's insufferable. I can't wait to get out of the restaurant and ask Connie what the hell he's thinking of, to tie himself to such a man, and to go so far away from everyone who cares for him.

But I don't get to ask, because when Victor settles the bill, he informs us he's asked for two cabs, one to take me and Viv back home, and the other for him and Connie.

"The day is young," he says with a greasy smile. "I'm sure you'll see him before we fly on Friday."

"Friday!" In all our discussions, Connie never mentioned they were leaving so soon. From his expression, their departure date is news to him, as well. "But that's two days from now."

A yellow cab pulls up at the curb. Victor waves for us to take it. "I'll make sure you have time to say goodbye."

There is a finality in the sound of the door closing. Viv looks at me. "We have to stop this."

It would be easier, it turns out, to stop a speeding train than a man like Victor Weston, possessed of two airline tickets and a portion of our friend's heart. Connie spends Thursday night at our house. He's supposed to sleep on the sofa, but after Viv and I change into our pajamas, we spirit him upstairs, where we share a bottle of wine and talk until we're weepy.

"I don't want you to go." Viv falls forward until her head rests on his thigh. "We're the Three Musketeers."

"I know." He gulps air to keep from crying. "I hate myself, I really do. But there's something mesmerizing about Victor. I can't explain it. I need to be near him."

Mesmerizing is the right word; he stared at Connie like a snake until my friend saw nothing in his eyes but his reflection.

"There's nothing we can do to change your mind?" I've tried crying, which nearly always works on Connie. When it didn't, I tried guilt, also to no avail. I even said that if the issue was not wanting to move to New York, Mama would rent him Viv's room once we were gone. He lit up at the idea of being part of a family, then shook his head.

"I'm sorry." He dabs at his eyes, then takes a healthy swig from the jelly jar that serves as our glass. "I'm going to be a mess tomorrow, thanks to you two."

"Can we see you off?" Viv rolls to one side to look up at him. "I can call out sick. I'll probably *be* sick."

Connie shakes his head slowly. "Victor wouldn't like it. But neither would I. I don't want to cry in public. The sight of the two of you, waving me off like little orphan waifs, would do me in."

When we stumble down to breakfast, he's already gone. Mama smirks as we slide into our chairs, holding our fragile heads.

"You look as bad as he did." She turns from the stove, placing loaded plates in front of us. "I fed him before he left. He insisted you sleep in."

"But he's leaving today!" The smell of bacon makes my stomach turn over, but I reach for my fork. I haven't been drunk often, but I know that greasy food is the cure—along with copious amounts of coffee.

"He wanted to go before you saw him." She gives us each a steaming mug.

Viv drinks as if her life depends on it. "He's not going to be happy, Mrs. Byrne. The man he's going with is awful."

"You have to let people live their lives." She sits down at the table and looks from Viv to me. "Interfering won't make him love you more. Just be there if he needs you. This won't last forever."

"Maybe we'll go to Hollywood next." Viv spears a piece of bacon and munches it disconsolately. "If Victor makes him a star, he can take us in."

That is so unlikely I can't even bring myself to think about it. One thing at a time. "Are you going into work today?"

"I know I said I'd call out," she says with a grimace. "But it's a few dollars more, so I'll go."

"Someone is bound to come in today who'll want to see every dress we have. Then she'll buy one right at closing time and demand to have it fitted by tomorrow morning." I look at Mama with new understanding. "Listening to the seamstresses at Wanamaker's talk about alterations, I don't think I realized how patient you were with your customers."

"I'm not that nice anymore." She gives me a tight smile. "I don't need that salary to keep us alive, so if someone is too demanding, I can tell them to take a walk off a short pier."

She reaches for our plates, which are somehow empty. "There's coffee left, if you need it—and I'm sure you do. And don't forget that it's Friday. Supper at Claire's tonight."

"Do we have to?" I don't know if I have the strength.

"You don't have to." Mama tops off our coffee. "But Sofie's in town. It might be nice to see her."

Despite my good intentions, I've only managed to see Sofie on two of her visits home. Neither conversation led to a better understanding of each other. But she is, as Mama reminds me, alone in the world except for us. I think of Connie, with no one now but Victor, and feel a stab of sympathy for my cousin. I should try harder.

"All right, I'll go. Can Viv come?" I don't want her to be home alone if she feels half as bad as I do.

"You know Claire," Mama says. "The more the merrier."

We drive to Delancey Place and Pop parks up the block. Aunt Claire's door is already open and she's waiting for us on the front step between two tall concrete planters filled with flowers.

"What is it?" Mama asks as we get close. "It's not like we're going to get lost, Claire."

"Come in, quick!" She grabs my wrist. "You, too, Vivian."

She tows us into the living room, where Sofie is curled on the sofa, composed and self-contained as a cat. There is a book open in her lap. She glances up and greets us, then returns to the page.

"Sofie! Not this time," my aunt says impatiently. "Tell the girls what you told me earlier."

With a sigh, she puts the book aside. "I'm moving to Boston next month. I start law school in the autumn."

"Congratulations." Sofie's academic aspirations are as mystifying to me as dancing and acting are to her, but I'm glad for her all the same.

"Yes, yes, darling," Aunt Claire interrupts. "Tell them the rest of it."

"I'm looking for someone to take over the lease to my apartment. The couple I've sublet it from live in Italy and it will be too difficult for them to find new tenants."

"An apartment," I say. "In New York."

We can't possibly afford it. Or if we can, it will be terrible and full of roaches or spiders. Viv's hand creeps into mine.

"Well, that is where I live, Thelma." Sofie looks at me over her glasses. "It would not be in New Jersey."

We sit down and Viv and I pepper my cousin with questions. Where is the apartment? How big is it? How many bedrooms? Is there a kitchen? And most importantly, how much does it cost?

Her answers come dizzyingly fast, until I am nearly overwhelmed. The apartment is in the West Village, a somewhat familiar area. It's small, with one bedroom, a living room, and a tiny separate kitchen. And it costs—miracle of miracles—fifty dollars a month.

"We wouldn't even need Connie," Viv says in wonder. "We can do this, Thel."

This time I find her hand. "Yes, we can. Tell me again, Sofie, because I don't think I was paying attention. When are you leaving?"

33

Pearl meets our train and supervises the loading of our luggage into two taxis with her usual understated ease. "You're certainly committed," she remarks. "Did you leave anything behind?"

"Hangers." It's the complete opposite of what she did—when my sister came back from Paris with a husband and a new wardrobe, she took almost nothing with her, whereas I've brought almost everything I own except Flora. When I moved home, Grace gave her back, but I decided it was time to put away childish things.

"Thank you so much for taking us in," Viv says. "We'll do our best not to get underfoot."

"That will be impossible." Pearl slides into the back seat and I follow. "But as you said, it's only a few days. Sofie leaves on Tuesday, so we have the weekend to get you acquainted with the city."

The taxi zigzags its way west. Viv stares out the window at the passing streets. "I thought you lived in New York?"

"We do." Pearl laughs. "It's not the New York you're used to. We're on the Upper West Side, over by Riverside Drive."

"Is it hard to get around?" she asks. "Being so far from things?"

"Nothing is far away here. It's a short walk to Broadway. From there, you have three subway lines. You can get anywhere you need to go."

"It's also close to the West Side Highway," I put in. "Pearl and Julian have a little place out on Long Island where they go on the weekends."

"Not this weekend," Pearl says. "Though I may send Julian on his own. Having three women in the house might send him over the edge."

I doubt that. My brother-in-law is the most patient of men, especially where indulging my sister is concerned.

"Don't you like living in the city?"

"We do," Pearl says, "but Julian likes to sail. It isn't practical to keep a boat in Manhattan."

Our towering pile of luggage—mostly mine—takes up the bulk of the living room. We each drag a single suitcase into the guest room, wedging everything into the tiny dresser, and hang our dresses on the back of the door. There is no closet.

"Your cousin's place can't be tighter than this." Viv sits and falls backward, rumpling the immaculate quilted spread.

"Even if it is, it will be all ours." The apartment *is* small—even their bedroom is tight—and the living room wasn't large before we filled it with suitcases and a trunk. But their priorities are different: Julian's job keeps him out all day and Pearl has a tiny closet of a room where she writes. At night they either stay home or go out with friends; on weekends, they leave the city entirely.

It's a small life for such a big city. Even arriving at the train station, I could feel the energy of New York, so different from Philadelphia. It made my blood fizz like champagne, but in this quiet, third floor apartment, we could be almost anywhere. I look forward to throwing myself into the current of New York and being carried wherever it takes me.

After two days, I don't know who is looking forward to our move more, us or Pearl. She insisted Julian drive out to Long Island on Saturday morning, and since then she's been familiarizing us with the city's different neighborhoods. Most of the time we get around by subway, which is faster, but I'm looking forward to learning the city on foot and finding the places that will make New York belong to me.

On Sunday night, Sofie comes for dinner, looking around at the chaos we've created and laughing. "Where will you put all this?" she asks. "Should I get rid of the furniture?"

For fifteen dollars, she has agreed to sell us the contents of her apartment. Most of it, she says, was secondhand to begin with and not worth taking to Boston. There's an insult in there somewhere, but I choose to ignore it. Sofie is who she is. Even though she looks at me differently now—my silliness about the stage might be a career, after all—we are far too different to ever see eye to eye.

Pearl dishes up an appetizing pot roast and we sit down at the petite kitchen table, which has been extended to seat four. Extra chairs have been carried in from her dressing table and office.

"You aren't set up for company." I add green beans to my plate. "Will you be happy when we're gone?"

"I'm happy you're in the city, so we can meet whenever we want," she says. "But I'll be glad to have my peace back. I'm running behind on my next book."

"You will catch up when they are gone." Despite fifteen years of exposure to my family, Sofie has never acquired tact. Even when I find her annoying, I appreciate her determination to remain her own person.

"I will," she agrees, "but I'll also miss them. It's been nice to have sisters again. If we had a bigger place, I'd be happy for you to stay longer."

Viv speaks for the first time. "I think Julian might disagree. He also misses the peace and quiet."

"What he misses is me being able to do my work," she says contentedly. "He knows what makes me happy."

After dinner, Sofie bolts at the first available opportunity to do some last-minute packing. Viv offers to do the dishes so Pearl and I can have some time alone. We take the elevator down to the street and walk toward Riverside Park.

A fresh breeze blows off the Hudson, ruffling our hair. We walk in silence until we reach the park.

"It may not feel like it, but I am glad you're here," Pearl says. "You've wanted this for so long."

"I have to try." I don't say it felt impossible to remain in Philadelphia after everything that's happened over the last year; she is closest to our mother, so she undoubtedly knows everything Mama knows. "And it's good to have someone to share it with."

"I like Viv. And I'm glad you've made friends."

Pearl was always one to surround herself with people. She had a core group of girlfriends in high school that she's close with to this day. Even the one who became a nun keeps in touch.

"I wish Connie was with us," I say. "He'd be a much more considerate houseguest."

She turns onto a trail leading down to the river. "I met him at the opening for *You Can't Take It With You*," she reminds me. "There was a lot happening that night."

"There was." I don't like to think about that night; those memories still hurt.

"I'm not sure how he'd fit in Sophie's apartment. In ours, we'd have to fold him up and put him in the kitchen cupboard."

"He would probably let you."

We've heard from Connie once since he left, a scrawled postcard addressed to the two of us with a return address in Burbank, California. I worry that he is so under Victor's influence he won't see that he's unhappy until it's too late.

"I need to sit." Pearl heads for a bench. "I'm not used to all this walking. You two have worn me out this week."

"It's nice that you have a park so close by." When I think of New York, I think of Central Park, but this long, narrow strip beside the river, with its view toward New Jersey, is lovely in its own way.

"I come here to think when my characters aren't behaving." She crosses her ankles and turns her face to the late afternoon sun. "I'm not sure if I should say, but Mama told me what happened with the man you were seeing. I'm sorry."

"It's not a secret," I say. "And his name is Stan."

"Do you miss him?" Whenever Pearl asks questions about my personal life, I hesitate, wondering if I will later find myself in one of her books.

"Wouldn't you miss Julian?"

"Yes, but he's my husband."

"And Stan was someone else's husband." I don't expect people to understand that the relationship suited me as it was. "It didn't matter, really."

She makes a sound in her throat. It could signal disapproval; it could also mean she's thinking about how to turn my love affair into fiction.

"When was the last time you saw him?"

"At the after party." That's not exactly true. As we were preparing to board the train at Thirtieth Street, I hugged Mama one last time and swore I saw him over her shoulder, standing at the far end of the platform. When I looked again, he was gone.

"Hopefully, your life here will keep you so busy that you won't dwell on him."

Rather than talk about Stan any further, I ask if she's heard from Toby, whose reserved status meant he was called up by the Navy. I don't understand much about what's going on in Korea, but when he announced his departure, George told him he was nuts to volunteer to fight in another war.

"Not a word," she says with a worried look. "But you know how he is. We got three letters during the entirety of the last war. I hate to think of Mama worrying about him."

"Do you think George will get called up?" In 1941, he used his brother's identification to join up at sixteen. Now he and Ruthie are trying for another baby so he can plead hardship.

"I hope not. And thank God, Teddy is too young." She follows a boat on the river with her eyes, clearly thinking about Julian. "Dan has a theory about Toby, you know."

"I need to hear that." Toby and George set themselves apart at a young age and constantly have to be drawn back into the family. "What's his theory?"

Pearl gets up, dusting the back of her skirt. "He thinks Toby feels guilty because he had an easier war than George, so he won't be content until he sees real action."

Good Lord, the things men will do to prove themselves! Women are so much easier.

I follow her along the river path. The sky is bright, but the sun is lowering. It's not yet the golden light of autumn, but there's been some indefinable shift since we arrived. Soon, the season will change.

To distract from thoughts of war, I tell her about Grace Kelly's agent and my plan to call him as soon as we're settled. "And I need to find work, regular work until I get an acting job."

"Do you want to stick with department stores?" She seems pleased at the change of subject. "Goodness knows there are enough of them. I would recommend Bergdorf Goodman."

"Why?" I've heard the name from Aunt Claire, but I've never been there.

"You look expensive. If you're going to continue modeling, they're the most high-end store."

Being called expensive looking is an odd compliment, but I know what she means. Pearl and I are alike in the same way Mama resembles Aunt Claire; there are similarities in our faces and in the way we move, but we don't look like sisters. When I consider the Dior dress in my sister's closet, I regret how dissimilar we are; it makes Pearl look both taller and more slender, but it would hang on me like a sack.

"Is it close to the apartment?"

"Fifth Avenue and Fifty-Seventh," she says. "Macy's is closer, but you'll make more at Bergdorf."

In the morning, we take another two-taxi trek down to Christopher Street, a block of worn brownstone and brick buildings with substantial front stoops. Small stores are tucked in at ground level in some buildings, while others appear to be apartments or converted houses. Sofie's building, just shy of the corner of Greenwich Street, contains a small coffee shop on the ground floor.

She meets us at the door. While the drivers unload, she says, "Let me introduce you to Gabriel. He runs the coffee shop and takes messages for me."

"You don't have a phone?" Viv looks around with a broad smile; this looks much more like the New York we were expecting. "How do you manage?"

"Gabriel takes messages for me," she says again. "I suppose you might want to get one if you are going to be waiting by the phone."

A telephone is an unexpected expense, but we will need one eventually. In the meantime, we smile at Gabriel and accept pastries from his mother, then troop upstairs behind Sofie and two wheezing, well-tipped drivers.

We climb the creaking wooden steps. The walls might once have been painted white, but years of smoke and city air have turned them a mottled yellow. A door leads to the main hall, where several doors are visible. Off the landing, three more steps take us to Sofie's apartment.

"What are the neighbors like?" I ask, knowing she will have no idea. But she surprises me.

"The first apartment is Mrs. Bowden," she says. "Widow, elderly, four cats. She'll take in your mail and judge all of your house guests."

"Well, we won't be having any of those straight away." Viv takes a suitcase from the driver and he heads back down the stairs. "Anyone else we should know about?"

She shrugs as she fits the key into the lock. "There's a young couple upstairs. Their baby cries a lot."

The door swings open, revealing a small, square room with a faded burgundy couch and a mismatched armchair. It has pockmarked walls, uneven floors, and the faint, pungent smell of five decades of tenants' dinners. It's terrible and I absolutely love it. The curtainless window faces north and allows a flood of light into the room. There is a miniscule kitchen off to the left, with a two-burner stove, an ancient icebox, and a rickety wooden pantry cupboard.

"It's perfect." It's not, but it's ours.

"I would not say that," Sofie says, "but it is enough. I have been happy here."

Considering she never seems happy anywhere, that is an enormous compliment.

"What about the bedroom?"

Back through the living room, a second door leads to the room we will share. It is darker, but there is a wide bed, a dresser, and two more doors, one of which is a decent-sized closet.

I can already see how I will arrange my programs and photos on the wall so I can see them from the bed.

The second door opens onto a bathroom so miniscule we can sit on the toilet, soak our feet in the tub, and wash our hands at the same time.

"Thank you again." How am I ever going to get all my clothes into that closet? We will either need to find more storage, or I will have to take some things home when I go for Thanksgiving. Except this is home now. New York. I am a New Yorker and I will learn how to live in this small space. "I don't know what we would have done if you weren't moving."

"I am pleased to have had my problem solved so easily," she says. "Now do not damage the apartment. The landlord doesn't care about the sublet, so long as the rent is on time and you don't break anything."

After we solemnly promise to be punctual with the rent and not to break anything, Sofie picks up two small suitcases from the threadbare carpet, bids us farewell, and follows the taxi drivers down to the street.

"Not the sentimental type, is she?" Viv throws herself down on the sofa and immediately scrunches up her face. "Springs!"

"She never has been." I look around the impersonal space, wondering how much my cousin has taken with her or if she has always lived with this little. "We're going to need curtains."

"We're going to need a lot of things. There's bound to be a second-hand store around here somewhere." Despite her complaints about the couch, Viv hasn't moved. "Should we unpack or go exploring?"

I hear my mother's voice in my head. *Once begun, half done.* "Unpack first," I say firmly. "We won't want to face it later."

34

We spend a week settling in, making an appointment to have a telephone hooked up, buying the few bits and pieces we deem necessary for our comfort, and getting acquainted with the city, both together and alone.

I walk so much my feet swell, but my hip doesn't hurt at all. Apparently, my body approves of my new life.

We visit theaters, making notes of what's on their call boards, and find a cafe near Times Square where all this information is posted in one convenient place. Viv and I make a point of being friendly to the staff and stopping in nearly every day for a coffee.

I find the actors' church on West Forty-Ninth Street, and duck inside to say a prayer that Grace Kelly's agent will contact me.

My first attempt to reach him was from Pearl's apartment, but after we moved, I called twice from the coffee shop downstairs, and now I try his number again from our telephone.

"I have your previous messages," the calm female voice says when I give her my name. "All of them. Mr. Edwards is out of town."

"Can I make an appointment for when he gets back?"

"I'm sorry, but he's all booked up."

"For how long?" The smug satisfaction in her voice increases my determination. She doesn't realize how hard I can dig my heels in when I want something. "I'll take the first available appointment he has."

"I'm sorry, Miss Byrne," she says. "I don't know when that will be. Please feel free to call again."

I throw myself down on the uncomfortable couch. "He's not back," I call to Viv, who is taking a bath. "But I'm welcome to call again."

Her rude comment is drowned by the splashing as she emerges from the tub. "Honest to God," she says, "that thing makes me feel like a giant."

"Think how I feel, then. You're a pipsqueak compared to me."

The realities of our apartment have begun to sink in—the toy bathtub, the lumpy mattress, the kitchen tap that drips only at night when we're trying to sleep. It's wonderful, it's just no longer perfect.

"So what are you going to do?" Viv wanders out wearing nothing but a towel. "Keep trying with him or start auditioning?"

"Both. Grace gave him my name. I'm not going to let go of this until I see him." She's all pink and rosy from the bath. I'm envious, knowing how I will have to contort myself to be completely submerged. "Did you leave any hot water?"

"There wasn't much to begin with." She shrugs. "Maybe?"

The next day, I stop in at the theater district coffee shop and talk to the young woman who has been at the counter on my last two visits. "I'm looking for someone," I tell her. "An agent."

"Aren't we all?" Like me, she's an aspiring Broadway star. "Any agent in particular?"

I explain I've been trying to get in to see Mr. Edwards, but I can't get past his secretary. "One of his clients recommended me to him, but that doesn't mean anything."

"You need to get past her," she advises. "Find him outside the office if you can."

"How? I don't even know what he looks like."

"Hmm." She slides a cup of coffee into the counter. "You should try the library."

"The library?"

"They'll have back issues of newspapers. There might be pictures of him."

It's not a bad idea, but I don't want to spend days inside a stuffy library looking through newspapers for a photograph of a man who won't see me.

As I walk back to the apartment, I find myself thinking of Stan, something I try not to do very often. Instead of focusing on him, however, this time I remember the desk clerk at the Clinton Hotel and how happy he was to take my money in exchange for information.

Abruptly, I change direction, my steps picking up speed until I reach the building where Mr. Edwards has his office. I'm thankful it's not one of the enormous skyscrapers, where it would be impossible to see everyone coming and going.

There are several people at the desk, making deliveries or asking questions. I wait, looking at the directory on the wall.

Neil Edwards, Talent
Suite 803

When the desk clerk is alone, I approach, giving him a winning smile. "I'm looking for Mr. Neil Edwards."

"Eighth floor," he mumbles without looking up. "Eight-oh-three."

"I know that." I press both hands on the desk, my shell-pink nails gleaming in the overhead light. "But he's not in."

"Of course, he is," the clerk says. "Just came back from lunch ten minutes ago."

I think several unpleasant thoughts about his secretary before acknowledging she is just doing her job.

"Well, *I* can't get in to see him," I amend. "And I need to."

He shakes his head and cracks, "Because he's going to make you a star?"

"A girl can dream." I try the smile again, and this time he sees it. "And you can help."

I sit at home all morning, hoping my surrender of the equivalent of a month's worth of groceries will amount to something. At half past twelve, the phone rings. I snatch up the receiver.

"He's gone out," the clerk says. "He'll be gone at least an hour."

Already dressed in a dark blue dress and heels, I grab my purse, the folder with my headshots and a few pages from Aunt Claire's scrapbook, including the *Inquirer*'s review of *You Can't Take It With You* that mentioned my performance, and run for the subway.

When I arrive, breathless, in the lobby, the clerk winks. "You got wings under that pretty dress?"

I sit on a bench inside the front door and try to slow my breathing; it will do my cause no good if Mr. Edwards's first impression of me is sweaty and out of breath. A quarter hour later, a finger snap echoes through the marble-floored lobby. As the brass and glass revolving door starts to move, I rise from my seat and head for the elevator.

"Afternoon, Mr. Edwards," the clerk says. "Nice lunch?"

"Good enough." He comes to stand beside me, fidgeting with his watch.

The dial ticks down and the doors open. He waits for me to enter, then follows, pressing the button for the eighth floor. The doors close.

"Mr. Edwards." My words tumble out in a rush. "My name is Kimber Byrne. Grace Kelly said she was going to talk to you about me."

His brows lift. "She mentioned you."

Second floor.

"I've called your office several times, but apparently you're out of town."

Third floor.

I glance at the emergency button. If I push it, it would give me extra time, but he would also see how desperate I am and would choose never to work with me.

"I am out of town for those without appointments."

"But I can't *get* an appointment."

Fourth floor. The door opens and a man gets on, nods a greeting. He presses the button for the seventh floor. Inwardly, I bless him.

"Miss Byrne, do you have any idea how many young women arrive on my doorstep each day, every one of them thoroughly convinced that I can make them a star?"

Fifth floor.

"Mr. Edwards, all I want from you is an opportunity. If you give me that, I'll do the rest myself."

Sixth floor.

He laughs unwillingly. "What will it take for you to go away?"

"Five minutes of your time," I say as the door opens on the seventh floor and the other man steps out, clearly wishing he could stay and listen to the rest of our conversation.

When the door closes, Mr. Edwards sighs. "I shouldn't drink at lunch, it makes me soft. Five minutes. No more."

The door opens one last time. I follow him out, still talking. "I've been working in Philadelphia for several years now, but I've recently moved to New York. I want to work, Mr. Edwards. I'm not proud—I expect to work hard. I was a dancer. I understand hard work and discipline."

The waiting room is crowded but silent. Four young women and nearly as many men are seated on straight wooden chairs, a variety of folders and cases clutched on their laps. At the agent's appearance, they all snap to attention.

"Mr. Edwards," his secretary says. "Your two o'clock—"

"Will have to wait." He sweeps past with me at his heels. "The persistent Miss Byrne waylaid me in the elevator."

He takes a seat behind his desk. "The clock is ticking."

I place the folder on the blotter and bring out my photos. They are new, taken by Davis before my departure—for cash.

"I'm a quick study," I say. "I've taken classes in Philadelphia and would appreciate a recommendation for a good acting class here in New York, because I'm never going to be done learning.

"I know what I look like, but I can do comedy, as well. In my most recent show, I played Essie in *You Can't Take It With You*." I produce one of my precious clippings, pasted onto a sheet of notebook paper. "You can see that I was mentioned prominently in this review."

He glances at it and pushes it aside. "A small production of an old chestnut. I'm not impressed."

I sit down without being asked. "What did you see in Grace Kelly that you don't see in me?"

That stops him, momentarily. "Talent, for one," he says. "It was obvious. Steel, for another. You think *you're* persistent. And beauty." He looks at me, his gaze sweeping my face and body with no purpose other than an evaluation of my worth. "You've got that in spades, but as for the rest..."

Do I even want this man to represent me? The stress that has built up over the last weeks spills from my lips.

"Why is it impossible for a woman to get anywhere in this business without dealing with men who, for one reason or another, refuse to see us as human beings?" I snatch up my photos and the review. "I'm sick to death of having men like you determine my value. I'd rather audition every day for the rest of my life than put up with this."

When I slam the office door, everyone looks up. I turn to his secretary. "He's ready for his two o'clock now."

35

Losing my temper was worse than if I'd pressed the emergency button in the elevator. Not only did I show myself to be desperate, but I undoubtedly came across as unbalanced, as well. What agent wants to represent an actress who loses her composure? My hasty words have likely cost me everything that I came for.

Instead of walking home to lick my wounds, I go straight to Bergdorf Goodman and apply for a job as one of their store models. After that, I stop at Macy's and do the same.

When I finally reach Christopher Street, my steps are dragging. While I know Viv will do her best to jolly me out of my bad mood, I hope she's not home. There is no place to hide in the apartment. I need time to cry this out of my system before I have to put on a brave face.

I pop into the coffee shop to see if there are any messages; not everyone will know yet that we have a telephone. Gabriel shakes his head—*no messages*—then says, "Someone is waiting for you at the back table."

It must be Pearl. No one would think of meeting us here but Sofie, and she is settled in Boston and gone from our lives until Thanksgiving, if she comes home then.

It is not Pearl. Seated at the back table, looking entirely too large for the spindly chair, is a gangling, beloved figure.

"Connie!"

He jumps up so quickly that he knocks into the table, catching his mug before it crashes to the floor.

"Thelma! Sweetheart!"

We are hugging and crying and making a complete show of ourselves in the middle of the coffee shop, to the point that when we finally separate, several patrons break into spontaneous applause. Being who we are, we bow in every direction before sitting down again.

"What are you doing here?" I ask. "You're supposed to be in California."

"I've been on a Greyhound bus for two days." Connie rubs his forehead. "I look like death. I smell worse."

"You do look tired," I grant him, and then take a healthy sniff. "But you don't stink. Somehow."

"I feel like I do." He drains the last of his coffee and looks pleadingly at Gabriel, who appears with two fresh mugs. "I would have walked here, if I'd had to."

"What happened? I thought you and Victor were happy." I know what probably happened, and I'm glad it happened before Connie was more firmly enmeshed in that man's life.

"Exactly what you and Viv thought would happen." He spoons sugar into his mug. "He liked me in bed a lot more than he liked me out of it. Of course, it turned out to be mutual."

"Oh, Connie." I take his hand across the table. "What about the screen test?"

"There was always a reason it couldn't happen. He was too busy or the producer was out of town. Then they cast someone who looked too much like me." Connie scrubs at his eyes. "It shouldn't have taken me so long to see I was being used."

"But you're here now." At least he'd stayed in California long enough to have received my letter with our new address. "That's what matters. Viv is going to be over the moon when she sees you."

"Is she working? Are you? I rang the bell when I first got here, and no one answered."

A large suitcase under the table pushes against my knees. We're going to have to find space for it—and him.

"She's looking for work, same as I am." I push the coffee aside. "Let's go upstairs and get everything settled, so we can surprise her."

By the time Viv comes home, lugging a bag of groceries and a black cloud similar to mine, Connie has bathed and I've made space for his things in the empty bookshelf in the living room.

"We'll have to buy another dresser," I said. "Can you sleep on this couch?"

"I've slept in a bus seat for two nights," he said. "Right now, I could sleep standing up like a horse."

When the door opens and Viv sees him, she lets out a shriek that must have made Mrs. Bowden pop her head into the hall to see if one of us was being murdered.

"I'll stay if you want me," Connie says when we finally begin to run out of words. "There's not really room, is there?"

"We'll save up and find a better couch," I say. "You're not leaving."

"Thelma's right," Viv says. "We let you go once and look what happened. You got your heart broken. We're not right without you. Now that the Three Musketeers are together again, everything will start to come together."

This calls for a celebration. Even though it's barely dinner time, Viv fetches a half bottle of gin from the kitchen cabinet and sloshes some in three glasses. We settle ourselves on the couch and raise them in a toast.

"Wait," Viv says. "Weren't you trying to see that agent today? What happened?"

I take a sip and let the gin burn a path down my throat. "Nothing good. But I did apply for two jobs."

"You're not giving up, are you?" she asks sharply. "You're the reason we're here."

I struggle to sit up, but the sagging cushions hold me fast. "What do you mean, I'm the reason? We decided on this together."

"Yes, but you're the talented one." She reaches across Connie to grab my hand. "You're the one who's going to make it, Thelma."

"Don't be ridiculous." The failures of my day build up behind my eyes, and I take another mouthful of gin to drive them away. "We're all talented. They just don't know it yet."

The next day, the phone rings while we're eating breakfast. Bergdorf and Macy's both ask for interviews. Connie comes along and occupies himself in the men's department while I present myself to the manager of better dresses, speak pleasantly, change into an evening gown and heels, and model it for an imaginary audience.

"Who do you think will hire you?" he asks as we duck into Penn Station. I'm trying to teach him the subway.

"Both, probably. I'm going to spend the rest of my life modeling dresses I can't afford for women who will sit in theaters that won't hire me."

"Don't be bitter, you'll get wrinkles."

The train creaks into the platform and the doors shudder open. I sit and Connie stands beside me, swaying with the train's movement.

"Do you ever miss your family?" I raise my voice so he can hear me over the noise.

He looks down. His hair has grown enough so it flops in his eyes again. "That part of my life is gone, like Victor and California are gone. You can go home, Thel, but it's not your place anymore, either."

"I know."

Instead of going back to the apartment, we take the train all the way out to Columbia University and walk for ten minutes until we reach Pearl's building. She'd asked me to bring him over when she heard he'd joined us.

Without two extra people making the apartment strain at its seams, it has regained its customary peace and tranquility. Afternoon light streams through the windows, bathing the living room in a golden glow. Vases of fresh flowers fill the air with fragrance. The sofa is laden with soft cushions, inviting comfort and confession.

My sister may more resemble our mother, but she's learned a thing or two from Aunt Claire about how to make a home. I want to burrow into the cozy space she has created and not move until I feel better.

"What's wrong?" she asks as we make tea together in the kitchen. "You're looking a little peaked."

"Nothing." I hesitate, then tell the truth. "It's not as easy as I'd hoped. And now Connie's here—it will make things more crowded, but we're so happy to have him."

"It will certainly make things easier financially." She pours boiling water into the pot. "Are any of you working? Do you need help?"

"We're all right." I don't want to take money from my sister. "Viv found a waitress job—she always does—and I interviewed at two stores today. Connie's still learning his way around, but he'll find something soon."

"What about auditions?" Her mouth curls at the corners. "Grace wrote to me once, when I was in Paris, that you snuck out of school and took the train to New York for a show."

"I tried out for the Rockettes." What happened to that girl, so fearless she cut school and risked her mother's fury to audition for a job she had no chance of getting?

"You aimed high." Pearl puts the sugar bowl and a small pitcher of cream onto a tray. "There's nothing wrong with that."

"I had a very inflated sense of my own talent." I sigh and shake my head. "I'm a bit more down to earth now."

"And yet your talent has only grown." She sets the tray down and puts her arms around me. "What I saw on stage a few months ago was something far more special than the skill you had as a dancer."

"Thank you." I am on the verge of tears again.

"New York is a hard city, but there's no place like it. You'll learn its rhythms soon enough. Don't let it get you down."

There are days when the flight up to the apartment seems endless. After three separate showings at Bergdorf's in a single afternoon, my feet ache and my temper is frayed. I unlock the door and step inside, appreciating the threadbare secondhand draperies that soften the light from the window and make the room feel snug as a cave.

The quality of the silence tells me no one is home. Kicking off my shoes, I walk to the kitchen and retrieve a cold bottle of Coke from the icebox. Soda is a rare treat, but I've earned one today.

It doesn't occur to me to check the message pad on the counter until I've downed half the bottle. In Viv's curling handwriting are the words, *Mr. Edwards, 2:20, call him back!!!*

It was too late to call the day before, so after a night of little sleep and many anxious conversations with my friends, I dial the agent first thing in the morning. Viv and Connie huddle behind me, barely giving me room to breathe, much less talk.

"Could I speak to Mr. Edwards, please? I'm returning his call."

"Your name, please?" It's the same secretary who has fobbed me off multiple times.

"Kimber Byrne." If she doesn't put me through, I'm going down to the office to wring her neck.

"Just a moment. He's finishing another call." I hear voices in the background. "He'll be right with you."

I put my hand over the receiver. "He'll be right with me."

Viv squeals and Connie claps his hand over her mouth.

"Miss Byrne, good morning." Mr. Edwards's tone is matter-of-fact, as if he hadn't recently watched me embarrass myself to death. "I was wondering if you could come in sometime this week."

I can't speak. My lips move but I can't muster enough breath to make words. Finally, I gasp out, "When?"

"How about Thursday at two? Does that work?"

"That's fine." I'd been given Thursday off because they want me in for a fashion show on Saturday.

"I'll see you then." He waits a moment, then adds, "Leave the drama at home. I see enough of that on stage."

I turn to my friends, my eyes brimming, and they wrap their arms around me as we all shriek with joy.

The secretary closes the door behind her, leaving us in uncomfortable silence. From far below, the sounds of city traffic reach my ears. I sit on the edge of the chair, my hands folded in my lap, my emotions firmly under control. "May I ask what changed your mind about seeing me, Mr. Edwards?"

"This." He holds up a card and lets it drop to his blotter. "It fell out of your folder when you bolted."

It's Stan's card, the one he gave me back when he ran into me at Wanamaker's. I've kept it as a talisman all this time, tucked into the scrapbook with my reviews and programs. It must have got stuck to the papers I'd brought with me.

"Do you know Mr. Arkright?" I would have never used Stan's name as an inducement for Mr. Edwards to take me on as a client—I was uncomfortable enough using Grace Kelly—but the sight of his card makes me feel as though he's here, watching over me.

"Years ago," he says, "before he gave up on New York and moved to Philadelphia. I haven't heard from him in a long time, but I saw his name on the review before you snatched it away. When I saw the card, I decided to call him and see what he had to say about working with you."

There is a knot in my throat large enough to choke me. "And?"

"He sang your praises." Mr. Edwards shakes his head as if shocked. "Talented, hard worker, even-tempered. I questioned the last one, but he swears you never gave a moment's trouble."

"That's very kind of him." Warmth seeps through my nerve-frozen extremities. I want to do this on my own, but where has independence gotten me so far? Ignored. Unemployed by anyone other than Bergdorf Goodman. Rejected again and again in favor of girls who knew better how to play the game.

Wouldn't it be nice, just this once, to play the game, too, and let the weight of Stan's name carry me forward?

Leaning back in his chair, Mr. Edwards looks at me appraisingly. "If what he says is true, what happened the other day?"

"Desperation? I'd left so many messages—when I finally saw you, I tried to get everything out at once." I shrug. "I'm much better when the words are someone else's and all I have to do is memorize them."

"I'd believe that." He nods as if making a decision. "All right, Miss Byrne, I'll give you a chance. With Miss Kelly gone, I'm short a cool blonde, and those are always in fashion." My heart leaps in my chest. Then he continues, "I'm not going to take you on—not yet—because I want to see how good you are. Check with Miss Terry on your way out. She'll give you the names of a few teachers. Three classes a week for a month and if I get a good report, I'll send you out on auditions. If they go well, then you can consider yourself as having representation."

The shaking begins in my middle and spreads outward. I twist my hands together so he doesn't see them tremble. "Thank you so much."

Mr. Edwards rises and holds out his hand. "Thank you, Miss Byrne. You've certainly livened up what can sometimes be a surprisingly monotonous job."

I shake his hand and thank him again, then go back to the waiting room, where his now-smiling secretary offers me a sheet of paper with a list of names. "Mr. Edwards approves them all," she says. "Good luck."

The elevator deposits me swiftly into the lobby and I walk out, barely noticing the smiling desk clerk, onto Seventh Avenue. Ignoring the waves of people washing along the sidewalk, I move to the curb and glance down the street toward Radio City Music Hall, the culmination of my childhood dreams.

All I want is an opportunity and I'll do the rest. That's what I told him, and that's what I'll have to do. I'll work and pay for classes and hone my craft and show Mr. Edwards—and myself—what I can do.

New York is a hard city, Pearl said; I just need to learn its rhythms. But I understand rhythm. If I take a breath and listen, I can hear it. I look at Radio City one last time, then turn away and plunge into the moving crowd.

Epilogue

A dozen young women are seated backstage, each with a script balanced on our knees. The air is over-warm: radiator heat and too many excited bodies packed too closely together. The mix of perfumes would be enough to make my head swim, if I let it, but instead I focus on the scene we've been given, reading it over and over, trying different inflections in my mind to see what might work best.

Although Connie's arrival made our apartment more crowded, it has been good for us to have him there. I'd always thought female friendship was something to be avoided, that competing for something meant we couldn't be friends, but she and I are as close as lovers, and yet we throw ourselves into the battle for New York and for Connie's attention like greedy girls. It feeds us far better than our half-hearted attempts at cooking.

Each week, we draw straws. The winner chooses a play, and then we work on it at night in the tiny living room, trading the parts back and forth. We've done Shakespeare and Ibsen, Chekhov and Tennessee Williams; I've played Falstaff and Cleopatra, Nora and Masha, Stanley Kowalski and Blanche, all in the comfort of my home.

Viv has a surprising flair for Shakespeare's comic characters, while Connie is going to break hearts with his big wet eyes and floppy hair. I'm not sure what I'm best at, but fast, clever dialogue lights me up. Noël Coward is my current favorite.

This is the first audition I've had. After spending eight weeks in the most challenging classes I've ever taken, I finally feel ready. Mr. Edwards agrees. It's unlikely, he said, that I'll be selected for this role, but the casting director is a friend and will give him an honest evaluation of how I put myself across.

I'd prefer him to evaluate me himself, but I'm limiting the thoughts I voice aloud these days.

After my first meeting with Mr. Edwards, I dropped a note to Stan's office, a few impersonal words in case his secretary opened it, thanking him for his reference and giving him my address in New York.

Two days later, the bell rang. I went down to find a young man cradling a white florist box. "Miss Byrne?"

The roses were parchment-pale, with pink tips. They made the entire apartment smell like springtime.

A name is called and the girl next to me springs to her feet, the script crumpled and damp in her hand. She smooths her skirt and looks around, her eyes wide with panic.

"You look good," I say softly. "Go on, now."

She nods stiffly and disappears. I listen to her audition, to the voices of the auditors, and try to remember how to breathe. Within two minutes she is back, pale but smiling.

"Kimber Byrne!"

I get up smoothly and walk onto the stage. It's larger than I'm accustomed to, but the same table and stool are in the center and the same insufficient spotlight shines just off-center. I walk to the table and look out into the darkness at the faceless men.

"Can you see me?"

Author's Note

Well, this was a ride!

In addition to the usual suspects (my husband and my friends, Marian Thorpe, Dianne Dichter), I would like to thank Laury Silvers for allowing me to place her father at Palumbo's, and for the stories she shared. During that time period when he appeared in these pages, Phil Silvers was on Broadway in a show called *High Button Shoes*, but he would have had Sunday and Monday nights off and could have easily traveled to Philadelphia to hang out with Frank and his pals.

The Downbeat club closed in 1949, but opinions on the precise closing date vary. The inability to verify the date gave me license to use the club as I saw fit.

The theaters where Thelma works are also fictional. When I started researching this book, I was shocked to learn how many theaters Philadelphia once had. Of the real venues mentioned in *Shifting Stages*, only the Academy of Music, the Walnut Street Theatre, and the Forrest Theater are still around. But those venues, and most of the others for which significant documentation exists, existed to host out-of-town productions bound for Broadway. As much as I wanted to use a theater with which I'm personally familiar, I didn't feel comfortable placing Thelma's imaginary—and completely local—shows in a venue that would not have hosted them.

Youngest sister Grace's story is up next. I can't wait to find out what she has to say.

As always, thanks for reading. The hardest part of being an indie author—after finding readers—is getting reviews, so if you feel moved to leave a review on Amazon or Goodreads, I would appreciate it so, so much.

About the author

As an only child, Karen Heenan learned early that boredom was the ultimate enemy. Since discovering books, she has rarely been without one in her hand and several more in her head. Her first series, *The Tudor Court,* stemmed from a lifelong interest in British history, but she's now turned her focus closer to home and is writing stories set in and around her native Philadelphia.

She lives in Lansdowne, PA, just outside Philadelphia, where she grows much of her own food, makes her own clothes, and generally confuses the neighbors. She is accompanied on her quest for self-sufficiency by a very patient husband and an ever-changing number of cats.

One constant: she is always writing her next book.

Follow her online at karenheenan.com and sign up for her newsletter to receive a free novella and updates on what's next.